SOME HELL

SOME HELL

A NOVEL

Patrick Nathan

Graywolf Press

This publication is made possible, in part, by the voters of Minnesota through a Minnesota State Arts Board Operating Support grant, thanks to a legislative appropriation from the arts and cultural heritage fund, and a grant from the Wells Fargo Foundation. Significant support has also been provided by Target, the McKnight Foundation, the Lannan Foundation, the Amazon Literary Partnership, and other generous contributions from foundations, corporations, and individuals. To these organizations and individuals we offer our heartfelt thanks.

Published by Graywolf Press
250 Third Avenue North, Suite 600
Minneapolis, Minnesota 55401

www.graywolfpress.org

Published in the United States of America
Printed in Canada

ISBN 978-1-55597-798-6

2 4 6 8 9 7 5 3 1
First Graywolf Printing, 2017

Library of Congress Control Number: 2017938025

Cover design: Kyle G. Hunter

Cover images: iStock.com

Thanks, Mom

I've thought about death a great deal. One day in the snow I felt so tired. I thought, "Damn it, I'll sit down. I can't go on. I'm tired of living here in the snow and ice." So I sat down on the ground. But it was so cold I got up.　　—JEAN RHYS

But is that because I *do* think it possible that someday someone I love who loves me will read my journals—and feel even closer to me?　　—SUSAN SONTAG

SOME HELL

Two days before their father shot himself, Heather foretold her brother's death. By then, Colin was old enough to not believe her, to not fall for every lie or story. He could have rolled his eyes and left the room. He could have called her full of shit. Instead, he chose to hear it like the truth.

"It won't be long after your sixteenth birthday," she said. "At the end of fall, when it's cold. It'll start to snow when it happens. That's how we'll know, Paul and Mom and me." She leaned toward the window above her bed and let the breeze charm the smoke from her throat, past her lips and out the window and into the neighbor's yard. "I can't tell you the exact day. It doesn't work like that. But I can see the snow, and that's the end."

The leaves outside—something in the wind had excited them and they chittered among themselves, as if they'd been listening. Heather eyed Colin as though he were a thing, a piece left over from a puzzle. She brought the pipe to her lips and spun the wheel on her lighter. Their brother, Paul, sat between them, quiet as the furniture until the buds began to burn. He reached for the flame but Heather was prepared. As she took Paul's hand in hers and traced a circle on his palm she gave Colin that smile—*Just watch*, it said—and she winked when his shoulders sagged, when his eyelids fluttered. Paul had grown stronger in the last year but he was still easy to control. "There," she said, and he sat slumped and still as though she'd switched him off.

Colin loved it when his sister smoked. He loved that every day after school he could listen for that same music, muffled and muted by the Sheetrock. Heather kept her weed in an old jewelry box—a gift left over from her ninth birthday—and when its song began to play Colin knew it was safe to let himself into her room.

Instead of threatening him or throwing a pillow she'd pat the bed next to her. He loved that she would talk to him. He loved that he was there to share a piece of some curious wisdom. He loved the smell. Paul must have loved it, too. Whenever Heather put the lighter to the leaves he brought his pimpling face close to hers and groaned in the way they all knew meant he was happy. It was the only time all three of them were together anymore.

"Three years," Colin said. He turned to the window to watch the leaves but they'd fallen into their piles and places like they too couldn't believe it. "That's all I have."

"You're already thirteen?"

He brushed his hair behind his ear. There was so much he could tell her—every last thing about his life she'd never before wanted to know. "I'll be thirteen in nine days."

She leaned back to the window. The lighter and the pipe each gave a sharp thump when she placed them on the nightstand. Paul reached out and again fell short, her hand on the back of his neck. "Yes. Three years is all you have."

Colin hadn't told anyone about this other Heather. According to the rest of the world, she never stopped being a bitch. He'd forgotten when he discovered it, when he first followed the smell and found the Heather who didn't hate him. Things weren't always this way. When they were young, their mother warned them not to exclude Paul just because he was autistic. But Colin knew he and his sister had been a team. Paul was just the kid who tagged along. Even when Paul grew taller and his language of groans dropped two octaves he was still that kid, that baby. Somehow, Colin too had become someone Heather tried to hide from her friends.

It must have been exhausting to look into the future. Every afternoon, after she told him what she knew, Heather would lean against the half dozen pillows on her bed and fall asleep, her hand twitching as it guarded her heart. For Colin, it was no longer enough to talk to her, and he searched the room for clues as to how she achieved her power. One day, he'd trap the new Heather in this world for good, and she would thank him for setting her free.

Lately, Colin found most of his clues in the magazines scattered across the carpet. Heather was obsessed with bodies that to Colin looked like they belonged to men, even though she used the word *boy*. Heather's magazines were supposed to be about girl fashion and girl relationships and girl interests, but there were more of these grown boys than anything. She folded the corners on certain pages, and these Colin studied more closely.

That Friday afternoon, after she told him about his death, he knew not to press her for more. As he eased off the bed he was already thinking of the next afternoon, maybe Monday, when she could tell him exactly how it would happen. *You need to stay away from planes*, he imagined her saying. *Never fly at night.* But he wouldn't find out today. As her breathing took on its rhythm he placed the pipe back in the jewelry box. Beneath the ballerina's feet, the cylinder lined with bumps like braille set the little metal reeds rattling. The battery hadn't been changed in eight years and every time he opened it he was terrified it would stop. He snapped it shut and went over to the magazines. Paul groaned when he heard the rustling pages but didn't turn away from the window, waiting for their mother's car so he could run outside and bang on the windshield.

Heather had dog-eared another perfume ad. The male models standing in their underwear looked like a royal court from some fantasy island, surrounding a young woman who touched her collarbone and looked to her left. Colin thought of what he looked like without his shirt, how his chest and stomach looked nothing like hard wet clay. His eyes traced those muscles to the light strip of hair slipping into each waistband. He touched his stomach and let his hand drift lower, into his briefs, down over the smooth drum of skin where he'd told his friend Andy his hair was already turning black, just to make him jealous. He looked at Heather's boys. He imagined them without their underwear. He'd caught glimpses of his father and he knew what it meant to grow up, but maybe there was something about one of these grown boys he'd failed to understand. His hand drifted still lower and he felt unbearably lonely.

No matter how much he learned about Heather, every one of these afternoons seemed a little lonelier than the last. When she rolled onto her side in her sleep he dropped the magazine and wrenched his hand out of his underwear. If she knew he was going through her things—if she knew what a little pervert he was—she'd never tell him anything. He grabbed Paul by the wrist and dragged him out of the room, even though he couldn't stand the way his brother moaned when you took him away from whatever it was he loved, the smell of weed or the sound of Heather's breath.

Life was full of things that weren't real. He was almost a teenager and he knew monsters were for little kids, made up to fill their nightmares. He knew, sitting in the car next to his mother, that scrunching up your face at a stoplight wouldn't make it turn green. Yet how many times did he try it? How many times, even in the last month, had he run up the basement steps as though something was breathing on his bare calves?

It wasn't like he was stupid. Colin knew about puberty, but when he looked at someone like Paul, who had warped and bent into a bad drawing of the Paul he'd known for years, he couldn't help but think it was impossible for a boy to just grow into a new face, a new body and skin, and for months he thought of reptiles. In the world he imagined, boys stepped out of their old skin and that was the end. Never for a second did he believe it was real, but that didn't stop him from looking under Paul's bed for moltings, for an empty shell of his brother as he'd known him. It didn't stop him from worrying about the day he'd unzip his own skin, like they did in cartoons, and ever after be an oily, angular creature no one could love.

In the bathroom, he looked down at himself. He'd never thought of it as small but now it felt that way, like a pink snail he'd pulled from its shell. In stories he read online, men referred to their dicks as six-inchers, eight-inchers, nine-inchers. Once, he'd snuck a ruler into the bathroom and frowned in disappointment. It was absurd to imagine something resting at the ninth notch. He ran his finger along its side, and when it responded he stuffed it back in his underwear as if he were afraid of it.

As he washed his hands he thought of the models in the ad, the briefs they were wearing, how the front looked like a heavy, stuffed bag of laundry. When he stood in his underwear there was nothing to see, just a wrinkled petal of cotton. He looked at his face in the mirror. *You look like a girl with that haircut*, Heather always said. He stretched his jaw to create an angle, to see if he could harden the softness in his face. The idea of being mistaken for a girl suddenly disturbed him, and he made sure the door was locked. He watched his reflection as he took off his shirt and looked closer at all the discrepancies. The muscles weren't there. Heather's boys looked worn and weathered; Colin saw only his pallor and its road map of veins underneath.

A pounding on the door made him flinch. "Hey, dickwad," Heather said. "Phone."

Colin swore as he tried to put his head through the sleeve of his shirt. "Okay. Hang on." He smoothed his hair in the mirror before he opened the door.

"Sorry to interrupt the bishop flogging." She handed him the phone. "It's your stupid friend."

Colin slipped by and held the phone to his chest until he reached the living room. "Hello?"

"Did you see the fight today?" Andy asked.

"No."

"It was wicked. Tyler stopped Jeff in the hall before third hour and called him a faggot, so Jeff spit in his face and Tyler punched him real fast, like bam bam bam three times in the face. Then Jeff kicked him in the shin, and when Tyler bent over Jeff kneed him in the face."

"You saw it?"

"Pretty much. I got there right when they were taking Jeff to the nurse."

"Cool." Colin passed from the living room into the foyer. Sometimes you had to agree with whatever Andy said. He was always excited about something, and if you didn't act impressed he'd use it against you. As he passed by the mirror near the front door he looked at his face again, as though it might have changed. "Do you know what bishop flogging is?"

Andy grunted *no*. "Sounds like a dumb game."

"Maybe I'll ask my dad later." Colin locked and unlocked the front door, flicking the deadbolt back and forth.

"I thought I'd spend the night at your house tomorrow," Andy said. "Will your mom care?"

"No. I'll tell her." A laugh track played through the phone. "What are you watching?"

"That stupid show about the stupid kids who live in the hotel."

Colin walked back into the living room and switched on the same channel. It was like sitting together on the couch, only you didn't have to worry about anyone looking at you. He listened through the phone, and when Andy laughed at some predictable mishap he laughed along with him, even though it wasn't that funny—not something you'd laugh at, all by yourself. The treetops in the backyard were burning as the sun sank across the street on the other side of the house. Colin watched a crow disappear into the flames.

At the commercial break he asked, "What do you think we'll look like when we're older?"

"Dunno. I'll probably grow a beard or something. My cousin has a beard. Why do you care?"

"I don't know."

"You're being weird."

Instead of saying something even more incriminating, Colin sank back into the couch. When the commercials were over he turned up the volume. They weren't laughing anymore, and Colin at first tried to figure out why, as if he'd done something wrong.

But then Andy laughed again, and the skin on Colin's neck went all pin-prickly as he laughed with him.

Later that night, he stopped himself in the hallway. The door to Heather's bedroom looked stolen from a horror movie, a solid black rectangle rimmed in light. It was too soon to ask, but he knocked anyway. "It's me," he said, rapping with his knuckles so their parents wouldn't hear. "I have a question."

He heard the turning of a page. "Get lost."

"Please?"

"Not a chance in hell," she said. "Now go away before I make you go away."

Colin looked at the light under the door. Another page rustled from inside. The little hairs on his arms stood on end as he tried to imagine the page in front of her, if it was one he'd seen, its corner long creased, or if it was something new—something so startling, so revealing, he'd know her even better than those boys who looked like men.

She'd tell him eventually. He only wished it would be before he boarded that plane or got in that car or swam in that river, and even though each of those things seemed strange, like things he'd never do, he could picture without even trying the plane shredding itself as it plummeted, the car smashing through the guardrail like a BB through its paper target, and the black river water.

On Saturday night, after dinner, three movies, and a game of Monopoly, Colin and Andy lay in the dark on the living room floor. Colin pulled his sleeping bag up to his neck and sank into it, listening to the clock above the fireplace and the humming furnace somewhere below. A half hour before, Colin's father, Alan, had walked down the hallway in his boxers and a T-shirt that wasn't white anymore and warned them to go to bed. What Colin couldn't help but notice, after he switched off the lamp, was the creak on the door's hinges. Living in the same house all his life, he knew the basement door's creak over the bedroom's. His father hadn't gone to bed.

The boys could hear each other not sleeping. Colin's foot was twitching, and he could just make out the bat of Andy's eyelashes against his pillow. He wet his lips and pulled them into his mouth, between his teeth. He couldn't take it anymore. "You want to know something?"

"What?" The word came instantly. Andy had been waiting.

"It's kind of a secret. You can't tell anyone."

"Just tell me already."

He took a breath. "I have three years left to live."

There, he thought.

He stared at the ceiling fan, or the ceiling fan's shadow—he wasn't sure which was which in what little light was left. His heart sped up as he imagined his friend's response, his pity and concern and maybe even his grief. He wanted his grief.

"Wow," he said instead.

"I know."

"How do you know? Are you sick? Did you go to a psychic or something?"

"I didn't have to go anywhere. Heather told me."

Andy lowered his voice. "Your bitchy sister?"

"She's different when she tells me this stuff. She really knows what she's talking about."

"When does she tell you?"

"When she smokes weed."

Andy laughed, his hand over his mouth. "Dude, you're a retard. She's just high. Hallucinating or something."

"But she knows for real. A lot of what she says is true."

"What's one thing that's true?"

"She told me Dozer would run away about a week before he did. That came true."

"So? She could've let him go."

"Dude, she didn't let him go. He ran away. We were at school."

The trembling in the air stopped when the furnace went quiet. Colin could hear his blood knocking against something in his ears, or maybe his brain. It unnerved him, the thought of his blood moving around in his brain.

"So three years, huh? How're you gonna bite it?"

"She didn't say."

"So you have no idea how it's gonna happen?"

Colin shook his head.

"That blows." Andy propped his head up with his hand, his eyes now lit by whatever light was outside. "I wonder what dying is like."

Colin thought about all those images of heaven, its golden gates and its angels. Was it really like that? Was hell a burning cave deep under the earth?

Andy grinned, his teeth almost blue in the dark. "Do you think there's sex in heaven?"

"Shut up." Colin swung his pillow.

"I'll bet there is. Lots of sex all the time. Maybe you should ask Chelsea. She's the authority on all the God stuff." Andy's hair rustled against his pillow as he rolled onto his back. "I bet we go to heaven and bang girls nonstop. They could line up and beg for our dicks, one by one."

"You're sick."

"Hey, I'm a man and I have needs. I always forget you're gay, sorry."

"I'm not gay."

"There's probably a cloud where all the dudes have sex. Except— oh man, I forgot. They don't allow you guys into heaven." He sucked in a deep breath. "Yeah. Nice knowing you."

Colin bit his lip to keep from laughing. "I'll send your gay ass to hell right now." He shoved his pillow onto Andy's face. He wasn't sure if he was angry or just pretending, or if it mattered.

Andy pushed the pillow aside. "Hey!" He sat up. "Let's see what dying is like right now. You hold the pillow over my face until I tap out. Then I tell you what it was like to almost die. Then we can switch."

"Okay. How will that work?"

"Just shut up and do it." Andy lay flat. "I'm ready."

Colin looked at him. The light had gone from his eyes, and Colin assumed they were closed. Andy lay there in his pajama shorts and tank top, and it occurred to Colin that he might play a prank or do something cruel when he was helpless like this. He thought about punching Andy in the balls or farting on his head. Instead he placed the pillow over his face as he'd been told and held it down in the center. He was squinting to read the clock when he heard something mumbled through the cotton, like a voice in the next room. He moved the pillow. "What?"

"I said I can still breathe. You gotta do it hard."

"Whatever." Colin returned the pillow and pressed down on each side until his knuckles met the carpet. He watched Andy's chest swell up and down until he started squirming. With a jerk of his hand he tapped on the carpet three times. Colin let go and Andy gasped.

"What was it like?"

"I almost died. There was this tunnel of light and my grandpa was asking me to step into it."

"Liar."

"It's true." Andy grinned. "He said, 'Make sure that homo friend of yours doesn't come this way or I'll beat his ass.'"

"Shithead." Colin hit him across the face with the pillow. He held up his arm as Andy swung with his own. They laughed as Colin moved in and tried to suffocate him again, as though giving him a hint. It didn't seem fair that Andy wouldn't suffocate him, that he didn't get his turn.

When the lamp flicked on they turned to face the doorway, both frozen and squinting in the light like night animals caught digging through the garbage. At first Alan said nothing. He stared with his eyes half open, leaning against the wall. The lamp flickered when the furnace clicked back on, and it made him look like an actor in a movie where a frame had been spliced out.

"Go to bed," Alan said. "It's almost four." He flicked off the light and shuffled down the hallway, his slippers crackling with static. Colin waited for the creak, and when he recognized the bedroom door he gave Andy a nod. Again they lay there, again quiet, again alone even together as they listened to the furnace and the clock. Colin didn't want to, but he thought of heaven, all those people who weren't allowed in, of their only everlasting alternative. He saw the way the shadows in hell's caverns would flicker as though they too were flames.

It wasn't long before he heard Andy's snores beside him and felt terribly alone. I'm the only one awake, he thought. There's no one left to talk to about hell. He tried to not think, ultimately focusing on the ticking. Sometimes he'd count to sixty, telling himself how that was a whole minute, that if he counted to sixty fifty-nine more times it'd be an hour, and that if he repeated that cycle twenty-four times, a day would have passed. It was nothing you could stop.

It was the bedroom door's creak that woke him, the basement's that wouldn't let him go back to sleep. The light was too grey to tell if it was just after dawn or late in the morning. Outside, the last leaves holding on to their trees were shaking in the wind, plucked off one at a time like part of a child's game. He still hadn't raked the yard, as he was supposed to, and he tried to imagine all the ways out of it. It was Sunday and he knew his father wasn't going downstairs to check on a fuse or a pipe or even to start the dryer where there was always a heap of wrinkled clothes. Colin knew he wouldn't be at breakfast. He knew he wouldn't move from that room—what he called his office—until dinner was on the table and they called down to him. Only then would he sit down and smile and tell them, *This looks delicious.* After that he would talk. He'd make jokes, and even though they were stupid jokes Colin wanted to hear them. On the following morning he'd go to work, come home, eat another dinner, and live through that week as though there was no reason to hide in a wood-paneled room with no windows. Maybe he'll forget about the yard, Colin thought.

His father had been writing for over a year but nobody knew what he was writing. It wasn't as if they never asked. At least once each Sunday Colin crept downstairs to peer through the slats in the door. *Hey*, he'd say, running his finger along the slats so they rattled. *You writing a manifesto?* Colin knew it was something serious, as though his father was about to make a discovery or invent a new way of travel. But Alan paid no attention and only went on writing.

Now, in the light of morning, time didn't seem so concrete. Colin tried counting the ticks but couldn't pay attention long enough to make it through a full minute. The house was still quiet. If the sun was outside it didn't move. He thought this might be what *forever* was like, after you died and had to go on existing. Why wasn't heaven whatever you wanted? Couldn't he choose to turn it off?

He stopped listening to the clock when Andy's breath quickened. Colin looked over and saw him as he whimpered into his pillow, as he mumbled words that weren't words, his whole body shaking in his sleeping bag. He watched until Andy cried out a single and final *No!* before he shuddered and fell still. Colin thought he should squeeze his hand, maybe even wake him up, but he didn't want him to get the wrong idea.

It was a while before Andy woke. He looked at Colin and blinked away the light. "Dude. Were you watching me sleep?"

Colin forced a yawn. "I just woke up."

"Man, I gotta piss like you wouldn't believe."

"Me too."

Andy unzipped his sleeping bag. "Well, me first." Colin watched as he took delicate steps down the hallway, almost like the floor was on fire. The furnace went silent again and Colin could hear the torrent that fell from his friend. Andy too had a penis, resting right now in his fingers. For some reason he'd never considered it before, or if he had it never seemed so significant, even crucial. Colin knew that Andy would be able to hear him as well, and when it was his turn in the bathroom he aimed at the porcelain instead of the water, and didn't make a sound until he flushed.

As he passed his parents' room he heard the bed creak. He paused in the doorway and his mother rolled to face him. "Morning," she said as pushed herself up with her elbows. She opened her mouth to yawn but tried to smile at the same time, her teeth bared like a dog's.

"Morning." Colin noticed the other side of the bed, its covers pulled up to the headboard, its pillow centered with too much care. "Can we have pancakes for breakfast?"

Diane squinted as though she hadn't heard. "Pancakes? I haven't made pancakes in forever. But I think we have everything. Except buttermilk, but regular milk is fine." She brushed her hair back with another yawn. Her bathrobe was draped over the footboard and she pulled it over her shoulders. "Come here a second."

Her legs were crossed and still buried under the sheets, her knees sticking up on both sides like two cats sleeping under the covers. She pulled him into a hug, her breath warm through his shirt as her hand traced a circle beneath his shoulder blade. He could tell she was looking at the right side of the bed. "Did you see your father yet this morning?"

"I heard the basement door."

Her arm squeezed tighter. He wished he hadn't told her. This was one of those times when lying might have been the right thing.

Diane put her head against his chest. "That's what I thought." She patted his back. "Give me ten minutes and I'll have the batter in the bowl." Then her hands were on his shoulders and she was looking up at him, her eyes too wide. "Why don't you go downstairs," she said with a smile that was all wrong. "Tell him we're making pancakes. Say they're his favorite. Maybe that'll change his mind."

Without warning, Colin kissed her on the forehead. Only after, with horror, did he realize this. As he left the room he didn't look back. He didn't want to see what she felt.

Sometimes Colin thought of what was happening to his father and felt a kind of pride, like they were evolving or mutating, one by one. First, Heather could see the future; now their father had become secretive, no longer the pun-making man he'd grown up with. It was something in their genes, Colin decided, and thinking of all the ways it might show up in his own body or consciousness charmed the pale hairs on his arms until they stood up straight. He had come to imagine that this is what his father was writing— all the truths he discovered and all the things that would happen. Whatever book came out of it would not be some random piece of the future but a history of everything that hadn't happened yet, their entire lives.

He was thinking about his father's future as he trod down the stairs—quietly, both out of habit and because he liked to sneak up on people. No one else was allowed in the basement office. They could only glance through the door and see, shelved on the far wall, Alan's leather-bound notebooks, no labels on their spines. To Colin it looked like the secret archive in some old spy movie. It was easy to pretend he was rescuing stolen plans or launch codes, and he slunk along the wall to avoid unseen trip wires. You couldn't sneak up on the evil archivist by strolling out in the open. He shook his head and came away from the wall. Lately he'd had to remind himself not to be such a stupid kid. He pushed his hair out of his eye and approached the door, stepping into the bands of light from inside.

His father wasn't writing. There were two open notebooks, one written in and the other blank. The brass pen he used was erect in its holder, next to his brass lamp. His arm was resting on the desk, and Colin immediately saw the gun in his hand. He stopped breathing and leaned closer, careful not to press his nose against the door.

He didn't look tense, his father. His posture suggested bore-dom, more than anything. He was leaning to the left, resting the non-gun-holding arm on the arm of the chair. The barrel faced the blank bulletin board hung on the wall between his desk and the overhead cabinets. The way he aimed it made Colin think of jokes from movies, like *I got six little friends and they can all run faster than you.* Then the gun came up off the desk as his father leaned back in the chair. When he bent his elbow and put the barrel under his chin Colin lost a little drop of urine. As if they'd rehearsed it, both closed their eyes and took a simultaneous, silent breath.

Colin had never heard a gunshot before, and when he heard nothing but a click he thought the sound was so loud he'd been deafened. *It's like a bomb going off,* his uncle had once said, making fun of an old western on TV. *Guns don't sound anything like little toys popping, like kids' fireworks. They sound like goddamn bombs.* When Colin opened his eyes, there wasn't any blood. His father was still in his chair, skull intact, barrel resting in that soft, ticklish spot neither chin nor throat. The furnace next to the office still humming. The fluorescent light buzzing at the top of the stairs. Footsteps on the floor above like nothing had happened or ever would. Alan sighed and straightened his arm, the gun leveled once more at the bulletin board. Either because he'd decided to live or because the gun was broken he pushed the chair away from the desk, slipped the gun into its bottom drawer, and took up his pen. Colin watched as he wet his lips and reached for the mostly blank notebook.

He thought about silently running up the stairs and making noise on the way back down. He could even whistle something, as if he hadn't just seen this terrible thing. But when he pictured his father at the breakfast table trying to make conversation his heart felt pushed through an opening that was too small. There was nothing Colin could say to him. There was nothing he wanted to hear. If his father sat down with them Colin would leap across the table and gouge out his eyes, smash plates over his head, slash him up with a butter knife. He left before he burst into tears and punched the fake door into fake splinters. When he came back upstairs, Andy was staring up at the ceiling. Colin thought of how afraid he'd been in his sleep, how you could see through him when normally he blocked out your light. "How'd you sleep?" he asked.

"What do you care?"

He shrugged. What did he care? "I had a couple weird dreams."

"Oh yeah? Who's the lucky guy?"

Colin rolled his eyes to make himself look annoyed. He knew Andy expected him to say something back, or maybe to come over and try to suffocate him one more time, but the concept of suffocation seemed more serious now, more permanent. If you did see that light, it was already too late. He began to shake, and if it wasn't for his mother, calling from the kitchen, he might have suffocated anyway, with no one's help.

Diane was pouring circles of batter onto the griddle when they heard Alan's coughs from below. It sounded recorded and played back through blown speakers. Colin looked down at the linoleum as though he could see straight through, down to the basement. Andy went back to reading the movie listings on Diane's laptop. Paul had already turned back to the table and taken a swipe at the stick of butter.

"He better not be getting sick again," Diane said as she cracked an egg into a frying pan. "He doesn't have any time left."

Colin was holding his brother's hand flat on the table when Heather walked into the kitchen, straight for the refrigerator. "Sounds like someone's got the black lung," she said.

"That's your father," Diane said. "Can you see if he's okay?"

Heather swallowed three gulps of orange juice and put the jug back on the shelf. "Why don't you see?"

"Can you please just check?"

"Whatever." Heather slammed the refrigerator shut, rattling the empty cookie jars on top. The house sounded it as if it were collapsing as she ran down the stairs. For a moment all Colin could hear was the popping noise as air tried to get out from under the eggs. Then her feet were on the stairs again, the basement door shut so hard and fast there was no time for it to creak. "He's smoking," Heather said when she returned. She looked to their mother for an explanation.

Colin hadn't told anyone about the gun and it was getting to be too late. *Why didn't you say something sooner?* his mother would scream.

Diane set the spatula on the counter next to the stove. "Can you watch this for a second?"

"What am I supposed to do?"

Diane tightened her bathrobe as she crossed the room. Her footsteps on the stairs were different, Colin noticed—heavy like his sister's, but slower. He understood what that meant, and he put his bare feet on the floor so he could feel their argument. When he heard his mother's weight return to the stairs and the door slam once more he crossed his legs and covered his toes with his hands. She frowned at him as she walked by. "You know that smoking is bad for you."

"I think I burned this one," Heather said as she poked at a blackened lump of batter.

"Let me do it." Diane took the spatula and scraped the failed pancake off the griddle. "It's times like this I wish we still had Dozer." She slid it into the trash can hidden under the sink.

Andy leaned in over the computer. "Your dad smokes?"

"I guess so."

"What are you two ladies whispering about?" Heather pulled a chair away and sat down, her feet on the chair across from her. "Declaring your eternal love?"

"I was telling Colin that the fortune-teller just walked in."

Colin tried to kick him under the table.

Heather rolled her eyes. "What are you talking about, faggot?"

"Heather," Diane said without looking up.

"So how does Colin die? It's getting run over by a bus full of nuns, isn't it?"

"How the fuck should I know?"

"Heather!"

"But you said he'd be dead in three years."

She put her chin in her hand and batted her eyelashes. "And when did I say that?"

"I don't know." Andy frowned. "I just know you said it."

"You two need to find something better to do than invent conversations with me, 'cause that's pretty lame."

"But you said—"

"Mom," Colin said. He pulled his brother's hand away from the butter dish. "We're gonna go to a movie. Is that okay?"

"I don't care." She tossed another pancake onto the pile next to the stove. "First batch is ready." She brought the plate over to the table. "Everybody gets one for now. More on the way." She stood next to Colin's chair. "Ask your father for money. Hopefully he didn't spend it all on cigarettes or a new convertible or something stupid." The way she looked at him made him feel like they were all alone in the room. She was trying to be angry, he could tell, but her eyes drooped in the corners and she bit her lip. "I don't know," she said.

Colin thought he could make it through the rest of the day without seeing his father. He'd prepared himself for the next morning, when he would find once more the father he knew—the one who'd make jokes you couldn't even call jokes as he poured cereal into four bowls, who'd never pointed a gun at his own face. But when Alan knocked on his sons' door before bed, Colin froze as though the police or the Mafia had found him. He stayed bent over his homework and pretended he hadn't heard. Paul went on sitting on the bed like a statue or a sad ghost. Their father let himself in. "Hey." He shut the door behind him. "Just wanted to ask how the movie was."

Colin stared at him. He couldn't remember the last time his father had even mentioned a movie, much less cared about one. "It was okay?"

Alan stood next to the bed. The room's only light came from a penguin-shaped lamp on Colin's desk. In that shadow his father looked unshaven, old, tired. He glanced down at the piece of paper trapped under Colin's hands. "Homework," he said.

"Yeah."

"What subject?"

"English."

Alan ran a hand through his hair. "I never did that well in English. Is it a book report?"

"Kind of. I gotta answer some questions on the book we're reading."

"What book?"

Colin bent over and opened his backpack and pushed aside folded papers and snacks. He came up with a small white book and handed it over.

"*The Catcher in the Rye*." Alan laughed. "They're still making you read this stuff?"

Colin nodded.

"I read this when I was your age." He thumbed the pages. "I remember the scene where he invites the hooker up to his room but doesn't—but doesn't, you know. I never got that."

"I don't think we've read that part yet."

"Oh. Sorry." He set the book on the desk.

"Whatever."

Alan sighed and sat down on Colin's bed. Colin watched him as he looked around the room reading posters and studying models of lunar outposts and spacecraft, almost as though he'd never been in there before. He tried to remember what he was going to write. Alan touched the wing of a fighter on Colin's headboard and watched as it bobbled, hit during battle. "So school's going okay?"

Colin turned back to his desk. He stared at the book and listened to his father shift on the bed. "I guess so," he said. "It's just school."

"I hated school when I was your age. Well, all through childhood really. I didn't really like it until college, when we could do whatever we wanted."

Colin thought about a school like that, where kids just got up and left when class got too boring, or where the boys who smoked didn't have to sneak into the trees by the highway. That was almost worse than school, having to choose.

"I miss it, though. All of it."

Colin shrugged and tapped his pencil on the paper in front of him.

"But I'm glad it doesn't bother you. Having one kid who can't stand school is hard enough."

Leafing through the book, Colin caught the word *fuck* toward the end. He read that paragraph.

"I mean Heather. I pointed at her wall but you're not looking."

"Totally," Colin said into the book.

"And you're not listening, either." There was a slap as Alan pushed off his thighs and got to his feet. Colin turned and saw his father standing next to Paul, pushing a willful lock of hair behind his ear. Paul's eyes were half-closed. Colin knew they were saying things to each other that nobody else could understand. He wanted to break the pencil in half and throw it at them.

"Did you rake the yard?" Alan asked.

Colin turned back to his homework, putting the pencil to the paper as though he finally knew what to write. "No. There wasn't time."

"Goddamn it, C."

"What? I'll do it after school tomorrow."

"That's not the point." The floorboards groaned as he moved for the door. "I asked you to do one thing this weekend and you can't even do that."

"Uh . . . sorry? I didn't know it was the end of the world or anything."

His father was standing by the door, his hand on the knob. It was hard, now, to picture him with the gun. Colin had let himself forget it, rolling his eyes at his father as if to say, *Work? You want me to work?* For a second it seemed like the whole thing could have been dreamed up, like he hadn't crawled out of his sleeping bag that morning until he heard the clang of a whisk in a metal bowl as his mother mixed pancake batter.

"Goodnight," his father said.

Colin nodded at the notebook paper. He wrote, very slowly, the title of the book, adding a loop on top of the *C* like he did when he signed his name, as though he would write *The Colin in the Rye*. His father lingered a few more seconds before he left, and Colin plugged his ears so he couldn't tell what room he went into next.

For the first few months after his father began to write, Colin tried, every time Andy came over, to pick the lock on the basement office. It wasn't something you could do alone. Someone had to watch the stairway or listen for footsteps. Before long, the boys tired of bending paper clips into shapes they didn't understand, arguing at the foot of the stairs. Besides, it was only a room full of notebooks, Andy pointed out. Not worth their time. They gave up and went back to watching television and smashing batteries with rocks on the back patio.

Now, as he stood outside that office and looked through the slats, Colin had never before wanted so badly to know what his father was putting on those pages. A notebook had been left on the desk. The lamp made parts of the room look like an unfinished drawing. Unable to sleep, Colin had heard what sounded like the basement door's creak, and he invented an entire conversation with his father. He would creep down the stairs with his silent bare feet and surprise him, right outside the door. *I'll rake the yard tomorrow. Sorry I wasn't listening.*

But he'd heard the wrong creak. It was instead the bedroom door, with its wooden groan at the end as the door frame pulled back against the extra weight. He'd gone to bed, his father, leaving the lamp and the notebook here to wait for him when he came back, maybe early in the morning, before breakfast, or maybe not until next Sunday. Colin leaned closer to the door and squinted at the notebook.

For the first time in months he thought about picking the lock. He was thinking of how he'd have to jiggle the paper clip until something clicked, and out of instinct he reached for the knob to test its strength. When it turned, he looked down as if there were something he'd missed, all this time. He opened the door and went inside. The cigarette smoke had already attached itself to the foam ceiling tiles, but it didn't smell as bad as he expected.

The notebook was open to a page marked "Curious Parasitoids" where his father had written, in a list: Emerald Cockroach Wasp; The Eponymous Alien; Sacculina; Lancet Liver Fluke. Colin had to read it several times to make sure it was English. Aliens? His heart picked up as he put together the scenario, his father working for the CIA, sorting through government secrets. He flipped the page back and found another list merely called "Notes." The first point said something about fixing the crack in the foundation under the kitchen window, and the second point advised him to "put bullets in separate place." Colin flipped the page back to "Curious Parasitoids" and tried to center the notebook where he'd found it. He felt judged for reading it, like the time he and Andy had found a copy of *Penthouse* when they were ten and burned it when they couldn't handle the secret any longer.

He opened the bottom drawer of the desk. His father hadn't followed through on his task. There the bullets were, right next to the gun. His eyes widened at its weight. "Jeez," he said as he shifted it into his grip. He aimed out into the basement's dark, finger on the trigger. For a second he thought about putting it under his chin, but his stomach panicked at the idea and he brought it into his lap. It was a revolver. He knew that if you pushed the cylinder to the side you could load it. It made a crisp little noise as he did so, light peeking through the chambers. When he and Andy were younger they pretended to be marines, marooned on an alien planet, and a marine's utmost skill lay in how fast he could reload his gun. Colin looked down at the bullets. In the heat of battle you never had much time. Every second lost meant one more second you could catch a bullet or fail to toss a grenade out of your foxhole under the ping-pong table. He took six bullets from the box, surprisingly small in their plastic cartridge. Loading them wasn't as graceful as you'd expect, and he dropped one or two on the floor. He returned his finger to the trigger. His heart had never felt so big, pressed up against its cage of bones as though it'd finally outgrown it. Then he began to sweat. He quickly put the gun and the box of bullets back in the drawer. When he realized the gun was still loaded he heard a door's creak—definitely the basement's—and he jumped up from the chair and darted out of the office, hiding behind a stack of boxes in the far corner. As he watched his father step into the light, he bit down on his tongue until it hurt. Alan didn't even look at the door. He didn't even ponder it, wide open like that when he'd left it shut. He didn't look around the basement when he reached out for the door and pulled it closed behind him. When his shape, sliced into pieces by the door's glowing slats, sat down at his desk, he didn't even pause as he reached for his pen and went back to writing. Colin, swift and silent without shoes or socks, ran upstairs before his breath gave him away. He lay awake all night waiting for the sound like a bomb going off.

Colin had always thought the word was *parasite*, but when he searched online he learned that *parasitoids* were a unique subset of parasites that, over time, "ultimately sterilize or kill, and often consume, the host." He wished he could see the list again—the long word his father had written before "alien," the *sac* thing, something about a liver. After a few days had gone by, the words *emerald cockroach wasp* hatched in his head, and he said them over and over until he knew where they came from, whispering to himself while Paul rocked back and forth on the other side of the room.

As part of its reproductive process, the emerald cockroach wasp delivers a paralyzing sting to its prey—the cockroaches of Africa, South Asia, and the Pacific Islands. With the roach briefly incapacitated, the wasp delivers another sting to the ganglia, targeting a precise fold of the brain. At this point, the roach is technically able to escape—no longer paralyzed—but will instead begin to groom itself as though the wasp has moved on. The wasp's venom blocks its victim's octopamine receptors, neutralizing aggressive or defensive behavior, including any desire to flee. The wasp then chews off half of each of the roach's antennae and proceeds to lead it, as though by a leash, to the wasp's burrow, where it deposits an egg on the roach's abdomen and leaves to find another roach. Meanwhile, the larva emerges from its egg, burrows into the roach, and begins its gestation process. To prolong the life of its host, the larva feeds on the least life-threatening organs first. Once the roach is hollowed out, it uses its body as a cocoon, emerging several days later as an adult wasp. Colin even watched a short video of the whole ritual—the wasp leading the roach away, *Here, come with me, there's nothing to be afraid of*, and the roach as happy as you could imagine a roach being, and so calm.

At the funeral the following Saturday, Colin's grandfather mentioned his black eye. "I used to get in fights when I was your age," he said as the two stood in front of a bulletin board full of photographs. He wasn't looking at Colin. He didn't introduce himself in case Colin had, over the last ten years, forgotten he existed. Instead he sipped his coffee as they looked at all those pictures of Alan—most with his children. Colin leaned closer and looked at some Christmas morning, six or seven years ago. His father was holding a boxed set of Legos. Only now did Colin remember how his father had read the back while he waited, describing the city workers and their vehicles. The bulletin board began to tremble and Colin looked down at the carpet to get himself under control. He still hadn't decided if he'd killed his father.

"I got it from my brother. The black eye." He licked a tear from his lip and turned back to the photographs, as though someone had dared him to look into the sun.

"Do you and your brother fight often?"

Colin shook his head. "Paul is retarded. I mean"—he looked at the floor—"he's autistic."

Quentin frowned at the pictures, as if he no longer understood them. "I forgot about that."

The word *retarded*—Colin knew better, and he knew his grandfather was ashamed, filing Colin away with the rest of the world's middle school boys. But he was different from them, and he wished he could prove he was different.

"I'm sorry about your father."

Colin hid the twitch he'd developed whenever he heard the word itself, *father*. When he looked up again Quentin was gone, across the parlor's entry hall. How long could Colin hide, a murderer in plain sight?

His mother was sitting on a bench by the door, surrounded by her friends and Alan's two sisters. If you didn't know them, his mother and his grandfather, you wouldn't have noticed the way he turned his head when he walked by her, how he didn't nod or smile, and it wouldn't have seemed strange. You'd have thought he was only a distant relation come to pay his respects—an old coworker, maybe, or a college professor, rather than her father. Colin watched as he continued into the main room. Piano music came through the overhead speakers, rattling on the high notes. He watched his grandfather take the row farthest from the pulpit, just inside the door. The way he laid his suit coat over the chair next to him and smoothed it with his hands made Colin's skin tingle. It made him think he was saving the seat, even though he said he'd be alone. There was family out there Colin didn't even know he had.

The night before the funeral had been long. As she read aloud from a letter that'd come in that day's mail, Colin's mother stubbed out cigarette after cigarette in a beach glass ashtray as the remains of their family sat around the dining room table. Diane had taken up smoking only two days after it happened. Colin had been heating soup in the microwave when she began coughing in the next room. It'd made him shiver, like a déjà vu you heard instead of saw—an already-heard—but it was the smell, more than anything, that made him want to fly apart in every direction, to throw dishes through the windows and overturn the table and its shingles of unopened sympathy cards. She was on the couch, cigarette in hand. Standing in the doorway, Colin thought he was the only one to scold her, to tell her she was a bad influence. Instead he put his head in her lap and cried until he fell asleep.

He watched her now as she took long, deep drags and held on to the smoke before exhaling. The smell was already familiar as the dining room gathered it up against all its clefts and furrowed places. He held his breath and wondered how it felt, but he knew he'd never try it. It was too hard to not picture it as his father's ghost, grey and shape-shifting, pulled into you and drawn out again like it was looking for something. *Why did the gun go off?* it wanted to know. *Why did I die?* It wouldn't stop searching until it found the answer, billowing out between his mother's lips. Someday that ghost would find its killer and wrap its tendrils around his neck.

"I just don't think he should come," Diane was saying, glancing over the letter again. "I haven't talked to him in . . . oh God, four years? It's too much at once."

"Where does he live?" Colin asked.

"In town. Over in Minneapolis."

"So he's not coming a long way?"

"No. Not at all. Why's that important?"

Colin took the letter and looked for clues that might reveal their relationship, his father and his grandfather, but there was only sympathy—no memories, no stories, no affectionate names. Colin traced the signature—an elaborate Q followed by a jagged line. It made him think of a seismic reading or a heart monitor.

He could feel his mother watching him. "I don't know what to do," she said.

"I don't get what the big deal is," Heather said. She put her phone in her pocket and collapsed onto the table, her head resting on her arm. She spoke into the wood and Colin felt it in his elbows. "Are we supposed to hate him? I know it's been like ten years but I don't remember him being, like, deformed or anything."

"Don't start," Diane said.

"Don't start what? I'm just saying he's not this horrible monster. He obviously wants to pay his respects or whatever."

"Please, Heather. I don't need to hear this."

Heather pushed herself away from the table. "Fine. Do what you want. I'm going to my room." She reached over and thumped Colin's head with her knuckles. "And don't bother me."

"I wasn't going to!" He swung at her, too late, and called her every name he could think of as she slipped through the doorway.

Diane waved her hand in the air as though she'd made Heather disappear. "Just leave her alone." She lit another cigarette and spoke out of the side of her mouth. "If she wants to be a little—a little brat, that's her business."

She was already good at smoking, Colin decided. It'd become something he could watch without crying or even thinking of what his father had called his *new habit*. Right now, it helped him not think of how she and Heather had turned against each other. Nobody had laid blame but it was something you felt coming. They were waiting for the right time to say it, and it made him feel worse to know they'd blame each other for what happened, passing over the real culprit.

"Can you blow rings?" he asked her.

"What?"

"With your smoke. Can you make smoke rings?" Colin dug his hands under his thighs and sat on them. He kept wanting to point at the cigarette, like some kid.

"I don't know. I don't think so." She flipped the cigarette in her hand, glancing at the glowing end. "Let's give it a shot. You're the judge—tell me how I do." With a tap of her finger she ashed into the tray between them and took a long drag, concentrating on a picture of a sheep on the far wall. She tilted her head back and blew a single, shapeless cloud, or what a cloud might look like if you vacuumed out the inside. Colin watched as she took another breath, but when she formed her lips into an *O* she broke out in a laugh and lost the rest of her smoke in a coughing fit. "Guess not," she said.

"Five point six," Colin said. "Promising, but needs work."

She smiled and set the cigarette in the ashtray where it sent its gnarled signal into the air. This probably wasn't true, but it felt like the first time she'd smiled all day—all week, even. It felt like something he'd given, and he let himself believe it. He needed to believe it when he'd taken so much.

Sometimes he was terrified, alone with his mother, that he might vomit out his confession without warning, with no way to control it. *I loaded the gun!* his mouth would suddenly say, and there'd be no way to take it back. Thinking of it, he clenched his teeth until his jaw began to ache.

Paul rocked at the other end of the table. "He needs a shower," Diane said. "His last one was Sunday night. Shouldn't have let him go that long, now that he's older."

It embarrassed him, her saying *older* like that and everything it meant. Colin looked down at the table to hide his blush. "I can set it up for him," he said. "If you need me to."

"Look at his hair. He can't go anywhere like that. Especially a—not a funeral."

"I can put him in the shower," Colin said, almost at a whisper.

She was chewing the inside of her cheek. "Alan used to do that."

"I can do it."

She sighed—so loud it made him flinch. "I guess you'll have to," she said. "You're the only man I can count on now." It came out almost recited, a line from a movie that had worked its way into her life. With her free hand she reached for his and traced his veins, small and submerged and more lavender than blue. All they heard right then was Paul's chair continuing to creak and somewhere the rumbling of Heather's stereo. The ash crept backward, and if it wasn't for its sudden heat next to Diane's finger, that might have become their future, sitting there forever like a painting.

In the bathroom, Colin laid Paul's pajamas in a neat pile on the counter. He'd gone back to rocking and was staring at the scale opposite the toilet. It felt like he was babysitting a toddler, and he was grateful, at least, that Paul could dress himself once you picked out his clothes. Colin felt the water. When it was hot enough he backed away and put his hand on the counter.

They could adjust, all of them. They could each learn something new.

Colin looked away when Paul stood and took off his shirt, but his eyes drifted back when he heard the zipper on Paul's jeans. More curious than cautious, he let himself watch, and when Paul pulled down his briefs Colin stared at what uncoiled. He hadn't realized how much time had passed since he'd last seen his brother naked. His heart felt wrung like a rag as he let his eyes snag in all the wrong places. It wasn't even the same color as his skin, which made it look fake, like a doll's arm fused to his flesh with a charred, wiry scar. It occurred to him that if he wanted to know what it felt like, if it was as heavy and coarse as it looked, nobody could rat him out. His own, bent painfully in his briefs, felt smaller than ever.

Paul turned toward the shower. Ringlets of steam fell over his shoulders. With this new part of his brother hidden, Colin felt like life could go on. "Go ahead," he squeaked, and coughed and said it again, but Paul didn't move. Colin told him once more that it was okay, it was just a shower, stupid, and when that didn't work he reached out and placed his hand on Paul's shoulder to nudge him forward. He was met with a shudder as Paul swung around and drove his fist into his brother's eye. Colin fell back against the door, and then both of them were screaming. When his mother knocked on the door he felt like a failure.

"Is everything okay? What's going on?"

"I don't know!" Colin shouted. He wiped tears out of his eyes. "He hit me!"

The doorknob rattled. "Open the door."

"But he's naked." Paul was hunched over and hugging his knees but Colin could see everything. His cheeks burned on his mother's behalf.

"I gave birth to him," she said. "I've seen it all."

Colin sighed and got to his feet. With one hand over his eye he unlocked the door. "What happened?" Diane asked as the hallway sucked the steam from the room. He closed the door and leaned against it, happy to have his mother between them like a shield.

"I told him it was okay to get in the shower and he hit me." He pressed his hand over his eye and wiped away a tear with the other. "I didn't even touch him and he hit me!"

Diane bent down to Paul as he grabbed his elbows and moaned at the floor. "Honey," she said. "Paul." She stroked his hair but took her hand away when he screamed. "What's wrong, Paulie?" She clasped her hands together and they trembled, held out in front of her heart.

"Honey, you have to get in the shower." The toilet gave a clunk when she sat on its lid. "It's been days and you have to get clean."

She brought her hands up to her face, covering her mouth and the end of her nose. "Please," she said, her voice muted by her hands. You could tell she had no idea what she was doing.

Paul moaned again, as though that explained everything.

When they first walked into the funeral parlor that morning, everyone spent a long time staring. Even though Colin had held the ice to his face until his hand and head both ached, he couldn't escape the broken blood vessels that left a purple ring around his right eye. At first he wanted to tell people he'd beaten up a kid in his neighborhood—an older kid—but when they didn't ask, he didn't offer. Eventually, everyone stopped looking at him, and when the service started they stared straight ahead, at the pastor, at the flowers, at the *body*.

Alan's brother delivered the eulogy. It sounded like all other eulogies ever written, both real and made up—from those who'd died and from movies he'd seen. His uncle choked on the word *brother* while he told a story from when they were boys, but Colin knew it wasn't anything like the word *father*. All he had to do was think it—*father*—and it rose up in his throat like a poison. His uncle talked about the strong man he knew, almost as if he were trying to persuade them. Colin squeezed his fingers together, thinking of the last time he'd spoken to his father. He could've said something, done something—and nobody would have died. Or he could have *not* loaded the gun, and *not* killed his father, and nobody would've died, his father wouldn't have died. *Father*, he thought. He opened his mouth to breathe but with it came a gasp he didn't expect, a quiet moan, and his mother pulled him into her warmth of smoke and perfume. There he cried not caring who could see or hear.

After everyone came forward one by one to touch the coffin's screwed-shut lid, they closed the doors to the main room. Nobody was supposed to notice the parlor's staff carrying the body out into the hearse. Colin thought about the body, which was supposed to be separate, now, from the soul. His father's soul was the real thing, a translucent and colorless copy of what he'd looked like on Sunday night. A soul would go to heaven or hell. His grandmother once said how sorry she was that her old friend from grade school had gone to hell after swallowing a bottle of pills: "When you don't respect life, you have no respect for God." But was it suicide? Instead it would be his own soul, Colin's soul, in the years to come, dragged down into the earth's cracks and fissures, held down by these gaunt hands that looked like shadows but weren't.

Colin searched the room for a distraction. His mother was in that chair by the door again, accepting tissues from in-laws and cousins and even young children who understood. To his right, his grandparents were talking. He'd never seen them together before. Their voices weren't reaching him and he tried to read their lips but couldn't get through the first sentence. Instead he imagined what they were saying. He knew she'd remarried—he was there when Ron slid a ring over her spotted finger—but, out of an unexpected ache, he hoped. *I miss you*, he imagined his grandfather saying as he sipped from his paper cup. *I miss you too*, she'd say, and right then she smiled as though she really had said it. Colin closed his eyes and there in the dark they embraced. When he opened his eyes they stood apart. She shook her head as she looked at the floor. Quentin frowned and picked at a protrusion on the cup.

Colin went over to his mother. Before he could speak she reached out and pulled him tight. He felt a tear slide down the back of his shirt and seep through the silk. When she released him she began straightening his hair. Then she laughed and touched the spot under his eye. "I can't believe you'll look like this, whenever I think back."

He wasn't expecting her to say anything—let alone laugh—so he went through with his plan. "I want to ride with Grandpa Patterson to the cemetery," he said. The way her face changed made him regret it. Offended—that was how she looked, as though he'd called her something obscene.

"Colin."

"I haven't seen him in a long time."

"You haven't seen him for most of your life. Why do you have to see him now?"

He looked at the floor and wiggled his toes in his shoes, watching the light crease and fold back into itself.

Diane looked over Colin's shoulder, where he assumed his grandparents were still frowning at the floor between them. Then she shrugged and took up her purse. She dug around inside for the cigarettes she'd inherited. "If it's that important to you," she said with a cigarette in her mouth, "I'm not gonna stop you. Just don't get too used to him." She turned her attention back to her purse and he reached into his pocket and put his hand forward. The lighter lay in his palm.

"You left it on the table."

She smiled, her eyes ringed in light, and wiped away her tears with a disintegrating tissue. "Thank you." She took the lighter from his palm and examined it before giving it back. "Step out with me for a second. If you're going to be a gentleman, you might as well light this for me."

He might have realized, then, that he and his mother were alone, in their shared way. Knowing just how easy it was for someone you thought was permanent to completely disappear made him want to latch onto her like he'd done as a foolish, wailing boy who couldn't bear to be dropped off at preschool. They had to trust each other.

When Colin came back into the parlor, his grandmother was walking away from that private corner. Instead of the grimace or frown he expected, she brushed a white lock of hair from her face. She looked thoughtful, as though she liked whatever it was she was thinking about. She saw Colin as he passed, and as she touched his shoulder her face switched back to that of his grandmother, the woman with a warm distance. He came up to his grandfather and stood behind him until he noticed. "Can I ride with you?"

Quentin tapped his finger on the side of his cup. "I don't think your mother would approve."

"She said it's okay. I asked her."

He looked past Colin, his eyes searching the room.

"She's outside smoking."

Quentin took a sip of his coffee. "That's new. Well, if you don't mind riding with me and only me, I guess you can. We're going to Roselawn, correct?"

"Yeah."

He looked down at Colin and pursed his lips, as though he was expected to entertain him or impart some great lesson. "I'm sorry about your father."

"Don't."

"Sorry?"

"Just don't." Colin shook his head as though it was in there—*father*—like a gumball machine's loose coin. He put his hands in his pockets and shrugged, waiting for the procession to get moving, but it wasn't anything he could fake, right then, and he began to cry. His grandfather was smart enough not to recoil, and when Colin threw himself at him, wrapping his arms around his waist as tight as he could, he was still human enough to wait until it passed.

For nearly a week the image of his father had been the tangled heap of blood and limbs on the basement floor, half-covered by his overturned chair. This he'd seen for less than a second before his mother pushed him away and screamed at him and Heather to go upstairs. Call 911, she said from inside the office, as though her husband had simply sliced open his thumb or stepped on a nail. Colin imagined the sense she was making of his face, or what was left of his face. He vowed to imagine it forever.

Now his father was a long, rectangular block of polished wood. Now there was a pastor who stretched out his long vowels in a way Colin hadn't heard before. Now his father sank like an island into a calm, green sea. Now the clap of a slammed-shut Bible echoed out over Roselawn. Now the sky was blue from treetop to treetop, even though all the funerals he'd seen on television took place on overcast days. Now his father lay where Colin couldn't touch him, and people he didn't know were offering roses they'd brought at Diane's request. Now his mother nodded to the pastor, who signaled the two men behind him. Now a noise was pulled from Colin's throat as the first mound of dirt hit the coffin. Now the earth was swallowing his father and his blanket of roses. Now the two men packed the dirt with the backs of their spades, and only then did his mother push back her hair and make for the car. Only then did anyone dare move. Now his father was buried.

When they arrived home that evening, nobody spoke. His mother stood on the deck out back, smoking at the sky, and Heather went to lie on her bed, no music and no magazines. Paul had never been so still, sitting on the carpet in the hallway like something heavy you'd dropped out of exhaustion. Since the burial, the word *parasitoid* was stuck in Colin's head. In the living room he read about them online, clicking on article after article until his eyes felt crossed. *A common characteristic of the parasitoid is an alteration of host behavior*, he read, and he clicked on the example of *Sacculina*—a word he recognized from his father's notebook. The *Sacculina* attaches itself to the male crab's rear thorax, near the reproductive organs, and begins to molt. Having shed its outer shell, the soft-bodied *Sacculina* pierces itself into the crab and begins to grow. Over time, the *Sacculina* secretes a series of hormones that sterilize and castrate the crab, nullifying all reproductive behavior and redirecting any energy wasted in searching for a mate. The crab now exists solely to serve the *Sacculina* and will care for its eggs, growing inside of the sac, as though they were its own. After the eggs hatch and the larvae emerge, the crab expels them and ensures their survival. Once the larvae are on their own, the crab is no longer needed. Colin couldn't figure out if this meant it died, was eaten, or just wandered away. When no one was watching he lifted the laptop and reached into his underwear. He felt his testicles as though something might be dissolving them from the inside out. They might have felt bigger than normal, and his continued research led to articles on testicular torsion, cancer, infertility, and hernias. His heart felt like it was crawling out of his throat and he was sweating, a cold drop etching an itch under his arm. His father must have been a genius to put together all this information. And what if he'd observed the rest of them, like a scientist observing his rats or monkeys? How had he judged and classified and taxonomized his family? Colin knew he'd have to read every single one of those notebooks.

As he lay in bed, the two images coalesced—his father in the wooden box and his father alone in the basement, writing at his desk. The palimpsest morphed into his father buried alive, his fists pounding against the wood as the groundskeepers dumped their shovelfuls of bad dirt into the grave. There was nothing after that darkness but waiting. How long would it take someone—a grown man like his father—to use up thirty cubic feet of oxygen? Colin knew it depended on how scared you were, how desperate each breath. He shivered in his bed and tried to force the idea out of his mind. *My dad is dead*, he told himself. *He shot himself in the head on Monday, October 13, in his office, in this house.* It occurred to him that something might have changed his father's behavior, a creature that had perhaps attached itself inside of him and was controlling him. Or it controlled Colin. Perhaps a parasitoid had given him the impulse to load that gun, to ruin a life, a family of lives. His father was now three things—a man writing, a man bloody on the floor, and Colin's own reflection hanging from the ceiling as he touched the coffin's cold surface, a woman in line behind him muttering an *oh* that cracked in her throat before he let go and shied away. What was living inside of him? Colin tried to listen to his heart, to his breathing, to his blood. He touched his eyes, his ears, and put a finger in each nostril. Was something using him? Would something hatch? Perhaps that was how he'd die—the three years Heather warned him about. Something would crawl its way out of him, and by then he would have long been under its control.

He got out of bed and went to the bathroom. In the nightlight's glow he looked barely there, but when he took off his shirt the light of his skin made the room brighter. Nothing seemed attached to him. Nothing was burrowing its way inside. He touched each armpit, the space behind his ears. He listened to the house, and when it seemed quiet enough he slid his pajama bottoms to the floor. Slowly, he crawled up onto the counter and stood right up against the mirror. Everything was still there, all in the right place. He couldn't tell if anything hurt or if he was just making it up. Nothing seemed wrong. He'd never watched it get hard before, and as it grew in the mirror he didn't feel pain, exactly, but it wasn't the same as always. He knew he should get dressed and go back to bed. He knew this was the wrong thing to be doing. He'd always hidden his body, even from his brother, with whom he'd shared a bedroom his entire life. *Nobody's seen this*, he thought as he held his erection in his hand, and somehow his fist knew to tighten, his legs knew to straighten, his knees knew to lock. His heart knew to pound, right then, and his body knew what it was doing. Everything was in working order.

Diane sighed as she looked over the waiting room. Even the sign above the reception desk—Jacobson Family Therapy—was sans serif and without color. It was hard not to answer sarcastically as she filled out the insurance forms, signed the privacy policy, put an *x* adjacent to *Struggling With The Loss Of A Loved One*. She returned the clipboard and smoothed the wrinkles out of her vest. Against what, she wanted to know, was she supposed to be struggling?

In the beginning, she thought she could handle it. Winter had helped, settling in soon after his death. Winter even found its way into their house, the snow quieting not only the yard and the street but also the living room, where she slept, and the bedrooms at the other end of the house. Colin did well in school. Heather did poorly. Paul rocked when the teachers spoke to him. It was as if nothing had changed, especially when you imagined that Alan had simply banished himself downstairs, back to writing more nonsense in those notebooks.

When Jack London first saw snow, he wrote that "one could not survive it." Born in California in 1876, on a warm January day, he began traveling when he was sixteen. First to Japan, on the schooner *Sophie Sutherland*, and—in July of 1897—to the Canadian Yukon. Like tens of thousands of other would-be prospectors, he did not arrive until the summer of 1898, malnourished and stricken with scurvy. He likened snow to a "silent assassin" that could "slit a man's throat." Since she'd read this, scrawled in Alan's hand, flat on his desk as she waited for the police, Diane had welcomed snow in all forms. It *was* silencing. You could hear it hush the neighborhood, even the traffic on Lexington Avenue a few blocks away, like it'd come from behind and put its hand over the city's mouth. Alan had written this between a list called "Curious Parasitoids" and a quote copied out from the *New York Times*: "Louise McPherson, head of the department of entomology at the University of Illinois at Urbana-Champaign and a participant in the study, said that examination of dead bees had found residues of more than 100 chemicals, insecticides and pesticides." Alone with his remains, she couldn't decide if her husband was a genius or a madman. She kicked his leg and called him a *fucking idiot*, and she kicked him again until it no longer felt like kicking a person, someone who might kick back. It was just an object on the floor.

His office was how he'd left it. The gun was now emptied of bullets and returned to the bottom drawer, against the investigator's advice, against her mother's wishes, against her own sense of self-preservation. But she would never go that far. She knew that the moment she found him. Standing over his body, she'd looked into the future to see if she too could end her life. Instead, the future conceded to Heather and Colin, standing just outside, and Paul somewhere upstairs making a noise she'd never heard. She left the gun in his hand and waited for the police. *He's gone*, she wanted to say when she let them in—or, *Help him*—but she only shook her head.

Almost every night she went to bed early, carrying her pillow and her blanket to the couch. It was snow, or the thought of snow, that kept her asleep until morning, even when it wasn't falling. It wasn't until spring came, quickly with a week of forty-degree rainy days, that she began to worry. She'd always loved spring and its morning thunderstorms, its birds you heard on the way to work. Even though she'd given up gardening for motherhood, she loved spying on the neighbors in their flowerbeds, wiping their gloves on old jeans, cradling geraniums or snapdragons like infant animals as they untangled their braided roots. But that spring, watching them trade spades or boxes of growth hormones, putting words to their silent bickering—she felt cheated. She no longer slept through the night.

As they approached summer she still woke up sobbing three nights a week. Against the May sunshine and evening warmth, her grief was suddenly abnormal, and her friend Shannon came armed with the name of a therapist.

"What can a therapist say that you can't?" Diane asked, moving her mug in a gentle circle to watch the coffee inside try to catch up. They had brewed their usual Sunday-night decaf and sat with the windows open.

"You'd be surprised at what they come up with," Shannon said. "When me and Frank were fighting a few years ago—nonstop, you remember—we tried it out. It wasn't like he knew something we didn't, but without him it might not've worked. They're just good listeners."

She tried to be patient as Shannon listed on her fingers what was left of Diane's life as though symptoms of a common infection. "You haven't stopped smoking," she said after Colin came into the room to light her cigarette. "You're spending how much a week on this? Without your husband's income?" Diane rubbed her hand on Colin's shoulder as he slipped the lighter back into his pocket, hoping he wasn't ashamed for supporting his mother's habit. But he wasn't ashamed. She could tell by the way he raced to find her, every time she called to him, and even when she didn't—even when the crinkling cellophane was enough.

"I'll quit eventually. I know it's stupid."

"You're still sleeping on the couch. It's been—" Shannon looked down at her coffee. It was clear she knew how a word like *months* could be offensive, just like *weeks*. Right then, Diane felt like *years* would be offensive, or *decades*. A *lifetime*. "I don't know," Shannon said. She took a sip of her coffee. "Are you still missing a lot of work?"

It was hard to get people like Shannon to understand. Diane would talk about things like the kids, her job at the plant, how the car took three turns to start on a cold morning, her trays of makeup in the bedroom. These were things that hadn't changed. Everything, except one thing, had stayed the same. "That's the cruelest thing of all," she'd tried to tell Shannon. "Talk about God's mysteries." Even now, on the way to therapy that very afternoon, she had the wind knocked out of her by the sight of a maroon Oldsmobile with rings of rust around the wheel wells. In high school she'd suffered anxiety attacks; a grief attack wasn't all that different. Her vision glossed over and she missed her exit, one hand on the wheel as she dug through the glove compartment for a napkin. By the time she turned around and got back on the freeway everything around her looked strange, as if she'd never been there before, and she was no longer bound by love.

Just as she began to grow impatient, shuffling through the leftover issues of *National Geographic* on the table next to her, a man emerged from the hallway across the room and smiled at her as he passed. He approached the receptionist, who surrendered Diane's clipboard without a word. As he looked over it he touched the upper ridge of his right ear. Diane saw him gently fold the cartilage there, like a girl testing a flower petal's strength. When he'd read enough, or had come to some conclusion, he returned the clipboard to the receptionist. Diane looked away as though she'd been caught peeking into a window.

"Diane?"

As she turned to face him she arched her eyebrows as though surprised. "Yes," she said. She saw that he was tall and growing a beard, that he wore glasses, his hair more grey than not. He wasn't that different from the man she had imagined, and this disappointed her.

"Thank you for seeing me," she said.

"You don't have to thank me." He waved his hand. "After all, let's not forget that it's you who's paying me. So I guess I should thank you for coming."

Diane forced a laugh and looked at her shoes. The whole thing seemed like a waste of time, despite the week spent thinking it over. That same Sunday, she told Shannon there was no way. "Can you imagine me sitting on some couch blathering on about my life? It's so self-involved." She laughed, then laughed at how her laugh sounded fake. "Sorry. That's just not me."

She'd been saying that a lot—that something wasn't *her*, that she wasn't *something*. It was a convenient way to stay at home or be alone. What she couldn't figure out was the mysterious something that would fit into her life. What was that word, *Diane*, supposed to represent?

"Come this way," the therapist said. His office walls were mostly bare, like he'd just moved in, and the only significant thing in the room, other than his metal desk, was a round table with two cushioned aluminum chairs. There was a small bookcase in the corner, its shelves cluttered by models of classic cars.

"Have a seat." He pointed to the far side of the table, next to a box of tissues.

She nodded and eased into the chair. She kept her eyes on his hands, watched them center a large legal pad on the table in front of him, watched them lay a black pen parallel to the top binding. *A waste of time and money*, she was thinking, even though she'd finally received, just last week after a long battle, the insurance check for Alan's life. All those zeroes, and for the first time in her life she couldn't think of a single thing to spend them on.

He looked up and she met his gaze. "My name is Tim Jacobson," he said. "This whole process works much better if you call me Tim." He smiled.

Diane only nodded. His eyes were brown with a green tint. A tooth in the corner of his mouth was discolored and eerily matched his eyes.

"That was just a joke back there," he said. "About payment. Sometimes it doesn't go over well. I should really stop using it."

"That's okay."

"So." He placed his hands on the table. "So I understand you've lost someone."

Diane looked over her fingers, searching for imperfections, uncultivated cuticles, uneven nails, the importance of which seemed suddenly imbalanced with everything else in her life. *I could be doing laundry*, she thought, running her thumb across the nail of the other.

"Diane, why don't you tell me about yourself?"

She placed her hands flat on the table, a mirror image of Tim. "I have three kids."

"What are their names?"

"Heather is the oldest." She pursed her lips as she scraped the top of her mouth with her tongue. "Paul is in the middle. He's autistic. Colin is the youngest."

"That sounds like quite the family," Tim said. "Does everyone get along?"

"Of course."

"Of course?"

She shrugged. "I don't know. Is this important?"

"It could be."

"Maybe Heather and I don't get along. I don't know what the hell to say to her. But I guess I don't know what to say to Colin, either, so maybe I'm totally clueless."

"How old are they?"

"Heather's seventeen," she said. "Almost eighteen. So that makes Colin . . ." She looked at the ceiling. That she sat there calculating embarrassed her. "He's thirteen."

"That's a tough age, thirteen. Is he starting to go his own way?"

She shook her head. "Not really. Except he wants to see his grandfather. My father. Something I don't really approve of." Her neck cracked as she turned her head to look at the wall, and for the first time she realized the room had no windows. She imagined Colin *going his own way*, as Tim put it, screaming at her like Heather, calling her names and telling her she was ruining his life. "But that's not why I'm here," she said.

"I know that. At least, I know a little."

She looked down at the table.

"May I ask who?"

Diane was silent. She arched her fingers with a slow grace and flattened them again, stretched out against the fake wood.

He'd always liked her hands, Alan.

"Diane, if you'd rather—"

"My husband." She let the word settle into the room's vulnerable spots. It still tasted like ash. "He went downstairs and shot himself one night, last fall, while everyone was home." A smile crossed her lips and she shook her head, almost like she'd malfunctioned, just for a second. She closed her eyes. "I don't know what to do or what to say or what to think and that's why I'm paying you." There was a sound like a ruined bell as her voice cracked on the final word. When she opened her eyes she focused on Tim's hands. They reached for the pen but pulled away.

Her heart kept beating. It wasn't like she expected it to stop, but she noticed how it didn't. She looked down, ashamed for smiling, a moment ago. "I'm sorry," she said.

Tim looked at her and took a long breath. When he spoke he articulated each word as though giving instructions. "I'm sorry this happened. You say you don't know what to do—that's good. To be honest, there wouldn't be many people in your position who *would* know what to do." He put his hand over his mouth and looked at her, then let it fall back to his lap. "Death is a part of life, but it also puts a huge dent in it. The death of someone you love is hard, but it isn't fatal to family and friends. You're still here, Diane, and you'll see there's still a lot of life left to live. You might not see it right now. I'd be surprised if you saw it right now. But you will."

She put her hands on her kneecaps and tried to hold them still. The clock on the wall made her silence feel incriminating, and she exhaled and looked at the legal pad. She no longer felt vulnerable. She felt like saying something funny, maybe making fun of his office or asking what was wrong with his secretary. *Who wears sweaters with cats on them?* she wanted to ask, then thought again that she shouldn't be here. His speech sounded canned, as though for someone's grandmother who'd passed away in her sleep. That's what he was used to, she could tell—Tim's patients' loved ones just *passed away*. It was *their time*. She shook her head and reached for a tissue, her eyes suddenly wet. "This is just a lot to deal with. I'm sorry."

"You don't have to apologize. We'll get to those things soon enough." Tim picked up the pen and tapped it against his temple. "Let's just take it easy today. Tell me more about your kids."

Diane wadded the damp tissue in her hand. "Colin is such a sweetheart," she said, scanning the room for a wastebasket. When she saw it under his desk she tossed the tissue and swore when it landed on the carpet. She stood up and threw it away with a petulant flick of her wrist. "I think he thinks he has to protect me," she said as she sat down. "Like he's the man of the house or whatever. I mentioned Paul? Autistic? It's very sweet, the thing with Colin. I just wish he'd forget about his grandfather."

"What's the issue there?"

Diane touched the back of her hand and traced a vein, alarmed at how far it protruded from its place under her skin. "I don't"— she frowned and shook her head—"I don't want him around my kids. He has no sense of how to raise a child." She thought of her weak moment, right after the service, when she let Colin ride over to the cemetery with her father. She kept wondering what they talked about, what he told her son that made him want to spend more time with him, why Colin was so adamant. He'd asked her twice each week since November to drive him over to her father's house. He'd begged her to invite him over for Christmas, even though Christmas was nothing special. They hadn't even wrapped their presents.

"I take it you had difficulty growing up with him?"

She looked at him like she'd been interrupted. "What do you mean by difficulty? It's not like he beat me or anything."

"That's not what I meant." Tim wrote something on the pad. "We don't have to into that right now. I made a note. We'll go back to it sometime. Just tell me more about how this affects your son. You think he'll feel the same way you did?"

"I don't see how he couldn't."

"A child's relationship with his grandparents is very different from the one he has with his parents. Grandparents are there to share their knowledge, or *wisdom*, as some people call it. Parents are there for protection. Guardians. That's not set in stone, but that's usually how it works. Across a lot of cultures, actually."

"And?"

Tim shifted his weight. Diane was glad she'd made him uncomfortable. "My point is, your father's impression on you might be very different from his impression on . . ."

"Colin."

"Colin. He might view your father as someone entirely different." Diane looked at the calendar across the room. There was nothing written on it—no days crossed off and no reminders in the little boxes. It made him seem fake. A real therapist would listen more closely. He wouldn't forget Colin's name. She cleared her throat and sat up straight. "I don't think he should spend time with him. You don't know him the way I do, so I don't know how you can say these things."

Tim nodded. "That's fair. I'm not here to push you. I understand that you know him better than I do. If you're truly not comfortable, I'm sure it's the right decision. It's usually your heart that knows what's best. I will say, though, that no one ever grew by staying comfortable." He smiled and reached for his pen. "Tell me about Paul."

Diane pursed her lips and looked him in the eye, trying to make him uncomfortable again, but she'd lost her power. *This is stupid*, she thought as he kept smiling. Her insurance would only cover the first ten sessions of therapy, no matter where she went. The clock kept ticking, asking her to say something. She thought of all the phone calls she could make, the therapists she could seek out who could actually help her. She wished she'd done her research and not taken Shannon at her word. Tim was still waiting, though his smile had begun to shrink. It would be a long hour.

"Paul is autistic," she said as though he'd forgotten.

The strongest recorded earthquake occurred near Lumaco, in southern Chile, on May 22, 1960. Its name—the Valdivia earthquake—comes from the city it most devastated. It's possible that Valdivia weathered the earthquake itself, holding on as it buckled roads and toppled churches, but there are no photographs that show the disaster before the proceeding tsunami, which, only an hour later, scraped away whatever hope the survivors had with thirty-foot walls of water and debris. In photos taken after the tsunami, the houses still standing have to lean against one another. Bent parking meters reach out of the rubble like the dactyli of dead squid. Fishing trawlers are docked in the cracked streets and cars look to be gliding down man-made canals. Casualty counts are in the thousands but there are no bodies. Outside of Valdivia, centuries-old Spanish forts crumbled into the ocean, landslides turned farmland into swamps, and the region's electrical and utility systems collapsed, leaving Valdivia without drinkable water for weeks. The waves continued across the ocean to Hawaii, killing 61, and Japan, killing 142. Two days later, nearby Cordón Caulle erupted and fed the sky with ash for two months. Today, from Ruta T350, you can still see the mast of the cargo vessel *Canelos*, brought under by the waves. During the earthquake, the village of Toltén vanished altogether.

Four years later, 143 died in Anchorage, Alaska, after a 9.2 earthquake struck the region. Tsunamis measuring up to twenty-seven feet affected several other Alaskan villages, as well as British Columbia, Washington, Oregon, California, Hawaii, and Japan. Evidence of the earthquake—the second most powerful in history—has been noted on seismographs all over the earth.

The third-strongest earthquake, Colin's father had written, occurred forty years later, in the middle of the Indian Ocean. Waves approached a hundred feet and killed more than 230,000 people in fourteen countries. Colin was in kindergarten at the time, but he remembered it. It was the first thing he encountered, in all of his father's notebooks thus far, that wasn't like a note from a history text. He could point to it and say *Yes, I remember* and nobody could argue it was fake. It made it easier to believe the world his father described was the world left in Colin's custody.

In no time at all, Colin had become an expert at picking locks—or at least one particular lock. He'd also mastered the open loops and uncrossed *t*'s of his father's handwriting. It still felt like spying, but Colin convinced himself of the task's necessity. Even now, he was looking for the future, or at least a way to prove his father would have loaded that gun, one way or another.

He had spent the rest of fall and half of winter haunting Heather's room when she was out with her boyfriend. Or boyfriends. There was no point in telling them apart. Each would pull up in his rusted sedan with plastic over one rear window, and each was sitting inside without a coat—only a T-shirt and a black stocking cap. Colin felt hypnotized by their arms: bicep wider than his calf muscle, forearm with its vein like a vine climbing a tree. They stared at Colin until he backed into the house. When he could no longer see them, down the street, it was safe to let himself into her room.

It'd been months since he sat on her bed and listened to her wisdom. The batteries in the jewelry box had finally died and now there was nothing to hear through the wall, no way for her to translate his future. Instead, he began to go through her things. Aside from candy wrappers and shoes there was nothing under the bed. He rummaged through her dresser until he found a box of tampons and immediately closed it. On most afternoons he found nothing, and soon gave up pretense and only went in there to jerk off. His rule was that he could look at the men in her magazines, but only if there were women in the picture with them. If it was an ad with only men, he was supposed to turn the page. Like most of his rules, he couldn't follow it.

Colin blamed his brother for his failure as a human being. Even now, as he tried to finish his homework, his brother was distracting. It wasn't like when they were kids, when Paul would rearrange the Lego men on his headboard, their plastic feet click-clicking against the wood. Colin had learned to ignore that years ago. The new distraction was the heap of clothes on the floor, as if his body had vanished in that spot. Paul had been sleeping naked for months, Colin had discovered. Without their father to select Paul's clothes and convince him to get out of bed, Colin was left in charge. His strategy that first new morning, back in October, was to throw back the covers and yell, "Time to get up!" Instead of pajamas or underwear, Paul wore nothing but a dark red erection that reached past his navel. He screamed as Colin ran out of the room. Colin still thought about it every night when his brother slid under the covers.

It didn't seem fair. Paul's side of the room remained cluttered with toys and books for children. Back in November, Colin had boxed up his model starfreighters and battle stations. When he peeled his film posters off the walls, they left behind bright matte rectangles. That was his childhood—*Colin's Stuff*, in his neatest hand, written on a stack of boxes. He felt proud to see it on the basement floor next to *Heather's Stuff*. How long until *Paul's Stuff* would join them, if ever? He listened to his brother's breath, thinking maybe he'd go right to sleep. *He'll never have a girlfriend*, Colin thought, and—as if the word *girlfriend* were on a flash card with a translation on the back—*He'll never have sex*. Colin switched off the lamp. He gathered his pajamas from the floor and brought them to the bathroom to change.

One of the few things left on Colin's side of the room was an angel—a drawing in colored pencil on a stiff sheet of card stock. When he returned to school the Monday after the funeral he felt like an exchange student. Some came up and hugged him, some said they were sorry this happened, but most avoided him. Nobody mentioned his birthday or asked him how it felt to be a teenager. No one could look him in the eye—not even Andy. But his friend Chelsea was different. She stayed with Colin as often as possible, smiling next to his desk until the bell rang and she was late for class. She told him she was sorry, he shouldn't be angry, there was nothing to be afraid of. "I've been praying for you every night." Chelsea's parents took her to church every Sunday and Colin thought this made her wiser than the rest of his friends, as though she might know more about death. If she told him his father wasn't in hell and that he needn't worry about things like revenge or punishment, he would believe her. She touched his hand in a way that made him smile, even when he tried to keep himself from smiling.

At the end of that first day back she met him at his locker and slid the angel out of her backpack, unpeeling it from two sheets of waxed paper. "I drew it last period. She'll watch over you."

Colin remembered her eyes, how they darted away and came back to him like fish hovering around a hook.

He'd tried praying. It wasn't my fault, he told God, kneeling on the bathroom rug because that's how people prayed. Dad would've done it anyway, he whispered at the ceiling. His prayers sounded like questions, lilting up at the end as though God might simply pat him on the head. There was too much to worry about, his worry itself a growing thing—an infected organ inflamed and toxic. Please take it away, he whispered to where he thought God hovered. When he asked God to rewrite history, it was only so he hadn't loaded the gun or even discovered it. It never occurred to him to ask for his father's life. I had nothing to do with it, he said to himself, or to God, or to whoever was listening.

The prayers didn't work. God was ignoring him. God was furious. God was planning his punishment. Colin thought about this more than he didn't, and it made life a hard thing to live.

When he came back from the bathroom, Paul hadn't moved, his breath still steady. Colin shook his head and crawled under the covers, glancing once at the angel. She glowed there in the oval of lamplight as though really in heaven. His grandmother once tried to explain angels in her way of using words like *celestial* and *hierarchical*. But had they been people—those who'd died and gone on to be graceful—or something else, something more secret? When he pictured his father, clad in light and floating on two white wings, he closed his eyes as if to stop the image there. But his father's wings burned up. His robes shredded themselves to rags, and those shadows of hands wrapped around his soul and pulled it down through the earth's fissures. Colin had thought of this enough, and dreamt of it enough, to know this was real. This had happened. There were always hands waiting, and they waited for him, too. All he wanted was someone to see this, to watch it play in his head, and call it fake, call it made-up. *You still believe in this shit?* he wanted to hear. He wanted to be laughed at and ridiculed. He wanted someone to tell him how it was, to take away every last shred of authority and order him to feel better. *Think this,* he wanted someone to say, and to lay out his new life.

Then he noticed it, the change in Paul's breathing, the bedsprings creaking beneath him. It didn't take Colin long to figure out what he'd discovered on his last night as a twelve-year-old, standing in front of the bathroom mirror, and as soon as he researched *masturbation* he heard Paul do it every night. At school, boys talked about their pervert brothers or cousins who jerked off all the time, and Colin laughed at their depravity while he watched the snow outside the cafeteria windows. They talked about going blind and he began to worry for his health. *I have to stop,* he told himself, but he only had to hear his brother pant like an overworked dog to break his own promise. Over a long weekend, back in January, he stopped for three days. Then, on Monday afternoon, his mother still at work, he couldn't keep his hands away. They turned against him, his hands. He rubbed up against the couch cushions while he watched the stretch of cartoons after school, and for an entire hour he listened to his heart scream for help. In the end he cursed himself and went to the bathroom. *I can stop tomorrow,* he'd thought.

Colin listened to Paul breathe. He moved his erection so it was flush against his belly. He tried to think about something else—about school or Heather or Andy—but again his hands rebelled. When he heard Paul's breath hang on a familiar note he crept out of bed and headed for the bathroom. *This is the last time.*

As he was cleaning up, his mother knocked. "Are you okay? You've been in there a while."

"Uh." With a handful of toilet paper he dabbed at his penis, wilting in his hands like a plucked dandelion. He thought she'd fallen asleep. "I'm fine?" The paper landed with a smack in the water and glided there like a wet swan. When he flushed and opened the door she was leaning against the opposite wall. "Goodnight," he said, about to brush past her.

She stopped him with her arm. "Colin. Hang on a minute."

He motioned to put his hands in his pockets but realized his pajamas had none. Instead he crossed his arms and looked down at the carpet.

"Sometimes I feel like"—a noise came from her throat that could have been a growl, her lip curled in though—"like there's too much going on at once. Too many things that need me?" She covered her face with her hands and her voice came out muted and airy. "I don't know."

Colin frowned as he looked at her feet—bare, too white, the carpet coming up between her toes. He saw the real color of her toenails, like pale lavender, when for years they'd only ever been red or pink. He knew she'd been to therapy that afternoon. *Just to see what it's all about*, she said. All night, he'd thought about what Shannon had told her, over coffee—what he'd overheard as he'd hidden in the dining room, pressed against the wall.

She sighed. "It's like I'm being pulled in all directions by mules or horses or whatever they used to do to people. Do you know what I mean?"

Colin thought of his father, coming to his room all over again to ask for help. His heart beat hard, just once, as though struck by the little hammer doctors use to test your reflexes.

"I don't know," she was saying. "There's just so much to deal with. What I mean is I'm sorry I've been weird lately."

"It'll be okay," he said quickly. "We'll be okay." He hugged her and clasped his arms together on the other side, squeezing until she had to tell him to let go.

"You're too quick to forgive," she said. Her hand landed in his hair. "But I don't know what I'd do if you weren't." She kissed him on the forehead, and he knew she was smelling his hair. "If you want to see your grandfather, that's fine with me."

He looked up at her.

She let go and stood up straight. "If you want me to help you contact him, I can do that."

In the morning, she stood behind him as he wrote at the kitchen table. "It has to be a letter," she said. She pulled stationery and a fancy pen from the desk by the refrigerator. "He'll like that." Colin felt like he was being tested or trained as she watched him put together his sentences. "You don't want to make any mistakes." She put her finger on the paper. "There's no apostrophe when *its* is possessive. Only use an apostrophe when it's a contraction, when you mean 'it is.'" She took up the letter and began to read. Colin played with the pen, thinking how stupid she was for believing someone would actually care if you forgot some dumb little mark on the page. "Don't forget to sign it," she said. He tried to impress her with his cursive but it looked like something he'd written in a moving car. He felt her lean forward, felt her lips touch the back of his head. He wondered what made her want to be near him all the time. Then he wondered if one day she'd smell it on him, the perverted leftover semen scent of a boy who'd lost all self-control. *Rats,* he had read in his father's notebooks, *can sense things like cancer and disease, even several generations back, in their mates.* Sometimes he wondered if his father had passed something down, some genetic defect that would switch on and ruin his life. He squirmed until she let go and reached for her cigarettes, and he pulled his father's lighter from his pocket, like a lock of hair cut from a victim.

His grandfather's reply was short—single paragraph short—and said little but *I'd love to have you over for lunch this Sunday.* The letter came on a Thursday in July, so long afterward that Colin was briefly confused when he saw his name on the envelope. From then on he couldn't stop thinking of the funeral, how he'd used the word *retarded.* He felt like he had to make it up to him. While watching television or mowing the lawn, Colin talked out loud as if his grandfather were there with him, and his grandfather said things like, *You sure are smart for your age.* He said, *I've never heard a young person say that.* As he wiped sweat and grass blades from his forehead, Colin went over it until it felt real and he liked who he was in his grandfather's eyes.

What he would discover, he hoped, was that his grandfather and his father had been close. There had to be some clue, some keyword, to unlock his father's second, secret history. *I didn't know you were so grown up*, his grandfather would tell him, cleaning his glasses with his shirt. *You don't know this, but your father and I—we knew each other quite well.* In the car ride over, Colin couldn't stop fidgeting. He still hadn't figured out that keyword, that smart thing to say.

"I hope you have a good time," his mother said as they pulled up in front of the house. She smacked her cigarettes against her palm and he offered the lighter. They hadn't tired of it yet, this game, he the gentleman and she the lady. But she didn't thank him now. She didn't change her voice to sound how they thought was rich. Instead she looked over at the house. It was older than their own and nestled closer to the neighbors' houses. Colin grabbed his backpack from the floor. His mother's eyebrows were raised as if she'd asked a question, but Colin only nodded and gave his good-bye. He waved from the sidewalk but she was messing with the radio. By the time he reached the front steps she was halfway down the street, and that's when he panicked. Was it the wrong address, the wrong house, the wrong part of town? The neighborhood no longer seemed like a nice place. He rang the bell and tried to look through the window in the door, but he wasn't tall enough.

Quentin looked younger, no longer in mourning, in a pale-yellow dress shirt with grey slacks. Colin, in his T-shirt and jeans torn at the knee, felt underdressed. Before they left, his mother had pulled a button-up from his closet but he put it back: "Doesn't fit." Now he wished he hadn't lied.

"Good afternoon," Quentin said. He looked at his watch. "Actually, it's still morning for a few more minutes. Good morning."

"Morning." Colin tried to meet his eye but the door was using the sun to blind him. He put his hands in his pockets and looked down at the welcome mat, already out of things to say.

The whole thing seemed suddenly stupid. All those times he'd asked his mother to please call Grandpa Patterson, to invite Grandpa Patterson to Christmas, to come with them to church on Easter Sunday because it felt strange without a man completing the parenthesis of two adults, three kids in the middle—and what for? During their ride to the cemetery, they'd only spoken one word between the two of them. Approaching the gates, Quentin had switched off the symphony playing on the stereo. "Respect," he said. Yet in the last several months, this man had, in Colin's head, come to know his father better than anyone else alive. In reality, his grandfather was one more person from whom he'd have to keep his secrets. Even thinking the word, *secret*, made Colin feel looked at and lit up, like one arrowed sign should say *Pervert!* and another *Fag!* and another *Murderer!* The sight of his grandfather's smile only filled him with shame.

"Well," Quentin said. "Why don't you come in?"

Colin swallowed and stepped into the house. Through a large doorway you could see the living room, where everything matched and belonged. Even the books on the coffee table were stacked in pyramids, the largest on the bottom and the smallest on top. In the foyer, afraid to touch anything, he looked down at his grandfather's pale-yellow socks. "Shoes?" Colin asked.

"If you don't mind." Quentin opened a small door to his right while Colin pulled off his shoes without untying them. "I just had the floors refinished two years ago."

Colin followed him into the living room, glancing at the floor as though he was impressed. He sat down on the couch and brushed his fingers over the eggshell fabric. "You have a nice place."

"You should have seen it when I bought it. It was almost a lost cause." He sat down in the chair opposite the couch and immediately stood up again. "Anything to drink? Iced tea? Juice?"

"Do you have any pop?"

"No. I don't drink it. All that corn syrup is terrible for you."

Colin looked down at his lap. He crossed one leg over the other and touched the top of his sock, where the elastic had lost its stretchiness. "What kind of juice do you have?"

"Cranberry."

"I guess I'll have water."

"Water." Quentin nodded and left the room. Colin listened to his grandfather in the kitchen, a cupboard door opening, a glass meeting the countertop, the refrigerator door's condiments shaking against each other. He tried to lean back into the couch but it was too deep for his thighs. He perched on the edge of the cushion and sat erect, then sighed and slouched into himself. He was reading the spines of a book pyramid when Quentin returned with two glasses of water.

"When I bought the place it was practically condemned. It was a duplex at the time and the landlord had done nothing to take care of it."

Colin tried to be interested.

"It's taken years to get it to look this way. I almost have it the way I want it now." He looked around the room as if something might have changed without his knowing. "When I'm done I don't know what I'll do."

"Have a party?"

He laughed, Then he realized Colin was being serious. "Probably not," he said, tapping his hand on the arm of the chair. "No. I'll just sell it and start over with a new one."

Colin looked at the tile surrounding the fireplace, pretending he lived there. He thought of convincing his mother to buy the house, but it was too nice. They'd ruin it.

"Well," Quentin said. He set his glass on a coaster that looked like a ship's rudder wheel. He stood up and brushed the wrinkles out of his pant legs. "Would you like the tour?"

Colin carried his glass close to his chest as his grandfather explained the changes he'd made, the walls he'd moved, the colors he'd chosen, with names like *Hampton Blue* and *Thirty-Year Merlot*. He nodded in a way he hoped looked thoughtful, asking questions when the timing felt right. He tried to remember everything he was told but when he repeated these things in his head he realized he was missing new information. Eventually he stopped listening and let his grandfather's voice give him the shivers. Voices could do this, if they were deep enough, and when his body began to like the voice he let out a small gasp.

"Are you okay?" They were in a small alcove between the living room and the kitchen. One entire wall was a window, floor to ceiling, and the other two walls were books.

Colin shrugged and walked toward the window, shifting his legs to try to hide it. "Yeah. I just thought I saw, um, a bird."

"I get so many birds here. I'm close enough to Lake of the Isles that I've seen bald eagles, now and again."

When he could, Colin turned around. The sun was letting itself in through the window, and when it was sparkling all over the shelf he realized his grandfather's books were bound in leather and gold leaf, like in some wizard's library. "Pretty," he said, without meaning to.

"You like books?" Quentin asked. Colin knew better than to disappoint, and he nodded as his eyes traveled over their spines, all names he didn't recognize. "These are my babies," his grandfather was saying, and he let his hand fall on Colin's shoulder. "If you want to borrow one, you're more than welcome."

Colin sucked a breath through his teeth. If this wasn't a test, nothing was. How was he supposed to pick, to pretend this was all old news? *Oh, everyone's read Dickens*, he imagined some snobby, alternate version of himself saying. Left of Dickens was Defoe, and before that Dante, a book called *Inferno*. This sounded familiar and Colin plucked it from the shelf. "Good choice," his grandfather said, and Colin felt the hand on his shoulder give a quick squeeze before it disappeared. "Let me show you the kitchen."

As they walked into the next room, Colin peeked into the book. Anywhere else, he would've groaned aloud when he saw the long column of text. *Poetry*, he thought, and wished he'd kept searching. He let the book fall to his side, where he carried it like homework, an assignment that ambushed him. *Inferno*, he thought, again losing his grandfather's words in the voice itself. Why did he know it? *Dante's Inferno*—a pair of words he'd heard or read before. "Well," Quentin said, in what must have been the last room. "Time to make lunch!" He stepped down the stairs with a new kind of energy. Colin's heart was winding itself up in his chest. On the way through the living room he saw a small bathroom and stopped.

"I'll be right there," he said. He went red when his grandfather told him to hold the handle down when he flushed, and locked the door with the softest of clicks. He didn't have to pee, as he thought, and after too much trying there was nothing he could do but finish in a fury, biting his tongue so he wouldn't pant. *What's wrong with you?* he demanded of his sick, criminal soul. *Why are you doing this?* On the other side of the wall he heard the clang of metal bowls. "Mmm," he said when he came. Already, he'd forgotten his grandfather's advice and watched his handful of toilet paper circle and float back up. More than anything, that was shame. *Look what he was doing!* the scene seemed to say, as though the entire world didn't already know.

He was still cheerful, his grandfather, smiling as he whisked together herbs and oil and vinegar. "You'll love Dante," he was saying, but Colin couldn't look him in the eye. *You'll disappoint me*, is what he heard, and he wished there was some way to believe it wasn't true. He glanced again at the first page, its stupid words like *e'en* and *discover'd* and *forespent*. Then he turned the page. If you ignored the names, it was easy to tell what was going on. "There's a bag of greens in the bottom drawer," he heard, and he snapped the book shut. "On the right."

Colin looked into the refrigerator. He found the bag—unmarked, reusable, plastic, a paper towel folded in with the leaves. "This doesn't look like lettuce," he said. His skin still felt a shade of bright, incriminating red.

"It's not iceberg lettuce, which is what you've been raised on. Iceberg lettuce isn't good for you at all. It's mostly just water."

He held the bag closer to his face, looking at the dark, flaccid leaves. "Iceberg," he said.

"I can't believe anyone would eat that stuff. This will probably be your first real salad." He reached into a high cupboard for a salad spinner. "If you wash it, I'll chop the walnuts."

Colin took the strange, soft lettuce from the bag and placed it in the spinner. Quentin stopped him at the sink, his hand once more on his shoulder. "You'll want to take out that one," he said. "The brown wrinkly one. And that one. If it feels slimy, get rid of it. That's the rule."

Colin took a deep breath, almost as though he was learning to biopsy a cancer patient or cut precious stones. When his grandfather let go he missed his hand, like when a blanket creeps up your legs and bares your feet. He'd ruined his chances—that he understood—but maybe there was still time, before his mom picked him up, to hear what a smart young man he was. As he washed the lettuce he tried to conjure the comment or observation that would elicit this praise. None of them were smart enough. None of them were good enough.

The waiting room was exactly as she remembered it. But it had only been two months, Diane realized. Why should it have changed?

Back in May, as she was leaving, Tim scheduled her for a second appointment. She'd intended never to come back, and in June, when the receptionist called to remind her, Diane spewed every nicety: how sorry she was, how foolish she felt, but she was just too sick to make it. What she hadn't expected was the perseverance.

"We'll put you on the schedule for July," the receptionist said over the clatter of computer keys. Diane wasn't able to lie fast enough, and by the following month she'd forgotten what Tim looked like—only that something about his smile made her grind her teeth.

Since May, she'd considered the transaction of therapy. Where was the advice on how to go on living, how to get out of bed? Those things weren't a problem for her—at least not literally—but a therapist was supposed to understand what it meant to lose someone you loved.

After that first appointment, she drove miles out of her way before going home, first into the northern suburbs, then back through Roseville. She passed the house and imagined she could see through its walls: Heather smoking her future away, Colin and Paul ignoring each other. She went back toward the freeway. When she got close to Minneapolis she turned around. It was almost nine o'clock when she arrived home. "I went to therapy," she told Shannon over the phone, expecting a *That's wonderful!* or a *Congratulations!* Instead, Shannon called it a first step and began to outline future steps. Diane, cradling the phone against her neck as she folded the boys' underwear, felt defeated.

Shannon was right, she realized. The session with Tim had lasted an hour but they hadn't talked about anything. She was still sleeping on the couch, waking up every time the motion light in the neighbor's backyard clicked on, staying up for an hour as she went to the kitchen for a glass of water and a cigarette. The street outside was different every night. When it drizzled, the streetlights looked predatory, like those monstrous fish in the ocean's darkest places, a school of black raindrops lured to their light. On clear nights you barely noticed the streetlights at all, and when the moon was full there was so much to look at that she lost track of time until she watched the sun rise, neither romantic nor adventurous.

She was still smoking, Shannon never failed to point out. *Your teeth will get yellow*, she said until it meant nothing. On a morning in June, when they met at the doughnut shop down the street, Shannon showed her a printout of a calendar, something scribbled under each day of the month. "You smoke a pack a day. Estimate that at five dollars a day." She pointed to the calendar. "If you carry it over, you get a hundred and fifty bucks every month. Stop smoking, and in a year you can take the kids to Florida."

"I hate Florida."

"California then, I don't care. Do you see my point?"

Shannon's point was clear, but her own was not. She promised she would try to quit, but when she walked into the house and took her cigarettes out of her purse, the cellophane brought her youngest son into the living room like a dog who'd caught the smell of meat. "For you, Madame," he said, using the fancy pronunciation. It made her want to grab onto him and tear him apart in her hands, just to bring him closer. Her arms twitched when she hugged him, as though they weren't being used. She didn't know why you couldn't love someone without wanting to pulverize them.

Another step was the basement office, unopened since October. Every time she did laundry she had to walk by the door, the gaps between its wood slats dark. Before she locked the door in October—there was a gun in there, after all—she'd thought about turning on the lamp and leaving it on forever, even if that very thing terrified her. Because his writing terrified her. It might have been when he bought a crate of notebooks from a wholesaler that she knew he was lost. Even if she hadn't known for months he was suicidal, it was one more signal, one more stupid, obvious thing she'd chosen to ignore. The gunshot shouldn't have surprised her at all.

Looking at all those therapeutic steps, the future they climbed to seemed pointless. Even after she scheduled a new appointment she was apathetic. Nobody wanted to add anything to her life.

Shannon only talked about taking things away, like how Colin lit her cigarettes, or the regularity of going to work every morning. "Take a vacation," she kept saying, as if something were waiting for her in a godforsaken place like Florida. As she sat in the waiting room she imagined Tim saying the same thing. Already, she was preparing her defense, how Florida or California or heaven itself would be a waste of time.

When Tim was ready, she followed him down the same hallway to that same office. "I'm sorry I missed you last month," he said as they sat across from each other. "I was looking forward to hearing how the rest of your spring went."

"I was sick." It sounded more petulant than she meant it to. "I just—I didn't feel well."

"That's what Kathy said."

There was a creak as she leaned forward in her chair to scratch her ankle, another when she leaned back. Her eyes fell to his hand, wrapped around the pen. He clicked it once as if to get her attention. When she looked up at him he was smiling and she felt cruel for giving the impression that she could be helped.

"I see my husband's car everywhere," she said. The air in the room sharpened and she reached for a tissue. "Sorry."

"It's okay. I'd be more concerned if you weren't crying."

"What do you mean?"

"I mean that it's normal to be emotional. It would bother me if we discussed your husband and—" Tim frowned and looked at his notes. "Forget I said anything."

"Did you expect me to not cry?"

"I didn't expect anything. You try not to go into a relationship like this expecting anything."

Diane didn't like the sound of the word *relationship*. "Do you really think that if I don't cry, it means I don't feel anything?"

"That's not what I meant at all. Like I said, just forget it. It was inappropriate and I'm sorry. You said you see your husband's car everywhere. You mean cars that look like his?"

She set the crumpled tissue on the table. "It feels like it's the only car people drive," she said. "It's all over the damn place." The tissue didn't look right and she closed her fist around it. "I hated that car. I kept telling him to buy a new one. It was loud and it stunk. I started to hate him for not listening. Sometimes he was so easy to hate. I know that sounds horrible."

"It doesn't sound horrible. It sounds like you were in love."

"Sometimes he was an idiot," she said. "Like just before he—I heard him coughing, all the way down in the basement. I go down there and he's smoking. I ask what the hell's he doing, what's Colin supposed to think, I guess a red convertible is next, all that stuff. He just said he thought he'd try it." She laughed. *Step one*, she said to herself. "Who the hell starts smoking when they're our age?"

"He just started smoking? Out of the blue? Don't you find that strange?"

"I did. I mean I do." She pulled her lips into her mouth. How to confess, if even a confession? "I started right after he did, so I don't know. It's strange, but I can't comment."

Tim made a note on the pad. "Before or after?"

"Before or after what?"

He looked at her.

"After." Her eyes fell to the table. "A couple days."

"It's certainly a unique reaction to grief. Your smoking."

She scrunched up her face and leaned away from him. "It's stupid."

"Maybe not ideal, but it isn't stupid." He shifted in his chair like someone who'd found his topic of expertise at a dinner party. "I know it seems a little mysterious to you, and frankly it's mysterious to me, but when you look at the big picture it seems very natural. It's an ironic thing to say, but you could even call it healthy."

An unattractive laugh burst out of her and she covered her mouth with her hand. "Healthy?"

"Like I said, it's kind of ironic. People do strange, beautiful things when they're upset, so it's understandable."

"You don't seem to understand it."

Tim shrugged his shoulders. "I guess *understandable* is the wrong word. Intuited?"

"I feel like I'm making fun of you. I'm sorry."

"You don't have to apologize. And you're not making fun of me. Not everything you say offends me, you know."

She rolled her eyes, then realized her childishness and began to shake her head. "Whatever you say." The room felt as though it'd shrunk and she sucked in a long breath. Her hands felt empty. "Thanks for listening."

"That's my job."

"I know it's your job. I just thought—I don't know." She glanced at the door. She sensed her purse waiting under the chair. "To tell the truth, I could use a smoke right now."

Tim smiled. "If you want to step out for a couple minutes, that's fine with me. I'll put the session on hold. I don't have a four o'clock, so we'll go an extra five at the end."

"Thanks." She stood up and had her purse over her shoulder before she made it to the door. Halfway down the hall she was already slapping the pack against her palm.

It was a hot afternoon, the sun still an arm's length from the horizon. In the street's rising heat and exhaust the buildings around her looked painted on a curtain flirting with a breeze, even if the ash tapped from her cigarette told her there was no wind. She tried to focus on the world, on the sky coming down around her on all sides, sewn to the cityscape with an aberrant stitch. Strange, beautiful things, she thought as she sucked the cigarette down to its filter and dropped it in the ashtray by the door. She'd been *off* for a long time—dormant, powered down. It was clear, now, that she no longer had to keep herself that way. Coming back up the stairs, she thought of everything there was to mention. His car wasn't all, sold to the first carbuncled teen who answered her ad. What else could she talk about? What aspect of life had been dragged from its hiding place and beaten unrecognizable? The first thing that came to mind was the key she'd carried in her purse since October. She felt the urge to write it: *Key*, she imagined, all by itself, on a sheet of paper. *Office. Gun. Notebooks.*

I'll have to start a list, she thought.

> *Man can do violence*
> *To himself and his own blessings: and for this,*
> *He, in the second round must aye deplore*
> *With unavailing penitence his crime,*
> *Whoe'er deprives himself of life and light,*
> *In reckless lavishment his talent wastes,*
> *And sorrows there where he should dwell in joy.*

Colin knew he'd read it before. In his father's office he matched it up word for word. Like most of his father's notes, it had passed right through him. Now he looked at every word, but all it said was what he already knew: his father, for ending his life, was in hell. He thumbed the pages of the notebook and his grandfather's copy of *Inferno* side by side.

"I thought we weren't allowed in here." Andy's voice was too loud for that quiet, sacred room. He stood in the doorway, disrespect-fully unimpressed. "The Hag let me in," he said, pointing at the ceiling. "So here's the famous journal. Where's the good-bye-cruel-world part?"

"Shut up," Colin said when his throat unlocked. He slammed the notebook shut and backed the chair into Andy's crotch. "We're not supposed to be down here."

"You better hope I don't tell your mom then." Andy plucked an-other book from the shelf—one Colin hadn't yet read—and flipped through it as if it were a guidebook at a gas station.

"It's the room where he killed himself," Colin said, because noth-ing else made sense. It hollowed him out to say it, as though some-one had drilled a hole in his stomach and siphoned everything out. *Right here, in this chair.*

Despite his efforts, he couldn't unconvince himself that this was still a matter of life or death. He still believed, against his will, his sister's prophecy. Even though he told Andy she was full of shit, he thought about it every night. In a little more than two years it was supposed to take him by surprise, and two years wasn't a long enough life to make up for what he'd done.

Since he'd first picked the lock, early that spring, he'd done as little as possible to change the office. When he plucked a new notebook from the shelf, he moved the others a fraction of a centimeter until they stood together more loosely and you couldn't tell anything was missing. It felt like a museum exhibit, a room preserved from an earlier time. "I bet we find some porn," Andy said. He dug through the desk's top drawer, shoving things forever out of place.

"Leave his stuff alone."

"Come on, dude." Andy slammed the drawer and opened the second one down. "I don't wanna be rude or anything, but it's not like he needs his porn anymore. Do you think he had DVDs or magazines?"

"Shut up. You're such a fucking perv." The notebook lay on the desk, unprotected if Andy decided to take it. The words *Man can do violence* called from inside.

"You're just mad 'cause your dad wasn't into gay stuff. You just want a movie with a couple of fat guys cornholing each other."

Colin stepped in front of him and tried to look menacing, but Andy wasn't paying attention. "You're gonna make me throw up." He reached over and pushed the notebook against the wall.

"You know you love it." Andy dug through blister packs of pens, loose business cards, half-used pads of sticky notes. "Two guys blowing each other, or maybe some kind of orgy." He laughed as he closed the second drawer and opened the third, and even without seeing what was inside Colin knew why his mouth fell open. "Jackpot," Andy said. It wasn't much more than a whisper.

From the beginning, Colin had known it was there. You couldn't not know. Its being there was like a black hole that bent the room's reality, or a chunk of some radioactive element that made you weak.

You couldn't not think about it, every few minutes, and say to yourself, *It's in here*, and at the same time be too afraid to touch it, as though by taking it in his hands he would lose all control of himself, march upstairs, shoot his brother between the eyes, his sister in the back as she ran for help, and, when she walked through the door and produced a cigarette for him to light, the only person in the entire world he couldn't live without.

"Dude, don't touch that." Colin reached for it but Andy fended him off. "Seriously."

Andy picked it up and pushed the cylinder aside. Colin remembered their days as soldiers who saved each other's lives. Andy clicked it back into place. "Don't worry. It's not loaded." He aimed at Colin and closed one eye.

Just seeing the gun made him shake. He reached out but Andy leapt backward. "Just let me hold it," he said, his voice more vulnerable than Colin had ever heard. "I've never held a real gun." He pulled the trigger and Colin winced. He pretended to blow smoke from the barrel. "It's heavy as fuck."

Colin wanted to agree, but as far as Andy or anyone else knew, he'd never held a gun.

"My mom would kill you," he said.

"She won't be home for a while." Andy had no way of knowing but he'd have said anything to get his way. He put the gun down the front of his shorts and tried to draw it quickly, like a cowboy, but lost his grip. The steel-on-concrete clatter echoed through the basement and, Colin was sure, all the way up the stairs, outside, across the city. Colin grabbed it from the floor. Its grip felt familiar. Instead of wanting to vomit he felt his heart come alive, his lungs full of something lighter than air. He aimed at Andy and said "Freeze!" like he'd cornered a murderer returning to the scene of the crime.

"Don't shoot!" Andy grinned as he put his arms over his head.

"Turn around," Colin said. "Don't try anything funny or I'll pistol-whip you." He'd heard this on one of his grandmother's police shows and liked the sound of it. The only thing that mattered was how Andy did turn around, how he faced the wall on Colin's command.

He laughed—more of a breath of air than anything—and tapped Andy on the shoulder. "My turn," he said. "Pretend you're robbing me."

The gun kept them busy until late afternoon. It was only when Andy asked for the bullets that Colin insisted they go upstairs. "She'll be home any minute," he said. He locked the door with his paper clips and blushed when Andy called him an evil genius. The house seemed quiet and fake, like the set from a movie, and they went outside where the freeway's traffic and the rustle of leaves confirmed that life was still happening. They lay in the yard, ripping up handfuls of grass until Andy called him *lame* and *boring* and went home. Right away he sank back into the basement, picked the lock, and returned the room to its natural state. He put the notebook back in its place and reached for the next in line. He began to page through it, standing by the shelf.

His mother had described panic attacks to him, but he imagined what he felt right then as something far worse. Each breath felt like it came through a stirring straw and the handwriting in front of him split itself in two. Then he heard the garage door and stuffed the notebook down his shorts. After burying it under his mattress he came into the kitchen and tried to look bored. "Your turn to make dinner," his mother said. As he rummaged through the refrigerator he repeated the words in his head, unable to unsee them. When she wasn't looking he mouthed them to himself, just to prove they were real. They felt thick on his tongue, like a mouthful of custard. *Things I've Seen in Hell.*

He didn't have a chance to read more until later that night. Dinner hadn't gone well. "This looks good," his mother had said, and then their plates were empty. Colin lit her a fresh cigarette and she leaned into her fist and smiled at the three of them. "So I thought we'd all watch a movie," she said. For a second it felt like nothing at all had happened to them.

"Sure," Colin said.

She nodded. "We haven't done anything as a family in a while. A movie sounds perfect."

Heather glanced at her phone, pulled halfway out of her pocket. "Sure."

Diane scoffed. "Put that away."

"I was just looking to see what time it was."

"There's a clock above the doorway."

Heather looked. Colin could tell she was surprised. "Well, I'm used to using my phone. You don't have to get all pissy about it."

"Pissy? I'm pissy because I want to have a nice meal without my daughter talking to her friends?"

"Whatever."

As soon as Heather said *whatever* you knew it would turn into a fight. It wasn't long before their mother brought up college, which only led to the same shouted argument he'd heard for months. When Heather wrenched her plate and fork from the table she was glaring at all of them. Nobody flinched when they heard her plate shatter in the sink, and nobody knew if Heather looked remorseful or proud of herself.

He was thinking, now—as he put his head against the new notebook and listened for its heartbeat—that he could've done more. *It's just past seven*, he could've said before Heather pulled out her phone and derailed the night. *We could watch something long*, he could've said, knowing the four of them would fall asleep together on the couch.

After dinner, he tried to clean the shards of ceramic from the sink. "Don't cut yourself," his mother said as she bused the remaining plates from the dining room. "I'll take care of it." After that, nobody spoke. It was as if they'd died and could no longer see one another, listening for each other's footsteps so they knew when it was their turn to leave a room or pass through the hallway. Winter had come back, just for one night, and it made Colin want to cry into his brother's shoulder. But he knew Paul would scream, or maybe blacken his other eye.

With a deep breath he propped himself on his elbows and opened the notebook. He couldn't waste time reading through all the normal stuff—his father's facts, stories, collections of words he didn't know—and thumbed straight to the list he'd seen downstairs. But he'd remembered wrong. It wasn't a list at all. Instead, his father had written in paragraphs, and after the first page Colin couldn't tell whether his father had died once before and had come back to life, was dead and haunting their basement, or had been to hell while he was still alive. He'd even drawn pictures of things he couldn't describe. In hell a demon kept him company, leading him through the parts you couldn't navigate alone. *The demon is kind*, his father had written, and you could feel the sadness with which he'd noticed this. When Colin turned the page he saw the demon, sketched in faded pencil. How could you not stare? It wasn't until he saw the burnt feathers tremble at the touch of his breath that he blinked. He looked again. Its feathers were still, cemented in grey strokes and shadings. He closed the notebook with a clap. Paul moaned at the noise and rolled over. Colin switched off the lamp. He didn't want to read anymore.

In hell's twilight he could see its gates, pearly as those in heaven but in hell reflecting the red rock and the red dirt and the flames. They began to close. In hell the ground gives like moss, and before long his legs were too tired to run. With each flutter of wings behind him he pushed himself harder, one more step, another, another. At the gate he'd fallen to a crawl, and when he reached for its rusted metal he felt hell's hands on either side of his ribcage and he cried out in the bedroom's silence. In the dark he looked around. Paul rolled over once more. The tree outside still cast its shadow on the wall and the shadow still bristled at the slightest breeze. The room hadn't changed.

He'd forgotten about it by morning, when the sun forced its way into his eyes. It was like any other Monday: breakfast while he scoffed at his mother's list of chores; setting out Paul's clothes; starting the shower and masturbating to his reflection while the water grew hot. It wasn't until he was in the shower that he remembered, that he felt again that monstrous grip. He saw again the words his father had written, the images he'd sketched. He considered hell and all its splendor, touching with his timid fingers the bruise just under his ribs.

In September 1848, construction crews near Cavendish, Vermont, broke ground for the Rutland & Burlington Railroad. For each blast, the men bored holes into the rock, poured a layer of blasting powder, threaded a fuse up to the surface, and covered the hole with sand. Afterward, they packed each charge with a tamping iron—a rod just over an inch in diameter and four feet from end to end. At approximately four thirty in the afternoon, a twenty-five-year-old foreman named Phineas Gage struck a spark and detonated a charge. The tamping iron, worn to a quarter-inch point on each end, passed through his left cheek and the roof of his mouth, up into his skull—just behind the left eye—and continued, just as cleanly, out of the top of his head, landing in the brush more than eighty feet away, "smeared," his men said, "with blood and brain." Within minutes, Gage spoke coherently, got to his feet without help, and was upright and conscious for the three-quarter-mile trek to Cavendish. Dr. Edward Williams, the first physician to lay hands on Gage's skull, noted "the pulsations of the brain being very distinct" and observed how, at one point, "Mr. G got up and vomited; the effort of vomiting pressed out about half a teacupful of the brain, which fell upon the floor."

Only a month after his accident, Gage was out of bed and venturing outside. By November, he swore the pain in his head had gone. Dr. John Harlow, who assumed care after Williams's initial examination, reported in November of 1848 that Gage "appears to be in a way of recovering, if he can be controlled." Though first-hand evidence is scant, Gage is remembered as the catalyst for studies in cerebral localization and advanced neurology; until his accident, it had never occurred to physicians that damaging specific regions of the brain—without considerable threats to one's health—could alter personality. He died of cerebral convulsions in May of 1860.

Diane wished she'd read none of this. It was one of those stories that bubbled up whenever she was trapped alone with her thoughts. In Tim's office she closed her eyes and tried to picture something else, tried to remember what movie she'd watched last night with Colin. There was a stream of air coming from a vent in the ceiling that wasn't warm or cold, just dry, and she shifted to avoid it. The room was making its familiar noises: the fluorescent light, the clock, the strokes of Tim's pen like small rocks tumbling down a hill. They were best together, but if she had to choose one sound over the others it would have been that of Tim writing. Even if it was disturbing—the thought of what he was writing, why she was there. She still asked herself what notes he kept. Trying to read them had become a game, eyeing the legal pad as he wrote, but his handwriting was too small and masculine; upside down it looked like ancient runes. Still, she tried to cheat and see herself through her therapist's eyes. She wanted to know whether or not her revulsion and her disgust and her fear were justified, or if the Diane she thought she was, at heart, was just a grief-given illusion, and that it was time, once again, to become the Diane everyone wanted her to be. "If for no other reason than for the sake of your spine," her mother called to say, "you have to stop sleeping on that couch. Have I told you about Cheryl?"

Yes, she'd heard about Cheryl at least twice since January— the point, apparently, at which her friends and remaining family had decided she should start behaving like the old Diane. That first month, they did everything they could. In November they were still dropping by with baked goods, mailing cards with hidden, unmentioned checks, and tidying up while she smoked at the kitchen table. "That drawer over there," she'd have to say, or "Above the toaster," as they unloaded her dishwasher. In December they delivered tins of store-bought cookies. "How are the kids?" they wanted to know, and it was everything she could do not to sigh and say, *You tell me.*

They didn't know her. Shannon spoke like an office manager trained to deliver bad news. Every week she arrived with something printed from her computer—an article on how cows reproduce or a list of animals ranked by the length and intensity of their orgasms, pictures of hateful cats wearing sweaters—and for a half hour they'd laugh about this stupid thing that had nothing to do with them. Then Shannon would put the paper aside and say something an observer would call innocent—"I see you have an ice dam above your garage." But Diane's eye twitched as though it could look into the future and was wincing at the argument it saw.

It was the cigarettes people nagged about most, made worse because she never knew how to respond. To repeat what Tim had said about strangeness, about beauty, sounded gorgeous in her head, but as she began to recount that day in therapy, Shannon got lost in the details. "You're saying he didn't smell it on you? He didn't say anything about patches, or gum?"

It was the cigarettes that convinced her to take the key from her purse and walk down to the basement. Even though it felt wrong to be moving around the house at two in the morning, tip-toeing down the stairs to read those notebooks by the desk lamp's light—even though she knew they'd give her hell for this, too—it felt close to healing. Yes, she found horrible things like the story of a young man's brain sloshing out onto the floor, but it felt like something she was supposed to know. When she connected it to her husband—when she imagined that he'd tried to replicate Phineas Gage's luck, that with a surgical gunshot to the brain he could kill everything that was Alan but go on living—she tried to swallow it as wisdom, or at least pity. And what if he'd written something about her, about the woman he'd perceived her to be? Her skin felt covered in bugs when she thought of their final night, when she shrugged his hand away. "You stink," she told him, and that was the end, the last thing she said to him. A vacuum opened up behind her as he rolled away, the sheets stretched between them as though it was only one more fight in their history of fights. Her back still broke out in goosebumps at the thought of his silence, his acquiescence, no matter how tightly she wrapped herself in blankets on the couch.

How was she supposed to tell someone that? How was Tim supposed to write that?

Finally he clicked the pen closed and set it on the table. She was happy to have her thoughts interrupted. "How were the last few weeks?" he asked.

"Fine. The boys started eighth grade."

"I thought Paul was older?"

She shook her head. "We kept them together. Remember?"

"That's right. Sorry. Does either of them ever have a problem starting school?"

"No."

He nodded and made a note. "Anything else with your kids? How's Heather?"

She looked at the door. *How about your kids, Diane? How about Heather the burnout, Colin the time bomb, Paul the complete fucking mystery?* A part of her knew that Paul was a problem she was ignoring, that soon he'd get out of hand. Had she thought about special schools, her mother had asked over the phone. Had she thought about *what the boy really needs?* Had she thought about anything? "My kids are fine," she whispered.

She knew Tim was testing her, like a doctor who prods your wrist and says *Here? What about here?* as he looks for the broken spot. "Diane."

"Sorry." She cleared her throat. "I've been feeling strange lately."

"Strange how?"

"Strange I don't know." There was a piece of lint on her slacks and she picked it off and set it on the table in front of her. "I feel like everything's slowing down or something."

"It's normal to feel that at this time of year. Autumn does that to people."

"Is isn't that. I mean it's autumn, yeah, and it came by surprise, but—I don't know."

Tim picked up the pen. "Are you sure you don't know?"

She pulled her bottom lip into her mouth and rolled it between her teeth. She did know, and it irritated her that he didn't. With a sigh she reached for her purse. Her lipstick clacked against a compact mirror. The car keys jangled. She felt her way past half-empty packs of gum, receipts, a screw, and pulled from the bottom a wrinkled piece of notebook paper. The last addition was on the back—*Oct 13 soon*—in blue ink.

"Is everything okay?"

"In a week he'll have been dead a year." Somewhere she'd read that the minute a phrase leaves your mouth it becomes true. Theories like that were hard to discredit as Tim's face and everything around him, the calendar, the bookshelf, took on a wet tremble. It didn't feel like she was crying, but when she looked down there were little black circles on her slacks. "Sorry."

"Is the memory getting stronger? The memory of his suicide?"

She winced at the word. It still made her panic, even when she saw it in its most benign forms, like part of a song title, or on the giant billboards that warned of depression's fatal consequences. She let in a breath and looked up at him. "I can still hear it."

She was expecting him to say *Hear what?* or *Do you actually hear it or do you just recall it?* but thankfully he only put his hand over his mouth and looked back at her.

"I think about it all the time."

"I can imagine," Tim said, even though they both knew he couldn't. "Is that what you've written down on that paper?"

She glanced down. "This?" She turned it over, then back to the front. "No, this . . . this is nothing." She returned it to her purse, shoving it back to the bottom where she'd found it.

"Nothing."

"It's stupid. I write these things down and forget what they mean." With her tongue she traced the sharp parts of her teeth. It felt like they were talking about something different now, and she was glad for it. The thing she'd come to talk about was sinking back down to its place. She tucked her purse under her chair. "I never remember any of it."

"Is it stuff that bothers you? What kind of things do you write on the list? What's one of them? What's one you don't remember?"

"I don't know. One of them says 'orange rind.' Another says 'flirting.' Well." She shook her head. "I guess I know what that one means. A few weeks ago I actually flirted with someone. A new hire at the plant." She looked over at his desk. "His name is Daniel and he works in AP. I don't know why I'm telling you this." She covered her face and her voice struggled through her fingers. "I've done it a few times now. I know I shouldn't. I don't know what's wrong with me."

"Why shouldn't you?"

She looked at him, her glare sharper than she could control. "My husband just died."

Tim reached for his pen but decided against it. He looked at her for too long, as though she was one of those optical illusions and he was waiting for her secret code to jump out at him. "I know you feel like you're betraying Alan," he said finally. "But that just isn't true." He folded his hands together and placed them under his chin. "The human spirit can only grieve for so long. Alan has been gone for almost a year. And you're still in mourning. You're still smoking, even. I'm not saying there's anything wrong with that. We all move at our own pace. Just that there's a point when the heart, like any living, feeling thing, needs nourishment. Maybe it's time to listen to your heart." He smiled and took up the pen, so pleased with himself. "You flirted with a coworker. Tell me about that. How did it start?"

Listen to your heart. She couldn't believe she was paying over a hundred dollars an hour for someone to quote love songs. Nor could she believe he didn't even feel sorry for her.

"Diane."

The seconds were ticking by on the clock. She counted them like pennies dropped into a jar. There was something awful about his patience. Finally she rolled her eyes in a way that reminded her of her daughter. "As plant manager, I'm responsible for giving tours to new employees. The new employee happened to be

Daniel. He started flirting with me. I liked it. I flirted back." She put up her arms like she was out of ideas. "That's all."

"So he initiated it?"

"Of course. Jesus. I don't go around flirting with younger men."

"He was younger?"

"Is that so surprising?"

"No. That's not what I meant. I meant that it probably made you feel good?"

She folded her hands and looked at the carpet. Her cheeks warmed at the memory, even though she was frowning. "Yes," she said. "It did. But it didn't mean anything."

"It doesn't have to. There's still a lot to take away from that. Remember, grieving is not your job. You have to allow yourself joy. You have to realize there's still a lot left in you. Men will see that, and they'll be attracted to you. They have every reason to be."

She looked up. She thought of these men and their schoolboy flirtation, regardless of their reasons. "Don't be ridiculous," she said, and to her the word *ridiculous* sounded ridiculous and she laughed at its ridiculousness. Her laughter felt inappropriate and she put her hand over her mouth as she shook her head. "It's so stupid," she said through her fingers. "But thank you."

"You're welcome. And it isn't stupid. There's a lot about you that would charm any man. Any sensible one, anyway." Tim shrugged and crossed his legs, bumping the edge of the table. The pen rolled toward her and they both reeled forward to reach for it. Their hands stopped no more than an inch apart, his holding the pen and hers poised to grab it, had she been quicker. For a second that's what they looked at, the other's freckled and vein-laced but very different, very unfamiliar hand. When they pulled away they both laughed like it was funny, even though it wasn't, and Tim clicked the pen in his fingers but wrote nothing new.

Diane reached for her purse. "Do you want to come outside with me?"

"What?"

"I need a smoke. Talking about this. My husband, a few minutes ago. I was gonna step outside, if you want to join me."

"I don't smoke." He clicked the pen once more and set it down. "But it's a nice day. Probably one of the last till spring. Why not?"

It *was* a nice day, though you couldn't mistake it for anything but autumn. Death always seemed dry in October, or crisp. It was a cloudless afternoon and the sun's angle gave each building around the parking lot a redness that crept up from the concrete. "It's gorgeous," Diane said as she dug through her purse. "Too bad it'll all be buried in snow a few weeks from now."

Tim checked for dust or bird shit before he leaned against the railing. "Don't say that. The sooner you mention snow, the sooner it happens."

She watched her breath rise up grey between them, curling back in on itself before the wind took it. "So you think it's normal for me to flirt with men."

"I don't see why not."

The leaves scuttled across the parking lot like blind crabs. When the wind reached her it carried with it the clean smell of October like sun-dried tree sap. She lifted her face to smell it again but it was gone. Tim was watching the leaves and her eyes fell to the buttons on his jacket, too golden to be gold. Out of seven billion people on earth, he knew her best. An animal image put itself in her head and she shook it out. She wondered what he would have said if the list hadn't distracted them, if they had gone on to talk about Alan and his basement office, the notebooks she was reading—one list in particular called *The Pros and Cons of Living*. The pros had run out pages ago, and—just like in life— you couldn't argue with him. For the first time since youth she'd considered it. The thought of her own brain, lapping loose in her skull like she was just a bowlful of gazpacho, made her feel faint. "I'm not interested in anyone," she said.

"Sorry?"

"Dating. I don't want to date anyone."

"Okay."

"I'm not interested."

"You don't have to be."

"Okay."

Tim shrugged his shoulders forward, as if he were cold. It wasn't that cold. "I'm gonna head upstairs."

She nodded. Behind her the door's hinge cawed like a rain-forest bird. There was a leaf trapped in an updraft across the lot, blowing in a circle. *He's been dead a year*, she thought, and it was true. The leaf fluttered to the ground to rest before it was tormented all over again.

It was Andy who brought Colin back to prayer. They were never a religious family, church visits limited to Christmas Eve and Easter morning, but Colin had long assumed God would understand how busy they were. He assumed God would listen anyway, that He'd have a genuine interest in helping him, and what he told God— after too much time with Heather's magazines or three showers in one afternoon—was that he'd do anything in exchange for one thing. He wanted to look at Andy without feeling like a creep. He wanted to sit cross-legged on his sleeping bag and talk about girls with the same enthusiasm, the same vulgarity, and he wanted to do this without the constant reminder of Andy's shirt, balled up under his head because he'd forgotten his pillow.

Looking at Andy had become difficult over the summer, and was made worse with the start of the school year. Colin couldn't get through a lunch period at Andy's table without him bring-ing up the length between his legs, holding his hands apart to show the other boys why he was superior. Day by day, something was tightening in Colin's chest, some wheel or hot coil. Almost as if it were part of his school day—the Pledge of Purity—he'd swear never to masturbate again, and fail before the day was over. He kept failing, every morning and night, sometimes not twenty minutes after lunch in a quiet stall while everyone else was in class. He liked to read stories printed out from the Internet and kept under his mattress, and when he thought about them later he modified the details until it was the two of them, best friends, stranded in the school for the night, or until it was Colin who slid to the floor in a movie theater at Andy's request. He couldn't fall asleep without failing, couldn't get out of bed. He no longer cared what Paul heard. His dreams and his nightmares often met in the middle, and after an evening spent rereading his father's account of hell Colin dreamt that he and Andy were trapped there and could only escape after they did whatever the demon commanded.

He continued with the other notebooks, but this one he never returned to its place on the shelf. It was something he referred to at least once each day, refreshing himself on some detail like the sparkle under hell's starlight as the grass collected dew or tears or sweat. *It was hard,* his father had written, *to tell them apart.* The fact that hell had grass—that it was more than a maze of granite and fire—made it feel true. That it had a sky full of stars that weren't our stars meant something but he couldn't pinpoint what. Colin felt if he read it over and over he could learn more about his father, as though this one entry, only a dozen or so pages, could tell him whether or not what he'd done was wrong.

It was hidden, the notebook, stuffed under his mattress with the wrinkled-up stories, a sci-fi book his father had never finished, and a yellowing T-shirt, all equally incriminating. He told his mother to stay out of their room, mostly because he didn't want her putting sheets on his bed. The way she looked at him—like he was so disgusting it was funny—made him want to list for her all his redeeming qualities. But there was nothing redeeming anymore, not with the notebook and not with the prayers Paul overheard, and not with Andy stretched out on his sleeping bag, the way the basement's one naked bulb spackled all his hollow spots with shadows. Nobody would hear them at this time of night, this far underground.

"Is little baby Colin gonna fall asleep without his angel to protect him?" Andy asked as Colin laid down the ten of diamonds. They'd learned blackjack the weekend before. "Hit me."

"You're just jealous. Nobody made you a picture like that."

"I don't want a picture like that. You only keep it 'cause you have a total boner for her."

It wasn't the best drawing of an angel—the colors faint, its wings like clumsy arcs of chicken feathers. In fact it sucked, but he kept it. "She's okay," he said, trying to avoid the trap.

"Dude, you know you want to fuck her. You probably lay here all night looking at the angel and beating off."

"I don't do that." Colin looked at the jack of spades, whose sterile profile couldn't tell when he was lying. He flipped over the next card. "Ha. You lost again."

"Whatever. Cards suck." Andy leaned back, his hands behind his head. He stretched out until his leg rested in Colin's lap. Colin felt the bare foot against his thigh, cool even through his jeans. He wasn't as pale, Andy. He wasn't as bony. You couldn't see his veins, and the black ellipse in each armpit actually looked like hair. Whenever Colin raised his arms in the locker room he felt ashamed of his light brown curls, almost invisible in the green fluorescents as though he was still a child. He shoved Andy's leg away. "Your feet fucking stink," he said, treasuring the little electric spot under his jeans, that circle of skin within a finger's length of his crotch.

Andy brought his foot to his face. "Mmm. Eau de athlete's foot."

"Anyway, I don't think Chelsea's into me."

"Well then you're fucking stupid." Andy sat up. "She's totally into you. She'd probably suck your dick if you asked. I mean, if she could find it."

Colin threw out his fist and landed a punch just below Andy's collarbone. He'd hit harder than he meant but didn't want to apologize. "She could find it," he said.

"Maybe with a microscope." Andy massaged the knuckle marks on his chest. "Sorry. I forget not everyone's hung like a porn star. Maybe one day I'll let you play with it, gay boy." He patted his crotch and made a face that cleaved Colin's heart in half. Then the normal Andy face returned, just mean enough to make you hate yourself. "Hey," he said as he sat up. "That reminds me. What do you think of Mr. Miller?"

Colin didn't want to answer. He wanted to pick up the cards and put them back in order, to deal another hand. He wanted Andy to keep losing. He wanted him to put his shirt back on.

"He's okay," he said. "He knows a lot. About science and stuff. I think he's pretty cool."

Andy grinned. "Figures you'd like him. My brother said he's a faggot."

Colin rolled his eyes. "They say that about all the dudes who teach."

"This is for real, though. He said when he was our age he saw Mr. Miller creeping on this kid in his class. He's a total homo. He probably rapes little kids when he's not at school."

"Whatever."

"Seriously!" Andy put up his hands, palms open. "I swear to God."

Colin pictured Mr. Miller, his button-up shirts always untucked, his hair parted down the middle. When he drew the diagram of a heart on the board he held the chalk like a pen, letting it rest against his finger. Colin didn't know what this meant. "He can't be gay," he said.

"He probably lies about it. I mean, it's not like he could tell anyone at school."

"Is he married?"

"If he is she's probably a dyke. Like they have an agreement or something."

"Whatever." Colin lay back on his pillow. "You need to find some new shit to think about."

"I'm totally saying something in class. I'm gonna see what he does."

"Don't be stupid. You'll get suspended."

"I'm not gonna say anything to his face. Maybe I'll call you a faggot in class and see if he gets all mad or whatever. Holy shit!" Andy slapped his knees like an excited toddler. "What if I got him to hit on me? What if I could get him fired and sent to jail?"

Colin looked at the ceiling and thought of his science teacher escorted from the room in handcuffs. "Dude, just leave him alone."

"But he's totally a rapist!"

Colin sighed and looked at the halo around the overhead light. He shut his eyes and there it was again, a green ring in the dark. He was thinking of Andy alone with Mr. Miller, after class on some Friday, their discussion of the human body and its rapturous mechanics. Blood trickled to his pelvis and he let his fingers slide beneath his waistband. He realized Andy might be watching and he scratched his pubic hair and withdrew.

"Do you think we should defend ourselves?" Andy asked.

"Just shut up already."

"I'm serious." Andy leaned over and prodded Colin in the ribs. "We might have to carry protection, you know. Like Mace or something." He looked over at the office door. "Or a gun."

"Don't even think about it. You're not gonna carry around a gun."

"Maybe just when we're not at school, like if he tried to follow us home or something."

"I'm serious. Forget about the fucking gun."

"Let's just practice with it," Andy said. "You don't have to load it. Let's just try hiding it under our shirts or something, and drawing it out real fast." He was folding the skin on his palms, looking at Colin like a much younger brother desperate to play. "We won't even touch the bullets, I swear. You know what? I'll stay out here. I don't even have to go in there. Promise."

"I told you to forget it."

"Okay, how about this." Andy leaned forward and made a fist. "If you don't get the gun, I'll punch you in the balls. And if you still don't get the gun, I'll punch you in the balls again. I'll punch you until you sound like SpongeBob. 'Hey guys! Has anyone seen my balls?'"

Colin looked over at the office door. He'd never shown Andy how to pick the lock, and now it was clear he'd never paid attention while he stood guard.

"You have five seconds," Andy said.

Colin groaned and retrieved the paper clips from behind the

furnace. Andy stood just outside the doorway, chewing his lip as Colin reached into the bottom drawer.

It wasn't long before they grew bored, aiming at a large strip of exposed insulation on the far wall that could've been a man's shadow. "What if Mr. Miller had a gun?" Andy asked, and pointed it at Colin. He imitated their teacher's deep voice, drawing out each word, only it sounded like someone who'd just learned to speak English. "Take off your clothes, kid," he said, and laughed when Colin lifted up his shirt and squealed *Please! Don't!*

"I got another idea," Andy said, already running for the office. He slammed the door loud enough to wake everyone in the house.

"You fucking idiot!" Colin whispered through the slats. He tried the knob but it was locked. "You want to wake up my mom?"

"She didn't hear it." There was a hollow metal sound as Andy opened the third drawer. Colin felt his hands go numb.

"Dude! The fuck are you doing?"

The drawer groaned again. Before Colin could remember where he'd put his paper clips the knob clicked from the other side and Andy pushed it open. The gun was tucked into the front of his underwear. *It's like a bomb going off*, Colin wanted to say, but it didn't make sense without the rest of the story, which he'd sworn never to tell.

"You're fucking crazy," he said.

"I didn't actually load it." Andy drew the gun and aimed between Colin's eyes. "I just wanted to fuck with you." He closed one eye and laughed. "You're totally shaking."

Colin felt like he was about to pass out. He looked down at the concrete and waited for it to look like concrete again.

"Or maybe it is loaded . . ."

"Not funny. Is it loaded or not?"

"Do you really think I'd load a gun?"

A year ago Colin would've known the right answer. He would've known that Andy, despite how he called Colin *faggot* and *pussy* and *fuckface*, wasn't all that different from himself. He would've known how Andy was scared of being alone in dark houses, how he laughed at the sight of blood and gore in movies but cried the day Colin sliced open his thumb trying to pick up a broken bottle in the woods. Today's Andy was a different Andy.

"I guess you'll just have to do whatever I say." Andy twirled the gun in his finger in a way that should've been graceful, but he had to steady it with both hands when he nearly dropped it. He pointed it back at Colin. "It's like truth or dare, except you're stuck on dare."

"Knock it off."

"I dare you . . ." Andy looked around the room. "I dare you to sniff the armpits on my shirt."

"Come on, man. You're being a dick."

Andy waved the gun, as if Colin could've forgotten it was there.

With a sigh he walked over to Andy's sleeping bag. The shirt was balled up in the corner, and when Colin unrolled it he could see the whitish spots from Andy's deodorant. He smelled those spots and let out a fake moan of ecstasy, even though they just smelled like shampoo and drugstore cologne. Andy wasn't satisfied.

"I dare you to take off your clothes," Andy said.

"What? All of them?"

"Every stitch." Andy touched the barrel of the gun with his other hand and stroked it, like an arch villain might stroke his villainous cat.

Colin looked down at the sleeping bag. "How about I take off my clothes, but I can be under the sleeping bag?"

"Sure. Whatever." Andy put both hands on the gun and held it steady.

After Colin pulled his briefs from under the sleeping bag he gave them a ceremonial twirl on his finger. "Ta da," he said, as though it was the most boring thing he'd ever done, as though his desperation wasn't pointing straight up at him. He tossed the underwear aside with the rest of his clothes.

Andy crossed the room and took Colin's shirt, jeans, and underwear and locked them in the office. He pulled the paper clips from his pocket. "Oops," he said.

"Not cool."

"Looks like you might have to come out of the sleeping bag after all."

"Fuck you, dickhead."

Andy shook his head. "Sorry, kid. If you want your clothes, you're gonna have to pay for it."

Colin rolled his eyes. He was sitting cross-legged in the sleeping bag, the fabric bunched up in his lap. "Okay," he said with a loud, fake sigh. "What do you want?"

"I dare you to blow me."

Colin looked down at his lap. Nobody could see his eyes right then, how they'd brightened and reached out for what they wanted. Nobody could see how he was struggling to breathe. "Um . . ." He tried to laugh. "What?"

"You know. Suck my dick."

He could almost forget about the gun leveled at his forehead. "You're not serious?"

"Why wouldn't I be serious?" Andy shrugged, like it didn't matter. Like this was as big a deal as cutting ahead in the lunch line. "You suck my dick, you can put your clothes back on. And, you know, I don't shoot you or anything."

Colin bit his lip. Then he smiled, as if he'd caught on to Andy's sense of humor. But Andy wasn't smiling, and the gun was starting to tremble.

"You don't really have a choice, dude. You're totally naked, at the wrong end of a gun. Plus, I could always tell the whole school how you boned up as soon as I said *blow job*."

Colin pulled more of the sleeping bag into his lap. He'd never dreamt this situation. He'd never failed at this merciless fantasy, but he knew if Andy touched him he'd burst as helplessly and iridescently as a soap bubble. He laughed and shook his head.

"You have ten seconds to make up your mind," Andy said. He stepped closer and put the gun against Colin's forehead. "One."

Andy's boxers were black with orange flames. A designer brand, the name stenciled on the waistband. With his jeans worn so low, Colin could make out the first half inch of his fly.

"Two."

He never got to three. There was nothing to say as Colin cast aside the sleeping bag, unzipped Andy's fly, and wrenched away jeans and underwear in one stroke. Colin had always suspected Andy was lying to the boys at the lunch table, but a dark part of him had hoped, all along. Even so, it was difficult for either boy to be disappointed, and long before it was over the gun was nestled among the sleeping bag's folds. Colin no longer cared about his clothes, not even with the certainty of hell ahead of him. Because Andy too would be in hell. They would be in love, and their suffering would only be suffering until each had swallowed the other's pain.

II

In November 1899, the *Boston Evening Transcript* reported the rumored existence of hundreds of cats, living in a mine near Butte, Montana, that had never seen the light of day.

Since the recession, many families have surrendered their horses to the desert. Those that don't die fall in with the wild herds already scavenging the plains for water—some ninety thousand horses. Without predators, the wild population doubles every four to five years, depending on rain.

According to his brother, six-year-old Sergei Nabokov adored Napoleon, and took a little bronze bust of the emperor to bed with him every night.

Kaskaskia, Illinois—the "American Atlantis"—will not survive another flood. The town's fourteen residents, most of whom are over sixty, are waiting for what they call the last flood.

The Voluntary Human Extinction Movement was proposed in 1991 as a solution to human suffering, as well as a precaution against the "extinction of millions of plants and animals." Choosing to stop reproducing, the VHEMT argues, "is a humanitarian alternative to human disasters." Here disasters are poverty, starvation, disease, and a planet that grows increasingly hostile as it tries to scratch its own back.

Who can blame them? his father had written.

As it grew colder and the birds and insects disappeared, Colin felt personally responsible, as though without him the seasons wouldn't change and nothing would have to die. But here he was, alive and killing everything around him, a year older as his birthday came and went with no one noticing, not even his mother. At the grocery store, a week afterward, she ran into a former coworker. "This is your youngest?" the woman asked. "How old?"

Colin and his mother spoke at the same time but gave two different numbers. "I mean fourteen," she said, as though it was funny. After they parted she picked up a small cake from the bakery and put it in the cart. "Colin, I'm so sorry," she said.

With the end of October came the season's first frost, and in November all the trees looked naked in the white slanted sun. Andy hadn't spoken to Colin since their last sleepover. They still had classes together, lunch together. They ate at the same table. Andy filled his followers' heads with lies and Colin still listened, every time thinking of the truth, of how Andy could fit gently in his hand. He knew there was nothing to say. Instead, he thought of how it should have gone, how Andy should have kissed him and said, "Now it's your turn." But that only made him sick with shame. He imagined that the right word could reset everything and bring them back to where they'd gone wrong. Even if they never touched each other again, he wanted that word.

The worst part was how nobody cared. His mother didn't ask, as the weeks went by, why Andy never came over. Heather never mentioned the kid who drooled over her. Their friends at the lunch table hung on Andy's every word, and had realized, maybe, that they'd never liked Colin in the first place. That same weekend, his grandfather accused him of looking *brighter* than usual—"Did you get some good news?" Their Sunday meals, with the cooling weather, had complicated themselves. He'd taught Colin how to *julienne* radishes, potatoes, something called *celeriac*. He'd shown him how to sear chicken without losing the skin to the bottom of the pan. When Andy wrapped his fingers in his hair, Colin had sworn never to forget it. Here was an image scratched into the backs of his eyelids, and he'd never go more than ten seconds without the most thrilling moment of his life knocking him out of place. At his grandfather's house, he was surprised to go nearly an hour without reminding himself of what had happened.

But his grandfather was just as clueless as everyone else. "I don't feel brighter," was all Colin said, and shrugged as if it didn't matter. He'd gone back to slicing the carrots and was thinking how something as soft as human skin would be so much easier to cut, so smooth. But his grandfather was waiting with the sauté pan.

Even Chelsea, who came over twice a week in Andy's place, seemed oblivious. All she wanted was to watch movies on the couch. "This is so comfy," she said as she dug through his mother's stock of extra pillows, blankets, quilts, and throws. She never seemed to move or even shift her legs, but by the end of every movie she was somehow right next to him, her thigh against his, her shoulder against his, her ribs trying to interlock themselves with the spaces between his. Once, when his mother wasn't home, she managed to slide her fingers up under the back of his shirt. "It gets so cold in here," she said, even though her hands were hot and slick with sweat. "I really like that you're so warm. You can be my heater." She laughed, and the suddenness of it, so close to his ear, startled him halfway down the couch.

Other people: more often than not they made him feel alone, and he spent most weeknights in his father's office. The more he dug into the notebooks, the more space they took up in his head. How is *this*, he wondered as he read about mummification rituals in ancient Egypt, related to *this*—a list of "Living Places" with bullet points like "Mojave Desert, dawn" and "another world's sun" and "Penn Station, rush hour." He read until his eyes crossed and the ink blurred. After locking the door, he would peer across the basement. How must it have looked, Andy's knees shaking as Colin licked and gorged like a starved dog? He shut his eyes and let it happen again, and even a little more as—in his head— everything went as he wanted.

By late November, Andy simply wasn't a part of his life anymore. During the last class before Thanksgiving break, Colin was watching him from the other side of the room. For a few days, Andy had been whispering, passing notes, and snickering with the boy who sat behind him. Instead of hurting less as time went on, it hurt more. Their science teacher, Victor Miller, warned the class of their upcoming unit, the human reproductive system. Those three words brought laughs from the back of the room, a few whispered words flipped into the air like a profane deck of cards. "I know, I know," Victor was saying as he reached for a textbook on his desk. "But what the human body can do is more beautiful than you can imagine."

"You should see what I can do," Andy said, and the kid behind him prodded him between the shoulders. The boys in the class laughed and the girls rolled their eyes. Colin was thinking, was picturing, could feel in his hands, could savor the taste all over again, of precisely what Andy could do. He wanted to die.

Victor ignored the comment. "Now, over the break, I want you all to read . . ." He stretched the last word as he thumbed the book's middle pages, raising his eyebrows at sighs that were anything but subtle. "Read all your recipes carefully." He closed the book and smiled at his students, immune to every groan and glare in their arsenal.

Colin watched as his teacher walked back behind his desk, studying the way his feet hit the floor. Over the last five weeks he'd looked for similarities. Was there anything in Mr. Miller's face that would have looked girlish when he was young? Did he chew his lip when he thought about something? Had he loved, against his will, the feel of his hair clenched in another boy's fist?

The bell rang and he flinched in his seat. He got to his feet and threw his backpack over his shoulder, but before he could leave Victor stopped him.

"Colin," he said. "Can I see you for a moment?"

Some of his classmates sneered as they walked out—the look every child learns by kindergarten. Colin put his hands in his pockets and thought of the beaker he'd broken and hidden. As he approached the desk he felt the room emptying. Who could he blame? Who couldn't prove it? It wasn't until they were alone that he thought of what Andy had said, the warning he'd given—that boy his brother knew who'd been hunted. He could scream, if he had to. Someone would hear it.

Victor wrote a note and stuck it to his computer. "You're not in trouble, so don't worry." The footsteps in the hallway paled from thunder into a clatter. The textbooks on the desk were left open to diagrams of the genitals or grainy fetuses drifting in kidney-shaped shadows. "I want you to know that as your teacher I'm concerned. You and Andy are best friends, are you not?"

What the word *father* had been a year ago: *Andy* was now that word. *Friend* was another. "I guess," he said, in a way he hoped sounded bored.

"Are you two having a fight? Is there something going on?"

He heard footsteps again. He hoped someone had forgotten something—a hat or a jacket. Instead he saw the earth sciences teacher hurrying down the hallway, an oversized red bag over her shoulder. How obvious they must be—Andy, the boy who always looked uncomfortable in class, and Colin, whose depravity had ruined everything, who wore it on his face. He thought about the classroom, how there might be nobody left in this wing, and only that one door.

He shrugged his backpack up onto his shoulder. "We're fine."

Victor folded his hands on the desk and tried to catch Colin's eye. "Are you sure?"

Colin looked away, as though Victor was too bright. If he wasn't careful, his teacher could cross the room and lock the door. He could pull down the blinds. He could take Colin in his adult hands and unfasten every button and zipper that kept him safe. "I'm okay, Mr. Miller. Really."

"I'm here to help. We all are."

Colin looked back at the door. "I should probably catch my bus before it's too late."

"Of course," Victor said. "Sorry to keep you." He leaned back and glanced up at the clock. "You may already be late. The buses leave at five to."

He looked up and saw that it was three o'clock. Paul would be waiting on the steps, alone while the buses pulled themselves into the street like immense yellow worms. He imagined the noise coming from Paul's throat, like a life raft's pinhole leak. It would be dark by the time his mother arrived, crossing the empty parking lot of a locked school to collect her shivering, stupid boys. He leaned up against the wall and banged the back of his head into it.

Victor stood and neatened a stack of papers. As he was slipping them into his briefcase he shrugged. "If you don't have a ride, I could give you one. And your brother."

Colin's scalp tightened. He couldn't tell which was worse—stranded at school and waiting in the dark, or accepting a ride from this man who may never take him home. He chewed the inside of his cheek as he looked at the clock and time moved forward, one second, two seconds, three seconds, on and on. Why should it stop? The halls were quiet now.

"If you want," Victor said.

He drove a black Toyota with grey upholstery. Colin guided Paul into the backseat, careful, by instinct now, not to touch him. Outside of the car he clutched his backpack like a shield, thinking of the ways kids disappeared, of basements, abandoned warehouses, parts of the woods no one knew about. "Ready when you are," Victor said. His gloves squealed against the steering wheel as he tightened his grip. Colin swallowed and slipped into the front seat. A fly landed on the windshield and flicked its wings. He reminded himself to go on breathing.

Victor backed the car out of its spot. "So . . . where to?"

A boy and a girl crossed in front of the car, holding hands and laughing. There were no cars in either direction and they were free to turn at any time. The sun slipped behind a cloud and the car's interior felt cooler. A car behind them honked. Colin sighed and surrendered his address. He hoped Heather was there waiting. He hoped the neighbors were out raking the last of the leaves before winter ushered them inside. He hoped his mother had come home early for the holiday, that she would climb out of her car just as he arrived.

Victor tapped his fingers on the wheel as he drove. Colin wasn't looking but he could hear faint puffs of breath as Victor mouthed words in a whisper, some song stuck in his head. The houses and the gas stations and the baseball diamonds crept by.

"You're not taking the freeway."

"I prefer side streets."

Colin could feel him watching. A route like this had what you'd call quiet roads—ones that snaked off to hidden places, playgrounds and parks that were empty this late in the season. He thought of how easy it would be, how it'd only take a sudden turn, a hand over the mouth, a threat. Everything would be lost. Stories came to him—the plots of movies where men would bind their victims' hands. He thought of the things they did to boys and felt his dismay between his thighs.

"I know what they say about me," Victor said.

Colin put his tongue between his teeth and bit down.

"The thing about rumors," he said, "is that they start with a misunderstanding."

Colin's leg began to twitch and he pressed it into the floor mat. When would it happen? How long would Victor make him wait?

"From there it's just an annihilation of trust." He turned to him. "Trust is important."

Colin nodded without taking his gaze off his knees.

"Don't believe everything you hear, Colin. You're too smart for that. Sometimes you just need to think things through for yourself."

The car was not quite silent with the tires' groan on the asphalt and the backseat's creak as Paul rocked back and forth. Even the stuffy, heat-scorched air they shared seemed to be muttering, as though it doubted them.

"Okay?"

Colin moved his lips but his voice had deserted him. He coughed and tried again. "Okay."

He began to recognize the houses around him—first one, then another, then every house on a block. His mother's car was in the driveway and he grinned like an idiot. Had he prayed? Was this God? Victor pulled his car behind hers and turned to face him. "Here we are!"

"Thanks." He clutched his backpack to his chest and reached for the door.

"Colin."

He stopped. The door handle—this thing of cold steel—felt beautiful in his fingers.

"There are people who care about you," Victor said. Colin wasn't looking but it was impossible to imagine him not smiling that smile. "Have a happy Thanksgiving."

He nodded. He hoped it looked like a genuine, thoughtful nod instead of what it was. The weak November sun tried to warm him as he retrieved Paul from the backseat. Colin didn't look back until he heard the car roll out of the driveway. He didn't know if you'd call it danger, or if this was anything like an escape, but his hands could barely guide the key into the lock.

The house was in a different state. Despite the sun's reach through the uncovered windows, all the lights were on. Closets had been left open. There were bottles and cans all throughout the house—Endust, glass cleaner, countertop spray. A bucket of dull water waited in the middle of the kitchen, its mop reaching for the sink. The floor looked like two floors stuck together, one shiny and one dull. The whole thing looked like an art installation his father had taken them to in Chicago. Where was that, in the notebooks? Where was a list with *Mop, Cleaning products, Half-mopped floor*? Why hadn't he cared enough to write the word *Colin*, or *Heather*? There were screwdrivers and old keys and batteries scattered on the countertops. He unshouldered his backpack and let it fall to the floor. The house smelled like lemons and ammonia.

His mother was scrubbing the carpet in her bedroom, singing beneath her breath. The words he couldn't make out. It sounded more like a lullaby or a church hymn than something you'd hear on the radio. The closet was drawn open and Colin could see his father's suits and shirts on the far right. He reached for a brown wool jacket, something you'd wear to a funeral. It felt scratchy and he rubbed his fingers to make the itch go away. Adjacent was a black dress shirt with grey stripes, and he saw his father wearing it. He didn't know what day of the week it was, or even what month—only the garage door roaring closed as his father came into the kitchen, the smell of lasagna in the oven, Heather's laughter from the living room. Colin looked at the other shirts, desperate for more, but they were only shirts—ones he had to imagine his father wearing, and that was just fake.

She glanced up. "You're home."

"Yeah." He slipped his hands into his pockets. "What're you doing?"

"There's a stain here. I've been meaning to get rid of it for years." She pulled a rag from a basket near the bed and pressed down as if the floor were wounded. "I came home sick."

The dresser and the nightstands had been polished, wet with light from the bedside lamps. The bed itself looked like something from a furniture commercial, its pillows centered on each side, the comforter flipped so you could see the egg-blue sheets. He couldn't remember if she'd left the sheets in a tangle since her sudden scramble for the basement, or if she'd made the bed a long time ago and this, right now, meant nothing.

"I forgot how sunny it gets in here this time of year," she said. She balled up the rag and looked at the carpet. The wet spot was a shade darker but there was no stain, if it had ever been there to begin with. She nodded and threw the rag back into the basket. With a groan she got to her feet and turned to the closet, pushing clothes aside as though he wasn't there.

"Therapy is going okay then?"

She paused to look at a green dress. "What do you mean?"

"I don't know. You seem different."

"Different how?" She shook her head and pushed the dress aside. Colin could see himself behind her in the mirror, and behind them both the window with its blanket of rusting sunlight. It occurred to him that maybe Victor hadn't left, and that he was spying on them from the other side of the light. It really had been an escape, his leaving the car. At any second, Victor could have pulled into a hidden driveway or parking lot and tied Colin's hands to the door, drawing from his boyhood whatever purity was left. He thought of the things Victor would've whispered in his ear as he held him down against the seat. That he was standing there, in front of his mother, with a growing longing for Victor set it all in stone: he deserved this pain, and more.

He touched his father's pillow. "Are you gonna start sleeping in here again?"

"What?" She flipped another hanger down the rod, the screech of metal on metal enough to make him wince.

"Never mind." In the mirror he got up from the bed and straightened his jeans. Boxed in like that, in the mirror's frame with the sun's orange rectangles thrown all around the room, he looked not like himself. He looked, he thought, like a boy who'd never done anything wrong. Like a boy his mother could actually love—not the deviant he'd become.

In victims of autism, scientists have observed a unique reaction to the world around them. Words appear useless, as does any expression of emotion—crying, yelling, laughing, putting one's hand over one's mouth. Six years ago, based on several decades of research, Dr. Ursula Alagóna made a previously overlooked deduction: "If their response to external stimuli is inconsistent with their surroundings, perhaps their surroundings are different from our own. Perhaps what they perceive to be the world is not what we perceive to be the world." In the photo from the newspaper, Dr. Alagóna seems radiantly tired, with the glow of someone who's just run a marathon. Perhaps Paul, his father had written, is in another world, and perhaps our speech, our methods of what we perceive to be communication, are to him nothing but white noise. I've often imagined the two of us sitting there, what his world must look like, what the darkness or blindness must be like, what the aloneness must be like, until he feels my hand in his hair or on the back of his neck. How does that world bloom the way mine blooms when he walks into a room? How does the sudden dissipation of loneliness look, in his world?

Colin remembered how Paul seemed a different Paul only when his father was there. His parents had always said they didn't play favorites, but it was easy, now, to see that lie for what it was. It hadn't occurred to him until then how lucky he was that his parent—the parent who understood the world to which Colin belonged—had survived.

"I'm gonna go hang out in my room," he said, pausing in the doorway where the blue carpet met the white carpet. His eyes met hers, in the mirror, and he noticed hers were full of tears. "Have fun," he said—the only words he seemed to know, right then—and he left.

That night, he decided that the only way to prove himself strong was to never again think of Andy, of Victor, of anyone else who inspired his body to rebel. It made the long weekend seem longer, his abstinence. His best defense was to remain at his mother's side. "You must have something you want to ask me," she said as he lit her cigarette. She reached out to brush his hair into place.

He took a step back and glanced into the kitchen. "There's lots of turkey left in the fridge."

"I know."

"Do you want a sandwich?"

She formed her lips into an O and sent a perfect ring of smoke sailing across the room. "That sounds lovely."

With a nod he slipped into the kitchen and took the plate of leftovers from the fridge. She likes mustard and mayonnaise, he was thinking as he washed his hands. The soap dispenser was plugged, and when he pushed harder it shot across the counter, a long pearlescent strip. It kept his attention as he pressed himself against the cupboard.

Somehow, he made it to Monday. Diane went to work. Colin and Paul went to school. Heather went to the mall to fill out applications. It had snowed a little in the night and the grass looked covered by a grey moth-eaten blanket. Thanksgiving weekend was over, and as he went from class to class he remembered what it meant to pay attention and take notes. Andy's voice, his smirk, his cologne—nothing had ever been so toxic, and Colin spent his lunch period in the library. He went the whole school day without eating.

The sight of his science teacher was no better. He too made Colin hurt the way only chaste bodies could hurt. Which fear was worse?—what the world would do when he closed his eyes, or what he would do to the world if he couldn't stop staring at Victor's crotch while he lectured about bodies maturing, of how they grow, of their industry, he said, their autonomy, their drive, their flawless systems? "The adolescent male must ejaculate several times per week to keep his sperm healthy," he was saying, and as the other boys in the class snickered—he could hear Andy's above all the rest like a favorite song in a crowded mall—Colin felt like tearing off his clothes and showing Victor just how healthy he could be. Or he could wait until the class cleared out, until it was just the two of them after school. He heard Victor's footsteps cross the room as he described the passage of sperm through the body. Colin steadied his hand as he wrote SPERM in his spiral notebook, as though a clue to acing a test.

At the end of class Victor passed back a graded quiz from the week before. Colin was indifferent to the A+, but he noticed a note scribbled in the margin above his name. *Thank you for the conversation last week. Anytime you need a ride, just ask.* Colin flipped the page face down. He thought that maybe for some untold reason the bell would ring early, just this once. Victor smiled at him, and with a pirouette placed another quiz on another desk.

When the bell did ring, Colin remained. He folded the quiz into his backpack, pausing to read the note once more. He got to his feet and watched Victor erase vocabulary from the board: *vas deferens, epididymis, seminal vesicle*—all these things inside him he'd only begun to understand. The slamming of locker doors echoed from the hallway. It was hard to believe how fast the school could empty, like a spilled can of pop. He leaned against a desk and it groaned across the linoleum.

Victor hadn't looked up. "Did you have a question?"

There was still time to back out. Colin shook his head, leaning on another desk. Another groan. "No," he said. "I don't think so. No."

That same smile. "Well then, have a good night. You'll have to hurry if you want to catch your bus."

He nodded. The voices were fading again. His heart was pounding again. He shifted his weight from one leg to the other. The halls were quiet again. "I was gonna ask for a ride."

Victor's eyes were on his desk. Colin could see his tongue move along his teeth. He saw how he, too, shifted from one foot to the other. He began filling his briefcase with books and assignments. "You could still ask."

Colin looked at Victor's hands. His eyes passed to the desk beneath the briefcase, to the chair behind him, the front of his khakis.

"Go get your brother. I'll be ready in a minute."

When Victor delivered him to his house untouched, there was no way Colin could hide his disappointment. He thought of Victor's hot breath on his neck, what it must feel like.

What made the night hard was solitude. Heather was out. Not long after his mother came home, she took Paul to the hospital. He'd tripped and landed on his finger—a simple dislocation, she said, *but with a son who screams every time you touch him, what are you supposed to do?* Colin wished he'd gone with her. Alone, it felt like he was sweating out a fever or infection. He tried a cold shower but only shivered in the stream thinking of someone watching, the naked boy they would see. For a half hour he sat on the front steps knowing he couldn't try anything in public. Then it began to snow and he came inside. At eight o'clock he called his mother's phone but it went straight to voicemail. With nothing left to do he went to bed, spending the next hour with another of his father's notebooks. He held it close to his face so it blocked out everything else. When he felt tempted he put his free hand behind his head and thought of his virtue, how this might redeem him from everything he'd done. It was just after nine when his eyes grew tired. He slept in his jeans and pretended they were made of iron, that he couldn't touch it even if he wanted to.

Whenever you thought hell was something you could understand, it did something new. The wings and burnt feathers of his father's new frame were softer than anything he'd ever touched, and, gathered up in their embrace, Colin shivered. In hell the moon is a dark lump of red-splintered amber and its light is scattered on the grass and in that dream he closed his eyes to its splendor. He felt touched on all sides, touched all at once, and there was nothing he could do but moan his wordless prayers into the bedsheets. At five in the morning he changed out of his dampened briefs and buried the notebook at the bottom of his desk drawer. First he'd killed his father, and now this—a dream you couldn't pretend was only a dream. He spent a long time staring at himself in the mirror, chastising and berating, shaking his head, making promises even he knew he couldn't keep.

In ancient Rome, in colonial America, in twenty-first-century Thailand—since the invention of fire and iron—slaves have worn artful scars on their foreheads. A felony to harbor or feed a fugitive, a slave is forever dependent upon one person for food, water, and shelter. Should that fail, most would find it difficult to run without feet.

Even though she'd dismissed them, back in October, Tim's words had followed her. They'd climbed into her car and sat in the backseat. "There's a lot about you that would charm any man," she said in her deepest voice, laughing at herself in the rearview mirror.

From then on her hands felt empty. She did what she could to occupy them, smoking more often, squeezing her fingers until they could hold a plush paper-wrapped filter between them, grinding her teeth until she could flick away the ash with a twitch of her thumb. There was always a song in her head and she tapped its rhythm against a tabletop or a steering wheel. Her knuckles never felt satisfied and she pushed her fingers forward even when they didn't ask to be cracked. She touched people. It was impossible to get through a conversation without removing a piece of lint from someone's sweater or asking to feel strange fabrics. When Colin came into the room she'd take up his hand and look at his fingers. "You still bite your nails," she'd tell him, running the pad of her thumb along his sharp places where she knew her skin would snag. She hugged him when he stood at the stove, when he washed dishes. Not long after Halloween, Paul stayed home sick. As he lay on the couch she couldn't help but part his hair how she'd always liked it. It wasn't as if she expected anything new or miraculous, but she sighed when he groaned and slapped her hand away. All day she'd carried the touch of his hair on her fingertips, that tingling like she was wearing gloves of spidersilk.

It wasn't until the first week of December that she realized what she was looking for. Cleaning the bathroom on a Sunday afternoon, she found a disheveled copy of *Penthouse* in the rack next to the toilet. Before she threw it away she remembered the night she and Alan had read each other letters, squinting in the candlelight. That was so long ago, she realized—back when he was still a good man, someone who smiled at her more than he didn't, someone who resembled the man she thought she'd loved. She locked the bathroom door and tried to conjure his voice, but she didn't recognize any of the stories. It wasn't until the air in the house changed, the front door drawing in an outside breath, that she realized she'd read half the magazine. She felt dizzy when she shoved it down into the bag, covering it with a gardening catalog, and as she left the bathroom her armpits prickled with cold sweat.

She drew a bath that night and was dragging a razor across her shin when she began to shiver. There was nothing new—the same old band of flesh flanked by shaving cream—but the water murmured when she rinsed the razor; it lapped against her breasts when she returned it to her leg. Her entire calf was tingling as though just woken from some anesthetized sleep. Her fingers felt stiff and she bent them back against the tub's fiberglass wall. Only one knuckle responded, but it rang out like a gunshot and sent pinpricks galloping down her spine. There were little white crests on the ripples in the bathwater. She turned on the faucet to silence herself.

Now, in the last days of December, she'd made a decision. Not something for New Year's—not an arbitrary promise or a vague resolution. Instead it felt like breaking a promise, as though she'd been good for so long and now deserved to treat herself to this one thing. That she'd been alone for over a year without the thought exploding inside her—wasn't that a mark of how she'd grown, over time? Hadn't she been the exemplary, chaste wife?

Tim was across from her, finishing up her notes. That's how Diane thought of them—her notes, not his. What wasn't there to like about her, or at least about the woman she scrutinized in mirrors? She was forty-three but didn't look it. When she narrowed her eyes, any man would know how sometimes the only thing for two people to do was fuck. She had read enough letters of serendipitous sex to know how to trick people, how to wear down their defenses. With what she hoped was a grin instead of a plain smile, she opened her mouth to speak.

"So how were the last few weeks?" Tim asked.

She didn't know how to answer. Her lips were still shaped into that grin but she'd lost the look, the heat in her eyes. "Fine, I guess," she heard herself say.

"Just fine? How's Heather doing? You guys still fighting regularly?"

The shaky feeling was gone. She sank back into the chair and frowned. "I don't know."

"You don't know?"

"I guess nothing's new. She mostly just stays in her room."

"This happens to a lot of families. It's usually the worst with the oldest child. There's no model for how it's supposed to work, so you both tend to hate what's happening."

Say something sexy, she commanded. Her tongue felt inadequate and she dragged it across her teeth. Now she was stuck thinking about Heather. "Are you trying to make me feel bad?"

"What? No. Not at all. I'm just trying to—I'm softening the blow, I guess."

"What blow? What are you talking about?"

"Forget I said anything." He took up the pen and rearranged himself in his chair. "How about the boys? Didn't one just have a birthday?"

"Colin's birthday was in October."

"Yes, Colin. He's . . ."

"Fourteen." After the supermarket she willed herself to remember it. She'd wanted to buy a bigger, more expensive cake, but all they had left was a six-inch marble cake with no flowers or footballs or even swirls. She still told him, all these weeks later, how terrible she felt.

"Fourteen." Tim made a note.

"My kids are fine."

His eyebrow jumped. He crossed a *t* with a quick swipe of his hand as though he was trying to cut something. "Your kids are fine. Is something else on your mind?"

There was a purring sound coming from the ceiling vent. When she sat back in her chair a rush of air caught her in the eye. "I don't know," she said.

Tim was tapping the pen against the legal pad. You could tell he had no idea how horrible it was, that sound.

"I don't know what it is lately. I keep thinking about things." Her whole method of seduction now seemed impossible, like when you set out to draw someone's portrait and what ends up on paper looks inhuman. "I don't know what it is lately." She cleared her throat and uncrossed her legs. She should've worn a skirt, even though it was winter. Her lips felt fused together and with a sound like an egg hatching she wet them with her tongue. How long, she wanted to know, until you regress into virginity? "I keep thinking about sex."

Tim's eyes fell to the notepad. He wasn't tapping anymore. "That's not so unusual."

"It is for me." She brushed her hair behind her ear. "I swear I didn't think about it once for a year. Then bang, it's everywhere." Her hands felt weak and she collapsed them into fists to verify her strength. She didn't sound sex-starved and manic, only sad. "I'm sorry."

"It's okay. You can talk about whatever you need to. What you're describing is very natural."

"I just feel so ridiculous. And stupid, like I should be beyond this. It just feels so unhealthy."

"Diane, it isn't unhealthy. It's very normal. It's sex. Why do you think it's unhealthy?"

Her eyebrow started twitching and she covered it with her hand as if deep in thought. "I keep thinking about people I know." She glanced up at him, under the shield of her fingers.

A door slammed in the hallway and sent a picture frame on the far wall into convulsions. Tim was reading his notes as if he'd already forgotten the first few minutes of their session. The clock's every tick sounded critical, like someone tsk-tsking. Hate, too, is like lust, and she wanted to overturn the table and give this man hell. *Have you ever actually helped someone? Do you know what that means—help?* She looked up at him, his sweater and his glasses and his faint greying stubble the purest picture of smug, arrogant, abstracted humankind. Tim was everything a lover was not. Why had she wanted this? When she imagined it, it was like the letters where people lunged at each other, where they smashed themselves together. That it was wrong made it even better, the perfect affair, and it made it easy to pretend she was still married. All through October she'd thought about what he told her—about men and their reasons. In their November session she'd watched him like an appraiser or analyst. Everything he did—smiling at her, leaning into his hand as he listened, touching his ear as he fell into thought—had become flirtation. Now it made him seem like an overgrown child.

She tried to remember the last time she felt the good kind of alone, truly unobserved and free to do whatever she pleased. When had she last thought, staring at something or someone she wanted: *Who gives a shit?* It would have been in San Francisco, when she was young. Twenty-two or -three, out of money, out of shits to give, she could have done anything, been anyone.

Finally Tim spoke. "I'm not going to ask who."

"Just people." She fell back into the chair. "The usual. That guy Daniel, always."

"You don't have to divulge specifics if you don't want to."

"I mean, who else would it be? I don't know anyone else." Her scalp felt as though someone was pulling her hair, one strand at a time. "Don't worry about it. Hormones, I guess. Maybe I'm getting to that age, I don't know." She plucked a tissue from the box. A habit, she realized. She was someone who cried after a confession, after sharing a memory. Instead she broke out in laughter, loosened from her chest like a strange phlegm. "It's been a long year."

"I'd imagine." His fist was clasped around the pen, his finger poised as if to make that awful clicking. *Just put down the fucking pen and listen to me*, she wanted to say. Her reflection was there in the corners of his glasses, translucent and cut in half by the light. She wanted to watch it laugh again, to put her hands to her face and laugh at how funny it was to be laughing, to be so stupidly controlled by boiling, bubbling chemicals in the body.

Often I worry I am a kind of cage or straitjacket, a way of confining or mummifying other people until they're no longer themselves. My wife has it in her to soar far above this life I've anchored her to, and instead I sit here and let her look out the window at the sky she's denied herself on my behalf. If she is a bird, I am her wings kept clipped.

If she is light, Alan had written, *I am the curtain. I am the shroud.*

"Anyway." She waved her hand in the air, her old magic trick. "Let's just forget about it. It was stupid anyway." She reached for her purse. The familiar clicks and clacks filled the room as she pushed aside those pieces of life. When she found her list she laid it on the table, pressing it flat to hide the way her hands had decided to tremble. She brushed her hair out of her eye and took on a different voice. Her mourning voice. "I keep thinking about this cologne he used to wear. I saw a bottle of it at Macy's. I just had to smell it again." She kept her eyes on the list. It wasn't a lie—she had gone to Macy's, and even brought the bottle home. She'd gently misted his clothes, leaving the closet door open so it could weaken as though it'd been worn all day. Thinking of it now was more of a pleasure than anything—her resourcefulness, the slow ritual she took in setting up an opportunity to remember, to immerse herself in something she'd loved so much. If she'd ever even loved it, or if now was the first time. Death had given her so many new things, she thought, and shook her head, there in Tim's office. Since she'd read that passage in Alan's notebooks it was hard to cleave from herself that image, light splintering outward from what was presumably her soul. There was so much, yet, to accomplish in this life that was newly her own.

"Is something wrong?"

"No." She bit her lip. "I mean, other than the usual." She sucked in a breath and pushed her hair back with both hands. "Life is so cruel," she said, in a lilt that couldn't hide her joy.

By Christmastime, Colin no longer pretended to have a reason to linger after the bell. Every day, Victor was waiting at the far edge of the lot, the defroster making its strange handprints on the windshield. Paul too got used to it, no longer rocking in the backseat until the ride was over. Colin watched his teacher's hands glide over the steering wheel as they came around sharp bends in the side streets or passed over the icy patches along the curb. Once, they got stuck in traffic and the car grew hot enough for Victor to take off his coat, revealing the short-sleeve button-up he'd worn in class. His bicep shuddered as he shifted the car into reverse to find another route. Colin looked out the window. He thought about his promises to God.

There was something easy in going straight home from school. He liked the way Victor talked about the heart and its blood, the blood and its cells. *There's nothing in the body more important.* Colin pictured his own heart—its panic at the sight of a road that led to a hidden park. The things he wished for, what he asked from another kind of god—one who understood him and would forgive his failures—made him think Victor could see right through his clothes. So far, just like any other prayer, nothing and nobody had answered.

He looked at Victor now. His eyes were on the road and Colin felt embarrassed not to be looked at. They passed by that same park and Colin imagined the turn, the bumpy ride to the clearing. There would be bluffs of snow all around them, pushed off into the parking lot's corners by the plows. Victor would hold Colin down, even if he begged him not to—especially if he begged him not to. After that, Victor would steal him. He'd smuggle him across the country, his purity a little more undone in each motel as they made their way west, east, back west. *You're sick*, he thought. *Stop being a perv.*

"It's oxygen that turns blood red," Victor was saying. "I'm sure you remember that from class. I just find it fascinating, when you look at your veins. How blue they are."

Colin nodded and smoothed a wrinkle out of his jeans.

"I don't know why you ride home with me every day. I probably bore you to tears."

"No." He looked up at Victor. "It's—it's interesting."

"You know in Minnesota 'interesting' means you don't like it, right?"

"What?" Colin laughed. "No, I didn't. Fine. It's . . . neat."

"A way with words." Victor tapped two fingers on the wheel. "Still, it's always me telling you things you already know. You learned all this stuff in my class. At least I hope you did. I'm not worth anything if you didn't. I just feel like one of those forest ranger mannequins they used to have at parks. Are you too young for those? The ones where you'd press a button and they'd start talking about the forest?" He swerved to avoid a squirrel. "What about you?"

"Huh?"

"Tell me about yourself. Talk to the park ranger mannequin. It wants to take a break."

He looked outside. A woman was shoveling snow, her lips moving as if someone were there arguing with her. "I don't know. There's not much. I get up and go to school and go home."

"I'm sure there's more than that. What do you like to do? Who do you spend time with?" Victor glanced over at him. "Do you have a girlfriend?"

How he said it—dragging out the word *girlfriend*—made Colin feel like he was back in the fourth grade. He rolled his eyes to show how little he cared. "No."

"I see you with that one girl all the time. I don't know her name. She's in Jeanie's class—Mrs. Morowitz."

"Chelsea?" He scrunched up his face and looked down at the floor mat. "She's just a friend."

"Come on, Colin. Don't fool yourself."

"What? She's just a friend." For a second he expected that fourth-grade joke: *Is she a girl? Is she your friend? Then she's your girlfriend!*

Instead Victor shook his head. "Frankly, I'm surprised. You probably have girls falling all over you. Maybe Chelsea scares them away. Just be careful." He peered at him, out of the corner of his eye. "Judging by the look of you, you could easily get yourself into trouble."

"Trouble?"

"You could get her pregnant."

Colin's next breath was too sharp and he coughed as it caught in his throat.

"You remembered what we studied. You are old enough, aren't you?"

There was an itch in his throat, maybe where the air had stabbed him. He swallowed and looked at his knees. He didn't want to ask but he felt like he had to. "For what?"

"Are you ejaculating?"

Colin wrapped his hand around the door handle and watched the houses creep by. The car had slowed with only a few blocks to go. Paul was rocking in the backseat.

"It's perfectly natural to do it. You don't have to be embarrassed. All boys have to do it or they'll do it in their sleep." He laughed. "You probably spend a lot of time alone in your room thinking about girls. Or the bathroom. The shower. All those places."

Colin's leg was twitching. He pressed it into the floor to keep it still.

"I'll take your silence as an admission. Girls probably drive you crazy."

The car came around a curve and Colin caught the eye of a man reaching into his mailbox. The man waved and Colin felt his skin go red.

"Maybe you don't like girls."

The houses had become familiar. They trudged by like doomed soldiers. "I like girls," he whispered. He could feel Victor looking at him as they crept around another corner. His house was only a block away.

"Are you sure?"

"You can drop us off here," he said, his voice cracking on the final word. "I'll walk. Me and Paul can walk from here."

Victor bit his lip. "Nonsense." The car returned to its normal speed—too fast for a residential street, Colin's father would've said. "I'll drop you off at home."

Before he could leave, Victor wrapped his hand around his forearm. "Colin," he said. "I'm sorry if I made you uncomfortable."

Colin stared at his hand. He was shocked that it could encompass his entire arm. Was he still a child, then? Had he grown at all? "It's okay."

"I'm just concerned for you. You always seem like such a loner."

"I'm fine."

"I know about your dad. I know what happened."

All those times he prayed for those hands to take him, and now Colin only wanted to listen to his sister complain, his brother groan. He wanted to light his mother's first cigarette of the evening, right when she walked through the door.

Victor's fingers, pale from winter, were wearing veins just behind the knuckles. It *was* fascinating, how blood was so brilliantly blue. "I have to go, Mr. Miller."

"Oh. Of course." He let go and leaned back to his side of the car. "I'll see you at school then. I hope you're still comfortable riding home with your science teacher. I've grown to like . . . it's really nice not listening to the same boring news on the radio every day." He flashed once more that smile, that kindness. You couldn't get away from it.

Fistulae of the Circulatory System: Cerebral Arteriovenous (in which an artery feeding the brain wears through its lining and joins a nearby vein, ferrying blood back to the heart); Coronary Arteriovenous (in which the carotid, brachiocephalic, or abdominal arteries fuse to one or more veins, overworking the heart until it wears out like a dry pump); Pulmonary Arteriovenous (in which an artery joins with a vein of the lungs, interrupting the blood's intake of oxygen). Cerebral fistulae will burst and hemorrhage until the brain is blanketed in blood. In pulmonary fistulae, the patient can go weeks without symptoms, unaware of why he can never catch his breath. In more severe cases, he begins to cough up blood, and is at risk of cyanosis—a bluing of the skin. None of this Colin learned from Victor. They were words he'd memorized, repeating them out loud as his father's notebook lay flat in front of him. As Victor's car receded from the driveway he asked himself what veins in his chest had come loose, what bleeding was inside him as he stood there barely able to breathe.

Heather was stretched out on her bed, bag of chips in reach, magazine between her elbows. Colin leaned against her door frame. The jewelry box was still there. The pile of dog-eared magazines. Colin's breathing was still labored, as if he'd run right from the school. "I had a weird ride home," he said.

"The fuck are you doing in here?" She waved her hand at him. "Go bother someone else."

"I just had a weird story. I can tell it fast."

"I don't give even one shit." She picked up the magazine and drew her arm back over her shoulder. "If I have to throw this, I'm getting revenge."

"It's about my teacher. My science teacher."

"So go tell your math teacher. Just get out. You have three seconds. One."

"Whatever. I'm going. You don't have to be such a bitch." He put his hands back in his pockets and wanted her to love him. *Remember when you used to dress me up as your cat?*

"Two."

Colin shook his head and left the room. He heard the pages crinkle as she straightened them out in front of her. "Hey, shithead. Can you close my door?"

"Fuck you."

Colin didn't know why he expected a response, but when he heard only another page as she folded its corner he let out a sigh and slammed Heather's door. After a muffled bang and a shout there was nothing to hear. He stepped into his room and closed the door behind him.

Paul was on the edge of his bed, staring out the window. The sun left a bright spot on the far wall with a Paul-shaped lump in the middle. "Our sister's a bitch," Colin said, as though Paul might have some wise counterpoint. Colin had always wanted a different brother, a wise older brother who'd been there, who'd seen it all. "I don't know if you knew that, but she's a total bitch. Like Bitch of the Year or something."

Paul wasn't someone you could talk to, but at least he was alive. Colin waved a hand in front of his face. He didn't even blink. His eyes only changed in the sun, as if someone had poured cream into their usual coffee color. "Don't look at the sun," he said as he stepped in front of his brother and blocked the light. "It's bad for you." When Paul inched over to see the street, Colin grinned. "It's bad for you, stupid," he said. "You're such a fucking retard." The word flashed in his head, *retard*. It was the only word for someone like Paul. There was nothing a retard could do, nobody he could tell. Before he could change his mind Colin lunged at his brother and put his hand over his eyes. "Got you now!" he said, wrapping his free arm around Paul's chest. The way Paul screamed— like a caged chimp at the zoo—was the funniest thing Colin had ever heard. "This is the death grip!" He was weakening as he laughed and he knew he couldn't hold on. Paul was wearing a pair of sweatpants and Colin peered down at them over his shoulder. "Got your balls!" he said, but before he could latch onto anything Paul broke free and elbowed him in the stomach. Colin was still trying to breathe when something slammed into his mouth, his eye, his cheekbone, his ear, and by then both boys were screaming.

"Fuck!" He pushed Paul away and stood up from the bed. "You fucking cocksucker!" It wasn't until he looked at his hand and saw the little oval of blood that his eyes began to burn. He left for the bathroom before Paul could see him cry.

In the mirror, Colin could see why everyone hated him. His lip was halfway swollen and a line of blood reached across his chin and down into his shirt collar. A red half-moon bordered his left eye, and both were bloodshot. After he took off his shirt and wiped away the blood, everything made sense. You couldn't help but hate a frail little faggot like that, a waste of the Y chromosome. "You're such a pussy," he told his reflection. He dried his eyes with his shirt and sat on the edge of the tub, his face hidden in his hands. "Total dickless piece of shit," he choked, but nobody heard him as he sat with his arms locked around his chest. Nobody caught the names he called himself. Nobody saw him put his hands together and nobody knew what god he prayed to, what promises he made. Nobody saw him unfold his hands and look at his wrists where the blood flowed fragile and breathless and blue. Nobody saw him look at his mother's razor hanging in the shower. Nobody knew what he was thinking.

If there is such a thing as too much goodness, his father had written, *it is the phrase I'd use to describe my youngest child.* That was it, all by itself on its own page. When, Colin wanted to know, had his father figured it out? When had he realized that Colin's goodness was only a ruse, that his youngest child—his baby boy—was the monster who'd finish them all?

When he returned to the bedroom, it was like he'd stepped back in time. "Sorry," he said to Paul as he tossed his bloody shirt into the hamper. He sat next to him on the bed. He'd never before wanted so badly to pat someone's thigh, like everything would be okay. That's what that meant, wasn't it? You just put your hand on someone's thigh and patted it twice: *Yeah, it's hard, but it's okay. I killed our father but it's not a big deal. Our mother's going crazy but it doesn't matter. I'm going to hell but it could be worse.* But he knew how Paul would react. Instead he looked out the window and tried to feel his brother's excitement, reaching into his own pocket and rolling the lighter's wheel in his finger as they waited together for the same car.

After winter break was over, Colin tried to prepare himself for the moment he'd hear Victor's voice or get hit with his smile, the second he'd break upon his disarming *Oh, Colin* like dandelion fluff on fresh blades of grass. He'd been wrong, hadn't he, to be so afraid?

When his mother came home that night he lit her cigarette as planned, but—before he could decide whether or not to tell her about Victor—she gasped. "You look like you just fought your way out of jail." She tilted his face toward hers. "Who did this? Tell me in the car. The last thing we need is a broken nose."

In the emergency room they stung him with cotton swabs and touched his face with cold, powdery gloves. They asked him to look here, then there. His shirt came off as they checked his breathing and his heartbeat. When they left he put it back on. When they returned they helped peel it off, even though he didn't need help. They checked his ribs for cracks, his back for bruises. "I think I'm fine," he said, but the two nurses ignored him as they commiserated over their sons' canceled hockey game. His mother sat in the corner, biting her lip as she tapped her fingers together. "I was sitting with Paul on the bed," he'd muttered on the ride over. "I might've bumped his leg or something, or maybe I wasn't—maybe I didn't think about it. I might've been stupid and patted his leg or whatever. Like, he was sad." Everyone else in his life was a good person. That he lied to them, that he hid who he really was, made him feel toxic. "I fucked up," he said, halfway to a choke.

"Don't say fuck," she warned. A few houses later she softened, putting her hand on his neck. But he had fucked up. *Want to know what I really fucked up?* he could ask, and explain what happened in the basement that Sunday night two Octobers ago. Thinking of it that way, those fourteen months opened up behind him like in movies when the ground splits in two. This is how you don't go back, he thought, and wanted to scream and smash everything in the car. He wanted to grab the wheel and swerve into a tree. Again that old compulsory feeling, as though his mouth might tell her the truth without his permission. Instead, as they neared the hospital, he began to cry. "We'll help your brother adjust," she said as she rubbed his neck. "You know he hurts, too."

While the nurses asked him to walk back and forth across the room, a policeman poked his head through the curtain and beckoned for his mother to follow. Colin's balance suffered, watching them through the curtain. The policeman's shadow was pointing at him, gesturing toward the curtain with his thumb. His mother was nodding or shaking her head. She bit a hangnail from her finger. The policeman put his hand on her shoulder. What had they learned about him? What had they found out? "Stop walking," the nurse holding his hand said, and she turned to the other. "This boy's fine." On the ride home his mother said nothing, and he knew that asking would make his punishment come quicker—his transfer to the cops when she surrendered him. Over the break, she spent several evenings in a row on the phone, locked in her bedroom. But that was all. Their Christmas, their New Year's—it was all as normal as they could make it, the disabled family that they were.

When school resumed, Colin went back to worrying about Victor. He tried to believe he'd misheard everything. But when he walked into his last class there was no Victor to confront—only a young woman shuffling papers at his desk. When class was over he found Paul waiting on the same steps, hunched over the concrete looking at the ice with the same stare. There was no black Toyota waiting. They caught their bus just as it pulled away from the curb. They sat in the front with the seventh graders and the kids who never spoke. Different houses and different street signs went by, no sight of that hidden park and no threat of his hidden life. He'd never been more bored. It hadn't even occurred to him, that he wouldn't ride home with Victor.

The next day he tried again. Again Victor was out. They day after that it seemed normal, this woman lecturing the class on mitosis and meiosis. When Colin began to think that Victor had been fired, that someone had found out what Colin had made him do, he couldn't look at the parking lot without wanting to cry. Then he saw him, the following week, nonchalant as he erased names and diagrams from the board. "Sorry to have missed you," Victor said when class was over, when Colin didn't move from his seat. "I've been sick."

They walked out together. The heaviness Colin had carried for three weeks was vanishing. Victor, too, seemed happier. After that, he didn't ask Colin about girls or what he thought about at night. Even when Colin and Chelsea briefly tried to be a couple, Victor didn't press for information. It was Colin who brought it up. "We've been going out for a couple days now," he said as they passed by that road—his favorite road.

Victor tightened his grip on the wheel, mouthing lyrics to a song that wasn't playing. "Good for you," he said. As they approached a stoplight he rapped his knuckles on the window. When they stopped, the car sat there trembling. The windshield looked chewed around the edges, frost scalloping forward from the trim.

"We haven't kissed yet. But I think we will this weekend." It was awful, how Victor wouldn't look at him. Colin wet his lips. "How old—" His voice cracked. "How old were you when you had your first girlfriend?"

The light turned green and Victor let the car roll into the intersection. "To tell the truth I don't remember."

Colin leaned back in his seat. The familiar houses skipped by faster than he hoped. When they pulled into the driveway Colin stalled, rifling his pockets for his keys even though you could hear them jingling with every sweep of his hand. "I can't find them," he said with a fake laugh, ashamed at how bad he was at lying. He and Chelsea broke up the next day—their friendship meant too much to her, she said over the phone, in tears while Colin watched TV.

Those afternoons went back to what they'd always been. Victor talked about the body and Colin listened, wishing he'd talk about *his* body. The neighborhood did what it could to hibernate. On the last day of the semester Colin was shaking, aware that if the errant hand or the dark question didn't come now it never would. Paul had stayed home sick and they were all alone, student and teacher. What he wanted was to tell Victor everything, to open up like a fish slit along the belly and pour every last secret at this man's feet. *I've sucked a cock before*, he wanted to tell him, and he wanted it to sound like he was the best cocksucker in Roseville. Instead he kept quiet while Victor went on about the heart, how it beats and beats for seventy, eighty, a hundred years without stopping. "Think of it," he said, opening and closing his fist. "Think about doing this for a hundred years, never tiring." When they pulled into the driveway Victor smiled. "Good luck next year," was all he said, and that was the end.

After that, Colin would go back to riding the bus, sitting with

Paul among all the other losers, listening to him groan and panic at the noise around him. He'd have to protect him from the thrown-around trash, the obnoxious kids who liked to flick each other's ears and thump each other on the skull. He knew he'd think of Victor while he sat there, how he came so close to knowing something so important—some crucial fact, he decided, necessary for survival.

Andy had been wrong. Victor wasn't dangerous. Here was a man who could tell you everything, if you knew how to ask. He could show you everything.

Colin hadn't figured out how to ask, and when he walked into the house he found he would be alone on those bus rides. "I didn't know how to tell you so I thought I'd tell you after," his mother said. There were boxes stacked along the foyer walls. Heather was leaning up against the kitchen door frame, her lip trying not to tremble. "Colin," his mother said, in that way that was supposed to soothe him, and he knew Paul no longer lived there.

Why all this? What it isn't: comprehensive, complete. Given that up. Image of life as one of my uncle's fishing trips. What he'd catch and what he wouldn't. "The one that got away"—he used this for everything. The car on sale that got away. The deal on cruise tickets that got away. His first wife, before I was born, who got away. As though there was nothing he could do. All the things he missed were the things he remembered. "We almost moved to New York when I was a baby"—as though New York was gone forever. As though it was beyond him.

As though he was helpless. Colin loved it when he found something in the notebooks that resembled the man he'd known. This uncle—Colin's great-uncle, he calculated—he had never met. He could be the great-uncle who got away, but he realized his father didn't want him to think of life like that. But how could you not? If his father hadn't died, for example, would God hate him like this? Would his best friend have seen through him, used him, and cast him out of his life? Would his mother have sent Paul to the *special home* for boys like him?

Would Paul—still at home and not at all angry—have kept Heather from leaving?

Even though she did nothing but call her brother things like *creep* and *fag* and her *bitch*, Heather's presence was a sad comfort. With Paul no longer home, Colin realized just how rarely Heather spent the night, anymore, and how some days she only stopped by to grab a clean sweater or a hat she'd left behind. Her bedroom was how she'd left it, but every time Colin went in to spy on her, something else was missing—a lamp or a pillow, a hairbrush, her stereo. It felt like she was vanishing, bit by bit, until one day she'd cease to exist altogether.

Their mother didn't seem to mind. "It's so quiet around here without your sister," she said while Colin made dinner. She was sitting at the kitchen table, watching as he sliced carrots. When Paul left, only two weeks earlier, it was a complaint. "It's quieter," she'd said as she blinked herself into feeling okay. Now it sounded chipper, as if they'd killed an animal that lived in the walls. "I never thought I'd have peace and quiet again."

Colin peered at her from beneath his brow. "You could be nicer to her. She might actually like being here, if you were."

The oven creaked like something inside it was trying to get out. Colin glanced at the temperature. When he turned back to his mother she was pushing herself away from the table. "You have no idea what it's like," she said. From then on they didn't talk about Heather. Paul they talked about but only as though he was on some kind of quest, backpacking all over Europe or going to school in Asia, not sitting in some locked room in a huge old house in Michigan's Upper Peninsula, waiting for his mother's car to wind its way down the endless driveway, through the frozen trees.

On his first afternoon alone, Colin switched every television in the house to a different channel. It sounded like one of the holiday parties his parents used to throw. That was all he wanted—voices. A man's baritone was most comforting, vibrating its way down his spine. The stretch of afternoon between school and dinner had never been so long. He began to read faster, half a notebook every day; and always, before bed, sneaking the one special notebook from its hiding place and reading, over and over, his father's account of hell itself. Without the arguing voices on TV, all he heard was each floorboard's creak as it called his name. All he saw were hands pushing their way through the cracks. *You're too old for nightmares*, he tried to tell himself. At least when he wasn't *too young to be reading this*—stories on the Internet that could waste an afternoon. What boys were for, he was learning from these stories: kidnapping, controlling, shaming, binding, tormenting, enslaving, and, in the end, rewarding.

At first he didn't answer the phone. Then he noticed how the same number—one particular number—called at the same time every day, ten or twenty minutes after he walked into a quiet house. Then he imagined that Heather had lost her cell phone and that she was calling, desperately, from her boyfriend's apartment. Something in her life had gone wrong and she needed Colin's help. The next afternoon, when he got home from school, he dropped his backpack in the kitchen doorway and waited. *She's crazy*, he'd say about his mother, but not in the way Heather wanted. *That's just who she is and she loves us and you should please come home.* And if that didn't work: *Let me live with you.* When it rang he jumped away from the desk. Would she be nice to him, like when they were young? "Hello?"

"Colin. It's good to hear your voice."

Even without seventh period Life Science, Colin still ran into Victor, passing from one class to another or walking by the lunchroom before the morning bell. Victor would smile and Colin tried to look happy and confident like everyone else. It wasn't as if he never thought about him, how his voice had felt in the confines of that Toyota. His legs began to tremble, standing there in the kitchen. His lips moved against each other but not in any motion you'd call a word.

Victor went on, energetic as ever. "I hope your last semester has been treating you well. It's a tough time for a lot of kids, middle school. Especially one like you. With your situation I mean. How have you been? The last couple weeks?"

"I'm—I'm okay."

"I'm glad to hear it." Colin heard a loud clack through the phone. Victor cleared his throat. "I've been thinking about you a lot, Colin."

"Yeah." He held the cord in his hand and wrapped its ringlets around his finger. His mother had always loved the look of an old phone. "I should go."

"You're growing up to be a good-looking boy. You're a lot taller."

Colin looked down the hallway. He wanted Heather to step out of her room, as though she'd been hiding all along. He wanted Paul to be there, dragging his hand along the wall. He wanted to hear the thump of Paul's fingers against the spot their father had always meant to spackle.

"Are you staying out of trouble? Adolescence is a difficult time. These in-between years. Sometimes you just can't trust yourself." Another clack echoed through the earpiece. Colin held the phone away and put it back to his ear, afraid he might miss something. "What I want you to know is that I'm here, Colin. If you ever have questions, concerns. I've been there."

"My mom is calling. Bye, Mr. Miller." He hung up without trying to intercept and decode whatever Victor might have said. He held his hand over the phone, waiting for it to ring again, unsure of his plan if it did. It didn't—not until the following day, at its usual time.

Image of life as a motor or machine missing one bolt, rattling itself further out of alignment until it hurtles itself in all directions, its weight diminishing, its pieces scattered. Image of life as the pieces themselves, nothing but leftovers. What was this? his father had written, as though he'd pointed at something right then, on the ground. And this?

Image of life, Colin thought as he closed the notebook. *A glass of ice water you can't drink. A knuckle that won't crack.* Anything could set him off: a commercial for boys' clothing, lifestyle magazines in the bathroom rack. And now Victor, who could teach him everything. He saw his future, little more than a pet Victor kept under his desk. "This is your life now," Victor would tell him, pointing at the handcuffs that kept him from getting away. He imagined Andy, curious about some assignment or upcoming test, peering behind the desk to find his former friend, servile and silent. Andy's old grin. The flash in his eyes that showed his talent for knowing what to take advantage of. Colin couldn't stand this, alone every day. From then on, as the phone rang upstairs, he did his time in the basement.

With the sound of the furnace, he could pretend the office was a control room deep inside a starship. The slight tremble in the floor, the door rattling in its place—he could be a captain on his way to the next system. Maybe his father was the captain, and all those notebooks made up the ship's log. Hell was a planet circling the galaxy's oldest star, one that wouldn't shrink or supernova, one that'd never die. They kept going back because there was so much to learn. It was a dangerous place, even if some of its demons were kind, as the captain had said. That's why he kept a gun. Even in hell, you sometimes had to fight your way out.

He felt stupid to think like a kid, to tell himself an ugly room in an ugly basement was part of a spaceship. But it felt worse to think it was only a house where three people of the original five had left. We've lost 60 percent, he calculated. It sounded like something he could add to the notebooks, if he ever had the balls or the malice to change them. We've lost 60 percent of the crew, he corrected, and it felt adventurous, it felt right. Nobody was watching. He could step outside the office and hold the gun as if he were exploring the ship, as if it'd been taken over when they docked. That's where Heather was, maybe, and Paul—taken prisoner by hell's marauders. The captain himself had been taken. There was still time to save him. Even without his lieutenant to watch his back—*Who betrayed me*, Colin suddenly decided, *who defected to the other side*—he could still put up a good fight. For a second he lost the fantasy, distilled to the image of Andy holding a gun to his forehead. *Image of life*, he called the eternity of seconds it took to unzip those jeans. He looked at the floor, where his father had lain, all blood and limbs. Not a captain. Not a hero. Just a man too weak to live. Image of life. That is life, he told himself. Whatever game he thought up, he knew now he'd never play it. He opened the drawer anyway, and there it was again: image of life, an empty drawer where bullets had once been, where a gun was supposed to be locked away.

That evening, his mother walked into the house like a movie star. Colin could tell she wanted him to ask why, but he didn't. "It's just one of those days," she said anyway, setting her purse on the counter with a deliberate, heavy plop. He was unloading the dishwasher. She put her fingers in his hair, letting her nails run apart from each other as they slid down his scalp. His shoulders contracted. He stood there on pause as his skin came alive. "I thought we'd order a pizza," she said. "I called on the way home. I hope you didn't start dinner."

"Mmm," he said, in their way that meant *no*. He pushed back into her hand.

"I was thinking"—she let go and crossed the room—"I was thinking you could call your girlfriend, if you wanted."

Colin went back to the dishes. He sighed as he smacked the plastic cutting boards together. "She's not my girlfriend anymore. I told you, she's just a friend." He hated this conversation, especially when he realized someone like Chelsea was convenient. Fags don't have girlfriends, was the middle school reasoning. He leaned over and began gathering up the silverware.

His mother sat down in front of the ashtray, its cigarette butts bent up and crushed like overcooked macaroni. Most wore the ruled, pink smudges of lipstick. Were a person's lips like her fingerprints? he wondered, every set unique? "Get real, Colin," she said. "You two are on the phone day and night. She's over here every couple days, or you're over there. It's love."

"Nobody says 'get real' anymore."

She frowned and pulled a cigarette from her pack. Right away he searched his pockets for the lighter, and she smiled as he neared the table. This wasn't forever, he knew. You couldn't sustain it or preserve it. You couldn't enclose this whole kitchen in glass, seal all the seams, and flash-freeze them both. He wanted to cry. The dishwasher was empty but he still gave it his attention, as if there were something he'd missed. "Did you have a good day at school?" she said.

"Yeah. I guess."

"You learn anything new?"

He shrugged and began rinsing the leftover dishes. "I guess. Isn't that what it's for?"

Why hadn't he understood, until now, that when she waltzed around the house, reached for things like a ballet dancer, sang half of what she said, and closed her eyes with each deep breath, his mother was at her most depressed? He glanced over at her purse as though he could see right through the purple sequined fabric. She'd never stash it elsewhere in the house. He knew, because he knew her, that the gun was with her everywhere she went.

How was he supposed to lose everyone he loved?

"Colin, I feel like we haven't talked for a while," she said. "I mean *talked*. Like . . ." The phone rang before she could find the word. He didn't want to answer it. He didn't want to hear him. But it was worse, wasn't it, to think of her talking to him, to hear his breath on the other end like some midnight's obscene call?

"I'll bet that's her now," his mother said. She scooped up the ashtray. "I'll give you lovebirds some privacy. It's not too late to invite her for pizza." She winked and left the room.

He held his hand on the receiver. The same number. Couldn't he let it ring? Would Victor only call back? He picked it up and listened, hoping he'd detect something—noises from some machine, maybe, that Victor was building in his basement, or the faint cries of someone he'd locked away. Some sign this was the biggest mistake of his life.

Only silence. "Hello?"

"Colin. I've been trying to reach you all week."

"I've, uh. I've been downstairs a lot. It's hard to hear the phone down there." He heard a creak—Victor leaning back in a chair, he guessed—and pictured him at a computer, all of Colin's information, his life, his past, everything onscreen as though he was a criminal.

"Are you sure you're not avoiding me?"

"No. I just—it's hard to hear the phone." The receiver felt hot and he passed it to his other hand, where it felt cool. He touched the hot hand to his face and wondered if he was getting sick, if he could stay home tomorrow. "I'm sorry," he told Victor. It seemed like the only thing to say.

"I want you to trust me, Colin. I really do."

"I don't. I mean I do trust you," he said. "I'll try?"

"Will you take the phone downstairs with you, when you go?"

There's no cordless, he could have said. There's no reception. The furnace is too loud. Instead he nodded, as though Victor could see him. "Sure?"

"I'm glad," Victor said. "You know, I was thinking of you—"

The doorbell, mounted right above the kitchen desk, rang out like a siren. Everything hit right then—how weak his legs had become, how his hands were coated in sweat. "Pizza," he said into the phone. "I have to go, Mr. Miller." He hung up before Victor could protest. The pizza man looked afraid of him, like he might get sick just from talking to him. Colin tried to smile but his mouth felt wrong.

She was already on the couch, clicking through the channels. She'd changed into pajamas and tied her hair into a ponytail. With her feet folded beneath her she looked ready for a slumber party. "Why, thank you," she said as he laid the pizza on the coffee table. It was the same voice she used when he lit her cigarettes. He grabbed a slice and sat across the room. She found an old, unfunny comedy and they ate until the pizza was gone.

It wasn't long before the sunlight retreated from the room and across the backyard. As it sank into the tree line the whole thing looked like a fresh scratch, pink with blood. His mother, alone on the couch, looked wreathed in slashed-up, watery rainbows. She smiled and patted the cushion next to her. "Sit with me."

"Why?"

"Just get your ass over here and sit with me."

With a sigh he crossed the room. He recoiled as she put her arm around him, but when she began massaging his neck it was hard to fight it.

"Relax. You're very tense."

"Whatever. I'm totally relaxed." He tried not to close his eyes and sink into that smell of cigarettes and faint perfume. But she was still his mother. When the credits rolled and the late news started, Colin's head was on her shoulder. His skin was tingling as though he was wearing some electric shield, as though nothing could hurt him. His eyes snapped open when the phone began to ring but she pulled him tight and rubbed his shoulder.

"Whoever it is, it's not important."

It went on ringing. It wasn't important, was it? He could hear her heart. His own slowed to match it. The television went quiet. There was a wisp of breath in his ear, the words all soft and squished together. What she said, he couldn't hear. The words themselves, though—he could tell they weren't what mattered.

She could protect him.

She couldn't protect him.

It was something Diane had learned over time—not her fault or his but just what happened to mothers and their children. Some nights, she felt everyone was right to hate her. *Here's your model of stability*, she thought, squinting to read one of Alan's notebooks in a shard of moonlight, the only one awake. *Here's a year of therapy bills.*

To have been a bee or an ant, a drone whose only inner voice is that of its colony—*Seek, Return, Attack, Defend, Gather, Harvest, Die. At least that you can trust*, Alan had written.

But it *hadn't* been a year, she realized one morning. She'd first seen Tim last May, after seven months of trying to mourn alone. She couldn't go back to that. Since leaving his office in December, she'd thought about her mistake every day. Washing the dishes or creeping along in rush hour traffic, the image of Tim resting his head against his palm came to her, his look of surprise like he'd encountered a new subspecies of humanity. "You don't have to divulge specifics," she repeated in her best Tim voice as she drove to work. All through January, she promised herself she could undo it. She could get him used to her again, old harmless Diane. On the morning of her appointment she glanced at herself in the bathroom mirror and felt, for the first time in weeks, no longer repulsive.

Just before lunch, she got the call from Kathy. "Tim can't see you today. His son is sick."

Diane dropped the phone in her lap and picked it up again. "Sorry. Hello?"

"Tim can't see you. He's taking care of his son."

A forklift in the warehouse beeped as it backed up. Whenever she heard it she thought of movies Colin watched, as if she were on a space station and something was failing.

"The earliest we have is the last week of February."

She sank into her chair. In her head, February was an entirely different color from January, stuck that way from all the calendars she'd hung in her office over the years. February was grass coming through the snow, streams and lakes thawing at the edges—photos taken in places far from Minnesota, where grass and flowing water were weeks into the future. February felt like a separate part of the year. She was chewing her lip when she heard the shout from the production floor below, the crash. The forklift wasn't beeping anymore. She stood up and looked out the window and saw a pallet overturned, a slow dark circle creeping out from under it. "Fuck," she said into the phone.

"Do you want to schedule an appointment?"

She reached for a list of emergency phone numbers. "Yes. Yes, put me down."

Kathy sighed whenever she put an appointment into the computer, a sweep of breath against the clatter of her nails on the keyboard. "You're all set. See you in a month."

Diane hung up and went to the window. There were six of her people standing around the spill and shouting at one another. They'd want somebody fired over this, and she was already grouping them into those she'd try to save and those she'd let slip by.

Two weeks later she slept with Daniel. The accounting department invited her to a happy hour on a Thursday, too cold to do much else, and as she wrapped her coat over her shoulders she made a list of excuses. *I had a flat tire*, she could tell her son. *I had to work late.* Two hours later, she realized she'd have to think of a better lie. In the bar they had to squint to read the menu, and when Daniel touched her arm as he asked her to split a two-for-one, she felt somewhere inside her that murmur, that voice bubbling up like tar and just as ancient.

As they made their way through his underfurnished apartment she felt as if the entire floor could hear her heart. Her favorite part, when she thought about it later, was the moment he removed his shirt. The way men, in their youth, looked broken into shapes—it was an odd thing to love but she loved it. Daniel was put together with ovals and rounded rectangles, the arcs around each bicep like sleeping parentheses. She began to squirm on the bed as he fumbled with his belt, and if that's all they'd done—if he had stood there unbuckling his belt for another five minutes—everything would have worked out.

"You sure can go a long time," she said, half an hour later, hoping it would be one of those things men can't hear without ejaculating. Instead it sounded like criticism.

He paused to look at her, propped up on his elbows. "Is everything okay?"

"Everything's fine." She traced a curve across his shoulder and down his chest. Up close, it was only skin. "This is fantastic."

He bent down to kiss her and she pushed his head into her neck. She forced a moan and he continued, slow at first but gathering momentum. Her eyes roamed the ceiling and she tried not to laugh or cringe as he kissed the spot under her ear. Each movement was so deliberate his entire body was shaking. There was a brown spot near the wall. Water damage, she thought, almost missing his soft convulsion, his absence of breath.

He sat on the edge of the bed, facing the window. "Well," he said.

"Yeah."

He scratched his lower back and turned to look at her. "Maybe next time will be better?"

She nodded and got out of bed, gathering her clothes from the floor. "This should definitely make things interesting," she said. Her fingers felt frozen as she fastened her bra. When she checked the mirror, straightening her hair, his reflection stepped behind hers. It annoyed her that he was still naked, but she smiled at him anyway.

"What?"

"Nothing. I just wasn't expecting this."

He came over and touched her shoulder, and when she turned

around she moved away from him, as though it was natural. "I'll see you tomorrow," she said, and she kissed him on the cheek.

She didn't see him the next day. They both called in sick.

For a while it distracted her: sex as a novelty, or a vacation. The human male like wearing skirts again in the spring, how you forget they exist and how much you love them after you remember. Later, she came to realize it wasn't even what she wanted. It was the wrong thing to want, and this made it easier to look Daniel in the eye, as if they'd only bumped into each other in the laxative aisle at Target. She'd been through ten months of therapy and she was well trained. *What is it that you really want, then?* she heard Tim say in her head. What did she think a man would do to her? What was Daniel, whose skill lay solely in his confidence—without which women were free to burst out laughing at his touch, to smirk at his eyes full of heat—what was he supposed to have done for her? He could fill himself with blood and fuck all night, but it was a stupid trick, just like men who can talk forever and—without once revisiting a subject—say only one thing: *Don't move. Don't escape.* What, instead, had she hoped for?

As February went on she began to worry. Last year, she spent Valentine's Day crying, unable to leave the couch. That was foreign now. Even as she stood smoking on the dock at work, her cigarettes felt like the present—not cheap tokens of the past. She told herself it was healing. She faced away from the wind and let the ash ride away, off toward the swamp and the freeway just past it. The pond out there was a white sheet of ice, and in the morning's light there were two suns, stacked one on top of the other, if suns you could call them. More like white stains on a grey T-shirt, lost in the clouds. She thought healing would feel better, or at least different.

She thought she'd be happier.

During their Valentine's dinner, she at least pretended to be. "I'm so lucky," she told Colin after the waitress had left. "So privileged to be out with the most handsome man I know."

He leaned close and cupped his hand around his ear. "What?"

"I said I'm privileged. You taking me out. Here." She waved her hand across the room. Shannon had sworn up and down about the Blue Pig, one of those restaurants loved briefly and defended violently like a bad boyfriend. Diane knew it would be closed in a few months.

"This is gonna be a good year," she said, and waited for Colin to lean closer so he could hear. "January doesn't count. Nothing until now counts." She raised her water glass. He rolled his eyes and raised his own, already empty. They clunked together and she understood they were cheap. Not plastic but that thick, clumsy glass you can find in the clearance aisle at the end of summer.

"To a superawesome year." Colin twirled his glass and slouched down in the booth. He glanced out the window, half reflection and half the sidewalk's dirt-encrusted bluffs of snow.

How were you supposed to raise a child? How could you turn them into young people you were proud to introduce to family or friends you hadn't seen in years? How could you prevent this? she thought, looking at her youngest, her last, whose look of contempt, when her eyes met with his reflection's, ruined everything. The waitress shuffled by their table and she stopped her to order a margarita. She was still waiting for it when the food arrived.

"Grandpa and me made something like this," he said as he picked apart his food. It was a giant hunk of meat with the bone showing on each end, almost black from hours of simmering. When he touched it with his fork the meat flaked off in slivers and she said it looked delicious. "Ours was better," he said with his mouth full.

She couldn't stay mad at him. "You're turning into quite the little cook."

"Stop saying that. You always say that."

"You're becoming quite the upstanding young chef." She tasted her own dinner. "Delicious."

"Restaurants are so boring," Colin said. He still ate like a teenage boy, barely letting himself breathe between bites. His dinner was already half gone.

"Shall I order the entertainment?" Diane asked. She waved her hand out over the restaurant as though, just behind the bar, at the far end of the room, was a troupe of performing chimps. "Or the girls? You want me to bring out the girls, Colin? Just like in the old days. Girls who dance around during dinner?"

"Shut up. What old days? You're being gross." He wrinkled up his nose and scarfed down the rest of his food. The way he looked at his plate, at the last pools of sauce, made her think he might grab it with both hands and start licking it. *No*, she'd have to explain, *this is inappropriate, this is not what human beings do.* But as he dabbed the corners of his mouth with his napkin she knew her father had already enjoyed the privilege of that speech, and likely many others. It was *his* movement Colin echoed, *his* way of clasping it in his hands, of delicately wiping his mouth.

How had she not spoken to her own father in six years? It seemed so impossible, something that shouldn't have happened. But I'm angry, she thought. *Be angry.* Instead she wanted to cry.

"What's for dessert?" she asked. She smiled and was suddenly aware of tears in the corners of her eyes. She blinked as though something was stuck in her eyelashes. "We could also get something to go," she said as she looked at the ceiling, her head tilted back. "Ugh, whatever this is, it stings."

"I—I don't think so."

"What? You don't want dessert?"

"Maybe we should just go home?" He shrugged and slouched back in his seat again, trying not to hear her. She hated this restaurant.

"Colin, did you bake a cake?" She realized it sounded like she was angry and she smiled. She reached for his hand but he wouldn't move, like a mistreated dog.

"It's too loud in here," he said.

"I didn't know you baked."

"Learning." He looked out the window. It'd begun to snow and more of the street was out there, its snow-caught light brighter than anything in the restaurant.

She didn't care about baking. Even the cake, waiting for them at home—which she knew would be the best cake she'd ever had—

didn't move her, one way or another. All she thought about was Colin peering into the window of an oven, watching batter bubble up into bread like lava cooling to rock, and her father standing just behind him. What he knew, he was sharing. It was the simplest of images like these, lately, that filled her with an immense sadness, but not grief. This wasn't like grief. She couldn't explain it. "How . . ." she said, her throat beginning to numb from the drink. She swallowed and sat up straight. "How is he?"

"Grandpa?" Colin shrugged. "Fine, I guess. We just cook. Or read sometimes."

"Does he ever mention me?"

He frowned and looked down at the table. "Um. Only like, you know, Your mother wouldn't want you doing whatever. Your mother wouldn't approve, blah blah blah." His Quentin voice was eerily accurate, the words cleaved from one another and enunciated like a stage actor's. She smiled, even though she felt terrible. They loved each other, her son and her father, and all she'd done was drive Colin back and forth.

"Anyway, he knows you don't want to talk to him. So he doesn't ask about you. It's taboo."

"Taboo?" She laughed. "Like I'm some controversy? To tell the truth, the whole thing's so stupid. Do you want to know what happened?" She waved her hand before he could nod or shrug or tell her how he didn't care. "It's completely stupid. You know Grandpa Patterson—you know he's . . . you know. Right?"

"Huh?"

She sighed and looked around the room. Nobody was listening. Nobody could if they tried. "He never remarried is what I'm saying."

"So? He lives alone. Am I supposed to care?"

"Colin, you're not getting it. Basically I found out something the hard way. I walked in on him. He cheated on my mother— Grandma Jean. It wasn't what we all thought. But it happened. A stupid grudge. Thirty years." She laughed again as though it wasn't most of her life, as if it were no big deal. "Thirty years I hate him, and for what? Six I don't even speak to him and why? It's nothing he could've done, you know? I think I get that now. Things were different when I was growing up. Anyway. It's all stupid."

"He's gay," Colin said, louder than he'd meant.

How he sat there, his eyes dead still—she knew he was using every last bit of energy to process this. She reached for his hand. He jerked it away. "Colin, look at me. I don't want this to change how you treat him. He's still your grandfather. It's a lifestyle, isn't it? Like I said, when I was your age this was all very different. Society's changing. It's normal now. Just different."

She'd made a mistake. He was too young, she realized—too mired in middle school where *gay* meant social death or torment. Again she tried to reach for him and again he evaded her comfort. Even in the dark of the restaurant she could see he was trembling.

"Different, but not wrong. Not bad." She felt as if she were talking to a toddler and she shook her head. "This wasn't appropriate. For me to tell you. But I'm kind of glad I did. I don't want you to treat him differently now. Will you still love him?"

"Shut up." Colin shook his head. "Just shut up, okay? I don't wanna talk anymore."

"Okay. I just—"

"Shut the fuck up!" He winced at the word and she let him get away with it. She knew it hurt him, too, and she was glad, at least, that he knew better.

The waitress brought the dessert menu but neither read it. None of it looked like words, all scratched into the card stock in a fake script. Instead she was thinking of what she'd overlooked, all these years Colin was alive. If you considered the stereotypes—he loved cooking, he spoke softly, he'd always clung to his mother, he'd never been in a fistfight—it was so tempting. And what had he said, when she mentioned bringing out the girls, as though the restaurant would fill with strippers and belly dancers? *You're being gross.*

"I'm sorry," Colin whispered. She couldn't quite hear it, but with his head drooped forward like that, his shoulders limp like he'd fallen asleep, she knew there was nothing else he would've said. She reached, once more, for his hand. He didn't pull away. She rubbed his palm with her fingers, found the ragged bitten-down edges of his nails. She wished there was room to guess or reinterpret, to be wrong, but she wasn't wrong. It was a sad thing and she grew angry with herself. This is my son, she thought, and he'd never appeared more fragile. Everything she wanted to say she knew she shouldn't. You poor thing, she thought, and brought his hand to her mouth. She kissed the back of it, right where the two bluest veins joined together. What was the word Alan had written? *Fistula*. Fistula, she thought, and kissed again that spot. She hadn't understood but still she carried the word in her head. *Fistula*, like a supernatural villain, or a kitchen utensil. All that life had dealt her, and now this.

As February went on and she neared her appointment, she tried, over and over, to broach the subject with the Tim in her head. *So life's gotten more interesting*, she thought she should say, but it sounded flippant and mean. Would he judge her? Then it was the last Wednesday of the month and she kept looking at the clock. Six hours, she thought. Four hours. Three hours. When the Tim in her head asked her how she'd been, what broke open in her head was Daniel, how she'd thought getting fucked would solve every-thing. There was Colin, her little gay son she couldn't protect. And there were, always, the nights she sat up reading her dead hus-band's ramblings, so convinced of his suffering, his wisdom, that she herself agreed, halfway to tears, how right he'd been to call it quits. To give up. *Two hours.* Just before three o'clock she called Kathy. "I have the flu," she said from the back of her throat. "I can't make it today." She held the receiver away from her head and coughed. "Can we shoot for next month?"

It wasn't a problem. For Kathy it was never a problem. A sigh, a drumroll of typing, an "all set," and Diane would be alone with her brain until late March.

Should their bodies make it home, soldiers are autopsied, washed, and scrubbed clean. From photographs—or in some cases firsthand memory—their living peers wire together broken bones and re-construct flesh, down to the last seared-off birthmark or split-open childhood scar. Their hair is shampooed and conditioned and brushed back into place. The dead are then dressed in full uniform, each ribbon and medal pulled from the Armed Forces Medical Examiner's overstock—something like a tool chest full of regalia instead of nails. Uniforms are pressed and tailored. Even for closed-casket funerals and cremations, the dead are worthy of salutation, as though they themselves are ready to carry a friend's coffin to a quiet, unassuming grave.

Only for soldiers. Hard to imagine anything so meticulous, so full of love, for ordinary men and women.

Have I made my decision? Does any of this matter? Time to give up the pretense?

Colin's father had written.

By March, Victor's phone calls were something Colin expected, like the mail carrier showing up every day around three. He kept the cordless in his back pocket wherever he went, answering re-gardless of what Victor interrupted. Mostly he just listened. *I saw you in the lunchroom today*, Victor liked to begin, or *I thought of you while I was out running errands*. It wasn't all that different from their car rides, except there was nothing to see—no houses, no-body reading mail in the yard, no roads to hidden parks. Often Colin paged through his father's notebooks, Victor's voice en-tangling itself with his father's notes and observations. *The dead are then dressed*, he imagined Victor saying, bent over Colin's still very alive, very undressed body. Once, while Victor described the blood's migration during physical arousal, Colin softly pulled himself to orgasm. "I have to go," he squeaked, his boy's voice re-turning when it was most incriminating, and tossed the phone away from him. "What the fuck," he whispered as he cleaned up his mess. "What the fuck what the fuck." If anyone deserved this, he decided, it was him.

When he wasn't hiding in the basement or lost in Victor's voice he scoured the Internet for traces of his sister. Heather's updates on social media were cryptic and vague. There was nothing about where she lived, or even who she was with. If she came by the house it was during the day, when nobody was home. Even if he'd wanted to surprise her out in public it was impossible. If she posted a picture of food, she never disclosed the restaurant. If she was out shopping it was always just *Out shopping!* with a smiley face. Her hidden life made Colin feel even more criminal, as if she were trying so hard to live and that if he had his way—if he found her and interfered with her life—she'd have to hide all over again and find a new life somewhere else. He commented on everything she posted but she never responded, not even when he stopped asking where her boyfriend lived or when he could visit, instead just typing *Hi* or *That's a neat coat*. He felt as though he wasn't supposed to exist.

On the first day it got above thirty, his mother walked humming into the living room. He clicked out of Facebook and pretended to play a game. "I was thinking," she said as she looked out the window, the backyard damp with sunlight, but she wouldn't finish.

He put the computer to sleep. "I'm going to my room."

"I was thinking it's been too long," she said. "We've hung around too long." When she turned to look at him she wasn't crying, and until then he hadn't realized that's what he expected—that's what he hoped to flee. "What do you say we take a vacation?"

Next to the window she looked like a photograph. It was something she'd always done. All you had to do was study the family pictures hung in the hallway, how in each she looked like someone had directed her. She always found the right light and stood as though she was being watched, her hands (at her sides, by her mouth, fiddling with her hair) like the hands of models in magazines with too much on their mind. Now she was half-lit by the sun as if in a commercial for heart medication, her arms folded across her chest.

"We could go somewhere nice," she was saying.

It hadn't occurred to Colin that they could go anywhere. As a family they never traveled—only once, to Washington, DC, but he didn't remember it. "Can we do that?"

"Why couldn't we?"

"I don't know. Isn't it, like, expensive?"

"It can be." She turned back to the window, her face dissolving into the light. "But it's not a big deal." Her eyes scanned the sky. She kind of grinned, or tried not to, her chin dimpling just beneath her lip. "We have a hundred and fifty thousand dollars set aside."

Colin didn't move. Sometimes his mother had a strange, stupid sense of humor.

"From the insurance settlement," she explained. "Your father." She took a long breath and closed her eyes as though she was smelling a flower. "The sun's starting to feel warm. Through the glass. On your skin, I mean."

"A *hundred* and fifty? Like . . . six digits?"

"Don't tell anyone. People change their mind about you when they know something like that. It changed my *own* mind, just having it. Please don't tell your friends or whoever. Andy doesn't need to know. Your grandfather. Chelsea. Just between you and me, right?"

"Me and Andy haven't been friends in forever."

"Why? What happened?"

"Forget it. So we're rich?"

"Hardly. And we're not gonna splurge. I was thinking San Diego or something. Cape Cod. I haven't been to San Francisco since college."

None of them sounded like places he'd care about. "What about Paris?"

"France? Neither of us have passports."

"We're rich. We could buy them!" Colin pictured stepping off a plane with the Eiffel Tower in the distance, being driven around Paris by chauffeurs who'd call them *Monsieur* and *Madame*. He walked over and poked his mother in the shoulder.

She shook her head. "Nah. I think you'll like San Francisco. I forget who, but someone called it the Paris of the West. It's pretty like Paris, all the buildings in rows. The streetcars, the hills, the palm trees, the flowers. Colin—" She reached out and hugged him without warning. "When's school out for you? June?"

He'd hoped when she said *vacation* it meant tomorrow. June felt like another lifetime, a hundred of Victor's phone calls from now, a thousand hours of his father's stupid notes.

"Can't we go sooner?"

"We can tour Alcatraz, ride the trolleys, all that stuff. Do you know about the crookedest street in the world? That's what they call it. It makes twelve or thirteen turns in a single block."

"Why?"

"It's just beautiful." She stepped back and looked him up and down. "Get dressed," she said, even though he was already what he'd call dressed—torn jeans, torn T-shirt, socks full of holes. "I want to get one of those guide things. The Secrets of San Francisco or whatever it's called, with restaurants and stuff."

"We can just look that up online."

"Just go get your shoes and your jacket. Put some pants on."

"Uh, these are pants."

"I can see your underwear. They're rags, not jeans. I guess we're going to Penney's, too."

On the way to the mall she talked about sourdough bread and how the seagulls swarm for it. She made him try on jeans and T-shirts before they went to the bookstore at the far end of the mall. He spun around for her like a drug-dazed runway model while she tried out what she thought was a British accent. "And the lovely Colin is wearing Levi's, ladies and gentlemen." She laughed until she began to cough her newly hardened smoker's cough.

"God you're embarrassing."

"Isn't he sexy, London? The man of any lady's dreams. Or any man's."

He stared at her. She was smiling, but not like it was funny. "Don't make me puke," he told her, and he slammed the dressing room door and shucked off the new clothes. Had he said something?

Did he sound funny? Did he walk wrong? In the mirror he tried to look mean like all the boys at school. He gave himself a don't-fuck-with-me look and hardened his muscles, which he now noticed, in the dressing room's light, finally looking something like muscles. He touched his belly, newly sectioned into shapes. When had all this happened?

She knocked on the door. "Honey, I'm sorry. That was just a bad joke. Are you okay?"

He tried to be angry with her as they walked toward the bookstore but it wasn't working. Her good moods were too rare. Whenever they walked by someone with stupid clothes or an ugly haircut she leaned in to whisper. "Do you think they stitched those pants onto her?" she asked about a girl who took up most of a bench, and they both snickered and snorted as they hurried on out of earshot. Sometimes he knew she was doing all that she could, that she was trying her best, that, despite the inexhaustible energy of love, one person can only do so much. He'd never felt so grown up—laughing with her at all the dumb, sad people who shuffled up and down the mall's courtyard on a Tuesday night—full of pity for his own mother, who for most of his life had been invulnerable, all-powerful, who had known everything a human being could have known. If they hadn't stopped for mochas and if she hadn't told him to sit up straight and to stop slurping, he might have cried.

At the bookstore she bought three guidebooks and a new road atlas. "We'll drive," she said as she handed it over. "Flying misses the point. You don't *see* anything." By the time they pulled into the driveway it was nine thirty and beginning to snow. A new sheet of clouds had blindfolded the stars. He'd barely taken his bags to his room when the phone rang.

How they'd done this for weeks was to pause. No *Hello*, no *Anyone there?* After they recognized each other's silence, Victor sighed and leaned back in whatever same, squeaky chair he liked to sit in. Colin pictured all the lights around him dark except for a computer screen.

"I had a dream about you the other night."

He sat on the edge of his bed. That he was already hard made him want to cut it off, to take the largest knife from the kitchen and get it over with.

"It wasn't that kind of dream," Victor said, and he laughed. "No. You were running. It was cold. I had to find you." Colin heard a pen tap against a hard surface as if Victor were ready to transcribe whatever Colin said. "There was something I needed to tell you, to show you. I kept finding these little drops of ice in the grass. I knew they were important. I picked them up and tasted them, and then I knew."

Colin gripped the phone. How Victor was breathing, how he was so sure of every word—how could you just hang up? "You knew what?"

"I knew they were yours. Your tears. You were so sad."

The bed creaked as Colin lay back. He glanced behind him at the angel above his lamp.

"Then I found you," Victor was saying. "You were so tired. Your legs had given out. You were huddled under a willow tree." He laughed a small laugh, if even a laugh—just a breath of air with a current of electric, undisguised joy. "You had strips of ice on your cheeks. Tears frozen under your eyes. What had they done to you? That's what I asked as I bent down."

Colin dropped the phone into the crook of his neck and fumbled it back to his ear. He pressed it close so he could hear everything, so Victor *was* everything.

"I reached for your hand," he was saying. "You pulled away. But I didn't give up. I took your hand and touched it to my chest. I don't know if it was the touch of warmth or the feel of someone's pulse, but your tears melted. You could smile again. You were happy."

Colin's blood surged in his fingertips like it wanted out. Who was he supposed to tell?

"Anyway, it was only a dream."

He closed his eyes. The room had begun to throb as if the walls were made of flesh. He wanted to see Victor at school, walking up and down the aisles of desks like this was only a lecture. Andy would be there snickering. Victor was Mr. Miller then, someone you made faces at every time he turned around.

"So how's your girlfriend?" Victor asked—the real Victor, who knew his phone number, who knew everything Colin was hiding. "I've seen you together. To be honest, I'm surprised." Victor wasn't surprised. There was no reason to believe he was that stupid.

"We've been together for, like, two months," Colin lied.

"Very surprising. I really didn't think . . . well, you know. I remember you, Colin."

Victor said his name like a holiday, or a favorite film. It stood out from all the other words, and not just because it was his name. It was like hearing *emergency* from the guy who interrupted songs on the radio. "Mr. Miller—" He swallowed hard and closed his eyes. "Mr. Miller, I don't think you should call anymore."

Why not? he expected to hear. *Colin don't be silly. Colin you know I'm only kidding. Colin sometimes you're so sweet. Colin, Colin. Don't you love me, Colin?*

But Victor knew when silence was the sharpest reply. Colin heard a pen stroke's quick scratch, a soft, bored sigh that might've only been a breath. "I—I mean—"

"Colin," Victor said. That laugh again. "I wish it didn't have to be this way."

He sat up in bed, wincing at the sudden rush of blood. "What way? Be what way?"

"I'll talk to you again soon, Colin."

All his life he'd hated the sound of a disconnected phone call. Now it felt like the earth itself had vanished. If he opened his door right then, there'd be no hallway, no house beyond that, no family at all. If he looked out the window there'd be no streetlights and no darkened houses. The only thing left was his bedroom, and his ears began to ring before the dial tone clicked over and droned on like a siren.

It had been months since he'd dreamt of hell. He thought he'd outgrown them, his dreams, waking up with a startled *No!* in protest of a calloused hand, the shuddering beat of wings. But that night he dreamt of ice, of running until it no longer mattered. He saw the willow and knew he shouldn't stop, knew he shouldn't crawl into its shadow. The demon's heart was not warm. It did not beat. It only hung like black fruit in that open ribcage. Colin felt his tears thaw against his will. They froze again before they hit the ground, thudding into the grass—someone's wet, thrown-away stars scintillating in the sky beneath their feet.

When he woke he tried to wipe the dream's tears out of his eyes, only to feel like part of him was still there, holding that heart. His throat felt glued shut, too dry to swallow, and even though the room felt as though it would grab him if he dared move, he got out of bed. His hand was still numb as he made for the kitchen.

The hallway was empty. The bedroom doors were closed. The kitchen was dark if you didn't count the barcodes of moonlight stamped on the floor. He moved in his old silent way, light on his bare feet, and drank orange juice from the carton so he wouldn't wake his mother in the next room. He wondered if her therapist knew she slept on the couch. He wondered if she told him the truth or if she said the same mindless, stupid stuff she said at home. Colin looked out the window as he drank. It was still snowing, but calmly, no wind at all and every flake moving together like the light from a tipped-over disco ball. The last time it snowed in San Francisco, he remembered reading in the guidebook, was 1976.

Before he went back to his room he went to check on her, like he used to. What he expected to find was her zigzagged way of sleeping, her knees bent and her back kind of arched, one hand under her pillow. Instead his mother was awake, sitting on the edge of the couch with a notebook open in front of her. It lay flat on the table and he squinted through the pale blue dark at the curlicues of his father's handwriting. Colin backed into the hallway where he knew you couldn't see past the shadows. She was holding the gun and was petting its grip with her thumb.

Why did life have to happen this way? What had they done to deserve this? When his mother took a deep breath and put the gun under her chin you'd think he'd be less sensitive to it, you'd think it wouldn't make his lungs seize up as if they'd filled with blood. You'd think that when she pulled the trigger and he heard that impotent click it would be no more of a surprise than her way of crying whenever she spent time in her bedroom. But you had to understand it. You had to see how perfectly she did it, how exact her imitation, as though she'd seen her husband do it not once but many times, a dozen times. Enough to study it. Enough to remember it.

When she began going to therapy, Diane swore it wouldn't be permanent. It was supposed to be a ritual she could quit at any time without feeling a thing, not become something she needed. She'd said the same, years before, about the chiropractor.

All those magazines whose headlines never changed, whose articles she never read—she felt helplessly giddy to be there. Being at ease in Tim's waiting room was like laughing when the person with whom you're furious tickles you under the ribs. She tried to compose herself into someone annoyed, someone anxious, someone horrified to be alive. Instead her skin had that tight feeling, as though she'd caught the scent of lemons or a soft, sun-bleached breeze. She looked into her purse but couldn't deceive herself into stepping outside for a cigarette. It was too lovely to be trapped, to have to enjoy.

Spring has saved me, she decided she would say—her witty opening line, because it wasn't yet spring. Tim would point this out. *Yes, but it's the thought of spring*, she'd say, and she'd explain how it helped to imagine the weather she wanted. The sun was higher every day, something the leafless trees couldn't hide. *Every time it gets above thirty I want to go for a walk.* She pictured herself in his office, legs crossed, hands clasped together as she spoke at the ceiling and said *um* or *uh* like a girl. *Anyway*, she'd say, much later. *The sex thing is all about, um, self-destruction. It's all about ruining whatever's good in my life, I guess, haha. I think I understand it. I think it's over.* She heard the door right then, at the end of the hall. Spring, she thought. Think about spring.

Tim eased into their time, smoothing out a new page, his pen perfectly parallel to the pad's top binding. There was a new calendar behind him—this one full of national parks instead of distant nebulae and constellations. She'd never seen a picture of the Grand

Canyon with a dusting of snow. Was the Grand Canyon on the way to San Francisco? She couldn't believe, in nine or ten weeks, she would pack up the car and cross half the country. Of all things, she thought of what she'd wear. It would be June. It would be hot. Start with fabrics, she thought, and tried to picture everything silk in her closet, everything jersey. When Tim shuffled in his seat she flinched and sat up straight.

"Did I scare you?" He was smiling, hands folded together in his lap.

What you need is something familiar, Shannon had said over coffee, only a week after driving Paul to Michigan. *Something routine. So much has changed for you.*

"Not at all. I don't spook that easy."

"I've noticed. I'm sorry about canceling. Back in January."

"I didn't know you had a son." It came out like a reprimand and she forced herself to smile. Tim looked down at his lap. "What's his name?"

"His name is Kale," Tim said. "Yes, like the vegetable. He's in fourth grade. Just turned ten."

"Ten?"

"I know," he said. "How does an old guy like me have such a young son?"

"That's not what I meant."

"It's okay. I get it a lot." He shrugged his shoulders. It was the longest he'd ever gone without making eye contact. That was his weapon, eye contact. It was why people gave him money. "I had a relationship with a younger woman. We had a son. Now I take care of him."

Diane set a hand on the table, ready to reach out. "Did she . . . is she . . ." She wet her lips and coughed out a little sound—*mmm*—as she assuaged the tickle in her throat. They could have so much in common. "Did she die?"

"What? No. No, she's still alive."

"Oh."

The room's white noise came back as she looked down at her

hands. She could feel the joints in her fingers grinding but she didn't want to sit there like she was nervous. She heard Tim scratch his cheek and it made her think of all the men she'd kissed, how every touch was different. Alan's cheek was always rough, even in the morning when he'd just shaved. Daniel felt like a high school boy. An image of his chest, streetlit via the uncovered windows in his apartment. She crossed her legs and fanned out her fingers, touching the wrinkled circle of skin around each knuckle.

Blouses, blue jeans, open-toed shoes, capris, jackets instead of coats, cotton socks instead of wool. *Spring has brought me back to life*, she thought she should say, but it was a lie. "What school does Kale go to?"

"Edina."

"Do you live by Southdale?"

"Diane, let's talk about you." He turned back to her and smiled without warmth. "How were the last few weeks—well, months? The last few months?"

Another Diane, she could be for him. "I keep thinking about spring," she said, and winced at how wrong it came out, bland and obvious and not at all clever.

"It is that time of the year." Tim glanced at the wall as if there were a window showing them the last days of winter, the sun melting the snakes of snow resting on staircase railings and the broken-up fences lining the parking lot.

"It is." Already, she'd lost interest. But she felt committed. "It's exciting to think of all the stuff I can wear again, all the clothes waiting in my closet?" She shook her head. "I'm sorry," she said with a laugh. "This is boring the shit out of you."

"No, no it's not," he said, in that way that meant *yes but don't worry*. "It's actually nice to hear you say it. To hear you so excited about something. If you want to know the truth—"

"You mean everything until now hasn't been the truth?"

"If you want to know the truth I was worried about you." His eyes fell to his notepad. He tapped the pen against the page but didn't click it open. "After our last session, in December. I felt like we left on a downer. And then we didn't see—I didn't see you for three months."

Diane felt touched. She felt ashamed for everything she'd thought about him, every time she'd labeled him uncaring or obtuse. "Thank you," she said. She pictured Tim at his house in Edina, likely someplace large and far away from whatever quiet street he lived on, worrying. He would tell Kale to get ready for bed, and he'd worry about her, she imagined. She moved forward in her chair, perched on the edge of her seat. "But you shouldn't have worried. The whole sex thing—I was way off with that one. It wasn't what I wanted at all."

"What do you . . ." Tim coughed and flipped back a page, then forward again without reading a word. "What would you say has changed?"

"What would I say hasn't? It's been a crazy winter. I even slept with someone, for fuck's sake. A coworker. His place, after a happy hour. It was so terrible. I mean it was nice at first but when we got down to it I just wasn't into it." She reached for a tissue but she wasn't crying. It felt greasy in her hand, pretreated with lotion. She laid it flat on the table. "I don't think I'll ever be with a man again. It just doesn't make any sense anymore."

Tim said nothing. Wanting him to speak made her feel childish.

"I've thought about it all, though. I've always been kind of self-destructive. I'm thinking that wanting to go out and fool around, you know, get laid, was just me wanting to fuck up my life. Meet the wrong person, get in trouble, get found out, have my kids— have Colin—hate me."

"Why would he hate you?"

"He'd think I abandoned him, wouldn't he?" She thought of Colin, waiting up for her the night she was out with Daniel. For the last few weeks they'd felt like roommates. "He's gay."

"He told you?"

"He'd never tell me. I just know. I haven't told him I know. I don't know that I can. He looks, all the time, like he's about to fall apart. Like one little push and he'll just fall over. He's getting so tall. His voice more and more like his dad's. But I feel like he'll just shatter if I tell him. He'll never talk to me again."

Tim had written nothing down. "I think you're being a little hard on yourself. About your relationships."

"They're not relationships," Diane said. "I don't have relationships."

"Any interaction with another person is a relationship," Tim said. "You've interacted with Daniel"—here he blushed—"therefore it's a relationship."

"But I only went after it to hurt myself, or someone else. It's my youth all over again."

Youth, she thought. A strange word that upset her.

Youth is an island. Where had she heard this?

"What do you mean, your youth?"

She frowned. "When I was young—a teenager, a girl, into my twenties, whatever—I asked God for horrible things to happen to me. I prayed once for cancer. When you started to hear about AIDS, how even straight people were getting it, I prayed for that. I asked God to run me over with a bus, to knock me out of an airplane."

Youth is an island seen through a telescope, stranded at sea without a sail.

Alan, she thought. You couldn't get rid of him.

"I prayed for natural disasters. Tornadoes. Meteors. For a nuclear bomb. I'd step off the school bus one day—I was maybe fourteen when I started fantasizing about this one—and everything would flash white. That would be it for me. I prayed for that. Then I had kids." *And then my husband cuts ahead of me in line.* She picked up the tissue she'd left on the table and began tearing it into little strips, letting the stray fibers and shreds pill on her slacks. "It's been a long time since I prayed for stuff like that. I mean, it *had* been a long time."

She thought of a family she'd read about who had lived in Phoenix. There were three of them living together, all siblings, all over fifty. When the firefighters arrived at their house the upper floors had already caved in, throwing themselves into the flames below. You could hear, reports said, the explosions of ammunition coming from the basement. By then, nothing could be done, and when they picked through the mud and wet ashes they found the remains of assault rifles, handguns, sawed-off shotguns, and a stock of homemade bombs. Neighbors reported no initial explosion, no sudden burst of flames. Two dogs had been tied to the bedpost in one of the upstairs rooms, where the brother and his two sisters, authorities calculated, had waited. So much of what Diane encountered she'd rather not know, but this, over the last several weeks, had been a strange, dangerous comfort. Before she knew what she was doing she'd underlined it in Alan's journal, his old handwriting with a bright blue streak from her own pen.

Tim had been watching her now for almost a minute, as if she'd pray, right there, for something she wasn't even sure she wanted. "I don't know what to say."

"You don't have to say anything."

He gave a light nod, his hand over his mouth. How his throat twitched—she could tell she'd upset him. She felt beyond repair. Beyond redemption. Beyond humanity.

"It's really not how it sounds." Only now had she begun to cry. She reached for a fresh tissue. "I mean I guess I'm a little fucked up, but it's not like—"

"You're not fucked up, Diane." Tim said *fuck* with an angry dart of air. "What I've been telling you, all these months, is that very thing. You're not fucked up. You're not bruised. You're not damaged. You're not crippled or maimed or whatever else you think you might be. You're a beautiful, kind woman who's been left to deal with more than she asked for. It's 'in sickness and in health' but not 'death,' Diane. There's no death. That's not part of it. This wasn't you. It wasn't your doing. Your wish to enjoy life, to go out in the lovely spring weather, to drink hot coffee on a cool porch, your desire to find partners for healthy sexual intimacy—none of this is wrong. What's happened, in your head, that you feel so ashamed to be alive?"

She'd never seen him cry and clearly he'd never wanted her to. She imagined the Diane he described, the hurt Diane, the alone

Diane, the Diane who only wanted to go on living her life, taking care of her family. The Diane who told her husband not to eat barbecue in a white shirt, who made sure the kids did their chores. She saw this Diane, who'd lost everything, like an actress in a film—someone it was painful to love, to root for, but you did anyway. You knew how hard life was for her. Tim comforted this Diane as she cried. He slowly raked a finger through her hair, circling around her ear and down her neck. Tim had seen the real Diane cry a dozen times, and she wished it mattered more, right then, that she'd fallen apart, that she couldn't speak, that her entire body trembled as the session went long. "I'm not letting you leave like this," Tim said when she pointed to the clock. "Everyone else can wait."

For the last year, Alan had filled her head with stories. Real people, she assumed, who'd died, who'd suffered, who'd achieved something great—men who invented machines or women who pulled fellow passengers from plane wreckage. Even in life, he'd never told her a story about herself, and she wondered where all of this had come from. How long had he kept these notebooks? How long had he harbored their facts? He'd always noticed things. He'd always observed the life around him. If it was so simple—if all a person had to do was tell her, *No, Diane, that's not you, this is you*—she would've asked decades ago. It was only a story, of course, a kind of fiction or a lie, but believing it stopped her tears and stilled her shoulders. It brought her to her feet. It thanked Tim via her smile and her weak, sweaty handshake. Outside, in the parking lot that clung to winter, it lit her cigarette and filled her lungs with warmth, and as she glanced down in her purse, pushing the gun aside, it reached in via her own hand and crumpled her old list into a little ball. It threw that ball into a bin with McDonald's wrappers and pop bottles and all the other trash. It said, *Go home.* It said, *Rest.*

In her previous life, she would have come home to find Alan asleep in front of the television or hidden away in a corner with a newspaper. All the stuff she'd fantasized might be fixed—the creaky cupboard door, the crack in the foundation beneath the dining room window—would be as broken as it was when she'd left. If she said anything, it would be a dig at him—*Sorry to disturb you*, or *Your servant has returned*—while she collected ingredients for a quick, flavorless dinner she was ashamed to serve her family. One more night of wondering why she hadn't yet divorced him. As she drove home, this imagined evening felt like a stone suddenly lifted from her chest—the relief of knowing it wasn't waiting for her—and then, with a wash of guilt, put back. *How can you be grateful for something like that?* she thought as she pictured his body, the remains of this man who'd never disappoint her again.

Colin was at the kitchen table and had already eaten, his plate pushed out away from him and the atlas in its place. He had a scrap of notebook paper next to him and was adding up the miles. "You know you can do that online," she said, tapping his calculations with her finger.

"This is more fun."

Diane set her purse on the counter, draped her coat on the chair by the phone. "That's because it's new for you. Can you imagine what it was like when we bought our first computer?"

"I was there."

"You were two years old. You weren't . . . you weren't really *there*."

"I'm pretty sure I remember it." He flipped over to Nebraska and traced a highway that wasn't the interstate.

While she ate, he outlined their route. He read from the scrap of paper next to him—what was special about Deadwood, South Dakota, and who'd eaten breakfast in Rock Springs, Wyoming. She saw how he bulleted his notes—the right-angled arrows and the method of underlining names uncanny, not his own. How were you supposed to be angry with the dead? How do you reprimand someone who's no longer alive? *You see what you've done?* she imagined herself shouting at Alan's headstone. Colin was telling her how in the desert you can see forever. Her mouth was twitching, and if she wasn't stuffing it with food it would've been no secret, how close she was to crying.

"I wonder what else we'll see," she said. "Maybe we'll drive through a ghost town."

"You don't really drive through them. But there's a few here." He pointed to a part of Nevada that looked, on paper, purely white. No green patches. No veins of highways. Not even a little grey pencil mark of a road.

"Wow."

"It's a big place," Colin said, as if she'd never left home. He gathered his notes and the atlas. She noticed the cordless, snuggled up against his chest at the edge of the table.

"You should put that on the charger."

"Whatever, it's charged." He picked up the phone and waved it at her and set it back down.

"It's bad for the battery," she said—something Alan had told her. She pushed a stray vein of onion around in circles with her fork. "The more you use the battery the faster it wears out."

"Um, that's bullshit."

"Colin."

"Sorry." He rolled his eyes and leaned into the atlas, his notes. "Bull*crap*."

For weeks now she'd wondered if, with Colin, she'd made all the wrong decisions. Heather, too, if she felt honest with herself. Even Paul. How much can a growing child take? How much can you place on his shoulders? She wished, right then, that they'd talked about Colin in her session instead of her own problems. She wished Tim had told her she was doing the right thing, or at least revealed there was no right thing to be done. That, too, she'd considered—what if all of this was irreparable? Colin turned the page to California and she looked at San Francisco, a knot of roads and parks and points of interest. What would she tell the world around her, should something happen to him? Colin radiated pain like no one she'd ever met. Perhaps there wasn't anything you could say. Perhaps there was nothing to understand.

"I should've done more," she said, and she smiled as she began to cry.

"Huh?"

"For you. I should've been there when you got home from school every day, you and your brother and sister. I should've stayed home with you when you were too young, not sent you to preschool. I should've—"

"Mom, stop it." He shook his head. "You're crying. Cut it out."

"I just feel so bad."

He'd stopped moving—no more fidgeting, no more eye-rolling. "I feel bad too," he said. "But whatever. It's fine. Stop crying. I'm fine."

She reached across the table and he recoiled, dropping his hands into his lap. "Colin," she said, her voice like a bent piece of metal. "Colin, I—"

"I said stop it!" He reached up with the collar of his shirt and wiped his eyes. "I'm fine, remember? Look at me, I'm fine." He sat up straight and put on a smile, so fake and so silly she couldn't help it—she laughed. "I'm just a normal kid," he said. "Going to school, learning stuff, making friends." He bent his elbows and swung his arms back and forth like he was marching or dancing. He made crazy eyes at her and that was it—she was done. *Thank you*, she wanted to tell him, but she knew it'd drag her back into herself, and instead she called him a creep.

"Son of a creep," he said, and stuck out his tongue.

She took her plate to the sink. There was a pile of pans and she began to wash them.

"I so can't wait to go on our trip," Colin said. "Like, just to get out of here?"

She pushed out a long breath. If you thought about it, their life was too much to believe. "No work. No school. No goddamn *dishes*."

"I've never seen the desert. Or mountains, I guess. Not the ocean, either."

"It's so beautiful. All of it." She felt like she should place her hand on his neck but it was soaked with dishwater and wet food. Instead she bumped him with her hip and he bumped back. "I wonder what all we'll see. Buffalo, I'll bet. Maybe some—"

"There actually aren't buffalo in America. We have bison. Buffalo live in Africa."

"Bison then, smartass. I bet we see some."

"There's a lot in South Dakota and Wyoming. We'll see some for sure. Antelope, too, and vultures, elk, mule deer, maybe a bighorn sheep."

"I'll bet we see some wild horses." The image of a herd came to her, galloping over an open plain, an earthquake of hooves like you hear in movies. "There's a resurgence of them," she explained. "With the recession their owners can't really take care of them, so they set them free. They're supposed to be all over the west, tens of thousands of them. I read about it in . . ." She swallowed and looked at herself in the window. It was still light out but the air had gathered enough evening to reflect her own hesitation, to show Colin next to her, his eyes fixed on the clanking bundle of silverware in his hands. "In the paper," she said.

On their own, these horses quickly fall in with the wild herds already scavenging the plains for water—some ninety thousand horses. Colin dropped the silverware into the little wire basket next to the sink. There were still plates clunking together in the dirty water, and then all the glasses and coffee cups to wash. *Without predators,* his father had written, *the wild population doubles every four to five years, depending on rain.*

"They're probably all dead," Colin said. He balled the dishtowel up in his hands and dropped it on the counter. "I'm done for now. I'm supposed to meet Chelsea. I'm gonna walk over there." As he left the room he stretched out the word *bye* as if he were speaking to a four-year-old. He was supposed to be a snotty, ungrateful teenager—an easy part to play if they didn't have to confront the truth. *Oh, you've read them too!* he imagined himself saying, as though it was a best-selling series. It was easier to pretend the notebooks had been written for him and no one else. As he slipped on his hat and his gloves he felt violated. Why couldn't the horses have belonged to him? "Leaving now," he called into the kitchen, and winced at his own strength as he slammed the door. He pushed his hands deep into his pockets and felt her eyes on his back as she stood at the window, but he wouldn't turn around.

It was still that part of the year when you were surprised every time you went outside. The sun was taking its time in setting. It no longer felt like winter, despite all the snow. Right away Colin zipped open his jacket. Halfway to the gas station it was folded in the crook of his arm. He still didn't know what he was doing. The trip to Chelsea's house was a lie and he had nowhere to go. At the gas station he bought a bag of cherry licorice and ate it as he kept walking, past the mechanics and auto-body shops, the thrift store that never seemed to be open, and the stray houses that filled the gaps between them.

At the next intersection, there was a strip mall set back from the street. In front of a chain restaurant he saw a boy he recognized shuffling away from a car. His mother—Colin guessed—shouted at him to *get back here right now*. He'd seen him in school, maybe the year before when Colin was still a seventh grader. It occurred to him that he might run into other classmates, wandering around like this, and he changed his demeanor. He tried not to slouch and he carried the bag of licorice at his side instead of out in front of his chest, like a child. Seeing this boy with his mother—an older boy he'd respected and feared—Colin felt embarrassed. He slipped into the coffee shop at the end of the strip mall.

It was too warm inside—fake warmth from the fake fireplace surrounded by fake leather furniture. Colin stuffed the licorice into his jacket and looked at the menu above the counter. Coffee was something he'd never understood. He was conscious of everyone in the room, imagining himself being watched, but nobody was watching. Nobody he knew was here. He ordered a large mocha and the barista warned him—because he looked like a dumb kid, Colin guessed, standing there with his hands in his pockets—that it had three shots. "Exactly," Colin said. The barista shrugged and made his drink. It was bitter but he got used to it, and by then—with the sky purpling and the western clouds glowing like coals—it was nice, at the very least, to hold something warm.

As he continued down the strip mall, glancing through the windows of the late-night bakery, a hair salon, the bar where everyone did pull-tabs, a fast-food Chinese place, and a store that sold used games, he realized he was hoping to see Andy. Only see him—from a distance or through glass, where Andy might glance up and see Colin out by himself, walking alone at night with a cup of coffee. For months, he'd tried not to think about Andy in the way that came easiest. He tried, instead, to imagine them as friends. It was his own fault that Andy avoided him. It was his own lack of self-control that had driven him away. But he could change that. He could not ask for him. He could not want him. At the end of the strip mall was a burger-and-fries kind of place, and he stood outside until his ears were cold, waiting for one Andy-looking boy to turn around. Colin blushed when she did, and she wasn't a boy.

Down the street was another strip mall—a tiny bowling alley, a greasy pizza place, a video store with empty shelves, more coffee, more bakeries, more restaurants. There weren't yet stars but it was dark enough for the treetops to look like mountains, miles and miles away. He imagined Andy at the video store, picking out a movie with some new best friend. Colin called himself stupid for thinking he could've just walked up to him and said *Hi, remember me, I'm sorry I sucked your dick, I'm not a fag, please don't hate me.* He laughed at how pathetic it sounded, but he couldn't ignore his heart. With every beat it felt jumped by a car battery. Andy, it seemed to shout, *Andy, Andy, Andy, ANDY.* He began to breathe too fast and too deeply and he had to stop walking. He rested his hands on his knees, bent over the salt-stained sidewalk. *Am I throwing up?* He wasn't throwing up. His heart slammed against the bars of its cage, the word *Andy* like a taunt from something free outside. He dumped the rest of his coffee and watched it melt the snow into a brown slush. At the curb, he tossed the cup into the garbage. He tried to think about homework. He thought about cooking with his grandfather, how it was getting close to spring and they'd start in with new recipes. By the time he got to the gas station his heart had calmed. His breath came slowly. He gnawed at a stick of licorice as he walked, his hands going numb with nothing to do. He saw the black Toyota before he saw Victor, swiping his credit card at the gas pump. It was dark enough for Colin to vanish—down another street or just into a shadow, out of the fluorescents. I saw you, he could say to Victor on some future phone call. Instead he stepped over the guardrail that separated the sidewalk from the parking lot and walked up to him. Normally, Victor controlled the world around him, pulling all of its strings as the threat of a grin hooked the corner of his mouth. Today he looked ready to cry and kiss the backs of Colin's hands with joy. "Colin!"

Colin only nodded. It was best just to wait for Victor to say all the things he liked to say, tell the stories he liked to tell. This was a strange comfort compared to his earlier panic. This was familiar, a part of his life he'd come to expect. He knew, next, that Victor would offer him a ride, and he knew he'd say yes, and he knew Victor—who was the most reliable, predictable person on earth—would push Colin's boundary just a little further. Only around adults did Colin feel astute, sharp, and observant. Around teenagers, he felt like a separate species.

"I can't believe you're here," Victor was saying. "Are you going to tell me what you're doing, walking around in the middle of the night when it's this cold?"

"It's like eight o'clock," Colin said. "And I don't know. I just went for a walk I guess."

"It's almost nine, mister. You staying out of trouble?" Victor looked at him askance. He lowered his voice and leaned in close. "Been up to no good?"

Colin stepped back. He shook his head. "Just . . . I dunno. Bored?"

"Does your mother know you're out wandering around?"

"She wouldn't really care." He slipped his hands into his pockets. The last of the licorice was still there, and it struck him how strange—how *normal*—it would be to stand there like any other bored-off-his-ass eighth grader, chewing candy while he suffered someone's concern.

But it wasn't concern. Victor's eyes were lit up in a way the harsh gas station fluorescents couldn't account for. This wasn't his duty.

"Anyway." Colin shoved his hands deeper into his pockets, stretching the polyester lining of his coat until it creaked. The pavement was discolored from years of spills and mosaicked with an entire winter's worth of pressed-down trash. His nose had begun to run and he sniffed it back. "It was nice running into you?"

"Colin," Victor said.

Like a word that halts every muscle, his own name. He wondered if Victor had hypnotized him, when they'd first met. *In a few seconds you'll be awake, but from now on whenever I say your name you'll freeze. Whatever you're doing, you'll stop in your tracks. Do you understand?*

"Why do you think your mother wouldn't care? After all you've been through? Your family? It's just the two of you now—how could she do that?" He took another step and put his hand on Colin's shoulder. If the power went out, Colin imagined, Victor eyes would light the entire block. He felt him give a squeeze, his finger finding a muscle Colin hadn't even known was knotted.

Victor wasn't wearing gloves, and even over the gasoline Colin could smell the drop of cologne he wore on each wrist. When he closed his eyes, Victor tightened his grip, finding pain underneath pain. "You're very tense," he heard, closer than he expected, and opened his eyes to Victor. Nothing but Victor. He'd eclipsed the gas station, the stoplight's bustle, every other car and driver. Colin knew what was coming, what Victor—who knew all the spells—was about to draw from the boy he loved. Colin saw it now, that love, and it saw him.

"Colin. You break my heart."

With his first sob his chest and throat heaved together. He shut his eyes to pretend it wasn't happening. But Victor was there. Victor knew and would know forever. He'd been through it all. Why hadn't he listened until now? Only an hour ago he'd peered into restaurant and store windows hoping to impress some fictional Andy, and now he was crying in a parking lot a half mile from his house. The real kind of crying. But all the people who might see, all the kids who might spread rumors—what did they matter? This was his life and only one person was trying to save it. No matter how hopeless it was, how doomed he'd been from the beginning—as Heather had warned him—he would let Victor try. He wanted him to try. He let his shoulders go limp and Victor knew to gather him up. Colin let himself be held. "I know," he heard, over and over, and he could've cried until they froze to death. He wished, right then, that he could feel Victor's heartbeat through his coat, but he'd been out a long time and was starting to tremble. He let go.

Victor lifted his chin so their eyes were again locked. "Colin," his entire world seemed to say. "You need to get home."

Colin let Victor wipe the tears from his eyes. He even smiled when Victor brought his thumb to his mouth. "They taste like I remember," Victor said with a private grin, as though their time in their respective dreams had been a first date or a honeymoon. "Are you going to be okay?"

He wasn't, and Victor knew it, but he swallowed the phlegm in his throat and blinked his eyes dry. His hand reached behind him, for the passenger door. Whatever Victor wanted, wherever he'd take him, Colin would comply.

Victor sighed and walked back to the driver's side. He dropped the gas pump back into place. He waited as it spit out his receipt, which he folded neatly and slipped into his wallet. "I'm sorry but I can't drive you home," he said, in his lowest voice. Colin could feel it, his voice, as it tolled through the car's cold steel. "Suppose I drove up, nine o'clock at night, and let you out? Your mother would misunderstand."

Colin let go of the door handle. "Whatever," he said, like there was nothing to care about, but his voice was uneven, hammered into bits. "I gotta jet then." If he was going to throw up he wanted to do it far from Victor, far from the gas station or anyone who might pity him. "Later," he said, the word wrinkled and wet. He cast his eyes on the concrete: one foot in front of the other, it wasn't far, only a few blocks, at least it wasn't January. His mother might not even notice the way he was trembling. She might not come to see. *How's Chelsea?* she might ask from the living room, blue and wavy like an aquarium. He wouldn't sleep that night— not with all the coffee, and not with the memory of Victor all over him. He'd stay up and read his father's notebooks. He would think of his mother reading those same books, how she would soon finger the next page in his same absent way. Why would anything change? Why would you ever hope? He wondered what it felt like to freeze to death. He walked slower, evaluating the deeper ditches. Not far away there was a path to an undeveloped spot, a small pond in a circle of trees. He'd be dead by morning, without a chance. He mopped his tears with his coat sleeve before—if this was even possible—they could freeze as Victor had described.

His mother was in the living room, the TV's glow splashed all over the walls. "How's Chelsea?" she called, and Colin called back. In his room he switched on all the lights, even the little red bulb that glowed in the penguin lamp's chest. Before he undressed he peered outside and scanned the street for his own body, as though he hadn't changed his mind and had died on the way home, his ghost now haunting his mother. Hadn't his father convinced him, by now, that the reasons to die far outweighed the reasons to stay alive? He touched his knuckles to the glass, its chill welling up on his skin like water. Here he was, safe in his bedroom, watched over by his mother, tolerated by his entire school. Why couldn't Victor have driven him home? Why couldn't he have needed him? His eyes, once again, began to fill with tears, and it was in their blurry light that he caught sight of the black Toyota, shaded from all the streetlights. That he laughed right then, and that he cried, too; that his heart seemed to spin like the *image of life* his father had described, defective and malfunctioning and hurtling itself in all directions—how had his father missed it? How had he missed this exact reason, this part of life? Colin lay awake without reading, without crying, but the sun came up before he'd figured out a way to let Victor in. By then, he couldn't figure out why it was ever a good idea, and the sight of Victor's car, sparkling in the morning frost, gave him the chills. "You look terrible," his mother said when he stepped into the hallway. She felt his forehead and his throat and frowned when he seemed okay. "You're staying home anyway," she said. "You need to sleep."

After she left, Colin watched the street from his bedroom window. When it was clear he wasn't going to school, Victor's car came to life and slipped slowly away from the curb. By ten o'clock Colin was asleep and he didn't stir until noon, when the mail slot woke him with a creak. There was only one letter in the bin, a small note in a hand he'd be stupid not to recognize. *Hope you're okay*, it read. *Hope you get better. Think we'd better talk sometime soon. Not on the phone.* The word *not* was underlined, a quick slash you could tell was important. Colin thought about saving it, Victor's note, but tore it up instead. The envelope, too, he shredded, and it was only in pieces that he noticed it wasn't postmarked.

You'd think putting a gun to your head would indicate the end, but as Colin watched his mother for the signs—the drifting around the house, the long silences, the little sayings that sounded like riddles—he was shocked to conclude she was happy, not at all like his father when he'd begun to die. She was *so glad* about everything. "I'm so glad it's spring again," she told him in the car on their way into Minneapolis. It was mid-May and all traces of winter were gone. Even the wet, wilted trash that flowered every year under the snowmelt had been swept up and hauled away. "I'm so glad you're spending time with your grandfather again," she said when he didn't respond. "I was worried you'd never want to see him again. I'm so grateful you can get to know each other like this. That you can learn from each other."

Learn from each other. His hand was already on the door handle, his backpack between his knees. They weren't even off the freeway yet. *I'm so glad you two fags can learn from each other.* He wouldn't look at her, and when she asked if anything was wrong he silenced her with a quick and curt "Shut up." Only when she dropped him off and drove away did he feel cruel, as though he'd stomped on a freshly bloomed flower.

His grandfather showed Colin everything he'd changed—new curtains in the dining room, a refinished mantel over the fireplace. He'd stripped the brick in one of the upstairs bedrooms, exposing what he called the chimney's "character." It was just a brick wall. "I don't know what got into me this year," he said while Colin fiddled with the straw in his glass of lemonade. When the tour was over it was time to make lunch. It was Colin's job to fetch the ingredients from the fridge, as if it were some kind of test. He'd had the whole afternoon planned out, Colin realized. There was an agenda, a way things were supposed to go. His grandfather suddenly seemed less than alive, a robot going about its tasks. Colin was wrong, he decided, to have expected wisdom or some lesson on life. He was wrong to suppose his grandfather could've taken away a fraction of his loneliness. His grandfather was useless.

"Usually spring doesn't affect me," he was telling Colin, slicing thin circles of brie from a round he kept in a little wooden box. "But this year it's rather different. I feel invigorated. That's the best way to say it. Rejuvenated, perhaps. It's what people are supposed to feel every spring. I usually feel it in the fall, when summer is finally over."

"Yeah," Colin said.

"I asked for thick-cut prosciutto. This is the kind of sandwich you eat with a knife and fork."

Colin could tell he was supposed to be impressed. "Wow," he said, carrying out his same old task of removing the wrinkly, slimy leaves from the rest of the greens. Why couldn't food be ready to eat, or simply compressed into a pill, like in movies? He smiled, thinking how much his grandfather would hate the idea, how he'd swear that society had lost its appreciation for life. *Why be alive at all?* he'd say, because he'd said it before. "Grandma usually just makes a protein shake for lunch," Colin said.

Quentin tossed the knife into the sink. "I never understood that. She's such a brilliant woman, but how can she do that to herself? One of the few pleasures in life you can control is good food. Why be alive at all?"

Colin laughed and finished picking through the leaves. His grandfather was smiling as if he'd said something clever when it was only a stupid trick, pulling a string in a doll's back.

Over lunch his grandfather went on about their perfect spring, how the weather couldn't be improved, how it was easier to get through the day without a nap, and how even literature (he could never just say *books*), which he'd read all his life, had come to mean more than it ever had. Colin made a point of yawning—six times, seven times—until there was nothing left for his grandfather to say, nothing left to care about. "Well, that was good," Quentin said to the remnants on his plate. As usual, it was too late for Colin to be sorry.

"It really was good," he said. "And I had fun making it." He put his plate by the sink, on top of his grandfather's, and noticed two wineglasses pushed back against the tile. Colin knew he washed dishes every day, and he knew, because you couldn't find a more predictable old man, that his grandfather only drank one glass every night. He looked at them for what felt like too long, the glasses, as though he could read the unique set of lip prints just below each rim.

The image of them—his grandfather and the man he must love—felt more domestic than even his own parents, whose "date nights" were like a bad play they'd put on for their children. Was he young? Colin wanted to know. Was he attractive? Did he lisp or could he pass for straight? Was he dressed like a teenager or like a businessman going to work? Did they drink the entire bottle? And what about after? More importantly, had Colin—with his hateful little act, with his derision and his display of contempt—ruined what could have been a perfect night in his grandfather's memory?

He turned on the tap and began filling the sink.

"I can get those later," his grandfather said, rearranging the dishes because there was nothing else to clean. "We can head into the library, if you brought something to read."

Colin shook his head. "I mean I did. Bring something I mean. But we can do the dishes now. It doesn't really bother me."

"I suppose if you insist," Quentin said. He went over to the oven and grabbed the dishtowel from the door handle. "I'll dry."

Nobody had to love you. Loving wasn't a law that'd been passed through the ages, and certainly no one could enforce it. To love was to hurt, Colin was learning, and you never chose to hurt more than you could stand.

Over time, Colin had learned something from his father's notebooks, and not just facts, dates, and stories most people had forgotten. He'd learned, more than anything, to observe people. To interpret. When Chelsea fought with her parents, Colin pretended not to listen, slouched in a chair while she fished for permission to go to the mall. She called her parents stupid and retarded. Once, she called her mother a bitch. Colin knew they loved her, their only child. Chelsea knew it too, and she used it to her advantage. But how long could that work? How far could you push it? Only five months away from fifteen, Colin felt like a strange, miniature adult. If there was any legacy his father left behind it was proof—thousands of pages of it—that everyone has his limit. Watching Chelsea fight with her parents revealed love for what it was: finite, limited, and fragile. Something nobody else in his family had figured out.

Nobody left alive, anyway.

"My mom said she's glad I come over here," he said, scouring a pan with a ball of steel wool. "She said she's happy we can do this. She said . . . she said it's good for us to know each other. That I can learn stuff, I guess." He coughed into his shoulder and let out a laugh—from where he didn't know—that made his voice jump an octave. "That sounds really stupid," he squeaked, and he cleared his throat back to normal. "Dumb voice."

When it was ready, his grandfather took the rinsed pan and held it close to his chest. He stepped away from the sink and stood by the far window, looking out at the shelf of herbs he'd built along the fence. There were more dishes to dry but he moved slowly, buffing until the pan shined. Colin went back to washing, stacking the wet plates next to the sink. Finally his grandfather let out a small click—something in his throat that'd come loose. "She said that?"

Colin nodded. "I know, right? I was like, Who are you? but she didn't want it to be a joke or whatever. She was serious, I guess."

The pan was long dry and Quentin held it at his side. He looked out the window until, as if a clock had struck and it was time for something new, he laughed—just a small laugh, but something Colin hadn't yet heard. "I wonder what changed her mind." He shrugged and walked back toward the sink, pausing halfway to hang the pot on the rack above the island.

"She thinks you're a good role model, I guess." Colin reached for the first of the wineglasses and rinsed loose the dried flecks, like river silt. "You never have two of these," he said, and he waited for his grandfather to understand.

Colin felt delicate, like a trinket you couldn't set too carelessly back on its shelf. He wanted this man who'd lived so long a life to make it easier, to say the magic words all doomed boys like him needed to hear, whatever they were. Instead he felt a hand on his shoulder. It felt limp, like a leaf blown in place by the breeze. Then he took it away. Colin washed both glasses and handed them over. Quentin dried them and set them on the counter. They were done. The kitchen was again perfect, as if no one lived there. "All clean," he said, and without warning began to shake, all over like a train was barreling through the house. In a half second Colin's arms were wrapped tight around his grandfather. Colin thought back to the funeral—the only other time they had hugged. He felt a hand on his back, tracing a circle as he sobbed. How much longer could he have made it through life if had he kept all this grief to himself?

Quentin patted his hand against Colin's back. "I don't know what to say," he whispered, his chin resting in Colin's hair. "At least you know. At least you're brave." At the word *brave* Colin cried harder. "It's not an easy life. I'm not going to lie to you because you're smarter than that. You're brighter than that. You deserve more than that. It's a goddamn hard life, if you want to know the truth." The clock in the dining room chimed two and they waited while it cycled through its song. "But it's the only life. There's no other."

Colin nodded and pushed away. He dried his eyes with the collar of his shirt. "I don't want you to treat me different or whatever, now that you know."

He tried to suppress it, you could tell, but his grandfather's mouth cracked upward in a smile. He hid it behind his hand. "Now that I know? Colin, I've known since the funeral."

Colin knew he looked angry but he was more shocked than anything. *Why didn't you warn me?* he wanted to know. *Why didn't you stop me? Why didn't you help me?*

"Why didn't you tell me?"

"You can't do a thing like that. You can never do a thing like that. Besides. Think back. Would you have believed me?"

In his head, the funeral was a collage. His own reflection in the polished wood of his father's coffin. His mother's breakdown by the front door. The smell of burnt coffee. A feeling like everyone, no matter where he hid, could see his guilt and pity his future. Not in a thousand years—if someone had placed a hand on his shoulder and told him not to fight something as unchallengeable as desire—would he have nodded, would he have considered this person sane. "I'm not a fag," he would've said, as he'd said all his life.

"You can hide it if you need to," his grandfather was saying. "Kids your age—boys especially, I'm sad to say—are vicious. They're monsters. Hide it if you think it's better for you, but don't fight it. Don't believe the lies you'll want to tell yourself." He returned his hand to Colin's shoulder, this time with a grip, and gave him the most open, vulnerable smile he'd seen in his short, endless life.

You can't divide yourself among others infinitely, Diane had read recently. She was only one person, only one soul. She tried to act the part her therapist had cast. "You sound so hopeful these days," her mother told her over the phone. Tim suggested she list small accomplishments. *I swept the driveway today*, she called to say, and *On Tuesday we bought a new valance for the kitchen*. Each she tried to sell as a struggle against victimhood.

"This'll be the year I fall back in love with gardening," she told Shannon. At the grocery store she asked whatever happened to them—their coffee and girl talk—and that Sunday they picked up where they left off. Shannon had given up coffee for tea—to calm her stomach, she said—and brought a small thermos that she clicked open and closed with each sip. "You'll see," Diane was saying. She waved at the window behind her, opaque with nightfall. "There's still flowers out there for me."

Shannon clicked the mug and sipped and clicked it closed. She'd always been perceptive, and right away Diane knew she saw through her. "You're not yourself," Shannon said.

"Myself wasn't working." She reached for a cigarette to kill the emptiness in her hands. "Besides, Tim has helped me understand everything that's happened. How I've been perceiving things all wrong?" As she popped the cigarette into her mouth she let her thumb crinkle the cellophane, an old habit even though she'd used her own lighter for months.

"No more young gentleman?" Shannon glanced down the hallway.

"He's gone. As soon as they turn fourteen it's over. Even the boys. You'll find out someday."

"You know Frank had a vasectomy. We decided years ago, remember? I asked your advice?"

"But before that," Diane went on as though she hadn't heard, "those eleven, thirteen, however many good years really are good. The best, if you want to know the truth. There's nothing like them." All at once she smiled and teared up—two expressions that, over time, had twinned into a single emotion, boring as all the rest. This was too much, she realized—too close to her heart—and she waved it away, the conversation, the memory, the future that threatened her, all of it. She sat up straight and put on her usual melancholy. Diane knew she'd lost Shannon as a friend. "It's been hard," she said as she watched the smoke above the table try on scarves of different light. "But I keep going. What else can you do?"

How, she wondered, were you supposed to convince anyone that life was just a thread or a chain you'd dropped, something you could simply pick up again—*Oops!*—and keep following, as though nothing had happened? *Lost my way, sorry, but here it is, let's keep going.* In what world did all these people live? How long before you couldn't take any more surprises? Before you'd felt too much for one lifetime? It was morbid, she knew, but she'd lost all control over that. She'd forgotten all the boundaries Tim had helped her establish. How long, she wanted to know—how much could you take—before you paled into a ghost, wandering from room to room long before your body died or shot its haunted brains all over the walls? What if you someday simply ran out of grief? What if—while there may yet be plenty to lose—there was no longer a way to grieve those things or persons lost?

Still, for the sake of those around her, she decided it was better to live as though each chore, errand, and conversation was an act of healing. On the last Wednesday in April, on her way to therapy, she sang along with the radio, and for a moment she tricked even herself. She believed that some wound had sewn itself shut, and as she searched for the reason—sifting through the last month for the truth—she realized it didn't matter. If the brain was this stupid, believing any lie you told, why fight it? If this was how she felt, why care? Before she rolled up the windows she cranked the stereo and had another cigarette, collecting, from the people who walked by: stares of surprise and concern, a thumbs-up, a fist pump as though they were at a concert, and, from one old woman, a frown usually reserved for teenagers. For years, Diane had never allowed herself any fun, and she stuck out her tongue as the old woman—not much older than herself, if she was honest— shuffled off to her car.

On the way upstairs the song wouldn't leave her. She hummed it to herself, stepping on the linoleum in time with a beat only she could hear. It was hard not to feel cheered on, the world suddenly with her instead of against her. Tim was waiting, resting his elbows on Kathy's desk. How they both smiled—she'd never felt so welcome, anywhere on earth. In Tim's office it was easy not to act, not to wear a costume of strength. Even his comments on the weather made her feel as if she'd stepped down from the stage and resumed her life. But it wasn't the same life. Right away she talked about a dream she'd had, in which she and Colin bought a house she hadn't lived in since she was ten. By the time they'd found the little tumor of anxiety at the heart of the dream, she realized he'd written nothing down. He didn't once reach for his pen. He did nothing to hide the openness of his eyes, begging for more of her light. "I always used to think dreams were garbage," she said. She'd worn a pair of sandals that showed off her toenails, shiny from a fresh coat of polish. "Just the junk you throw out at the end of a long day."

The rule is: at some point you have to confront the fact that you've fallen in love. What she wanted was this exact thing, for her to visit Tim's office once each month and keep that love a secret. For them both to know but pretend they didn't. Living with it could be its own mild pain.

"There's a variety of theories," Tim said. "Some think dreams are total rubbish, like you said. I like to read a little more into them. They don't come out of nowhere. But I'm also not going to base everything we know off some dream you might have of an old boss or one of your college professors. You're more than your dreams. So am I. So is everyone."

"I never went to college."

He smiled and took off his glasses. "You're a master at missing the point," he said as he cleaned them with his shirt. "Or a mistress, I should say. To use the proper term."

He'd gone red, and, if he wasn't helpless without his glasses (she realized that she had no idea, and this struck her as strange in someone she felt she knew so well), he would've seen her blush back at him. She knew she was reddest just beneath her collarbone, where her heart, it seemed, couldn't hide its heat. "Mistress," she repeated. How easily could he lean forward, slip his arm in the small of her back, and kiss that spot? Alan had once called it her sunrise. "The sun's coming up over the mountains," he said after their third time together. It was the most poetic thing anyone had ever said about her. Her eyes weren't blue skies, to him; her lips weren't rose petals: he'd seen something no one else had. He hadn't found it in a book or plucked it like a common chord.

"You know I got the point," Diane said. She drew her shawl over her shoulders as though she was cold. "I just like to tease you, is all."

Tim replaced his glasses and pushed them back with the pad of his finger. Had Kathy walked in, it would've looked like an honest therapy session.

"I've been feeling much better," Diane said. In truth she'd only felt better since the parking lot, but in her head she translated everything she'd said and done over the last month into expressions of hope. "Funny how the brain works. So much of it's the weather, I think. What was it? Only a month ago we had snow everywhere? I still don't know why I live here."

"I'm a fall person. All summer I feel like I'm just waiting for it. Hovering by the window like any second the leaves will change."

"Snow is just so disgusting. Months and months of it. Who was it? Jack London called snow a silent . . . a silent assassin. Something about it slitting a man's throat?"

"Sounds like I need to read Jack London again," Tim said. "I've read all his work. Most of it several times, since I was a kid."

"I'm just so grateful it's spring," Diane said. "I feel like I've melted with the snow."

"I wonder where in London's work he said that. If this was trivia night, I'd have lost."

"You wouldn't be the only one. Ask me the capital of Vermont."

"What's the capital of Vermont?"

"I have no idea." She laughed and coughed into her hand. With her heel, she nudged her purse under the chair as though Tim could see through its lining. *I've been feeling better*—her own words absurd in her head, those of a grown woman, a mother, who illegally carried a firearm everywhere she went.

"The lilacs will be out soon," she said. "Every year it's a thing for me." She clasped her hands together in her lap, staring at the ceiling as she tried to paint for Tim the perfection she'd never be able to find again. "In a perfect world they'd grow on the walls of my living room. If I was to come home someday, from work or whatever, and someone had filled the whole house with lilacs, I'd die. Right then. I saw this movie once where the main character filled this woman's yard with daffodils—her favorite—and I'm ashamed to say I cried." She teared up as she pictured the man standing in what she could've sworn was an entire country of daffodils. She placed the girl's movie heart on top of her own heart and its love for lilacs.

This is how she'd cry, she realized, if, some years from now—had they done something stupid and chosen to be together—Tim remembered this very conversation and donned their house with lilacs. She pictured them on the mantelpiece, the dining room table, along each baseboard, hung like purple pinecones on all the curtain rods and door handles.

"I saw that one, too," Tim said. "I can see it in my head. I thought the same, except it was something I would do for someone else." He closed his eyes as though it was playing on the backs of his eyelids, but Diane knew he was only waiting for the tears to sink back inside.

"This is crazy," she said, but when Tim asked *what* she wouldn't clarify. "I'm just," she said, and that was all. *Talk about the weather.* "It's like I haven't seen grass in years," she said, pinning Tim back in his role as therapist. By the end of their session he'd even taken a few notes, his crooked little arrows and illegible, underlined phrases like street signs in an otherwise strange city where you'd once spent a year abroad.

In May she began a new list. She kept it on the fridge, scrawled on the magnetic notepad Alan had used for groceries. Her first accomplishment was to convince Colin to get up at ten on a Saturday morning for a drive down to Roselawn. She pictured Alan's grave as the most neglected of the cemetery, overgrown and disintegrating under a layer of bird shit. At the gates she had to ask for the grave site. Since the burial, she'd meant to return, to bring flowers. That first night after the funeral she'd imagined her life as a series of sunny afternoons on a picnic blanket, talking to him as though he could hear. How hopeful that seemed, in hindsight—a way of healing you could put on a poster or a sympathy card. She wanted to go back in time and smack that Diane, to blow cigarette smoke in her face. *Give up now*, she wanted to tell her. *Take your kids to Mexico and start a new life.*

"It's this way," Colin said, tapping his finger on the map the attendant had given them. "Left here, then right, then straight ahead, then right."

"I suppose it's too much to ask for a cemetery to be on a grid system." She smiled at Colin but he was staring at the window. Every grave was different but they were all immaculate, with or without flowers. Alan's, too, looked as if they'd only just left, save for the grass covering the grave. She caught herself looking for the seam where they'd shoveled out the dirt, but there was only grass that went on to meet more grass, as though there'd never once been a way in or out of the ground. "It's chilly out," she said, and gathered the snacks they'd brought for a long morning. When they arrived home she took out a large black marker and crossed *Visit Roselawn* from the top of her list, and by the following weekend she'd planted flowers out front, sorted through the plastic tubs of photos in the basement, and packed for an overnight stay in Escanaba, Michigan, where Paul had lived without visitors for three and a half months.

"This will be kind of like practice," she said to Colin as they took the interstate into Wisconsin. "For the big trip."

For weeks they'd called it *the big trip*, as though it was a three-month vacation around the world. Colin had the atlas in his lap and was tracing the route with his finger. He'd already taken off his shoes and socks. As he sank into his seat he put his feet on the dashboard, the map resting on his knees like sheet music on a piano.

"Hopefully this little trip won't make us kill each other. If we can't handle eight hours we sure as hell can't handle four days, right?" She nudged him with her elbow. He didn't answer, instead flipping through the atlas to Nebraska, Colorado, Wyoming. As she toyed with the CD player she watched him out of the corner of her eye, memorizing each state's map. "Hey, buddy." She put her hand on his shoulder. "Don't go on the trip without me."

"Shut up." He slapped her hand away and sank further into the seat. Like his sister, he'd mastered the sulk. "You're going to take the 160 at someplace called Angelica," he said, "but it's a couple hours away." Wisconsin had never seemed so large—not even when she'd driven back in tears after handing Paul over to the nurses. *Don't touch him*, she'd said, wincing at how cruel it could sound. *I mean, he hates that.*

Where Paul lived it wasn't spring. All the towns along Lake Michigan had not yet found color, and in the occasional shaded ditch or back of a barn they could see lumps of snow, hiding as though in ambush. What the brochures promised was cherry trees in bloom, meadows of wildflowers, waves full of sunlight lapping at the shore's white rocks. That grey link between winter and spring was even uglier out in the country. Under an overcast sky, the old farmhouse her son shared with a dozen other violent, autistic boys couldn't fool anyone into believing it was anything but a prison. In the oblique January sunshine, she remembered, the glare on the windows had hidden the bars between the panes. There were guards at the main entrance and a security gate at every stairwell that could be closed off if there was, the attendant said, "a situation." They stayed as long as they could stand. The nurse led Paul into the room by his hand—something that no longer bothered him, drugged up as he was. She tried to smile as she sat with him, running her hand over his acned cheek. It was the first time she'd touched him since his father was alive, and she tried—even saying it out loud to Colin, "He's letting me love him!"—but it was impossible to ignore the truth. The boy she touched was not Paul. Even the human sheen of his eyes seemed to have dulled, and it was hard not to think the nurses had taken even his tears away from him, inconvenient as they were. At the hotel she paid for a separate room so she could cry alone. When they returned home she threw the list away.

After visiting Paul she wanted to give up. She didn't deserve her children. She didn't deserve to live. But—at the end of May—the Diane who walked into therapy was suddenly repulsed by that weepy, dying Diane. She'd seen enough of her, had suffered enough of her. When she entered Tim's office it was in high spirits. By then, she felt like her life was a treasure she'd dug up from the pale San Francisco beaches she now—with their trip only a week away—dreamed of every night. "I can't believe it," she said as he arranged his things for the notes he wouldn't take. "If you'd have time-traveled and shown me a picture of this"—she gestured to herself, lowering her hand down her side like she was a prize on *The Price Is Right*—"I'd have asked if I had a long-lost twin sister."

"You do look fantastic," Tim said.

"So do you." She patted her hand on the table as though it was his arm and he thanked her. "I've been—" She smiled and glanced down at her own hand, still resting on table. It was hard to believe that all it took to look younger was a coat of nail polish. "I've been looking forward to this all month," she said. "I never—and this isn't a reflection on you—I never thought I'd make it this far. I never thought I'd get used to telling a stranger all about my life." She laughed, within it the first choke of a sob. "To asking for help."

"Diane."

She shook her head and dried her eyes with a fresh tissue. She laughed again. It leapt out of her like the hiccups or a bad cough—something you had to ride out. "Anyway," she was trying to say, but it kept sounding like "and," as though there was something to add, some other secret. She waved her hand in the air but not to make it all vanish. If she was to ask for any power right then it would be to arrest the entire scene and keep it, like a bauble or an ornament, for the times—should there be any more times—when she'd need it most.

"If you want to know the truth, I've been looking forward to this as well. It's not common practice to have favorite . . ." Tim touched his pen to the tip of his nose, chewing his lip as he searched for the kindest, most unmedical word. "Favorite sessions. But sometimes . . . well, I guess for the first time, someone so magnetic comes along you can't help but fall into their magnetic field."

"That's sweet of you to say." She gathered herself higher in the chair, flashing a quick, insincere smile. Insincere only because she'd rather be grinning or laughing open-mouthed. She'd rather reach across the table with both hands and pull Tim's face toward her own. Instead she dug each hand into an arm of her chair. "Anyway," she said.

"Anyway," Tim said.

"I wanted to tell you about this dream—"

"Oh!" Tim placed his notepad and pen on the table. "I wanted to tell *you*." He pointed at her. In all these months he'd never once interrupted her, or if he did it'd never felt disrespectful. "That Jack London thing you quoted, about snow? Like I said, I've read it all. So I did some research. Actually asked a friend who's a librarian. They have all his work digitized now, you know. So I said, search for this, and I gave him the quote—word for word. Nothing. Nada. We tried variations. Jack London never said that. Do you think you got your wires crossed?"

She gave that smile again, insincere in another way, and looked down at her lap. Her hands were pale for May, the nails red in a way that looked, on second thought, vulgar, almost ghoulish. She pulled them toward her palms and rested her fists on her knees. "Apparently so."

Why could you trust nothing? For weeks she'd looked forward to crossing the country, to the chance at a glimpse of a wild herd of horses thundering—she wanted so badly for it to sound like thunder—over the trampled grasslands of the plains.

Last night, I watched my wife sleep for the first time. I can't say why I've waited so long. Perhaps because she's so remarkable a woman it scares me. You get to know her and love her and she turns you into a musical instrument, a cello or a harpsichord. Even in sleep she could pluck those strings. Whale on those keys. What more can you ask for? Once, she wrinkled her forehead, going out of her way to worry in a dream, to think something over. Wondered if it was me. Knew it wasn't. All that she'll go through—it can't not cripple you, but you know she'll walk away, in the end, more radiant, more beautiful, never defeated.

Her husband had written. Whether or not it was true, anymore, she couldn't be sure.

"Have you read about the wild horses, out west?"

Tim said he had. He said how they were starving, how they kept reproducing, damaging fences. "They're a menace, according to the *Tribune*."

"So they are real?"

He frowned. He leaned back in the chair, his hand on his chin. "Of course they're real. Is everything okay?"

"As okay as it gets, I guess. I've just—you know me." She put up her hands and shrugged. "I've been through some hell, is all."

"I understand. Believe me, I do." With a deep breath he removed his glasses. His eyes were smaller than she expected, and she realized, as he squinted in her direction, he couldn't see a foot in front of him. "Diane, I've been wanting to—"

"I never told you about that dream."

Anger, she had read in one of those suicide survivor manuals, *is a secondary emotion.* That Tim pressed his lips together—it wasn't only anger. *But do you love me?* she felt she should ask, just to see how it'd sting, because even an hour ago it would've stung for her, too. "No," he said as he returned his glasses. "No, we haven't discussed that yet." He took up his instruments again—his instruments of listening, he'd once called them—but he couldn't convince anyone, anymore, that he was merely her therapist.

"It's not an isolated dream. It's not the only one I've had like it." Her eyes traveled up to the ceiling, where the air vent, with a sound like a faraway cowbell, came to life. And what did it matter if it was only a dream? She could've written it in some notebook to be found in ten thousand years and no one would know. She could've called herself Eileen instead of Diane, or Jennifer, or—a name it always felt silly to love—Candace. To Tim, though, it was a dream, not part of *this*: the tissue box, the metal table and its cheap chairs, his posters, his bookcase with its bowed shelves, the bad paint job in an old building in a shitty part of town poisoning everyone with asbestos and lead and general despair. To him, the clouds catching fire were not real, nor the birds raining down like meteorites as they tried to flee the flames. How she'd stood with Colin on their front steps and watched it all happen—

that, too, was just part of the brain's garbage, no matter what meaning you tried to assign. "What I'm saying is I felt relieved," she told Tim, smiling despite the tears in her eyes. "I wanted it. I was so, so glad it was all over. I've always felt that. I think I told you how I used to pray for cancer, leukemia, all that? When I dream, the world is never safe. I'm never safe. And so often it's . . ." She sighed and sat up in her chair, pushing herself erect with her elbows. "You know, I welcome it."

On the wall where the window should've been, the clock was nearing half past four. Tim had nothing to say. She shrugged her shoulders, strangely happy to have laid it all out for him. Even if they were only a kind of armor, her dreams, she wore them like the gift of invulnerability. He was still speechless as she reached for her purse and rummaged for her cigarettes. The gun, nestled among her makeups and various attempts at lists, didn't even faze her, nor its companion box she'd stuffed with cotton to stop the bullets from rattling. She'd take it with her, she decided, all the way to California. Out there, at the edge of the country, she'd go on dreaming of the earth cracking open, the sun going out like an old lightbulb, plagues that finished off all life in days. Every morning, she would wake up to life. She'd always awoken to life, and it seemed she always would. But she was prepared. And even if she wasn't, she had *this*, right in her purse, like an astronaut's cyanide pill. In case of emergency, she thought, and a smile trembled on her lips. When she left, she said she felt like they made a breakthrough, and she saw how it hurt him, how the mistake he made had uncovered itself and shown Tim how stupid he was to love a woman who'd been dead her whole life. "Yes," he said, and she left.

As she walked through the door, Colin savored the look of shock on his mother's face when she found him huddled over the kitchen table, shoulder to shoulder with his sister. Heather had been waiting in the driveway after school, her car stereo annoying the entire neighborhood as she sat scrolling through her phone. The only thing Colin could think to do was show her their itinerary, tracing their route on the atlas with his finger. "I thought I'd stop in and say hi," she told their mother as she set her purse on the counter. "I ordered us all pizza."

"Your car is blocking the garage," Diane said. She smiled, but there was nothing kind in it and Colin wanted to hit her across the face with a chair. "Anyway! You look great!" She crossed the room and stood at the head of the table. His sister actually looked terrible, as though she'd slept for ten days straight.

"Thanks," Heather said. She looked down, at the atlas.

"What are you wearing? You're drowning in that sweatshirt."

"It's Eric's. And it keeps me warm. I don't know. I like it." Heather sank deeper into it and shrugged it up around her neck. Colin could feel how nervous his sister had become, like a rabbit newly aware of a predator.

"And Eric is . . ."

"My fiancé?"

The doorbell rang before their mother could respond, as if Heather had planned it. "Pizza!" Colin shouted, desperate to change the mood, and he bounced up from his chair. His sister was slow to get to her feet as she followed with a handful of wrinkled cash.

The story was that she met Eric at Kohl's, where she worked, just after moving in with Anthony. His name, from her mouth, still had that girlish lilt. Anthony's name came out like a sigh. She was careful not to say where she was living or where she'd gone to work after losing her job, or if she was working at all. "Is it weird I'm having so much fun decorating our apartment?" she asked. Colin noticed how her skin was lit up with a hot glow, like an electric coil. She dug her hands deep into the pockets of her sweatshirt. It wasn't even cold in the kitchen.

"I'm glad you stopped over," their mother said. "Glad to hear about your apartment, your relationships. Glad to hear you're alive, for Christ sakes. I'm . . . I guess I'm proud of you."

"You guess?"

"I'm proud of you, Heather. I'm proud of both of you. All of you." She was smiling. Colin imagined how, if they were a different kind of family, she would have pulled them both into a hug and convinced them, somehow, that life wasn't so terrible after all. Instead she eyed them like pests who'd found their way into the house. He looked down at the pizza. There was still time to make things go right, to have the family he wanted to have.

"Fight you for the last piece," he said, jabbing Heather in the shoulder. Right away she snatched it from the box and licked the bottom crust.

"You mean curl up in a ball while I take it? It's all yours—I just warmed it up for you." She tried to shove it in his face and he screamed and fell backward in his chair.

"Never mind," their mother said. "I'm not proud of you. In fact, I have no children." She smirked and lit a cigarette, urging the smoke out the window above the sink. Colin scraped himself off the floor. "You know I'm kidding," she was saying. "I don't know what I'd do without my kids." Her eyes were fixed on Heather like two tractor beams that held her in place. "Children are such a beautiful thing to happen to a woman. At any point in her life."

"Must be nice to have your own place," Colin said, scooting his chair closer to hers. "Be able to do what you want. Eat what you want. Buy what you want and all that stuff."

"Well, that takes money, Colin," their mother said. "You can be as independent as you want but it's miserable if you can't pay your bills. Or provide for your family."

"I'm not here for money, okay?" Heather gestured toward the pizza box, its lines of cheese and stray bits of pepperoni gone cold and colorless. "I mean, I bought you dinner—for the first time your stupid, poor, irresponsible daughter bought *you*, Queen Mother, Empress of the Universe, a fucking meal. So give me a break, okay? I'm not here to jangle my cup of change and dance like some stupid-ass bear."

Colin was clenching the seat of his chair, the veins on his arms gone blue and bulging.

"So why are you here, *Heather*?" Their mother's voice had that old, invulnerable ice to it, and for the first time in years Colin wanted him and his sister to unite and overthrow this woman who'd tyrannized them for their entire lives.

"You know what?" Heather stood up and kicked her chair back against the fridge. "I don't know! No fucking clue. Guess I made a mistake, once again. Stupid, useless Heather makes another mistake. Don't you have a list of them? What's this . . . four million and six?"

Their mother finished her cigarette and extinguished it under the tap. "Even if I did have money, I'd want you to earn it. To *earn* something, Heather. Just once?" She flicked the butt into the trash. "I came home to take a quiet bath. To think. To be at peace." She put her face in her hands and Colin imagined that now, right now, was the time to attack, to knock her to the ground. "You know I love you both," she was saying, "but I need a break once in a while. I need some slack. I need to put the world on pause, just like anyone else."

On her way out of the room she tried to hug them both and both refused. Her eye was twitching, and when she touched it to make it stop Colin saw a glint of liquid light latch onto her finger. *The lacrimal canaliculi are situated just between each eye and the bridge of the nose, ferrying grief to where all can see.* If she cried now, Colin thought—if Heather saw how they'd been living these last few months—they might as well go to Roselawn together and dig their own graves. But she left, and down the hall they heard the bathroom door click closed and the tub's faucet groan open. "She'll be in there for hours," Colin whispered.

"That's fine with me," Heather said. She'd put her own face in her hands and looked so much like their mother that Colin pried them loose and smoothed her hair away. It felt wrong to be so affectionate with Heather, as though she might pummel him into paste.

"Do you want dessert?" he asked.

Heather laughed and shook her head. "I'm already too fat," she said, and gestured at herself. "But I guess that's just what happens."

"When you move out?"

She was looking at their mother's purse, left on the counter across the room. "You really are clueless, aren't you?" she asked, and he only stared back at her, his eyes as open as possible to remember this, to remember her. It felt so much like the end. "Hey—" She pointed. "Go get me her purse. Come on—she'll be in the bath a while, right? Just go grab it for me."

In another life, Colin would've been the perfect slave. *Yes ma'am, yes mistress, yes master, certainly sir, no problem sir, yes sir.* He stood from the table without much hope and brought what she wanted, let it clunk heavily on the table with its terrible, unnatural weight. From her face he could tell she found the gun before she found the cash. "The fuck?" she whispered. Colin shrugged and shook his head—there was nothing to be done, nothing you could change. Suddenly, Heather had to go, she had things to do, Eric was waiting for her, she just had to leave. For the first time in months or maybe years she hugged her brother, who gasped as he finally understood. *Children are such a beautiful thing to happen to a woman,* he thought, his mother's voice crisp and cruel in his head. What kind of uncle was he supposed to be, weak-willed and sick and perverted as he was? "You're a good kid," Heather lied, and she took herself away, out of their equation, out of whatever morbid game he and his mother were playing, out of their lives so she could live her own, off someplace with a future.

During World War I, a German lieutenant named Stolle, who could no longer bear his Siberian internment without music, built out of scraps and garbage what he called a piano. No one could hear the music he'd gifted himself, his fingers gentle on the hissing, wooden keys; and—as Stolle himself was a mere note in a fellow prisoner's diary—no one now knows if that music was enough.

By the last week of school, Colin had packed for their trip. They were to leave that Saturday morning. "Nine days on the road," his mother said as she dragged her finger across the calendar. While she was at work, he snuck down to his father's office. There were four unread notebooks left on the shelf. Sometime over the spring they'd given up hiding each other's evidence, and it was obvious his mother had been down the night before. She was only six notebooks behind him. Not that the sequence meant anything. None of the volumes were dated, and his father could've shuffled them into any order. Except the last one: still open and half-blank, waiting on his desk. The worst part was that he knew, already, that those last pages would answer nothing, explain nothing. It would only be more scraps. More noise.

As he pulled the next notebook from the shelf he looked around the room. Despite everything they'd disturbed, it was still the same room in which his father had lived his last year of life. Over time, Colin had decided there were no accidents, and that he'd snuck downstairs that night with a mission. For that, despite his apologies, his prayers—his entreaties to a god he was no longer sure watched over him—he would suffer in hell. He was already suffering, in fact, and for months now he'd thought of his life on earth as hell. It made his dreams and only his dreams seem real, stripping away life's veneer. What life was, underneath, felt honest and deserved: a plain of ice that stretched to the horizon and met only itself again, somewhere far; the hateful sound of sharp wind; a yellow sky full of wet, inky stars; and a boy restrained, tortured, humiliated for all eternity, whose punishment worsened with every sound of approval and acceptance he let whine from his throat. When he woke, in the morning, it was obvious that Victor had walked into his life merely to collect him, to bring him gently to his punishment. In San Francisco, he thought as he packed, he would spend his last days as a free human being.

It was hell that kept him in love. Having his grandfather say it—*This is your life*—made it easier to admit. When he passed Andy in the halls, *love* was the word for the hurt flowering inside him. Naming it made it grow, and to go with his hell he now had a heaven where he and Andy had not parted but admitted to one another what they had, what they could be, and despite his shame he refused not to reimagine that night, not to rewrite it how he wanted. It felt even more real than his hell as it burst all over his chest and dried sweetly in a handful of Kleenex.

But his grandfather was right about teenage boys. They *were* vicious monsters, and like all animal life seemed to have scented out the intruder. He'd begun to notice a stare here, a joke behind his back there. He tried to find the giveaway, watching his hips in the mirror, his wrists. He spoke out loud to test his voice. Somehow they'd found him out, and he was starting to panic.

On the last day of school, Colin hoped everyone would forget. He smiled at girls when he passed them in the hallway. He kept his voice low, his words clipped. He should've kept Chelsea as his girlfriend. He should've made out with her in the library or on the steps out front. Summer was long, though, and by the time everyone was shipped off to high school, it was possible they'd forget about Colin. Everything about him was supposed to be invisible.

He ate lunch alone, eavesdropping on the next table, where the boys who'd once been his friends laughed at Andy's every joke and believed his every lie. On the way back to class, Colin passed him as he waited outside the restroom. It wasn't rare for them to make eye contact, to remember each other, but for the first time in months, whether he was tired from all he'd been through or sick with hope, Colin gave the smallest, briefest smile he could manage. Andy returned it.

They'd fought once before, when they were eleven. They went a month without speaking, shunning each other in the halls, trash-talking each other to mutual friends. Then, while they were waiting in line together outside the nurse's office, it was over. They'd called themselves blood brothers right then, but instead of blood rubbed spit into each other's palms while the nurse wasn't looking. For the rest of the afternoon, after that smile, Colin thought it was over. Sometime during the summer, Andy—like every summer before—would walk the mile and a half from his house with a backpack full of movies and junk food. It felt wrong to want more than that, but before his last class was over he was shaking with a wish to be alone. As he walked to his bus he searched the halls for Andy. He walked slower, glancing up stairwells, peering into classrooms that weren't yet empty. Even if he didn't see him, he could wait. He could pretend. He could walk to the strip mall near Andy's house and wait for him to go out for pizza or fast food. It was two fifty when he'd made it to the door, and before he slipped into the seething, body-hot vestibule he heard his name. In that second, all his stupid dreams were worth it. Andy hurried to catch him and they walked out together.

Andy was awkward but Colin didn't care. He scratched the back of his neck when he talked, staring down at the candy-wrappered, spat-on sidewalk. "About time it's summer," he said, and Colin was ashamed to feel like such a girl, swooning at this boy's every stupid word. Why couldn't they be like any other couple and embrace, right there? "So you have a good semester?" Andy asked. The buses would wait longer today, the drivers familiar with how teenagers said good-bye. Everyone on that sidewalk was hugging, playfighting, or shoulder to shoulder in their circles. Colin felt as if they were leaving for another country.

"It was okay," he lied. "Mostly just hung around. Did whatever." His hands were trembling and he clipped them under his backpack straps, holding on as to a mountaineer's lifeline.

"Summer?"

"Nothing. Just a trip out west. San Francisco. Mom wants to see it."

"Cool. Yellowstone. Glacier, I think."

"Glacier?"

"It's a park." Andy shook his head. "She wanted me to go to camp again. I told her no fucking way."

"That's bullshit." A boy bumped him from behind as he hurried to one of the far buses. "I hope you told her you're not a baby or whatever."

"She doesn't get it," Andy said. Colin liked that he was nervous.

He felt himself grow bold. If he missed this opportunity he'd never forgive himself.

"We'll be back in a week, though," Colin said. "Later this month? So I mean—I won't be gone all summer, if you—if you want to. Whatever. Come over sometime. I'll be home."

Andy nodded, his eyes still locked on the sidewalk. "Yeah, that'd be cool. I was, uh. I was thinking about that."

"Yeah."

"You know how we, um . . . the whole thing with the gun?"

You can come over. You can knock on my window whenever. You can stay the night. You can do whatever you want. It hurt to be so lucky, to have woken up expecting more hell and to have walked right into the clearest, most crystalline heaven he could've asked for. His heart he imagined like a machine or a generator, some fusion core at the aft of a starship restored to full power, brilliant blue-white and with a hum that'd take them across the outer reaches of space and time. "I think about it a lot," he whispered to Andy, and was shocked when Andy stepped in and pulled him aside.

"You know it's a total secret, right?"

Colin nodded and tried to laugh. "Duh," he said, but it came out as *dhhh*, as though he'd been slapped on the back.

"I was wondering," Andy was saying. His hands were white now and his lip was trembling. He kept glancing around him. Colin's back was to the crowd and he imagined all the other kids going off to live their stupid, boring lives, while Colin and his boyfriend—would he let him say it?—spent the entire summer in love. "I'm just gonna say it," and he laughed. "I can't believe it but I'm gonna say it." He leaned in. "Do you think if—if I came over, you could . . ."

"Suck your dick?"

It was like reciting a spell: his body switched over to its too-familiar mode, and he felt pinched and confined in his underwear. He knew if Andy had asked, right there, he would trade everything for it and drop down in front of everybody.

But the look on Andy's face wasn't what he expected. How his eyes were fixed on his, how they didn't blink—Colin thought he saw sadness. Then he laughed, Andy, loud enough for everyone to hear. He pulled his phone out of his shirt pocket and put it to his ear. "Did you guys get that? I fucking told you!" From across the sidewalk Colin heard his former friends collapse into laughter, cycling through all the slurs, fag queer homo pussyboy cocksucker fag faggot fag, they said them all. Colin knew enough to leave before he started crying. "Hey man, I'm sorry," Andy called after him. "They put me up to it. I couldn't resist. Hey—come on, dude."

Being hated would've been so much easier. He pushed through the crowd and stepped back into the school, its air stale and musty after the promise of never having to set foot in it again. He disappeared into the nearest restroom and cried until the buses were gone, until the footsteps of teachers and administrators had diminished, until the humming from the air vents stopped and the room went still. He could poison himself in the science wing. He could wander out to the freeway and jump off the overpass. Like a rat or some other vermin, he could drown himself in the toilet, leaving his body for the janitor to mop up with the rest of the scum and the slime. He wondered if you could die from ink poisoning and shucked his backpack to the floor to look for a pen, and that's when he found the note that'd been slapped there, when that boy collided with him: *I blow like a pro! Will deep-throat!* with a phone number. His actual phone number. He screamed out loud and shredded the note, beating fistfuls of it against his skull. He hammered the stall door with his feet until it broke off its hinges and fell against the concrete floor. He was trembling when he heard the squeak of the outer door, the clack of dress shoes echoing off the walls. "Colin," he heard, before anyone could've seen him, before anyone could've known.

"Let's get you home," Victor said, and collected him from the broken stall.

The parking lot was emptier than it'd ever been. Victor held Colin close, his arm around his shoulder as they walked out in the open. He couldn't stop crying. Even in Victor's car he sat with his face in his hands. "No one knows why we cry," Victor was saying, and went on about the release of toxins, what people once called *humors*. He described the lacrimal ducts as though they were trees in the background of a painting. *Ferrying grief to where all can see.* "Of course," Victor said, and Colin felt a hand on the back of his neck, "from a biological standpoint, it doesn't always matter." That hand moved in a circle and it felt too good to send it away. "Poor Colin," Victor said, as though of a bum found frozen in some alley. "You break my heart."

They were taking all the old streets, even passing by that old park. Colin glanced down the road into the circle of trees that lined the lot. He'd managed to stop crying, and in the afternoon light he could see the shadows of playground equipment, the shadows of neighborhood children as they leapt here and there like squirrels. Victor didn't even slow down, one hand on the wheel and the other on the gearshift. His fingers were still. He wasn't whispering along to the radio. "How did you know it was me?" Colin asked, his voice froggy from crying.

Victor turned to look at him. For once he wasn't smiling. "Colin," he said, and Colin turned away, already wishing for home. "Colin, look at me." He couldn't meet Victor's eyes and only stared at his neck, the low cut of his shirt revealing a necklace that, for all Colin knew, he'd worn from the beginning: a scorpion entombed in glass, pincers and tail poised in permanent attack. "There's something you should know." Victor took a turn Colin wasn't expecting. This wasn't a park or a road through a suburban wood. SELF SERVE, said a sign above a drive-through cube, and they were alone in the old car wash no one ever seemed to use.

"The car dirty?" Colin said. He fake-laughed at his own joke. "I'm all out of quarters."

Victor shut off the car. Straight ahead was the windowless back wall of an apartment building, behind them a tall trash bin for the restaurant next door. "I want you to be honest with me. Can you do that?"

"I guess so."

"Look up at me. Look me in the eye."

"Um, okay," he said, but his sarcasm was broken. He was still staring at the necklace when Victor reached forward and put a finger under his chin, lifting until they locked on each other.

"Can you be honest with me?"

It wasn't quite a yes, what came from his throat—only an "ahh" that Victor chose to hear as consent. He leaned back in his seat and looked out the window. Their view was a dirty wall of instructions, half in Spanish, half washed away from years of winter salt. "Do you think I'm a dangerous person?" He turned back to Colin, holding his gaze as though his hands were latched onto either side of his skull. "You seem so afraid. I just want to know."

Colin shook his head. He was trembling and he knew Victor could see.

"Do you think I'm going to hurt you?"

"No."

"Then what are you so afraid of?" Victor laughed and slapped his hands on his thighs. "I worry about you. That's all. I know how kids can be cruel. I know how they are to boys like you, how they don't understand. All I want to do is help."

Colin closed his eyes and saw it all, the fleeing from this life into another where he was a grown man's toy, his accessory. In that life there were no decisions. There was no family—no Paul, no Heather, no niece or nephew. There was no one he had to face or fear, no one he had to love. The thought of loving filled him with hate. It felt good to know that, if he asked him, Victor would kill the boy who'd broken his heart.

"You just seem so alone." Victor returned his hand to Colin's neck, let it drift down to his shoulder, his upper back. "You don't have to be so alone." He leaned in and kissed him, just a peck, on the forehead. It was a trap Colin couldn't not fall for, and—even though he knew every detail of Victor's plan—he walked into it.

He lunged forward and put his tongue in this grown man's mouth, ran his hand over his chest, and, if he'd had the strength, would've crawled deep inside him and hugged whatever it was at this man's core that loved—even so wrongly—lonely, stupid, evil boys. He begged Victor to take him. Somewhere, he said, anywhere, just take him, free him, fuck him, use him, kill him. It was nothing you could stop.

Victor pulled away and said he couldn't. "The trouble I'd be in," he said, considering the wall as if it were a faraway landscape, as if they were parked on a cliff overlooking an infinite metropolis.

"Please."

"And where would I take you?"

"I don't know. Anywhere. I don't care. Out west. Mexico." He wiped his eyes. Victor was waiting. *How am I supposed to help you?* his look seemed to say. "I, uh. We're driving to San Francisco," Colin said, and winced at the truth. "Me and my mom. Maybe . . ."

"It's risky," Victor said. His hand was traveling again, lifting Colin's chin, down his neck and across his clavicle. "Take off your shirt."

"What?"

"Your shirt. Take it off. Just for a second."

There was no lie to back it up. No plausible excuse. But it was a command to obey, and Colin had only ever wanted, hadn't he, to obey? He slipped it over his head and held it in his lap.

"Mmm."

"What?"

"Nothing. I just never thought this would happen." He laughed again—almost a giggle—and caressed the spot just under Colin's collarbone, where the bones and veins wove themselves into lace. "I knew a boy who wrote poems," he said when he found Colin's heartbeat. His voice was strained. "He told me something I didn't know." He pressed with his index finger, then his middle, feeling with each what lay pounding underneath. "Do you know what *iambic* means?"

"Um . . . uh . . ."

"It's something from poetry. Just a unit of rhythm, I guess, like da-*duh* da-*duh*. I thought, long ago, how the heart is amazing. How it keeps beating. Unstressed and stressed like in poetry." His mouth hung open, like a cat tasting the air. "From conception to death in perfect meter. A muscle writing an epic poem." He laughed and withdrew, back to his side of the car. "That's what he said, anyway. All those years ago."

If Colin had spoken his voice would've wavered. If he'd run, his legs would've failed.

"Take it out."

Victor was staring at him again. Colin knew his eyes betrayed everything. His mouth fell open but all he could do was breathe.

"I want to see it," Victor said. "You'd show it to me, wouldn't you? Unless you've got something to be ashamed of? A handsome boy like you?"

Freed from the fabric of his briefs, it stiffened like frightened prey. A little droplet appeared and caught the light from the western doorway.

"Excited, are we?" Victor laughed and started the car. He switched on the radio—a song they'd heard a hundred times. "Get dressed. Let's get you home before one of us does something stupid."

It wasn't much farther to his house but he thought of a thousand possible lives on the way. Victor showing up on some California street, stealing him away in that black Toyota. Victor abandoning him forever, embarrassed at his pasty skin or the freckles on his shoulders or how he snorted when he laughed. In one life, Victor used him over the summer and sent him off to high school where he was passed from boy to boy like a porn magazine or a joint. "We'll see what happens," Victor said as Colin left the car, but in his room—alone with the bags he'd packed for their trip—Colin knew the ending, and he knew Victor knew. He knew the regretful moan as Colin melted, but it wasn't about that at all, he realized. Victor wasn't the type to ask. He wasn't a man who wouldn't know. He'd come to him, Colin, because he wanted to watch. He wanted to know each gentle step along the way, each hopeful glance at a heaven he'd never reach. Like a true scavenger, he wanted to taste each drop of blood that fell from that wounded creature stumbling through the trees as it looked only for a place to die.

III

Origin of the phrase *some hell*:

At the coffee shop by the library, catching up on work. Diane at home with Heather and pregnant with Paul. Toward late afternoon, a group of men—nothing like you'd expect. A disheveled man in his sixties, a young guy with a backpack who could be in college, a forty-something man in a suit. It's not the greatest suit but you can tell he has a job, a house, kids. They take the big table that says *Reserved 4 Large Groups*—which, deceptively, means groups larger than four. The men get settled, seven or eight of them total. They take out folders with loose fistfuls of paper, creased and frayed. They introduce the young kid—I can't hear his name—as a new "brother of the program," and he mumbles a "few things about himself." After he goes quiet, the other men take turns and do the same. It's some kind of recovery group, but I can't tell what for. There's a boisterous one, and it's easy to hear him say *booze* but not how it brought him there, *drugs* but not what kind, *sex* at least half a dozen times. The young kid mumbles something and the boisterous one laughs. "Yeah, I've been through some hell," he says, and the old disheveled man claps him on the shoulder. A fellow veteran of waste, pain, and destruction. They've accomplished nothing in life but climbing halfway out of the pit into which they long ago cast themselves. *Some hell.* Just a little piece? Or, conversely, "that must be *some* hell you went through," to designate wonder or fear? Perhaps it was some hell of many hells. Perhaps it would've been better if I'd asked. He wouldn't have found it rude. None of them would. They were there to illustrate, to show the way. "The stories I could tell," he would've said, but not out of pride. More like an architect who marvels at the Egyptian pyramids' perfection—*I'm here, right in front of you, but can you believe it?*

I've spent years imagining his life, Colin's father had written.

Had he ever looked at his own son and thought the same? What was it like to be imagined?

They didn't go to San Francisco. A few miles south of the metro they hit traffic, a long, wavy line of cars that led to flashing lights. Colin had the atlas in his lap and had told his mother twice how they should take I-80 west when they got to Des Moines, in 219 miles. They'd been at a standstill for ten minutes when she turned to him with something like panic on her face. "If we went to Hollywood instead, how would we do that?"

He didn't look at the atlas. He wanted to show her how much he'd learned. "I-70, I think. Kansas City. All the way through, uh . . . Colorado?" He flipped the pages to Missouri. "Or there's a state highway. It goes through Kansas down into New Mexico. We'd end up on the 40, which is like . . . the expressway to LA."

"That sounds perfect. Frisco's too cold, don't you think?" The car behind her honked and she glared at the rearview mirror. It took over an hour to pass the accident—an overturned motor home in a ditch. They drove by just in time to see the medevac glide over a grove of trees. Colin watched them load the body into the helicopter. "That hurts my ears," she said. He rolled his eyes and said *of course it does*, like an expert, and she gave him a shove that he tried to dodge. He laughed. Every chance they got, these last few days, they laughed. He knew that she knew something was wrong in his life, just as he knew something was wrong in her own. That she changed her mind about the whole trip wasn't even a surprise. He knew not to protest when the entire idea of San Francisco vanished from their future, all his planning and research for nothing. As long as he didn't have to see her cry.

Diane had begun to think of Los Angeles a few days before. A long time ago she had read that the sun in Southern California is like the sun nowhere else, and the phrase "another world's sun" came loose in her head one morning. She'd woken up early and was drinking coffee in the living room, and for that whole day she tried to place it. At work she was certain it was a song lyric but the song eluded her. On her way home it joined itself to the word *California*, and she no longer cared. She dreamt up Los Angeles from how it looked in movies: palm-lined boulevards that brought you straight to the sun, people sitting at tables on sidewalks, that theater where you could see Bette Davis's hand-prints. *What dainty little hands*, she imagined saying while Colin took pictures. "There's a reason people fall in love with LA," she said as they passed through Des Moines and kept heading south, giving up I-80, San Francisco, bitter summer fog, and everything else that would now remain exactly as she'd left it, twenty-some years ago.

She didn't believe she was going out west to kill herself. At their first hotel—a chain in Dodge City—she tried to imagine how Colin would live. Whether she did it here or in the middle of Hollywood Boulevard—who would he go to? How would he ask for help? What would *help* even mean? In Kansas City they'd lost track of time, gorging on barbecue, and meandered through the southern part of the city where you could be in Missouri on one street and Kansas on the next. She wasn't impressed. They left the city as the sun began to dip into the freeway ahead of them. At some town called Emporia, Colin told her to turn off onto a state highway. He spent most of the night with his face against the window, looking at the stars. "Are you ever going to stop?" he asked around midnight. In truth she hadn't even thought about it, but as soon as she imagined the sign—some gold or bright blue blinking beacon in the shape of a bed, towering over an en-tire town—she felt tired. There wasn't much out there, and a little after one in the morning she pulled over so Colin could pee in someone's cornfield. He made her stand guard, her hands in her pockets as she looked one way and then the other, not a hint of headlights anywhere. This is how people get murdered, she thought as she heard Colin's splatter against the ground's carpet of husks. She was glad for the gun, driving past the walls of corn that led to Dodge City, and she was glad for the overweight teenage girl who sat up all night at the hotel, watching reruns, just so Diane could give her son a place to sleep.

Even though they'd gone to bed at three in the morning, Diane woke at dawn. She thought about letting Colin sleep while she sat in the lobby with a newspaper, but the thought of the two of them, packed up in the car and heading west, flushed her neck with heat. How the sun would look in the rearview mirror, still orange as though it was groggy from sleep; how she could pretend she was outrunning it; how when they got to the next town they could fill up on gas, doughnuts, shitty coffee—who wouldn't want this? Who could dream something better? "This is wonderful," she told Colin as he tried to burrow back under the covers. She poked him under the ribs until he got out of bed.

The first glimpse of the desert came just before noon, when they crossed from the Oklahoma Panhandle into New Mexico. "Not cactus desert," she explained. "Just sagebrush. Tumbleweeds and dirt." Far away they could see bands of lavender she called mountains, which might have been clouds. In some western states, she reminded herself, you could see for a hundred miles. Whenever the highway curved toward the slightest overlook she slowed so she could stare off into the distance. Rarely was there any proof of civilization at all, and Colin had to ask why she was smiling like an idiot.

In Clayton they had a late breakfast, driving up and down empty streets until they found an old hotel. The pipes hissing in the walls and the way the waitress tottered to the side made her think they'd have to gag down their eggs and pancakes, but everything was delicious. Colin ate as if she'd starved him for a month, ordering a plate of sausages when she tried to ask for the check. She let him try her coffee and he made puking motions with his hand over his mouth. "You have good taste," she whispered. "They may have good food but their coffee's shit." She drank what was left in one gulp and asked for more.

"I hope you're having a good time," she told Colin as the waitress brought another short stack—on the house, she said, with a hand on his shoulder. He was hunched over his plate with his fork in his fist like a child. He didn't even bother to lift his eyes while he chewed. She noticed an ashtray nestled between the condiments. "Don't mind if I do," she said, as though someone had offered. She'd known, maybe, that this was the only way to get a response out of him. It wasn't every cigarette, anymore, but when he was right in front of her it never failed. When he held out the flame she smiled and said again, "I hope you're having a good time."

"I guess so." He looked around the dining room. Everything was that color you could tell was once blue. Even the tiles on the floor, scraped and cracked into a dimpled chalk, had little bits poking through that were still the color of a hazy afternoon. It felt weird to be there, he thought, his mother across from him with her elbows on the table, with her cigarette smoke. They might as well be at their kitchen table back home, arguing over what to do while they were on vacation. But outside it was too big. Even the country in Minnesota was smaller, boxed in by fences, filled with cows and the occasional tail-twitch of a horse. Everywhere you looked was a billboard, a silo, an outlet mall. Even the abandoned barns, their roofs sagging like giants had rested there, had next to them new barns, a cleared spot of land for pigs, a massive *FOR SALE* sign that wouldn't be there the next time they drove out of town. Here, the abandoned barn's equivalent was a pile of rubble—splintered lumber and stones—nestled all by itself in the yellow spot between two hills where, he guessed, plants grew in the spring. It was terrifying.

Santa Fe was the first place she said she could live. It was still early in the evening and they could've driven—he said, measuring a stretch of freeway with his thumb—at least as far as Albuquerque. "Part of traveling is to get a feel for places," she said. He was trying not to get her lost but it wasn't working. He couldn't stop looking in the rearview mirror.

Santa Fe was also the first place he saw a black Toyota.

It followed them for a while, when they first drove into the city. Colin hadn't paid any attention to the car until it took a sharp right—only seconds after his mother had pointed up at a hotel. He wished he would've been more alert, more vigilant. Of course Victor had pursued him. Why wouldn't he get what he'd always wanted? As they circled around the block Colin looked up and down every street. He locked his door as they pulled into a spot behind the building. "Stay here," she said. "I'll ask about rates." He watched her cross the lot to the rear door. The thought of Victor— standing right outside the car window and pointing at the lock— was so real he could taste it. He knew he'd unlock the door for him, like a child who would no longer disobey, who would offer himself for punishment. And Victor would be so disappointed that Colin had lied about where in California they were headed.

At dinner, she said it again: "I could live here." They'd walked from the hotel to a steakhouse the concierge had recommended. The sidewalks were narrow and they had to walk single file. Whenever Colin looked back, his mother was taking something in—a school done in pink adobe, its windows black as the sun prepared itself to set, or someone's front garden of yucca and sharp flowers. "I just think it's a beautiful place. Not even that, maybe, but a place where they didn't forget to make it beautiful. You know? So much of the Midwest is . . ." She flicked her hand in the air as if to bait and hook the right word. "It's such an afterthought. You know, here's this nineteenth-century church, you don't think anyone will mind if we build a concrete cube next to it, right? It's a joke."

"It has rules," Colin said. He had interlaced the tines of his two forks and was rocking them back and forth. "You're not allowed to build anything if you don't use the mud brick stuff."

"Adobe."

He knew the word. It just sounded stupid and he refused to say it.

The restaurant was quiet. The mariachi music was turned down so low that all you heard was a little groan of brass now and then, easily mistaken for a creaky door. Most of the tables were empty. "I just get the feeling—" she began. When he didn't look up at her she reached over and unhooked the forks so they lay flat. "I get the feeling that life here is very laid back. Like nobody's trying to figure you out and they're not worried about you."

"Like no one cares?" He picked up the forks and held them away from her.

"Knock it off."

"What? I'm bored."

"So take advantage of the conversation your mother is trying to have. Jesus." She leaned back in the booth.

He could feel her leg shaking under the table—spasms from too much unused energy. "You really want to live out here? It's just dirt."

"It's more than dirt. There's mountains. The sky goes on forever. That's not exciting?"

"I don't know. I guess."

She ordered a glass of wine—"Whatever you recommend," she said with a smile Colin could tell was fake. He looked out the window while the waiter explained where each wine came from, using words like *fruity* and *earthy* and *tannic*. I'll have a nice tall glass of dirt, Colin thought, and he buried his face in his shoulder so she wouldn't see him smile.

"What's wrong?" she asked after the waiter left. "Are you okay?"

He turned back to her with one eye squinted shut, the opposite eyebrow raised in an arch. "Yeah-yus," he said. "I'll uh-have the-uh, Earthy Cabernet, uh, '78. I do hope it, uh, tastes like dirt. If you please-uh."

By the time their food came they were both red in the face and wiping tears from their eyes. "We'll move here," she said between gasps of breath, her hand trembling as she drizzled vinaigrette over her salad. "We'll buy a ranch and see how much money we can make from selling fermented dirt." She tried to do the silly voice. "It'll be-uh, very-uh grand." It didn't sound anything like it was supposed to, but he didn't want to correct her.

The next place she loved was Seneca Lake. He'd insisted they drive from Albuquerque down to Socorro and go west from there. He'd seen the Very Large Array marked as a "place of interest" on the map and recognized the name from movies, all those radio tele-scopes pointed at the sky. By the time they left the hotel he had the entire fantasy played out—parking on the side of the road and using his mother's phone to send pictures back to Andy, as though he'd walked right onto a movie set. Andy wouldn't recognize the num-ber, but he'd know deep down who it was. Andy would know, Colin decided, how cruel he'd been, and he would know that if he only apologized they could forget the last year. But whenever Colin imag-ined Andy's long walk over to his house, his knock at the door—the whole uncomplicated ritual of boy forgiveness—he infected it with the afterimage of him and Andy out of breath on his bed, each too tired to untangle himself from the other. In reality, the VLA facil-ity looked like a pasture sparse with gangly white animals. Only one telescope was close enough to the highway to make out as a tele-scope. The rest could have been the strange deer that kept leaping over the roadside fences. "Do you want to stop for a picture?" she asked as he strained to see through the driver's side window.

He slumped back in his seat. "What's the point?" Out the other window was another stretch of desert, wavy with sunlight. Maybe he could tear the page out of the map and write, *I WAS HERE*, and mail it back at the next post office. But it was the kind of thing that Andy would just throw over his shoulder for his mom to clean up. Too hard to figure out. Not worth his time. Or maybe he would understand who sent it, and understand—when for some reason Colin could not—how you couldn't be friends with someone who, at the most halfhearted command, would drop to his knees. Colin shifted in his seat. He hadn't been sufficiently alone for three days.

After the VLA, there wasn't much except desert. Mountains had gathered to wait along the skyline. "So beautiful out here," she said every half hour, pointing to a dried-up gulch or the crev-ice between two hills, thick with sagebrush. He was bored and everything was beginning to look sexual. He tried to scare him-self by thinking of the black Toyota he'd seen in Santa Fe, but it wasn't fright he felt when he imagined the phone call—Victor asking where they'd been, what they'd seen. *Not a lot of privacy*, Victor would say, and with his eyes closed in his mother's car Colin let out a soft breath of air, a groan without the groan, and let his lips imagine the taste of the dewdrop Victor would feed him before he made him beg to go on. "Arizona!" his mother shouted, and Colin's eyes flicked open to a smeared-white sky hovering over a smeared landscape, his heart beating so hard he had to look down at his shoes to catch his breath.

"I think I need a long shower tonight," he said. "I smell funny."

She pinched a cigarette from a fresh pack and leaned toward him, her eyes still on the road. While he searched for his lighter she made a sniffing sound. "Well, I'll be damned. It is you. Here I thought it was the cheese I bought for lunch."

He bit down on his smile. "Shut up." As he held the flame for her he kicked off his shoes. "I'll show you cheese smell," he said, and after her first drag she made a face as though she was trying not to puke. "This a bad time to say I forgot deodorant?" He raised his arms with a long *ahhh* sound as if relaxing, but he realized that his T-shirt was too small and you could see the little tufts of down that'd grown there. He put his arms at his sides and turned to look at the bags in the backseat. "You don't really have cheese, do you? I'm starving."

She was still laughing to herself, ashing out the open window. "There's no cheese. But we could stop somewhere, if you want. What's the next big city?"

He flipped to Arizona. "Uh . . ." He followed their highway as it dipped down into a large green patch, dotted with points of interest. "Nowhere? I guess Phoenix, but that's hours away. I'll be dead by then. We're about to head into the Apache National Forest. It looks big."

"Even better. What's the best way through it?"

"The quickest?"

"No. Like the prettiest. What're all those pink dots?" She gestured at the atlas with her cigarette. A dusting of ash fell onto the page, immediately swept up and out the window.

"Take the 77 when you get to Show Low."

"Show Low." She smiled as the wind pulled smoke from her mouth. With her free hand she reached out and felt for his shoulder, his neck. She ran a hand through his hair as he tried to get away. "I'm so glad we did this." You could tell it wasn't one of those things she said just to change her own mind.

The shadows were long by the time they caught their first sight of the canyon, not far from Seneca Lake. The road dipped down to the river, switchbacking to drop what must be—she kept saying—half a mile straight down. Colin put his hands on the dash, screaming at her to slow down. When he looked over at the guardrail he could see patches of river still lit by the sun.

"Didn't think you'd be afraid of heights," she said.

"I'm not afraid of heights. I just don't wanna die."

"We're not gonna die." She patted the steering wheel with her wrist. "Look, no hands," she said, and she burst out laughing when he turned and saw both of her hands firmly on the wheel. "Relax. Just look at all this. Couldn't you see us living here? In one of those houses on stilts maybe, right on the side of the mountain?"

"Just wait till there's an earthquake."

"Are there earthquakes in the desert?" She pointed over his shoulder at a house built on the summit of a hill. "There! Like that one."

"Of course there's earthquakes. Slow down! God."

"Can you imagine what the stars must look like here?"

"Slow down!"

"There's already a line of cars behind me. You don't want to be that car, do you? The losers from Minnesota who can't drive?" She eased her foot off the brake as they came close to another pass. "There we go," she said as the car whipped around the curve. "This could be my commute. Driving every day and seeing all this. Can you imagine?"

"I'd kill myself."

"Don't say that."

"Or buy a helicopter." He let himself peek out over the edge. They were close to the river now. All this for a single bridge, not much longer than a railcar. They crossed it in seconds, and it took nearly an hour to climb the switchbacks waiting on the other side.

They ate McDonald's in a town called Globe, right in the middle of the mountains as if someone had dropped it there and couldn't reach down into the cracks to fish it out. What little of the sky they could see had flushed pink. As they ate in the parking lot they could hear the breeze push away the day's heat. By the time they finished their fries Colin was shivering in his T-shirt. "Roll up the stupid windows."

She ignored him. "I think we'll sleep in Phoenix. A place with a sauna, since you've decided to bring—let me guess—shorts, jeans, and . . . what? Three T-shirts?"

"It's the f . . . I mean the stupid desert."

"Colin."

"What? I didn't say fuck. But it's the desert. You know. Hot. Sunny. You have to hide in the shade or you die. We've had the stupid AC on all day."

The car bounced as she pulled back onto the highway. "You're the one who told me it gets cold, doofus. For a while you were a little encyclopedia. In the desert this, in San Francisco that. Interesting how you get amnesia the second you face some responsibility."

She hated Phoenix, she concluded once they arrived, and refused to sleep there. "Big, boring, and ugly," she repeated to herself as he thumbed through the atlas, tilting it toward his window so he could decipher one city and highway at a time in each streetlight's flash. "You want I-10 west," he told her. "It'll take you straight to LA. Maybe we could—"

"Where's the Grand Canyon?"

"North?"

"How would we get there? Sometime tomorrow."

"You want I-17. It goes up to Flagstaff, then you go a little west until . . . I can't read this. You won't let me turn on the light."

She turned on the light.

"You go west until a town called Williams. Then north a bit, and it dumps you right in the park." He reached up and switched off the light. She'd scared him, years ago, into believing that switching on the light while she was driving would blind her and they'd die within seconds.

It was close to eleven when the last lights of the Phoenix metro disappeared. Eating had made him tired and he reclined the seat. He was careful, out of instinct, not to bump into his brother in the backseat, and as he watched the signs flit by above him he was sad. Agua Fria. Camp Verde. Sedona. *Sleep*, he commanded himself, but instead he thought of Victor. How could he have believed he'd left him behind? How could you hope that going out of town would keep you out of danger? He wondered if, in the rearview mirror, his mother could see the headlights of a black Toyota. His brain took him places that weren't even erotic, only terrifying. Their brakes failing. The car overheating because of some sabotage. Victor would eliminate his mother so he could have Colin all to himself, and for that Colin already felt guilty. His mother begging for her life, knowing, at the same time, what kind of son she really had, the one in whom she'd placed her hopes— how could he have done this? How could he have lured her out here? Victor was the kind of man who'd carry a gun in the glove compartment. Out in the desert, nobody paid attention to these things. She'd scream as he aimed it, but that wouldn't stop him from firing, nor could it prevent the silence after, when Victor glanced over at him, maybe with a grin. Picturing this future, he began to sob, doing everything he could to control his breathing, to let his tears glide to the corners of his lips where he licked them back into his body. It went beyond his father, he realized. His selfishness, his depravity—he would kill them all.

Just before dawn he was wrenched awake, and he quietly lugged his duffel bag into the hotel bathroom to change. By the time the sun came up nothing seemed important anymore. He'd only slept three hours but didn't feel groggy or even tired. She was still in her pajamas, and as she smoked a cigarette on the balcony he lay on his bed with his hands over his chest. *This is what people do when they're happy*, he thought as he looked at the ceiling. *They sit around and think about how happy they are.* She'd left the door open and he could feel the morning's chill on his toes. It was one of those things you hold on to, the feeling, and before long his eyes were closed and every shift in the room's temperature brought a smile. When he was younger, she would touch his face before bed, running her finger along his eyebrows, the bridge of his nose, and the soft spots under his eyes, just light enough where she felt so much more than human. He remembered this and began to giggle, and to cry. Some people were so bound up and twisted into terrible shapes that you could never hammer them back the way the were. Unhappiness, Colin decided, was just part of his world. By the time they packed the car, he was already thinking of how easy it was to die in the Grand Canyon.

They ate a late breakfast at the lodge, right on the rim. "So this is the wilderness," she said with a mouthful of eggs Florentine, pointing with her fork at the line snaking toward the buffet. "I was in New York once. Came up out of Penn Station, on that giant escalator to the street. That's the only place I've ever seen more crowded."

"I read you're not supposed to come here in June," he said. "Too many people."

"But we are here, and we weren't here in April. I hope the Grand Canyon isn't offended that we've arranged the trip around *our* schedule." She winked and took a sip of coffee. "Besides. All I want is to see the damn thing. Get a picture of you on the rim. I used to take pictures of you all the time. All three of you. You'd lose a tooth and I'd take a picture. Heather's first report card—I have ten pictures of it, plus the stupid thing itself, somewhere in a box. All your art projects. Everything that says 'Mom' in your crooked handwriting. Which hasn't gotten any better."

"Shut up. Here—" He grabbed a napkin and dipped his finger into his orange juice. He tried to drip MOM but it came out like a big blob. "That's special too," he said, and flung it across the table. But she didn't push it away or laugh. Instead she smiled at something nobody else could see, and he felt more cruel than he had in months. "Sorry," he told her.

"Sorry for what?" She folded the napkin into fourths and set it on the table. "Being a jerk? I'm used to it." She finished her coffee and clunked the mug on the table. "You can't raise kids without breaking your own heart," she said as they pushed themselves away from the table. It sounded familiar and he knew where he had read it. He was so distracted that he forgot all about leaping to his death, and even felt a tinge of vertigo when, as they stood right on the edge, a single, tiny rock rolled out from under the toe of his shoe.

"And that's only halfway down," some man said, putting his hand on Colin's shoulder. "Not what you bargained for, hey buddy?"

The man was smiling but Colin felt as though he'd been attacked. He was old enough to be his grandfather, only fat and dressed like someone from *Gilligan's Island*. "It's a mile deep," Colin said, and he shrank back toward his mother, who was already searching her purse for a cigarette.

"It really is an amazing place," she said as they sat in traffic, waiting to leave the park. They were on a spruce-lined road that would've been pretty on another day. The signs about mountain lions and coyotes would've been exciting. "The car in front of us stinks," she said. "If I get a migraine you have to drive." He buried himself in the atlas, plotting their next route to LA. They should have arrived yesterday, he calculated.

The best thing to do was go south, back toward the freeway. Instead she went north and took them into Utah, where everything—as if someone had draped a swatch of silk over the sun—was orange. Toward evening they were moving west again. "You have to find the 15," he kept telling her, and he put up his hands when she turned where she wasn't supposed to go. "You're gonna get us lost!" he shouted, just outside a place called Hurricane. A half hour later she pulled onto I-15, heading toward Las Vegas.

"This is a vacation, remember? We're supposed to have fun."

"It *would* be fun if you weren't trying to kill us." He was trembling, he realized, and sweating so badly he could feel it drip down onto his ribs.

"Kill us? Really? Who's out there trying to kill us?" She laughed at him and cracked her window, only an inch. The freeway's thunder silenced anything he could've said. He turned and glared out the window, at the desert, which he now understood grew in all directions at this time of day and looked surrounded by flames so hot you couldn't even see their licks and curlicues. The whole thing looked like an oven, as if they could drive in any direction and roast themselves alive. By the time they crossed into Nevada he no longer knew why he was so angry, and after they left a gas station he tried to make a joke about the slot machine above the urinal in the men's room, but she wasn't listening. As she drove she looked up at the sky, the sun now sunk beneath the mountains. "I believe that's Venus," she told him, pointing to the sky's only star. Of course it was, he said, as though she'd pointed to the road and said *pavement*. And it was like this, their moods out of alignment, until they came around the bend and saw Las Vegas nestled in the rocks like a handful of diamonds. "Wow," they said at the same time, smiling at each other. It was too expensive to stay, and they moved on.

"Tell me about a small town," she said, after night had fallen in earnest. "What's nearby? Something tiny. Way smaller than Williams. I want some hole-in-the-wall place."

"Uh . . ." He held the atlas close to his face, leaning into the clock's turquoise glow. "I think you, uh . . ." She flipped on the light and he blinked until the map made sense. "Go east on 164. It might be called Nipton Road. It'll take you to Nipton." He reached up and killed the light. In the vanishing glare they saw a pair of eyes glide onto the road. "Fuck!" he shouted as she swerved. He looked back and saw something step into the night. "What the fuck?" His muscles felt full of ice. "We almost died," he said, over and over as she sat gripping the wheel. "You don't even care!"

For the first time in years, she slapped him across the face. "That's enough."

It was after eleven when they reached the California border. A roadblock forced them through a checkpoint. Colin gripped the atlas like a shield. His mother rolled down the window as a man stepped up to the car. "Good evening," he said. His accent made Colin feel like they'd traveled much farther. Through the filmy window of the booth he saw another man waiting, a rack with two shotguns behind him. His ears began to ring.

His mother seemed oblivious. "Hi there. What is this? Some kind of immigration thing?"

"Not at all. Just wanting to know if you carry any fruits or vegetables with you today?"

She laughed and glanced at Colin. The way she smiled made him think they were going to die. "We have apples in the cooler, sir," he said over her shoulder. "And maybe an orange somewhere. I can look if you want." He gestured with his thumb toward the trunk. They wanted money, he was thinking, and they had nothing to give.

"You're seriously looking for fruits and veggies?" she asked. "Like they're, what—full of drugs?"

"Not at all, ma'am. Just fruits and vegetables themselves. Many carry bacteria, parasites, insects, pests. California requires tight control on incoming produce, you understand? To ensure no contamination?"

"Can you believe this?" she asked Colin, who begged her to unlock the trunk and give the man what he wanted. "This is ridiculous," she said as she got out of the car.

Colin watched them in the rearview mirror. She was bent over the trunk and the border officer stood behind her. He passed a flashlight over her hip and Colin saw a band of flesh as her T-shirt rose up above her waistline. The beam was resting more on his mother than on whatever was in the trunk. She'd left the door open and the car's urgent reminder to take out the keys was all he could hear. The man dumped an armful of apples into a drum with a biohazard symbol. He was smiling as he walked back up to the car. "You are free to go," he told her, and winked as she shifted the car into gear. "Have a lovely night."

"Thanks," she said, and began to roll up the window. *You're pretty*, Colin thought he heard. The man was standing in the road, watching them go, ignoring the next car in line. Not even a mile down the road she had to pull over so Colin could vomit out the window.

"Don't get any on the car," she was saying. She rubbed his back as he coughed up the last bit of their dinner, and even offered her sleeve as a napkin. The way he shook his head reminded her of the child he'd been, and as they drove the last few miles to Nipton her heart felt like a rock hurtled through the sky, disintegrating as it plummeted back down to earth. "You know I love you," she said, and she was glad to discover, as she glanced over at him, that he'd fallen asleep.

At the hotel in Nipton she rented two separate rooms, right across the hall from each other. There was only one other guest who never left her room. They stayed for three nights and she couldn't explain why, even when Colin paced up and down the dirt road, complaining that they'd just have to turn around and go back home, that there was no point in going to LA, that they'd wasted all their time. But by morning on the second full day he was lounging in the lobby in a pair of gym shorts, his feet on the edge of the couch as he flipped through an old *National Geographic*. She sat alone at the card table under the window, watching pillars of dust skate across the expanse of the Mojave below. In time she thought of them as ghosts made visible by the air's particulates, and in the evening, when the wind died down and the heat had abated, she walked alone in the empty field behind the hotel. The desert was full of garbage, she'd noticed a few days ago, but garbage so old it seemed like treasure. Rusted cans that must have fed cowboys a century before. Machinery she imagined was long obsolete. And shell after shell of something exploded—land mines, grenades, bullets. For the first time since Kansas she asked herself if this was why she had come. Her hand found its way into her purse, where the gun's grip felt like something she knew, something that gave comfort. But she knew the tangled mess of her life had been picked up, once more, and bent into some other shape. It would take time, as always, to study it like you'd study a gliding cloud, to find something in its abstraction that looked, to you, like a thing you could name.

She'd thought it would be picturesque—they'd roll into LA and see it all, right there: the buildings downtown nestled right up against the great white letters of Hollywood, and from there you'd only have to squint to see the beach. Instead, Los Angeles was like a tide that overtook you, a little at a time. "This is the LA area," Colin said as they passed a ranch here, a sewage plant there. They hit traffic on the other side of a small canyon. The hills were quilted in gardens whose caretakers could afford varying levels of water bills, their squares of growth overrun with profanely pink flowers, palms, and pines that grew next to cacti. After that, the freeway trickled through a colony of stockyards where the smell of ammoniac shit made her realize that nothing could be more beautiful than the Mojave Valley at dawn, like a bowl filling with light. As they inched through exurban traffic she felt the wealthiest homes before she saw them, the change in moisture pin-prickling her skin. Colin was looking left and right, as if the city they knew from movies were hiding just behind that curtain of smog.

They had a late lunch in Pasadena, and the sky was purpling when they arrived in what they later learned was the LA Basin. Diane paid far more than she should have for a motel a few blocks south of Hollywood Boulevard. "We're close to the action," she said as they lugged their suitcases upstairs. "You know, *Action!*" Colin wasn't listening. He kept looking over the railing, down to the parking lot.

"Everything's outside," he said. He pointed to the vending and the ice machines, tucked in a cubby beneath the stairs on the other side of the building.

"Well, yeah. It gets . . . what, sixty here? At worst?" She unlocked the room. "Tell me where we are," she said as she hurled her bags onto the bed. "Show me on the map. Show me *me*." Colin was halfway through the bathroom door and gave her a pained look, like he couldn't decide which was more urgent. "In a minute," she said, and waved him away. "Perfect time for a smoke anyway."

It was hard, standing on the balcony, not to imagine she was on camera. She knew the city did this to people. You couldn't avoid it, especially in the evening when the lights overtook the sky. The traffic inched along between the stoplights and made her think of blood, pulled a little at a time through the heart's valves and chambers. She held her cigarette more elegantly here. She rested her weight on the railing as though deep in thought. This was how things started, she told herself. This was the moment at which something was supposed to happen. A couple on the first floor was arguing in Spanish and the only word she recognized was *comer*. Someone's TV's light show at the far end of the balcony made the night seem as if it had already ended and she asked herself who was inside. A man here alone on business, or maybe exiled by his wife—or a pair of high schoolers pretending to be adults. She took a long drag and closed her eyes as it filled her. Sometimes she pictured the little pockets in her lungs the doctor had called *sacs*. She tried to feel them individually, exhaling inside of her. When she opened her eyes the TV was off and a maid exited the room with a bundle of sheets. The downstairs argument had fallen to a mutter, and Diane was no longer sure if *comer* meant *to eat* or *to take*, and if "to take," in Mexico, meant something like *fuck*. "Christ, you're pathetic," she whispered. She stubbed her cigarette on the railing and flicked it into a pot of magnolias.

For those first two days they behaved like tourists. They took a bus tour of Hollywood and Beverly Hills and snapped pictures with the disposable cameras they bought at the gift shop outside the Chinese theater. Colin wanted to see the La Brea Tar Pits and she wanted to walk along the Santa Monica Pier. Both were expensive and crowded, and they loved it. They ate dinner at a sidewalk café and ignored the smell of exhaust from passing cars. Early the next morning they walked up and down Hollywood Boulevard, photographing the names of movie stars they recognized and complaining about the ones they couldn't find. A man walked by who could've been George Clooney but nobody seemed to care, so she decided he wasn't. "I'm sure he's taller anyway," she said.

In the shower, late that afternoon, she began to hate the city again. It had won her over with a simple glance at the evening sky, but she wasn't that kind of person. She wasn't someone who peeked through celebrities' gates. Instead, in the morning, she would pretend she lived there. She wanted to wake up and act as though this was her neighborhood, and that her motel was a tucked-away townhouse with a dense little garden in the middle of a courtyard. Just as she'd lain awake at the Hotel Nipton—her window cracked so she could hear the coyotes and decide whether or not she'd ever find them comforting—she would find some-place with good coffee, a sunny booth, and terrible doughnuts. She would pretend the barista was someone who knew her name, who asked questions about her week or the weather. As she toweled off she muttered to herself the things she might say, one day far off, when this was her real life.

When she opened the bathroom door she heard the bed creak and the sheets rustle together. Something fell from the nightstand onto the carpet. She waited a few seconds so she wouldn't embar-rass him. At home this was easier to ignore: he had his own room, they each had a schedule. Traveling had made her uncomfortably aware of how much he'd grown up, not to mention his gross little habits. More than once, walking barefoot through the room, she'd stepped on a shard of toenail, torn from his foot with his teeth. He left streaks in the toilet bowl. Whenever he tossed a tissue or a candy wrapper at the trash can he missed. The faucet in the bath-room was sticky with soap residue. *And if you leave him alone for more than five minutes*, she thought, and shook her head. *Don't think about it.* When the other room was quiet she walked in and found him there, the remote in his lap and a look of fake boredom on his face. "All clean," he said, his skin flushing red. It was hard not to tease him or shudder in horror, but she smiled nonetheless, like he was still her little boy. His hands were shaking as he gathered up his clothes and she thanked God she would never have to face being fourteen again.

As he stepped into the shower, Colin tried to believe his mother was still her usual kind of crazy, simply overwhelmed by all these new places. But whenever they sat down for lunch or stopped to rest on a bench she talked about leaving home for good. First it was Santa Fe—how the "crisp mountain air" was good for her. Now, in LA, she promised that their lives would change, that there was so much more *opportunity* in a place like this.

"Think of how different it would be for you," she'd said that afternoon. "How much easier."

Easier how? he wanted to know, and she changed the subject.

He resolved to act more like a boy, after that. He refused to point at things that astonished him, like the store that sold nothing but wigs, or the white-as-a-sheet woman whose fur coat, on that ninety-degree day, could have been cut from the dragon in *NeverEnding Story*. Instead he sulked like she'd ruined the trip. When they saw a gay couple in purple shorts and flip-flops he nudged her and pointed out *those two fags*. "Colin!" she said, as though it was a swear word. For the first time since they'd left home he felt ashamed enough to want to die.

That she thought someplace like this would be good for him— for a little cocksucking sissy, was how she meant it—made him want to leave. He thought of living his life here, of going to schools where they stressed what they called tolerance, where the teachers warned them how *you love who you love*. It made his eyes burn. Somehow she'd figured him out and now she wanted to move away from everything they knew, too ashamed to let anyone see her son grow up all wrong. *He was my last hope*, he imagined her telling Shannon over coffee. *Colin would graduate, go to college, marry Chelsea, have babies. Where'd I go wrong, Shan? Dead husband, dropout daughter, both boys total dead ends.* Colin was grinding his teeth in the shower. *Don't ever have kids*, his mother would tell Shannon. The water was starting to cool and his skin felt wrapped in wet leather. As he dried off and styled his hair he tested various lies, new ways to convince her he wasn't ruined, that he could grow up how she wanted. At every conversation with the mother in his head he grew angrier. When he stepped into the room she was on the balcony, ashing into the parking lot. He slammed the hotel door and shouted how it was too cold, how she didn't care about him, how she only thought of herself, and when she didn't knock right away he sat fuming on his bed until, unable to stand it any longer, he wrenched open the door and heaved a bottle of shampoo over the railing. He stood trembling in the doorway, nothing left to say.

It was over when she pulled his head against her shoulder. "I'm sorry," he whispered, and he wished, as she led him back inside, that he was still small enough to be carried.

It was a little after six when Diane left the motel. As the morning pierced the room's dark funk of sleep, she told Colin, who rolled over with a groan, that she'd be back by noon. On her way downstairs she smiled at everything a person could accomplish, or even enjoy, in an entire morning. The sun had been up a half hour and she could believe she knew her way around and had lived there for years. There was a dry cleaner's on the corner and she took note, as though someday she'd drop off a coat or a comforter. Halfway down that block she saw a blue mailbox sandwiched between two palms. A little farther, a store that sold Mexican produce. In this other life, she would shop for groceries at little stores like these, green peppers here and the beef to stuff them from a nearby butcher. Here she was, walking by everything she'd ever need.

She wouldn't miss home. As she walked by a gate of flowering vines, behind which she could see Latino boys setting tables for breakfast, she knew she would never think back to Minnesota and ask herself why she left. *Except you'll never see your grandchild*, she thought, and the very word—*grandchild*—filled her with terror, as if the entire globe would fracture at any second and they'd all drift off into space.

A maid at the motel had told her about the doughnut shop. Diane was glad to see it was everything she wanted: a store on the corner, booths along one wall, huge windows hiding under blue awnings. Out front there was a plastic newspaper stand and she bought a copy of the *LA Times*. She tried to make small talk with the barista but the line was too long and she felt self-conscious. It was still early and she was surprised to find it so busy. In her booth, right up against the sunniest window, she laid the paper out in front of her. None of the headlines made sense to her, all follow-ups from stories earlier in the week—controversies she hadn't yet heard about, names of victims in unfamiliar shootings, political uproar that everyone, the article said, was already aware of. She pushed the news section away and thumbed for the arts. For a half hour she skimmed movie and play reviews, none of which made her want to spend money. It was only when she began searching again, looking for the travel section, that she realized it was Friday. Her coffee was cold and she wrinkled her face at the last gritty sip. They were expecting her at work on Monday morning.

If they left now—if they shoved everything in their suitcases and headed for the nearest highway—they might be able to make it. She'd driven overnight before, when Heather got sick on a Girl Scout trip, out in the Badlands. *Ten years ago*, she thought, and it sounded made up, as though someone had told her the folds of her brain uncoiled could circle the earth, or that whales have hearts as big as cars. There was no way she could make it home. Not as the only driver, not at this point in her life. She went to the counter and ordered another cup. The café had filled up and she was alone at her giant booth. She gathered up her paper and sat at the counter, next to an old woman who'd brought her sewing.

Why hadn't Colin told her it was Friday? This was the kind of thing that would get him worked up and anxious. Instead, he'd never seemed more relaxed. She thought of him back at Nipton, lying in the sun or playing solitaire on the porch. *Life must be so hard for him*, she thought, and the fact that her son too was suffering made her want to sever every tie to their old life. The thought of going home, dropping their bags in the foyer, turning on all the lights, cranking up the air-conditioning, and trying to pick up where they left off made her chest feel crushed. Having to live— for many years to come—above that room full of his notebooks, his bullets, and the leftover electricity of the incurable hatred he'd felt for his family, seemed worse than pitching tents in the desert and letting it all go to bill collectors, neighbors, and whoever else wandered into the abandoned house where that man, they'd heard, had shot himself in the head. Where that woman, they'd heard, went crazy and ran off to live in the wild. She pictured her house full of birds and squirrels, the walls varicose with veins of moss and mold. "You have no idea," she whispered out loud, and coughed like it hadn't happened.

"No, I don't," said the old woman. Diane pretended not to hear and read about new rocks on Mars that indicated running water. It was one of those stories Alan would've collected and transcribed, no date or source in the margin. Just a story to blend in with the others, real or made up. *Last night I watched my wife sleep*, she thought, and wanted to cry at the cruelty of knowing she'd never know. Had he or hadn't he? What was left of him, falling apart in the ground, that she could beat her fists against? On what could she inflict pain? How much of her future had he imagined? How far ahead had he looked to see if she'd make it?

Would she make it?

She didn't want to know. She shut off all of that, the world deep inside her. Here she was, in a room with other people. Turning pages, phones clicking and beeping, coffee gurgling in its percolator, waxed paper crinkling beneath the wet slap of falling-apart doughnuts. This was real and she forced herself to pay attention. She tried to have her morning.

In life, she rarely met anyone. The man who asked for the sports section was attractive but she tried to ignore it. *I'm trying to live here*, she thought. "This paper's mine, actually." She winced at her words. "I mean I bought it. But I'm definitely"—she thumbed through the sections again—"I definitely won't be reading sports.

It's all yours." She smiled as she handed it over. Long ago, she lost whatever ability she once had to talk to men, to charm them on the spot. He took a small table near the window and popped the lid off his cup. He'd ordered one of those foamy drinks, and—after his first sip—licked his lips in a way that, she convinced herself, would one day irritate her.

Every year, in the Peruvian Andes, locals gather in the small, steep-sloped mountain town of Coyllurqui to celebrate the Blood Festival. The living symbol of tying a wild condor to a furious, full-grown bull could date back centuries, long before the Spanish genocide, but is more likely an expression of resistance against colonial rule: the sacred Andean condor left with no choice but to peck to death the Spanish bull beneath its talons. The birds are captured a month in advance and fed a diet of entrails. If victorious, they are forced to drink *chicha*—a type of beer made from corn—before they're taken to the mountainside at the edge of town and cut loose in a gesture of freedom, whether or not they're still able to fly. *That's awful*, Diane thought. But so was the urge, coming to her without warning, to cut the story from that morning's paper and transcribe it in a notebook.

It was just before eight when she went over and sat across from him. She pulled the chair closer to the table, wincing as its legs scraped against the linoleum. The *Times* was folded under her arm and when it fell to the floor, next to her chair, she made it look intentional. "It's a strange morning," she said. He hadn't put down his paper—only peered over it as she acted out her little play.

"Strange, yeah?"

"For me, yes." She cocked her head to the side and read a headline on the outside cover, something about football helmets and dementia. "Strange morning in a strange city."

"You come to collect your paper? I was almost done but if you need to go it's all yours." As he began to fold it up she put out both hands and shook her head, wrinkling her nose.

"No, no—God no. I'll never look at sports. I mean, it's not my thing. Nobody in my—I just never got into it. Too many rules."

She inched forward in her chair. "You know when you're watching something? A game on TV? None of it makes sense to me. All those guys start running around like you unpaused a movie, and then they blow a whistle and they all stop. I never know where the whistle comes from—why they stop the clock or anything." She was fidgeting, she realized, and she ran her hands through her hair and down the back of her neck before she let them come together at her throat. "It's all Greek to me."

"Greek indeed." He tapped the newspaper, a photo of a baseball player squinting up at the sun. "It's just something we did, in my family. Dad put us all through sports—even the girls. But to me it's just . . ." His eyes went white as he looked out the window. The sun was everywhere and had bleached the sidewalk into the street, the street into the storefronts on the other side. "Just for comfort. Something I might watch or read about to empty my head. Like how some people do yoga. It's like my yoga, or my meditation maybe."

Diane nodded. She wanted to make a joke but there was nothing there, nothing in her head. She blushed and looked away. "Never mind. Sorry to have bothered—"

"You *are* having a strange morning." He sipped his coffee. "But strange is good. Strange is real." There was another faint line of foam on his lip and she wanted, maybe too motherly, to wipe it away. Instead she gestured to her own lip. "Strange," he went on, "in this city . . . you'd be surprised how hard 'strange' is to come by. Even the weirdest people"—he nodded out the window—"they just do it for attention. To get noticed."

"You have a little—some—" She touched her lip again. "A mustache."

He licked it away and wiped his hand over his mouth. "Thanks," he said. That he blushed made her feel like she was getting somewhere. "To be honest, I only asked for the sports section when I saw you wrapped up in A&E. Thought I'd give you a chance to finish up with it. If you want to know the truth . . ." His skin was still dappled with little flushes of red. He wasn't a young man. This wasn't Daniel Cartwright from Accounting. He had to be half-way through his forties, she realized, maybe fifty, and could still smile with reserve. He was searching for the right word, which she could tell meant a lot to him.

"The truth," she said. "Always. I love the truth."

"If you want to know the truth, I had plans. I was going to let you finish reading, but not finish your coffee. I was going to get up when you were near the bottom of your cup—you can tell by how people hold it when they sip. I was going to ask for the arts section. In the nicest way." He buried his smile in his coffee cup, where again he came away with that stupid foam mustache she'd already fallen in love with—that made the blood in her veins bubble like soda from a just-opened bottle. This wasn't at all what she had in mind when she got out of bed, and for the first time in years she was grateful for the stupid, desperate voice deep inside her.

They talked about art after that, or at least he did. She said she was only visiting and he pretended not to have known, not to have recognized her accent. He began to learn her story: divorced, two kids, looking to move somewhere more . . . more . . . "Cultured," he offered, and she smiled. "If it's culture you want," he said, "we'll start today," and by ten o'clock they'd whittled a list of six museums down to three, all along Wilshire Boulevard. She was in town for another week, she explained. There was nothing she could miss.

"It's a way for us to see the consequences of our actions on paper," the boisterous one explains to the kid with the backpack. This after their introductions, their stroll—they call it—down memory lane. The coffee shop is emptier now but they've lowered their voices. It's hard to hear anyone but the one man who wants to be heard. "Sorry"—he shakes his head—"the *potential* consequences. If you choose to give in to the voice in your head. Anyway, my disaster scenario begins with a phone call." He reads aloud from his future—a possible future. *Disaster scenario*: a way to calculate, from whatever *if* you're afraid of, the hell that will unravel.

For years I went back to that library, Colin's father had written. I haven't seen them since, he'd written. Colin set the notebook aside and exchanged it for the other one, the secret one he'd hidden in his luggage, and savored the details of his father's possible hell.

He'd woken from one of those dreams that can't be undreamt. At his new high school, tucked away in a mansion-covered hill, nothing was difficult. It was a special kind of school where there were pairs of boys and pairs of girls, but no pairs of both, and from the way the pairs took care of each other—picking sweater lint from each other's shoulders, parting one another's hair—Colin knew this was a sanctuary, a place where you could meet your boyfriend after class and kiss—lightly, chastely—next to your locker. Everyone would tell you things like *You guys look so cute together* and *I can see it's really love.* For a few seconds after he woke it was still real. He was still going there after a shower and his usual bowl of cereal. When the motel came back to him—and with it their drive across the country and the things they'd left behind—he couldn't do anything but lie there and wonder which, of all the ways, was best to die. Everything he'd learned in life told him he would never be happy. Through the cheap glass in the window he could hear traffic, kids screaming at a nearby playground, people chatting on the street. Lifelong misery was certain; wasn't it smart to end it now? He spent a long time crying before he got out of bed. But then, the motel room and the world in which it existed seemed changed. As he searched for clean clothes, killing himself was no longer the first thing on his mind. In fact, as he paced from the window to the television, he changed his mind about everything. At first it felt like a great loss, his future family—wife and children—ripped out of him, the house he was supposed to one day own crumbling into rubble. But when it dissipated, he felt welling within him something like air or light. He'd shed weight. He'd cut out a part of his body that never belonged, a vestigial organ infected and sick. He considered running away, then and there. Instead, he decided on a trial run: if it went wrong, he could go back to the way things were. If he pulled it off, he could live on his own. In the shower, he promised himself out loud that he was "washing away the past," as if someone might record it and hold him accountable.

Only a block from the hotel he bought two sodas from an outdoor vending machine and drank them both. By the time he set foot on Hollywood Boulevard he was thirsty again. Under an awning outside of a store called Star Glass he searched his pockets for more change. He recognized, nestled in the window display, pipes like the one Heather had used, back in some other lifetime. It hadn't even been two years, but he no longer recognized that stupid kid who swallowed every word of his sister's bullshit. Even if it hurt to think of Heather, the image of her soft and pregnant and kind—actually, sincerely kind—like a wound. Before he could figure out what to feel, a man with a beard down to his chest came out of the store and shooed him away.

Hollywood hadn't been like this two days ago. Now, whenever he glanced into a store, the owners told him to keep moving, to "come back when you're old enough." Stores full of tangles of lace people called underwear, others that sold nothing but bladed weapons. Nobody would let him inside. There were stars on the sidewalk and they had names like "Richard Gere" and "Meryl Streep," but it wasn't the Hollywood they wanted you to believe in. Twitchy women asked him for money. Sunburnt homeless men slept on bus stop benches. Colin could feel his heart climbing, as though he might puke. He'd never seen anything like this and he wondered if it was always there—if his mother, standing next to him, created some force field that covered it up, that made it safe. For the first time he felt that if he giggled at someone's pain he'd get punched or thrown against a wall. If he told a woman she was pretty she might slap him instead of smile. He had climbed down into the pit with the rest of the world.

By one o'clock he was convinced his plan had failed; there wasn't a world to join. Then, from one block to another, the street changed. The shops still hid themselves under black awnings, and they still had names bent out of neon, but the clothes people wore were brighter, and the people wearing them, even the people in high heels and miniskirts, were men. He walked by store windows lined with magazines wrapped in plastic, with swimsuits smaller than the briefs he was wearing, and with boots as high as his thighs. Here, everyone smiled at him, nodded hello, called him Sweetie and Darling. He wished, right then, that he'd already left his old life behind. He wanted to be carrying everything he owned and he wanted one of these men to take him in. *You can work upstairs*, he imagined him saying, and he pictured himself at some giant desk where he kept track of papers and files. Running away could fix everything. A life of long bus rides and adventures, of getting work wherever you could, of falling in love with boys like Andy without Andy's cruelty. *You'll get kidnapped*, he thought—this from some part of his brain his mother had put there. He conjured his favorite stories and pictured himself sold into slavery, kept as someone's pet. The breeze felt suddenly cool and he realized he'd begun to sweat. He backed into the shade. The store behind him didn't have a name—only a symbol on the door. *The male store*, he thought, and peered through the glass. Squinting through the glare he could see, along the wall, things his blood reached for, things that took the certainty out of his legs, and when a young man—early twenties, maybe, wearing a vest but no shirt—opened up the door and gave him that you-shouldn't-be-here look, Colin shuffled off, almost at a run.

In another block the neighborhood ended. Rather than walk through Beverly Hills he turned around. Before long he was back at that same store with the dark windows. The sun's angle had changed just enough for him to see the straps and restraints and locks inside. At the end of that block he could've kept going but turned back once more. The way he drifted made him feel depraved, but he liked it. On his fourth pass, the young man from before popped his head outside. "For your sanity and mine," he said, "you should probably just come inside."

The store was brighter than you'd think—the glass so tinted it looked like a nightclub from outside. He stood just inside the door, his eyes fixed on all the ways men could be tied up, locked together, pinned down, held apart, and—he saw shyly—plugged up.

"You look young," the man was saying, "so I didn't want you hanging around, drawing attention. I know you're eighteen and all, but it's better people don't ask, you know?" He was standing behind the counter, a binder full of CDs or movies laid out in front of him.

Colin looked at the floor. "I'm actually—I mean I'm not—"

"Because we're not supposed to allow minors in the store. So it's good that you're eighteen years old. Otherwise you'd have to leave. Right away."

Colin nodded. He slipped his hands into his pockets and came toward the counter, where the merchandise was graphically visible. Rings and bands and leather. Shiny, cold steel. There was almost nothing he could identify. He felt made of stone. The binder was full of burned DVDs, titles scrawled in black marker. "Porn," he whispered.

"We start in the afternoon." The man flipped the pages as though he'd never been more bored. "Just to get sales moving after lunch?" He plucked a disc from its sleeve and bent beneath the counter. The man wore some kind of jock under his jeans, but with a chain instead of a strap. A small moan fell out of Colin's mouth and he stretched his jaw to pretend he'd been yawning. A flatscreen he hadn't noticed, mounted in the corner, flickered to life. After several antipiracy warnings there was nothing he could see, in the entire world, except those young, young men as they undid each other's jeans without even speaking, without needing to.

"You look like you need to sit down."

"I'm okay," Colin said. He turned away from the television and looked down at the counter, trying to make sense of all those devices. It only filled him with more heat, more violence. He closed his eyes and counted to ten, twenty, now thirty.

The man behind the counter laughed—nothing cruel or pleasurable, just an honest laugh. "Maybe you shouldn't be here," he said. "Maybe I misjudged you."

"No." Colin shook his head. "No no, it's fine. It's—it's a hot day and stuff. Like I can't concentrate or whatever." He looked around the room as though nothing impressed him. "Oh, you have handcuffs," he said, crossing to a center display. *Stupid*, he thought, but he kept up the act. "The last place didn't have them."

"Where were you before?"

"Down the street?" Colin waved toward the window. The men onscreen were swallowing as much of each other as they could. "Just some place. It wasn't as cool as this one." He took up the handcuffs and pretended to read the back, instead transfixed on the young model in the photo, gagged with his hands behind his back. They'd tried to make him look worried, like a prisoner, but it just looked like he had to fart. Colin bit his lip as he threatened to smile, thinking of this guy letting one rip in the porn studio. He put the cuffs back and kept looking. There was so much he didn't know—why you'd want to stretch your balls or let someone put alligator clamps on your chest. The expensive stuff, under the counter, was even more baffling.

"Those are sounding rods. You slip them into your urethra after you're fully hard."

"Urethra," Colin said. He recognized the word, then its meaning. "What the fuck?"

"You're probably more into blindfolds and hot wax, huh? The Disney stuff?"

Colin shook his head. He'd moved on to something else—a series of rings with a hole for a lock. This he recognized, a unique type of cage. "I'm into it all," he said, his voice choosing this moment of all moments to crack and poison his cheeks with a blush. "I'm into everything."

"Absolutely everything." The man scanned the case as if he were looking for the most dangerous, terrifying thing they sold, and Colin could feel himself waiting for it. Instead the man shook his head. "Kid, how old are you?"

"I'm eighteen." He pointed to a door at the far end of the shop. "What's in the other room?"

"Just employee stuff. Fridge, office, WC, all that."

"WC?"

"Bathroom. Not for customers."

Colin glanced at the young men onscreen, now rocking against each other. He realized what most of their customers would do in that bathroom—himself included.

The man came around the counter and Colin saw he wasn't wearing shoes or socks. "You really should get a move on." He placed his hands on Colin's shoulders and spun him toward the door. "You have no idea what kind of trouble I could get in for this."

"For touching me too." Colin grinned up at him, but when the man let go he wished the word *touch* had rolled off his tongue like it meant *fuck* or *fondle*. He gave the man his best pout. "I'm gonna come back. What's your name?"

"You're not coming back. And my name's Arlene for all you care. Hey, I'm sorry to be so rude or whatever but it was dumb to begin with, letting you in here. You know, thinking with the wrong head and all that."

Colin turned around. He'd planned nothing, but plans can happen by themselves. His mouth felt stuffed with paper towels as he put his arms around this man whose name he didn't know, in this city where he didn't live. "Don't," he said, the word coming out like the creak of a door's hinge. He wasn't sure what it meant. *Don't send me away, don't let me do this, don't tell my mother, don't show me any mercy.* The man was stunned into paralysis. It was only after Colin placed his lips on his and tried to push his tongue into his mouth that he broke away and shoved him toward the door. It was one of those times his body played every note, as if someone had suffered a heart attack at its piano and collapsed on the keys. He giggled as his eyes filled with tears and his hands pulled themselves into fists. The man let him cry and lash out and laugh into his shoulder until he could function, once more, like a human being. Then he told him to leave.

"For real. Please don't come back."

Colin looked out the window where the street was dark and tinged a sick, haunted house green. "Fine," he said, and gave the name, intersection, address, phone number, and room number of the place where—for several more days, he hoped—he was sleeping. As he walked back down Hollywood Boulevard he was glad he hadn't told his mother, the night before, that they should turn back. *It's too late now*, she'd say with a sigh. *We might as well stay another week.* By now it was two o'clock and the sunlight felt like the inside of a microwave, boiling the blood in his shoulders and neck. "I need a shower," he said when he burst into their room. Only after he reached the bathroom did he realize he was alone. *What if she died?* he asked himself, and the fantasy of vanishing into the city to live as an orphan helped him enjoy his brief solitude. When it was over, all he could think was how he'd wished death on his mother.

For the first time in weeks it came back to him: the image of his father's burst-open skull like a squeezed fleshy fruit, oozing onto their basement floor, demon-winged from his dreams and colorless as he drifted over plains of ice—and all because Colin put bullets in what was until then an innocuous thing, a hunk of steel, a little gadget that made clicking noises. That he wanted his mother out of his life made him think he knew what would happen after he loaded that gun. Was there a half second, a tiny flash of knowing, during which his father understood? Did the explanation—*Colin!*—boom out over the gunshot? Was his name the last word that passed through his father's head, the name that tore his brain apart? Did he know?

He was in the bathroom throwing up when his mother walked into the room singing. She accused him of not feeling well. "We'll have to stay a few more days. You need lots of rest. Here at the motel." She tended to him—a rag on the forehead, a glass of water when he asked for it. "My boy," she said, and it sliced him into pieces. He flipped over and hid his face in the pillow while she rubbed the tension out of his shoulders. "You're so stressed out," she said, as though his hair was too shaggy or his nails all bitten down. As if he were a thing that'd stopped working. "I had the best day," she said as she kneaded ropes of muscle out from under his shoulder blades. The way she almost sang it felt like she'd extinguished a cigarette on his spine. He clenched his teeth as she talked about her stupid coffee shop, as she told him how much life there was left in her, as though it was his fault she'd forgotten it.

The first voicemail came at seven thirty on Monday morning. She was in that same coffee shop with Liam when she felt the vibration in her pocket. *Fuck*, she mouthed as she recognized the number. Liam didn't notice, making his case for *real pastries*. "The doughnut's a perversion," he was saying, resting his chin on his palm as he looked down at her plate. "Set it next to a Parisian beignet and you wouldn't believe it was food." He chuckled and went back to reading the paper. *Like a married couple*, she thought, and tried to expunge it. *This is what vacation does. This is all fantasy.* She pocketed her phone. Sometime around ten, when it was noon in Minneapolis, she would call her boss. There had to be a way, in those next two and a half hours, to come up with something plausible.

Her phone vibrated again only a half hour later, this time from her mother. At eight fifteen Shannon called but didn't leave a message. She called again at eight twenty-two and Diane shut off her phone. They ordered their refills to go. Museums were closed on Mondays, Liam explained—they'd have to find another way to pass the time. "I'm sure we can think of a few things," she said, and the tension between them felt sharp in her back. In love, Diane had always been fast—she preferred this word—and she couldn't think of any man she'd met with whom she hadn't made love on the second date or sooner. "How far a walk is the beach?" she asked as they stepped outside.

"I knew you'd ask that. It would be nice to walk, yeah? Sadly, it's more than twelve miles." He pointed over his shoulder, off into the haze. "Nobody ever walks here. It's sad. Terrible even. But everything is so far apart. It's not like New York or San Francisco. Or even Minneapolis, from what it sounds like."

"The tundra," she said. It was hard to think back that far, to conjure the numbness in her fingers as she stood holding a cigarette on the dock outside the plant. "You go outside and the weather tries to kill you. Murderapolis—they used to call it that back when everybody was getting shot. I pretended it was just about the cold. My finger fell off, you could tell someone. I barely escaped Murderapolis. It's a fucking joke." She plucked a cigarette from a fresh pack and sucked in a chestful of smoke that tasted, still, like funerals and long nights without sleep or sound. She thought of the voicemails waiting for her, all those people who expressed, now, such concern, but weren't to be found when all she had was snow under the streetlights.

There was an earthquake that morning and when they arrived at the pier they saw what it had done. She'd been asleep when it happened, looking up from her bed at the window's outline of light, just starting to purple. "Was that an earthquake?" she asked. Colin groaned *yes* from the other bed and she went back to sleep. It wasn't until she shared the morning *Times* with Liam that she thought, astonished, *I survived an earthquake.* "It wasn't even a four," Liam said. All Diane knew, in disaster terminology, was tornadoes. *Four* was a step shy of annihilation.

"It was epicentered a few miles out," Liam said, sweeping his arm over the horizon. "Epicenter is where the earth actually moved. What happens when it's in the water is the water shifts. It smacks together and makes a wave. That's what all this trash is. All the junk that washed up with the wave this morning."

There were trucks parked along the beach, people in neons bagging sodden garbage. From where they stood she could see the seaweed wrapped around the pier's wooden supports, a shredded tire, a car bumper. "Must've been pretty serious," she said, and stepped closer to the edge of the boardwalk where a wall separated the beach below. There was a line just above the lowest stones, dry now but crusted with the ocean's salt. She backed away. "Christ."

"This change your mind about the city of dreams?" Liam reached for her hand and tried to tangle her fingers into his but her palms were sweating and she shook him away. She felt the air open up next to her and she knew she'd upset him.

"Of course not," she said, still surveying the beach. "You should've seen Minneapolis after that tornado a couple years ago." She turned and found him leaning against a palm, his hands in his pockets as though any minute someone might take his picture and sell it to a magazine. "I can handle a little shake now and then, even some garbage on my beach."

"Just don't go to San Francisco." He leaned away from the tree and tried, again, to hold her hand. This time she let him. "They get all the big ones. My cousin was there in '89 when the freeway collapsed. She wasn't on it, thank God. Talk about a mess, yeah? More than some garbage on *your* beach. More than a few dead birds."

She glanced out at the water. She hadn't noticed any birds, but right then someone hoisted a tangle of seaweed. Before he stuffed it into his bag she saw the grey webbed foot. It could've been a lily pad, if Liam hadn't said anything. "We almost went to San Francisco instead."

"Yeah?"

"That was the plan. Then I got in the car and it wasn't the plan anymore." She turned to him, the beach at her back. "I was there when I was younger and I'd never been here, not even passing through. Something new, I guess, is what I wanted. So here I am." She smiled as if it were some great moment, but everything sounded like a bad script. She was aware of how hard she was trying to believe it was love.

Liam, back up against the palm tree, gave her a cockeyed grin. Over his shoulder she saw a girl waiting for the bus. The way she checked her phone looked straight out of a commercial. Everyone looked like a movie star, Diane realized, and she pushed back her shoulders. She'd never been gorgeous or even all that charming, but in a place like this you couldn't stop yourself from playing along.

He rented a room not far from the beach and afterward they

ate a long lunch—four courses plus a cup of coffee. Even when she reminded herself of things like endorphins and hormones and the body's cabinet of chemicals that exploded at another's touch, she swore, over and over, that it was the best meal of her life. This was the best *everything* of her life. The sun would be up for several more hours but the shadows had arrived. It was the long afternoons, if nothing else, that forced you to fall in love with the palms and the flowers, the cars without a speck of rust, the entire sky an orange she'd never seen in her life. Pollution—she never fooled herself it was anything else. But was that so bad? "I hope you still have that room," she said as they sipped their coffee, and she ignored the other room, waiting for her on what felt like the other side of the solar system. Her youngest was there and in that moment he seemed infallible—the most innocent, loving boy in the entire world. But not a boy you couldn't ignore, just a little longer.

Right away, Allie told Colin the rules. They could never kiss or even touch—he wasn't going to jail. He could never give him porn or merchandise, not even if he paid for it; Colin had to steal it or find it. And their clothes would stay on. All this after he'd picked him up at the motel, that first day. "Think of me like a guardian," Allie explained, and Colin thought of all the filthy stories involving teachers, Scout leaders, football coaches, family friends, pastors. As they lay on the garbage-covered beach he invented a world where Allie was some old friend of his father's, here to take care of them. He'd already convinced him to break one rule when he handed over the sunscreen and pointed to his back. From then on, he decided, it was all patience. He couldn't believe that only three weeks ago he'd cowered in his house as an older man—not much older than the one next to him—sat waiting in his car across the street. Victor was just someone with too much sadness—a bumbling, unsteady creature for whom everything seemed both too much and not enough. Colin no longer understood why he'd been so afraid. The world wasn't a monster that wanted revenge. His father wasn't a soul traveling through hell, trapped there because of his son. Hell wasn't waiting for him. It was just a thing inside you, and knowing this undid it. In his heart, hell's flames hissed and pinched themselves into pillars of steam, washed out by everything he'd learned. He'd grown up, he decided. All he'd needed was a friend.

Even so, there were leftovers: his silence whenever a black Toyota passed by, his weightlessness whenever he heard what could've been Victor's laugh.

When Colin woke up on Saturday morning he was planning to return to the shop on Hollywood Boulevard. His mother had left instructions—drink ten glasses of water, eat three oranges, stay in bed for four of the eight hours she would be gone, call if he needed anything—and he checked them off as he ate mouthfuls of day-old doughnuts from the office downstairs. The oranges he dumped into the trash and covered with tissues and torn-up paper. He'd just stepped out of the shower when he heard a soft knock that didn't belong, he knew, to housekeeping. The man from the sex shop blushed, and even though Colin, wrapped only in a towel, begged him to come into the room, he refused. "Not until you're 100 percent dressed," he said, and turned to look over the railing. Colin changed with the door open, right there for all the world to see, but the man never peeked. By the time he pulled on his shirt he'd gathered enough sweat for another shower.

His name—as Colin learned over breakfast—was short for Alyosha, which was somehow short for Alexey. "It's not like I understand it either," Allie said as he watched Colin eat a stack of pancakes. For himself he'd only ordered coffee and a fried egg, and every time Colin gestured at the plate in front of him he shook his head. "I'm not gonna go overboard and get fat while I'm at it." It took Colin a moment to realize that he himself was a vice, a thing Allie knew he shouldn't have. This he liked and it felt wrong to like it, which he also liked.

When the waitress came to pour more coffee, Colin leaned

over the table. "So am I your youngest boyfriend?" His heels were off the floor and knocking together. The salt and pepper shakers, the glass bottles of ketchup and mustard and Tabasco, the mug full of extra forks and knives—all of it was rattling. Allie ignored him and looked up at the waitress.

"We'll need the check, thanks."

After she'd gone, Allie leaned away from him. He looked out the window as he spoke. "We're gonna have to set down some rules. If this is going to work anyway." At that time, Colin had no idea what *this* was—only that it was the closest thing to what he'd most wanted for what seemed like his entire life. While they waited for the check, Colin did everything he could to caress Allie's hands, find his foot under the table, run his fingers on the soft spots of his wrists. "Definitely we can't touch each other," Allie said. How were you supposed to have sex, Colin wondered, without touching?

That first day, they spent most of their time going to coffee shops, daytime bars, and stores along Hollywood or Sunset. Allie bought Colin new clothes. "These should actually fit," he said, going two sizes smaller than what Colin had always told his mother to buy. For the rest of the day he noticed people looking at him. At first he felt self-conscious but after an hour he realized that, whenever he met someone's gaze, it was the other person who looked away. That morning, after his mother left and before Allie came to take him to the beach, he'd watched himself in the mirror. For years he'd thought his skin was permanently white, as though he was shrink-wrapped in a film that sloughed off all color, unless he burned. Since they arrived in LA he'd been outside every day on unshaded streets. He'd been to the beach twice and he hoped, now, that people wouldn't look at him like something washed up from the ocean's forgotten, lightless depths. His hair had paled to a younger color. All that was left of the pimples on his chin and forehead were the little white scars from too much scratching. When they arrived at the beach, he insisted they sit near the retaining wall, not only because of all the garbage but because, from there, you could see all the people who might turn to look at you. He'd never felt so important.

"You're a vain little fucker, you know that?"

"I'm gonna do everything I can to get my mom to move here," he said. For two days now he'd cultivated his alternate life— that school against the hillside. Now that he'd fleshed it out and peopled it with friends, he could believe in it. "But even if she won't, I think I'm gonna stay." Sweat was trickling into the well between his ribs.

Next to him, he could feel Allie thinking. "It *is* a nice city."

Colin shrugged and sat up, his towel unpeeling itself from his back. He bent his knees up against his chest and hugged them, scanning the beach for anyone who might smile at him. "Can we get Chinese?" he asked. He didn't want Allie's dumb lecture about what was best for him, how he should stay with his family and all that. *What family?* he wanted to say. It was starting to seem like a failing business, a lost cause, everyone jumping ship while they could: his father, his sister, his brother even though it wasn't his fault. Colin didn't want to be the only one left.

"Chinese Chinese or California Chinese?"

"Chinese. Just feed me. And a place without dog or cat or whatever on the menu."

"They don't actually eat dog."

"I read about it online." He rolled over and looked up at the retaining wall. The watermark was right at eye level, beneath which the ocean had left a few treasures: tiny seashells, knots of seaweed like cooked spinach, cigarette butts, and a new sheen that, as the sun moved west, splintered into rainbows. It was hard to call things like the ocean beautiful when it harbored this garbage and scum, this oily life. "And a shower," he said. "Maybe we could stop by the motel?"

Allie flicked sand off his towel with a tiny key-shaped bolt of driftwood. "I was planning to take you back there anyway. There's some stuff I need to do later on. But don't let me forget we have to make a detour, up to Encino." He reached into his pocket and glanced at his phone. "In fact we gotta leave now." He sat up and wrenched the towel off the ground. Colin saw something black vanish into the dimpled sand and he wondered what was underneath them, all along this beach—what was crawling and tunneling. He gathered his things, checked his shoes and clothes for spiders. "I should keep you around," Allie was saying. "Without you I'd have forgot all about Stanley. You should be my secretary or something. And not like that," he added, before Colin's eyes even had a chance to light up.

If you watched TV or loved movies, LA felt like a place you'd already been. More than anything you recognized street signs, and on the drive to Stanley's, Colin saw Olympic, Wilshire, Sunset, Mulholland, Ventura. The actors from whom he'd learned those names were giving directions in his head. His mother, driving through Hollywood, had made fun of people lining up to buy "maps to the stars." But once in a while he caught himself staring out the window or standing on his motel balcony trying to spot someone, just so he'd have a story when he went home. *If we go home.*

In Allie's sedan he tried to belong. He leaned back in the seat and put his bare feet on the dash. Even his toes had lost their normal pallor.

If she wouldn't let him stay, he'd leave her at the motel. It wouldn't take much—a new haircut and color, different clothes—and with his darker skin she wouldn't find him. That she'd sit at their kitchen table back home, months after giving up on her search, smoking her cigarettes with Shannon, with coffee—that she'd sit wondering what happened, how he'd done this—made Colin's head light and his heart stand out against everything else inside him. *He was always a good boy,* she'd tell Shannon. *Never in a million years did I think he'd go and do this. He was always too scared, too shy. I never thought he had the guts.* Allie's car was winding through a canyon, its hills and slopes parched from no rain, and Colin let out a long whoop through the open window as though he was already on his own. Allie frowned and said something the freeway's roar swallowed up.

Stanley's house wasn't a mansion but it tried to be one, its lawn laid out like someone's idea of a palace, the columns on the front steps wrapped in grapevines. When Allie pulled into the driveway he turned to Colin. "Stanley's my guy," he said. "Just so you know." He killed the ignition and got out of the car. Colin felt like someone had taken a scoop out of him, and he wasn't sure, when Allie walked him through the stained glass doors, whether or not he'd start bawling. *You mean nothing to me*, he imagined Allie saying as he and this Stanley caressed each other, loved each other.

But Stanley didn't act like the other men Allie had introduced him to. He wore slacks and a suit coat with a pink T-shirt underneath. There was a glass of ice in his hand he couldn't seem to set down. And he was old—too old to be someone's boyfriend. Colin sat on the couch and tried to look bored but the room was too beautiful, like a movie star's or a football player's. All along one wall were pictures of the same woman, over and over. Then he realized that *guy* just meant drug dealer. "My wife's a doll," he said when he caught Colin looking at the pictures. "Even *you* can appreciate that," he added, and winked when Colin scowled at him.

The plan had been to leave right away and get Chinese in the Valley but Allie wouldn't get up from the couch. He sat with his arms behind his head and watched Stanley pinch and crumble leaves into the glass pipe they'd decided to share. Colin shook his head when Stanley held it out for him. In an alternate universe, a not-pregnant Heather might be somewhere in Chicago, Milwaukee, Denver—anywhere—doing this exact thing. Outside, the shadows were longer. Stanley's pool, reaching through the hedges, was a white sheet of light. "Where's your bathroom?" Colin said. They were giggling about something, the noises coming out of them nothing but clicks and whimpers. He sighed and made off down the hallway.

The bathroom was lined with pictures of naked women, but not like women in magazines. Instead they looked out over cityscapes and lay reading on blankets in meadows. Once, he'd tried to read *Penthouse* as though it was medicine or therapy. "Get hard," he whispered, but it only lay against his thigh like a reptile that'd just fed. When nothing worked he decided he was too nervous, too worked up, and relaxed with a story about a kidnapped boy he'd printed from one of his favorite websites. The story he knew well and didn't even have to finish. He only had to read up to the part where the man, who'd been so kind, betrayed the boy's trust. Right then he looked at the centerfold and imagined it was her who made him come. These days, he no longer tried to pretend that girls or women could do it for him. Soon, he thought, he wouldn't have to.

Colin didn't want to go back to the living room. There was more hallway to his left. Every room was designed for a single thing—one full of records with a chair in the middle, one with a pool table, one with nothing but bookshelves and couches. He paused outside the gym, a treadmill and a weight bench back-to-back, mirrors on every wall. He could see a million copies of himself standing in the doorway. Then there were a million copies of someone else, just behind him. Stanley must have had a son or a nephew, someone who could've been Stanley himself thirty years ago. "You get tired of looking at yourself eventually," he told Colin. His voice, slow on the vowels and squishy on the consonants, gave everything away. Colin smiled and leaned back against the door frame.

"I was just looking for the bathroom."

"Bathroom's down there."

"I know. I mean I used it already. I was just—heading back."

"You have an accent. Where is that? It's like . . . I know where you're from . . ."

Colin swallowed and tried to iron it out of his voice. "Minnesota."

"That's adorable. Say 'rowboat' for me."

He shook his head. His skin, he could feel, was as red as it could get.

"Come on." He put his hand on Colin's shoulder. "It sounds so cute. Just say it for me. Say rowboat." He leaned in so Colin could say it quietly, in his ear. Colin said it and felt fermented laughter on his neck. "Say 'trash bag.'" For his age—early twenties, he guessed, no older than Allie—his voice was deep and carried into the person he spoke to.

"Trash bag," Colin said, and the man leaned closer as he laughed.

He took Colin by the shoulders. "God, you're cute," he said. "How old are you? Don't answer that. I maybe drank too much." He put his thumb against Colin's lips. Every part of his body that could shake was shaking, every part that could sweat was sweating, every part that could fill with blood as full as it could get. His lips made a sound as they let this strange person's thumb into his mouth, as he flicked his tongue to show what little skill he had. "Stan will be busy for a while," he said, and hoisted Colin over his shoulder like he was nothing but a bag of leaves. "Don't say anything," he said. It was more of a plea than a threat but Colin pretended it was life or death, and while it was happening he told himself there was nothing he could do, no way to escape, no choice but to lie there and suffer and wish all suffering was this. The man's bedroom was dark and half-underground, the windows little more than slits of light near the ceiling. Colin's clothes seemed to unpeel themselves from his body, these strange hands masterful and light upon his skin. It felt like the man was inside his head as well as his body, doing everything Colin didn't know that he wanted. Whenever Colin reached for his own cock the man batted his hand away. "That's mine," he whispered in his ear, and with only the occasional stroke kept him on the verge of coming for what felt like hours as Colin begged. He'd heard it was supposed to hurt but it wasn't pain he felt at all, this man moving within him. There were parts of himself he hadn't known existed, and for the first time his climax bloomed from the inside out. His eyes filled with tears as he looked down and saw himself in spasms, not a hand anywhere near it as it jumped and pulsed like a creature electrocuted, spilling his load all over them both. The man, too, was finishing, his groans leaping up an octave as he squealed *fuck fuck fuck* in Colin's ear. Never had he felt so cherished, so worshipped as the man pulled out and licked Colin's mess from his stomach and chest, from his thighs. "You're absolutely perfect," he said, more slurred than before, and Colin buried his face in the wealth of pillows just underneath him.

When they left, an hour later, Allie's eyes were bloodshot and his words all stretched out. But he wasn't stupid. "You don't have to hide it," he said when they pulled onto the freeway.

"Hide what?"

"Your grin. The red spots on your neck." Allie reached for the radio and found the overplayed dance music they both knew by heart. "I have more than one guy," he said. "I have more than one guy in the Valley, even. There's a reason I went to Stanley's." He turned up the volume and began to sing under his breath. Colin knew he wasn't supposed to speak. Instead he looked out the window where the afternoon had ripened into evening. The shops along Ventura had mirrors for windows. The sun filled the sky behind the car. As they sat in traffic Colin began to fidget, tapping his hands on his thighs, bending back knuckles he'd cracked only minutes before. There was no way his mother wasn't back at the motel, waiting for him. Would she, too, be able to sense it? Would she know what he was and what he'd done?

"You okay?" Allie asked when they rolled up to the next light.

"I'm totally awesome."

"I know we're late," Allie said. "Try to relax, though. Think of everything we've done today. Everything you've done. It's a big day for you." He smiled and reached over, letting his hand fall on Colin's neck. Colin closed his eyes as his skin broke out in shivers. Then Allie stopped and withdrew, coughing into his fist before he returned both hands to the wheel. "It's just a few blocks more," he said, as though the car ride was intolerable and Colin was just a dumb impatient kid.

How to tell him it was okay to drive forever? They could head down to San Diego, into Mexico. Colin imagined himself smuggled under blankets, folded up into the trunk. They'd cross the border and find a hacienda somewhere south. From there he'd send postcards. To his mother: *Happy, please don't worry anymore.* To his grandfather: *Reading lots of books on the beach.* To Andy: *Glad you're not here* and *Life without you is sweet.* He pictured Andy reading it. To him, Colin might be something like a hero, someone he'd wish he had held on to, and this imagined sadness—Andy's fake remorse—reached in through Colin's ribs and strangled his heart. Sex with Stanley's son or nephew—he hadn't even learned his name—wasn't what he expected. He did it and he liked it and he knew he'd like it again, but it hadn't changed him. As they crept through traffic he faced the window, afraid of crying. He wished his love for Andy had been fucked out of him. Because he still wanted him. He wanted Allie, in the seat next to him, to be the short, bony, obnoxious boy who used to sneak liquor from the cupboard above the fridge, who won a wrestling match by grabbing your balls or jabbing you in the ribs. He wanted them to have stolen this car, two fourteen-year-olds only halfway sure how to drive it. It should be Andy staring down at him as he writhed in pleasure, caressing Colin's cheek and calling him perfect. What he wanted was for them to outrun the cops, to evade the FBI, to send little hints home to show their parents they were okay, they were happy, they were in love. What he wanted was to be happy. And he wasn't, he realized. Even now he wasn't happy. He couldn't be.

By the time they parked behind the restaurant he was crying and Allie put his arm around him. Over and over he asked what was wrong. Colin slid closer and buried his face in the weed and coconut smell of Allie's chest. If they were ever going to have sex this was the opportunity, and for a second Colin considered it— reaching for Allie's fly, pulling out his cock. He imagined himself sliding right on, his hands on Allie's shoulders as he rode him right there in the street. But there was no point. He'd done what he came here to do and it wasn't enough.

Colin used chopsticks to nudge his pot stickers back and forth, chewing while he tried to think of some way to fix his life. Outside, the sunlight had backed itself against the eastern edge of the Valley. In what was left of the day's heat it had the look of a mirage—a bowl of black water you'd pursue only to find more stucco and palms, more waste.

"You're a moody little fucker, aren't you?" Allie asked.

Colin shook his head.

"I feel like something's my fault."

"Shut up." Colin pushed his plate away and rested his chin on his hands. But the food looked too good and he kept eating. He could feel Allie watching him like you'd watch a stray, starving dog, capable of anything. As Colin shoveled more rice into his mouth he gave him the finger.

"That's not very ladylike. You won't be the belle of the balls with an attitude like that."

"Dude, shut the fuck up. I'm not—ugh, you're being stupid."

Their waiter was an old man in a velvet smock who walked with his hands clasped behind his back. "Okay?" he asked, whenever he looked at them. Allie's eyes were still bloodshot and he was wearing a grin even now. "Okay?" the old waiter asked, and Colin wondered if he was smart enough to know the sweaty, tank-topped man who nodded at him was totally out of his mind. Then he wondered if it was safe to drive around with someone so stoned. It's not like getting trashed, Heather once explained. *Being buzzed,* she'd said—*it's just like being super chill. Like, wow, that car cut me off, whatever, that's cool.* Colin tried to remember the details—what Heather was wearing, how old he was at the time, what streets they'd driven on and how much snow had accumulated or melted or left the grass green or hopelessly brown. Los Angeles was beautiful but you had to have a certain kind of love for a place where the skyline was nothing but chimneys and gables and the occasional overpass peeking through the treetops. *You'll get out someday,* Heather had said, and Colin realized she'd been planning her escape for years. He scanned the room for a window. He wanted to see the city and verify that he, too, had escaped, but everything was covered in red paper that allowed in nothing but red light.

"How's your dog?" Allie asked, and popped a wet lump of chicken in his mouth.

Colin shrugged. "It's a little *ruff*," he said, and couldn't help but laugh at his terrible joke. "Shut up," he kept telling Allie as he laughed with him. His muscles seized up and soon his plate was a blur in front of him, and Allie too, so there was no warning when he felt two hands close on his wrists, when he felt his body pulled forward, when Allie's lips touched his own and stubble scraped his cheek. Colin opened his mouth to let in anything that might want in but Allie pulled back. He took Colin's face in his hands and dried each eye with his thumbs. How were you supposed to stay alive when it was impossible to know whether or not you wanted to live?

"I'm sorry," Allie said as they walked back to the car. "That was the wrong thing to do. You just looked . . ." He had his hand in his pocket and was doing something with his keys. The sky had lost most of its orange and was now something like melted ice cream with swirls of strawberry. Colin pulled his arms into his T-shirt. On the drive back to the motel it began to get dark. The traffic on the 101 hadn't cleared and the canyon was aglow with brake lights. Colin had undone his seat belt and snuggled up to Allie. "I'm cold."

"Put your seat belt on. We'll get pulled over."

"No one can even see me." Colin shrank lower until all he saw was the blue empty sky and the black mountains all lit up, as if the stars had finally let go and fallen straight to earth. "All hidden," he said. His head was lodged between Allie's hip and his arm, right against his ribs.

"Get up, for fuck's sake."

"Why? It's nice down here."

"Colin, get up." He pulled at Colin's shirt, but not that hard.

Colin shook his head, letting his hair rub up against Allie's jeans. He slid lower until his back was almost flat on the seat. "Too comfy," he said as he opened his mouth for a fake yawn.

"Seriously. Quit fucking around."

Colin propped himself on his elbows. "What was that? Something moved."

"Nothing moved, Colin. Quit being such a fucktard and get up before someone sees you."

Nothing had moved. Allie wasn't even hard yet, Colin discovered when he undid his fly and pulled it out, but within seconds that changed. For a while he just looked at it, letting his fingers move up and down, touching all the spots that made it unique. They were all unique, Colin was learning. Allie had gone quiet and was just breathing, slowly, deeply, with a little stab of air when Colin's breath reached the part that glistened under the streetlights. Colin licked the light away. The taste he already knew and he let Allie's moans guide him.

At first he begged Colin to stop but soon he begged him not to. Colin's own was hard and bent like a ruined nail in his underwear, but he didn't let himself touch it. He wasn't allowed, he decided, until Allie said he could. His hands were trembling and all he could smell was coconut oil and sweat. Allie's hand landed in his hair and roamed down his neck, along his back, his fingers just brushing the waistband of his briefs. It was really happening. Colin moaned when Allie grazed the base of his spine, and his moan traveled back into Allie. *I'm such a slut*, he thought, and the word felt hot in his heart. He wanted Allie, moaning above him, to call him a slut, a cocksucker, the best fucktoy he'd ever had, the perfect little cockslave. All the words he'd learned from porn were like firecrackers in his head. *Your mouth is made for cock. Your tight little ass is made for fucking.* It was exhilarating to be such a thing, to take a break from being a person. There was no way he could go home.

What could the *Titanic*'s passengers, still onboard at two in the morning, have thought? By then her bow was submerged and her keel out of the water. It wasn't possible, anymore, to deny the ship's future. Clutching railings, wrapping themselves around benches and other passengers, hoisting themselves into windows—what was it like to feel your entire world sinking out from under you? The ground underfoot vanishing—and so slowly, with ample time to watch it go?

If you eliminate the variable of hope, is death like a calm, glassy pool of water, as warm and soothing as a bath?

How long am I going to do this?

Opportunities, wait-and-sees, what-ifs—you can reach out into the dark and imagine that anything you've grasped is the much-longed-for lifeline, the sign from God to wait a little longer. If anything's infinite it's a list of excuses, of possibilities. Hopes.

Either I do this or I don't. All speculation is ornamental.

Alan had written.

It was after ten when Colin climbed the stairs to the hotel room. Diane could tell he was trying to be quiet but she surprised him halfway. The way he broke—just a squint in his eyes at first and then a cascade of tears, like a failing dam or a shattering vase—disarmed her, prepared as she was to punish someone so much less childlike. She latched onto him and squeezed, once again ready to crush him rather than let him get away. She'd been crying too, up waiting for one more person she loved who might have vanished forever. He didn't struggle. He didn't shove her away. Before they went up to the room she drew back and slapped him across the face. There was nothing she could do to feel safe, to feel like she'd won.

"Where the fuck have you been?" She slammed the door behind her and the wall shook with her rage. "Who are you, Colin? You're not like this. This isn't how I raised you."

He sat on the bed and hugged his knees. He still wouldn't look at her. "I was at the beach all day. Looking at all the garbage. There's all this garbage on the beach from the earthquake." With a shrug he wiped his face on his shirt and spoke into his shoulder. "I was there all day and I stayed too late. I missed the bus and had to wait like an hour. It took forever."

Not looking someone in the eye is a confession, Tim once told her. There was no way she could prove anything, but she knew everything he said was an absolute lie. She could smell the smoke on him. He'd always been her favorite child, the one who used to search her roots for the hairs she called *greys*. She stood with her hands on her hips and tried to control her breathing, to summon whatever wisdom was left in her to deal with this very normal, very adolescent problem. Instead she felt like leaping off the balcony.

"Anyway," he whispered, and he coughed and tried again. "Anyway, I totally need a shower. The beach was kinda gross."

She tried to loom over him, stepping closer. "You expect me to . . . what? Forget about this?" The urge to slap him, to strangle him, to whip him with a belt was welling up within her, climbing her throat like bile, and she tangled her hands together behind her back. "Colin, this isn't fucking funny. You could've been . . . well, how the fuck am I supposed to know?"

His eyes were still on the bedspread. That feeling again, as though he was only a child who didn't know right from wrong. She'd heard long ago that cuteness—in kittens, in puppies—was an evolutionary adaptation to avoid being eaten by one's parents. "I'm sorry," he said. His voice was small and pitiful, and it made her think he was doing it on purpose. "I—I didn't—"

"I don't want to hear it." She put up her hands and went to the window. "You could've been anywhere. I had no idea. Anything could've happened to you, do you understand?" She closed her eyes and saw all the possibilities, the multitude of ways the living body could be destroyed. "Go take your goddamn shower before I slap you again."

As though she'd released him from a spell, he sprang up and vanished into the bathroom. Through the window the balcony looked inviting and she helped herself outside for a smoke. The sun had long set and it was the ground's turn to light the sky. Earlier, as she waited for Colin, she'd scanned the hillside for plots of light they could never afford. How had she convinced herself that this was life? That what was left of her family would feel any better in this city? Days ago, she commented on how Los Angeles would be good for him. Now she'd seen what a place like this had done—the marks on his neck, the new opacity of his eyes. A mother was supposed to know the cure for everyone's ache, or at least what would help. She started to cry, out on the balcony, and rubbed away the evidence with the ball of her thumb.

For days now, even after her dinners and her afternoons with Liam, she recited everything—the good news and the bad—to an imagined Tim who sat across from her, listening like a rock you kept nestled in your favorite plant's dirt. Right now she was asking him what to do about Colin. *He's my last child*, she said, and reminded him how Heather had left, how—*we had no choice, you understand*—they locked Paul up in some faraway room.

Are you afraid you're pushing him away?

But he'd always loved her, and he'd always shown it. What had changed?

He's fourteen, the imagined Tim said. *It's just an age boys get to, a phase they go through.*

Diane ashed over the railing and tried to believe that Colin was out doing stupid things because he was a teenager, because he was at that insane part of life where the word *consequence* was just something your parents said.

Or parent, she thought.

It'd been a long time since she felt any use for Alan, any real absence, but right then she wished she had asked him about his own adolescence. *Tell me what's normal*, she would've said, and saw herself taking notes. She put the cigarette to her lips to suppress a laugh.

I noticed you didn't wish Alan was still alive, the imagined Tim told her as he crossed his legs. *You just wished*, he said, *that you had asked him something* when *he was alive*.

"I'm totally fucking crazy," she said out loud. She shook everything out of her head and looked at the city, every night the same shimmering treasure at the bottom of a black ocean. When she asked herself what kind of trouble Colin had gotten himself into, there were too many answers. When she tried to think of ways to chastise him—to be his mother—there were none. All these months she'd spent looking through Alan's notebooks for some trace of the real Alan, and there was none. It was a sad hope to have clung to for so long, the wish to know the man her husband had become. But now there was no more searching, no more deluding herself into thinking you could ever really know other people or see what was supposed to be their soul. Alan, Colin, Heather and Paul, Shannon, even Tim: all the notebooks had taught her was that there was nothing she could know about anyone. Instead, she only wanted Liam to take her somewhere fancy for dessert and coffee, even if that, too, was just a fantasy, a diversion. It wasn't hard for her to understand that Liam meant nothing and could have been anyone. Just another distraction from reality, whatever reality was.

Her stomach felt light as she remembered the phone calls that morning, all the voicemails she hadn't listened to. She switched on her phone and saw the messages pile up, but she wouldn't listen to them. Not tonight. Instead she began to dial, sucking the last bit of life from her cigarette before she flicked it into the parking lot.

That her mother was awake was a surprise she hadn't prepared for. She broke out in tears without saying a word.

"Diane. Thank God. Are you okay? Where are you? The hotel in 'Frisco said you never checked in, and I find this out *this morning*. You're alive?"

Diane heard Ron mumble something and she knew they were in bed, Ron asleep and her mother flipping through pages of all the books and magazines she never finished. She leaned against the railing and slid down to the floor. "Diane, you have no idea," her mother was saying. "I don't know what's happened but I'm so glad you called. Where are you? Wherever you are, you need to come home. Don't even go to your place. Just come here. You and Colin can sleep here, as long as you need, whatever's happened. I'll get the beds ready."

Diane smiled and tasted tears at the corner of her mouth. "Mom," she said, and heard a long sigh through the phone, something whispered away from the receiver. "We're in LA. We're fine. Nothing's happened. The car's fine. I'm fine. Colin's fine. Heather and Paul?"

"You don't sound fine. You were supposed to be at work today. You need to come home."

She closed her eyes and leaned her head against the railing. Somewhere downstairs that couple was arguing again, or maybe a new couple, with new voices and new accents. She listened closer and noticed they weren't even speaking Spanish. They'd been in this motel five days, she realized. "I think you're right," she said into the phone, trying to conjure something like happiness as she pictured Colin hoisting his bags into the car, as they drove out onto the highway and sat in the city's endless traffic, suburb after suburb on their way to the desert.

"Of course I'm right, Di."

"We're leaving tomorrow." Her throat cinched up. Joy or misery, the sensation was the same.

"You come straight here," her mother said. She heard the bed-springs creak through the phone. Her mother was going out into the hallway, flipping on the light, and would soon rummage through the linen closet for two fresh sets of sheets. There was another mumble or groan from Ron and the way she hushed him brought a smile to Diane's lips.

"I've been so stupid," she said. The word itself sounded absurd enough to laugh at. She covered her mouth so no one else could hear.

"Everyone's stupid now and again. Call in the morning and tell me you're coming."

"I will."

"You know I love you."

"You too."

"Of course, Di. Now I want you to go to sleep. You've never sounded so tired."

Was she really that tired, or was her mother just being a mother? They said their good-byes and Diane got to her feet. This city— was it something she would miss? Or—like the Mojave at dawn, like the mountains of southern Arizona—would it be some glorious thing she had seen on the way to someplace a thousand times better?

Life, right then, was the biggest branch on the oldest tree, splitting off into so many dead-end leaves you couldn't comprehend it. Had she done the right thing, coming here instead of San Francisco? She wouldn't have met Liam, but she would've met another Liam in another city. Further back she unimagined Colin, Paul, and Heather—even Alan—and pictured herself as someone young who could have backpacked the Pacific Rim or built hospitals in places like Africa or Bosnia. That she wouldn't have known how it felt to have Heather's alien little hand grasp a strand of her hair and twist it through her fat fingers turned into one of those God-or-no-God moments. If no one had told her, would she cry at the threat of His absence? She thought of everything she would've lost or missed and it was too much. For the first time in months she looked at the sky, from where God, presumably, could see her and love her, and she asked to be forgiven. She explained, as though He might not know, that she loved her family, that if it disintegrated any further—if she lost the only one left—it would be over and nothing would matter. "Amen," she whispered, and then clarified, like a postscript, that she hadn't meant it to sound like a threat.

She thought of going north, maybe, or returning to the desert. Even driving all the way up into Wyoming or Montana—huge, empty places where you noticed yourself, where you could tell what divided you from everything else. Then she thought of Mexico, where they could sweat on a beach. *How long*, she wanted to know, *does a hundred grand last in Mexico?* How long could she ignore her life back home?

Tim, had he been listening, would have pointed out how she just referred to *her* life, back home. As she lit another cigarette she tried to think psychologically. Why had this vacation become so urgent? She reviewed what she had learned: how she loved to fall in love; how it was easier to imagine a new life rather than live the one you built; how if she decided that Heather and Paul were really gone she would have to accept Colin as gone, someday. Already he'd grown and changed, and he would go through so many more phases of personhood there were none to which she could cling. She tried to instill herself with wisdom, and when she pinpointed the word—*wisdom*—she knew it was what she'd come looking for in the mountains, in the desert, in the palm-lined canyons of a city where wisdom would never come and she could lie to herself forever. "My mother is right," she whispered to Tim, whom she wanted so badly to be listening.

In the shower, Colin scrubbed his skin red with the washcloth and soaped up twice, the water so hot it felt like ice under his toes. Allie had dropped him off two blocks away from the hotel, unable to look Colin in the eye. He didn't pull away, though, when Colin kissed him on the cheek and touched his chest. In a more chaste life, this would have been their good-bye, but he'd sworn to go back, to abandon his mother and run away forever. "I'll see you tomorrow," he whispered, and slid out of Allie's car. In the morning, he would start his new life. It was instead his mother's violence that felt like good-bye, her wish to banish him from her life. It was for her own good that he was taking himself away.

You're bad for people, he told himself. It wouldn't be long before she realized she was happier without him. The worst part was how she looked at him, not like someone who shouldn't have been out all day doing the terrible things he'd done but like someone who could no longer be understood or even helped. In the mirror, as he dried off, he saw himself first as a muscle-wrought growing boy that men wanted all to themselves, and second as a pale malformed monster who chewed up and spit out those who tried to help him. He was the boy who'd made a man groan and the boy who'd made a man die. He imagined the smashed-up skull where once his father's brain and being had sat safe and intact. *You loaded the gun*, he told his naked reflection. In Colin's own skull was something just as fragile, a coil of every mean thing he'd ever done. There was nothing in the bathroom he could use to kill himself, and he didn't bother to imagine how he would've proceeded had things turned out differently, nor what his mother would've done, driving back alone.

His clothes were in a heap on the floor—not fresh, exactly, but the cleanest ones he could find. For a long time he sat wrapped in his towel. The mirror was losing its last scallops of fog and he could tell it was late, that people in the other rooms were asleep. After sex, he thought, and grinned like an idiot at the word, at the experience he'd acquired. It was only two weeks ago that he was terrified of all of this, that he prayed for God to set him straight, and now he craved, confidently, the feel of a man inside of him; he couldn't wait to be Allie's accessory, paraded around town at a series of parties with more and more men. It seemed like a lifetime ago that he'd wanted something like a family, a carbon copy of his grandfather's house but full of kids, a wife to take care of him.

In those words, it wasn't funny anymore. All that loss suddenly felt like someone's death. The good Colin's death. The room was starting to cool, the shower's heat long gone and the desert air crawling in through the crack under the door. He'd begun to shiver but couldn't convince himself to get dressed. What he wanted was for her to knock on the door, to ask if he was okay, to give him an excuse not to kill himself or cry. *Let's go somewhere*, she could tell him, as though this was just another dead end and they could turn around and keep driving. *If anything's infinite it's a list of excuses*, his father had written. *Of possibilities. Hopes.* Colin imagined that he could cut his own throat and die here on the floor. Or he could get dressed and go through with his plan, to try this other life and live as the evil Colin. He pulled on a T-shirt and jeans and stepped out into the hotel room. She was out on the balcony. *Soon you'll be free*, he thought. About himself or his mother, he wasn't sure.

He flipped on the television and muted the sound, not wanting her to hear. It was some show about the ice caps melting. Captions came out garbled on the bottom of the screen. *Mr. Ostrowski hat bent studying the glacier cents 1987* and *Only a few more degrease wood be catastrophic*. He left it on to feel like he wasn't alone, to see the movement out of the corner of his eye. His mother's laptop was on her bed and he cracked it open to distract himself. She'd been searching for information on missing persons—what to do in an emergency and how long you were supposed to wait—and he felt like carving himself up with the dullest, rustiest knife he could find. He clicked out of it and, without thinking, opened his messaging program. Chelsea was online and he hoped she wasn't paying attention, that she wouldn't notice his name. Andy, too, was awake. Over two thousand miles away, and all Colin had to do was type *hi, remember me? that piece of trash you threw away?* In the morning, none of this would matter. None of these people would hurt him again. They would never understand who he was or what he intended to become. He was about to close out of the app when a box popped up on the screen. *Mr. miller's in jail* was all it said, just beneath Andy's name.

Colin stared at the screen. In a hotel room in Los Angeles, in his bedroom in Minnesota, alone on an asteroid hurtling through space—wherever he was no longer mattered. His heart, his body and brain, jumped through space and time to be with Andy; and it was in Andy's voice that he heard those words—*Mr. Miller's in jail*—lying next to him on a sleeping bag, just any other boring night as though nothing had gone wrong. He wanted to respond but it felt like another trap, a way to confess what he'd done with Victor when they were alone.

Andy was typing, Colin could see from the animated icon. He was really there, existing across the continent. He was thinking about him. *Told u he was a pedo, raping some 7th grader who told his parents. He's totes fucked.*

That old image—Victor hauled away in handcuffs—felt more fiction than fact now that he'd seen it in his head so many times. It was absurd to think it had come true. Was he on some bunk now, calling Colin's house with his one phone call? Colin pictured their kitchen phone ringing and ringing, nobody there to pick it up, nobody to hear Victor's poison. Andy's words on the screen began to tremble and blur into the white space, as though he'd never typed them. There was a noise in the room he mistook for something outside of himself, a door creaking open or the TV no longer muted, but it was only his throat as it let out a long, slow groan like the wind had been knocked out of him. He wanted to crush something, to kill something. He wanted to squeeze the life out of a living creature with his bare hands. Why hadn't he foreseen rage like this? Why hadn't he seen this coming?

u there dude?

Knowing what it felt like—knowing how it worked—Colin pictured himself below Victor's frame, pinned to his desk or the seat of his car. Had Victor loved this other boy, too? Had he called him at home and told him about the human heart and its limitations? Had he dreamt of him? Did the boy feel, as Victor flooded into him, that it was all his fault? There in his head was Victor's classroom, its rows of desks and lab benches, microscopes, charts, and Bunsen burners, its order and warmth. *I knew a boy who wrote poems*, Victor had said. How many others had he tricked? How many, like Colin, were stupid enough to pity someone so paralyzed by what seemed like love, so charmed by the body's symphony of blood and come?

Colin wrote only *i'm here,* and right away Andy was typing again. *was he weird with u? did he make u suck his dick? guess the police r lookin 4 more witnesses or whatever. like it's . . . a big fuckin deal. Just thought i'd ask.*

In Victor's eyes, Colin was only another piece of fruit to be plucked and eaten, the core of him tossed aside. Nothing Colin could have done would have changed this. Victor had played all the right notes. He'd long learned what notes to play.

I hope ur not still mad at me over that joke, Andy said.

He'd last seen them both on the same day, Colin realized— Andy outside of the school and Victor in his car, as he'd driven him home. It was easy to see the streets and the trees, the houses of his neighborhood, and the school itself. How badly he'd wanted Andy to love him, and how easily Andy had sold him out for a laugh, for a chance at being talked about. What would they have done, all those boys, had Colin—the little fag they derided and pitied and would never view as equal—leapt for Andy's throat, knocked him down, and bashed his skull against the concrete? What would they have called him then?

Colin felt his hands fill with hot steel as though he'd use them, as though he'd leap across all the states between here and home and pummel the boy he loved into pulp. Instead he began to type, and he relished typing slowly, one letter at a time so Andy could sit and wait. *If you ever talk to me again I will kill you.* He clicked out of the app before Andy could respond and leaned back against the hotel pillows. It felt like he'd closed the door to a room. Here he was again, a boy about to run away. He closed his eyes and tried to see his new life, curled up in bed with Allie or hand in hand as they walked along Hollywood Boulevard. Instead he saw his bed at home, the maples of the street where he lived. *Either I do this or I don't*, his father had written.

It was almost an hour before his mother came back inside. The TV was still muted, transcribing a show about an island of garbage somewhere in the Pacific. He'd eaten several candy bars and their wrappers fluttered to the floor with the breeze. It was still difficult to look at her, this person who wouldn't give up loving him. She sat down on the bed and put her hand on his back, just between his shoulder blades. "What're you watching?"

"Some show."

"A show, huh?"

"It's dumb."

"Looks dumb."

With her hands on his back he knew she could feel him trembling. He knew she could feel his breath cut in and out of him like a saw. It wasn't fear he felt so much as relief, as he knew what she was going to say. He couldn't wait for her to say it. "Colin," she said, touching the spot where his muscles always tied themselves in knots. *Such a tense little boy*, she used to call him.

"Hmm?"

"We've been gone a long time."

He tried to shrug, as if time were no longer relevant or he hadn't noticed at all. Instead he went from trembling to shaking, a creature she had to hug to keep still. She'd put on perfume that day, for the first time in weeks, and it was that smell more than anything that brought him home, perched on the edge of her bed as he watched her in her makeup mirror. How had he thought it was possible, to leave this life she'd given him?

"Pack up in the morning," she told him. "I want to be on the road by noon. I want you in the seat next to me, telling me where to go. My navigator."

That's all it took. For days he'd thought about LA as his new home. He'd envisioned new schools, a new house. He pictured new friends as though he'd already made them. But when she squeezed his shoulder and said, "It's time to go home," he could tell *home* wasn't this place. She cried as she held him, and he could tell it was for the same reason he was crying. His mother too had convinced herself that she no longer cared for the changing seasons, for the restaurants whose menus you could recite from memory, for the house they'd lived in his entire life—despite everything, in the last two years, that'd gone wrong inside of it. He could tell she too had tried to forget everything that was right and all that could turn out right, in the end. "I know it's hard," she said as he clutched her in his arms, terrified at how close he'd come to leaving this woman who cared for him at any cost.

Yes, people who loved other people were tied together, just as hopeless as the silk in a spider's web, but that didn't mean you could control them absolutely. Colin felt his mother hold on to him not out of obligation or parental duty but as her own choice. Sometimes there was little you could do, he realized, to damage or save another life. Andy was going to be Andy no matter how much he loved or hated him, no matter how much you worshipped his body; Victor would desire and pursue no matter how far you ran, a predator acting on instinct. *They will all flourish without me*, his father had written, having made up his mind long before Colin even came into the world. All Colin had done was tell him it was okay, the word his father had wanted to hear from the beginning. *Yes, I relieve you of life. It's okay for you to die.*

The boy Colin wanted to be did flourish, but only briefly. Confident as he was—self-reliant, sex-starved, independent, and able to win the heart of any man—he was a boy without a future; he was a boy who wouldn't last. Losing an imagined life was a small death—your own death, one of the many fragments you'd made of yourself unable to go on. This was the boy his sister had seen, and while he died ahead of schedule it felt right, all the same, to watch him go, to see him breathe his last breath on the sundrenched streets of this unreal city. He knew his mother, too, was mourning her own failed version, the woman she wasn't supposed to be.

During a lifetime, we all have those rare dreams that leave us shaken for hours afterward, sometimes days. Yet there's no describing a dream like this, not to another person. The events themselves, when cleaved from the dream's emotions, mean nothing—are often laughable. But when you first wake with your leftover terror, your lingering sorrow or melancholy joy, there's no way to talk yourself out of that impression. You can't articulate your way back into reality. Lately, his father had written, with more and more of these dreams behind me, I wonder if that isn't death: waking from whatever lifelong dream this world is and being unable to rid yourself of its impression. Death, therefore, would not be an event so much as the ache one feels after the wound that was life, now finally able to heal. After all these years, his father had written, I am ready to heal.

In the books about death, survivors are advised to create a life as dissimilar to the old one as possible. They use seasonal metaphors and refer to natural cycles, natural order, natural chaos. In the few books about suicide, change was crucial. Survivors were to put the house up for sale. Routines must be undone and new ones established. These, Diane found, were written like instructions: *you will notice* and *it will help you*, as if she were a plant someone should move closer to the sun. The metaphors here invoked forests—the two of *you* wandering through this forest and only one making it out, the aftermath of the "accident" throwing the survivor deeper into the darkest parts of the forest through which *you* had to walk until *you* found the clearing, until *you* could see far ahead and find *your* way home. Then you were to find a new home.

After those first few weeks, when she began to read the books her friends and family had foisted on her, Diane couldn't take any of this seriously. Once, Colin found her in the middle of the night, having mistaken her laughter for more of her same old sobbing. "This is so ridiculous," she said. "Listen—" and she read passages aloud as though sex advice from bad magazines, enunciating words like *journey* and *rainbow*. "I've read all the books," she told Shannon. "But I'm still miserable. What would you think if I had someone paint a forest on the walls?"

She did change, though, and certain things did help as the books had said. There were parts of her life she began to notice. Eventually she could notice things without crying about them.

That morning, on her way to meet Liam—her last morning in California, she kept thinking—she threw away the gun. It was something she decided the night before, and it helped to think she brought it for this exact reason. She felt its weight in her purse like ashes in an urn. After Alan had gone into the ground she read something about cremation, how it allows you to find the right time to say good-bye, and she lamented one more thing—as she told Shannon—she'd fucked up. At three in the morning, while Colin snored in the other bed, she stepped out to the balcony. She wasn't in the mood but out of ceremony she lit a cigarette. With her free hand she reached into her purse, the cold barrel, the familiar trigger. She couldn't believe she'd kept it. She couldn't believe she'd considered it. There was too much to love. Even if she left Los Angeles after all, watching that other Diane come to life and die off was enough. While she always laughed—and laughed even now—at the big bad forest in those books on suicide, she imagined, right then, that the blanket of streetlights beneath the mountains was the starlit meadow at that forest's edge. *I'm healed*, she let herself think. After all this time, that's all it took.

There would always be a void, Tim had assured her. So had her mother. Even Shannon, who'd lost no one as far as she knew, had warned that things would never be the same. *You will always feel the loss*, the books instructed, but at least, over the last few months, she could feel more than loss. Only yesterday she'd made love that felt like genuine love, even if it wasn't. That morning, on her way to meet him at some old mansion, she accepted the sunlight and the rustling palms as pleasures she'd soon give up. How she'd explain it to Tim, in their next session, was by outlining the choice she made. *I didn't hold on to everything*, she could tell him. *I wasn't trying to hoard emotions, like you said.* The previous night, she'd pictured herself tossing the gun into some sewer or over the edge of a steep hill, standing for a moment in the breeze to say good-bye before going on with her life. Instead, her entire walk to the park was adjacent to rush-hour traffic, never alone. It wasn't until she got to the park gates that she felt everyone else disappear. There were handprints on the stone, just beneath the address number. They weren't imprinted in the rock, and in fact looked more like stains, but definitely stains in the shape of hands. Something stirred in her memory but crept out of sight before she could see it. She shook her head and walked through the gates. When no one was looking she took the gun from her purse and wiped it down with the sleeve of her blouse. Halfway up the walk she felt lightheaded. It was good for her, she promised herself, and chucked the gun into an overgrowth of ferns and flowers. It would look wrong to someone if she lingered, and she continued on. There wasn't much time to mourn as she walked up the hill to meet the man who would soon be just one more person she'd met on her way through the forest. She laughed out loud despite the looks people gave her.

The way Liam talked about the mansion was through movies. She noticed this about the people she met in Los Angeles. It wasn't only the tour guides and the shop owners; everyone shared a little of the secretly starstruck. It was their version of bringing up the weather. As Liam walked her through the grounds he kept gesturing toward the windows, inviting her to peer inside. "Do you recognize this room?" he asked, and when she shook her head he named the film and the scene. It wasn't like the museum trips. She didn't feel as though she was learning anything. She didn't feel as if there were worlds she was peering into. Instead he was showing her just how fake those worlds were. "It's amazing what they do with this place," he said, leading her through the flower garden where they filmed the shoot-out at the end of *Beverly Hills Cop*. It made it easier to fall out of love with him, if love you could call it. She felt as if she could leave with a bittersweet satisfaction, as if it were nothing but a delicious meal ending in a cup of coffee.

The plan was to have a picnic brunch. Already the shade was growing scarce but they found a place between the hedges that was still cool, under a large stone obelisk. Liam had made sandwiches. "Are you sure we can just sit down on the grass? This is like a museum."

"It's a public park, actually," he said. "They don't let anyone inside the house, but you're free to use the grounds how you like. So long as you're not an asshole."

"I'll do my best." She sipped the coffee he gave her—from the place where they first met, he said, but like a fact or another bit of trivia rather than something that was supposed to be special. There were doughnuts, too, for dessert. "All that's missing is the newspaper," she said, and he nodded as he surveyed the flowering vine woven into the hedge. It was hard to believe she'd been so mistaken.

Her plan was to just tell him, outright, how it wasn't going to work. *I'm going home today. Maybe we can stay in touch.* Now, she felt, all that wasn't enough.

"I never do this," she said. She shifted her weight onto her knees and leaned back on her thighs. "But . . . I don't know why. I just feel like . . ." She stared hard at the grass. She couldn't remember the last time she sat on a blanket, this close to the grass.

3460 Columbus Avenue, she thought without warning. She was shocked that she still knew the address. The handprints were on the foundation, on the north side of the house—a cluster of children's hands, in the same, dark stain, all over the concrete, just as she'd seen them on the park gates, moments ago. It was the last house they'd looked at, she remembered. Colin must have been nine or ten. When the agent arrived and unlocked the house it wasn't what she had imagined—large and gorgeous, yes, but run-down and poorly lit. *New light fixtures will make a world of difference*, the agent said, and Diane remembered his tone as weary, as fed up. They went down to the basement and despite the mold all along the walls she didn't rule it out. She was too curious and wanted to see the rest. Colin was running all over the place, opening one door after another in a basement that could have held a Minotaur at its heart. All four bedrooms were upstairs and all four doors were closed, and when they opened the last they noticed scratch marks all over the wood. *They kept something in here*, she remembered saying. *Something or someone.* The carpet was frayed in the corner and when Colin peeled it back they found a dead bird, not yet rotting. There was a door in the corner that led, the agent said, to the attic. She wished, now, that she'd opened that door, just to see, but at the time there was nothing she could do to convince herself. *I don't think we're interested,* she said, while Colin, like he was tucking it into bed, gingerly covered the bird with its blanket of carpet.

They'd looked at houses that entire summer, she remembered. 3460 Columbus was the last. *Now don't tell your father what we're up to,* she'd instructed Colin, her assistant, her companion, her little gentleman. *I haven't convinced him that he wants to move yet.* But she'd had no plans to tell him. She was thinking of leaving him, even then.

Liam cleared his throat and she flinched. "You feel . . . ?" he asked, his hand outstretched and palm up as though he was waiting for her to set her entire life story inside of it.

It was hard, walking down Hollywood Boulevard, for Colin to feel good about anything. He couldn't not think of LA as a test he failed. You had to be strong here and he wasn't. You had to be smart. There were parts of home he missed and would be happy to see, but so much of it would be painful to go back to. Andy he'd inevitably see, at some point—in school or at a restaurant, out shopping with their mothers—and he'd have to stay hateful. Colin would have to resist his eyes, his smile, the curved shadows of his body if they ended up, torturously, in the same gym class; he'd have to look like steel or ice, a living weapon. And then Victor, or Victor's absence. Colin wanted to be grateful that he'd never look outside and see that car ever again, waiting in the street, but without Victor there was no one else, he was ashamed to realize, who would give him what he'd come to know he needed. *Why couldn't you have waited?* he demanded of the Victor in his head. *Wasn't I good enough? Why wasn't it me?* Instead, when he went home, there'd be nothing but gossip, his Facebook and his friends alight with news about their *pedo teacher* who'd finally been caught, and how they all knew from the beginning. None of it had happened yet and already Colin was tired of the whole thing.

As he lay awake that morning, listening to his mother shower, he'd thought it all through. Right after she left, he wrote his note.

With the pen and paper in front of him, he was still tempted to write his good-bye. *Don't look for me. You'll be happier.* But when he pictured her reading it, he wanted to tear himself open and wrench his insides between his fists like wet rags. LA wasn't his future anymore. It was a hard thing to admit but he knew he had to go home, and instead his note became a good-bye to Allie. *Good-bye palm trees,* he thought. *Good-bye mountains. Good-bye blow jobs and getting fucked. Good-bye good life.* To Allie he wrote everything he thought he should—that he was sorry for bailing and happy for meeting him, that he loved the taste of his cock, that he felt like he'd grown more in the last week than in the last ten years. Even if it wasn't true it sounded amazing, he thought, and added some stuff about love and missing him forever. That he cried made him feel like this was the biggest mistake of his life.

It was just before ten when he arrived and the shop hadn't opened. The sun was already hot through his T-shirt and he leaned into the shade and tried not to look like a kid buying drugs. "People see a kid on his own and they think druggy or rentboy," Allie had warned him. "They think no one cares about him. No one's looking out." How he meant it was for Colin to be careful. He laughed, at the time. After all he'd been through, he was supposed to give a shit what someone on the street might think? "I'm serious," Allie said, and the anger in his voice was a sad thing to remember. He wondered if there might be a way, yet, to stay and be loved. The door behind him clicked. He touched the note in his pocket to make sure it was still there.

The way Allie looked at him—like a mythical creature or someone who'd died long ago, something physically impossible—made Colin feel ashamed and proud simultaneously, glad to shatter the image of the weak boy Allie thought he knew, but also pained to know he'd have to tell him the truth. "So you did it!" Allie said, and pulled him inside. It was always easy to forget how strong men could be, how they could pick you up as though you were nothing at all. He set Colin on the counter and looked at him with an undisguised, embarrassing joy. "I wasn't sure you'd be able to do it. I thought it was all just talk. How's it feel to be free? Jesus fuck, Colin, you're . . . is this for real?"

Colin could feel the trembling in Allie's hands. As he began to cry he couldn't look at his face. He didn't want to see Allie's disappointment, his sad realization that he was right all along and that Colin didn't have the balls to run away. He reached into his pocket and gave him the note. While Allie read it, he kept his face in his hands. For the first time since he arrived it was quiet and he could hear, right then, the groaning from the porn playing behind him. He peeked out of the corner of his eye and saw it was something different than before—not two young men caressing each other in some sunny place but instead an older man securing a younger man to a table, bending him over and fastening his ankles to the legs and his wrists to bolts on the opposite edge. Colin felt dizzy and he broke away. When Allie finished reading he folded the note and slipped it into his pocket. Colin looked up at him. He could feel his heart lashing every faraway part of his body with hot blood but he tried to ignore it. There was a reason he'd come there. "I'm sorry," he whispered.

Allie was quiet. His silence made Colin feel even worse, as if he'd tricked him or wasted his time. Then he felt a hand on his thigh, brushing the hem of his shorts. "Colin," Allie said. His voice was lower now, as though this was their secret even though no one else was in the shop. Colin looked away and again caught sight of the television. The tied-up man onscreen was moaning into the sock that'd been stuffed into his mouth. With a hand on his chin, Allie guided Colin's eyes gently back to his own. "I'll bet this is another one of your games, isn't it?"

"What?"

Allie's hands were traveling up his thighs, the tips of his fingers now beneath his clothes. "I think this is you playing with me. I think you want me to . . . detain you. To keep you here. We both know what you're into."

Colin closed his eyes at Allie's touch. He felt a breath pulled out of him like a rope or a chain caught in his throat. Then he opened his eyes. "Um . . . no I really . . . I really have to go. I'm sorry but I just can't."

The hands disappeared. Allie backed away. Again that look of disappointment, of betrayal—how did he keep doing this to people? Colin sighed and looked down at his lap.

"I wish I could."

"I understand. I really do." Allie adjusted himself in his shorts and walked behind the counter. "I'm sorry, too. I don't know what I was thinking, just now. I just . . . you showed up, cute as ever, and I really thought . . . fuck, I'm an idiot. I'm sorry."

Colin leapt down off the counter. In the cabinet were all the things he still couldn't name but—after his short education—could recognize and understand. Onscreen, the sex had begun, the older man's pants around his ankles as he slowly moved himself in and out of his captive. Colin made an effort to close his mouth, already dried out from too much breathing. The lump in his shorts grazed against the counter and he pressed himself against it. The older man withdrew and began stroking himself, right above the young man's back. Colin was sweating as he waited for his favorite part, but the TV went dark.

"Let's not make this harder than it has to be," Allie said, and then he laughed. "Harder. That was totally an accident."

Colin tried to laugh but he felt broken. He stood breathing, as though he himself had been switched off right before he came. It didn't feel fair.

"Are you really sure it's not a game?" Allie asked. He reached under the counter and came up with a bottle of water. It gave a little hiss as he opened it and Colin remembered how thirsty he was. Condensation dripped down Allie's chin. He must have noticed the look on Colin's face, and he reached down again and brought up a second bottle.

"Thanks," Colin said. He uncapped the bottle and drank half in one pull. Allie was staring at him as he drank and it made him feel like an animal, a dangerous creature. "I wish we could play," he said, in a way he hoped was sexy. He looked into the cabinet, all those toys and treasures. "I'm sad you never got to tie me up or use any of this stuff on me."

"Don't tease," Allie said. "Believe me—I was dying to. This one right here—" He pointed to a curved set of rings, nestled inside a velvet case. "This is what I was going to use."

Colin looked at it. He knew what it was from pictures he'd found on the Internet, but he wanted to play dumb. He bit his lip and peered out from beneath his brow. "What's that, sir?"

"Sir? Fuck, you're a little slut." Colin beamed at the word and then looked away. He wasn't supposed to do this. He was supposed to go home. "It's a chastity cage," Allie was saying. "You put one ring on the base, and the others guide you at an angle. It keeps you aroused but unable to get hard. Someone else has to unlock it. Perfect for boys who want permission."

"So you can't even jack off?" Colin heard himself say. He knew the answer and he knew he should turn around and leave. It was something he'd imagined before and he was trying not to imagine it now, what being trapped in chastity would feel like, how you'd do anything for the person who had the key.

"Not a drop. You just get hornier and hornier."

The air in the room felt different, the breeze from the vent like someone's light, expert touch, traveling up to his shoulders and his armpits and then down his spine. "I should get back."

"Hey," Allie said. His voice too had changed, as though it came from inside Colin's skull. "Maybe you should stay and try it on." His own heart he could hear, not like a drum or a boom but like the clang of a railcar's wheels as they dipped into a chipped-out spot in the iron. It was cool in the room but he was sweating as though it was a hundred degrees and humid—and the trickle over each rib enough to sigh over, it felt so good. Something was wrong but there were too many things to take care of first. He reached into his briefs. "Hey, hands off," he heard, and Allie came out from behind the counter and took hold of his wrists, placing Colin's arms above his head.

"I don't feel good," Colin said, searching for Allie's eyes.

"Yes you do."

"No, I mean I do, but I—I don't feel right."

"Keep those hands up." Allie's voice was bursting open from inside him, something he needed to listen to. He felt hands and fabrics and the vent's cool air. A truck went by in the street and rattled into his groin. There was so much touch, right then, that he didn't know he was locked up until he looked down and saw it, until Allie's open palm showed him the key. Just a tiny little key was all it took to belong to someone completely. Without that key, he could never go home. "Now," Allie said. "I need you to do everything I say."

They never left the shop but the room began to change—a new kind of light and the doors blocked off with bars. Colin knew he'd been drugged but he didn't care. He could only marvel at the warmth of the lights, the vibration of music through his body. Stand there, was an order. Shirt off, was another. Shorts too. And those. Don't touch. Kneel there. Give me your hands. Up above your head. Look at me.

Colin looked at him. He hadn't realized what a beautiful man Allie really was, a poured composite of tattoo and muscle and shadow that was painful to see. His jeans he was still wearing, and the realization—Colin hadn't had much time to think—that they were about to come off made him want to reach for it. But he was immobilized now, fastened to something in the ceiling, and had no choice but to wait to be given, to wait to be taken, to wait for the ache to be relieved. The thought that Allie might abandon him here, not worth his time, made him whimper, and as he watched those jeans glide down those thighs he began to sob outright. He tried to follow Allie with his eyes as he walked behind him, but then there was nothing to see, only fabric over his eyes, hot with the smell of coconut. Ask me, was the next order, and Colin asked for everything: *Let me go* in a voice full of sobs, *Please take this off* in something like a groan, *Can I taste it* between sharp, hysteric giggles, *Don't tell anyone* in a whisper he'd forgotten.

"Colin," Allie said, but the way it came out, so soft and so pleasant, it didn't sound like Allie at all. With the blindfold over his eyes it was easy to believe that Victor had escaped, that he was here to do to Colin what he should've done a long time ago. The smell of cock was right in front of him and he leaned forward, his tongue tasting the air like a reptile's, but it was out of reach. There was a laugh, then the rattlings of metals and plastics. "It's good you can't see these tools." Colin knew he should be afraid, but it was hard to care at that point, his entire body like a grinding knuckle that refused to crack. "I want you to tell me how much you need this," he heard. His life, Colin promised, depended on it. He couldn't live without it. He'd do anything, just please. "Will you be a good little slave for me?" By then there weren't things like pain, at least not the body's pain. If there was pain it was only the pain of being half-finished, half-fucked. There was only the excruciating threat of being half-loved. Each pinch and pinprick this man gave him felt like its own little orgasm; before long he was trembling with the agony of being undone. "Tell me why you deserve this," he heard, and Colin told him what everyone had wanted to know from the beginning: how he drooled after his best friend, how he'd sell his entire family for a fuck, how he'd killed his father and how he knew, as he loaded the gun, exactly what that gun would do. "It was just something I wanted to see happen," he confessed. "I killed him because I could." It was for this reason, he promised, that no one on earth deserved this torture more than he did, but the man above him was silent. And why wouldn't he be, here before this wretched creature? "Now please!" Colin screamed, and his body began to shake so terribly he felt sick. The D-rings on the straps that held him chirped against each other. Even the tools, in their tray, were jumping and banging out something you might have called music. "Holy fuck!" he heard, and something like a jet's taking off began all around him, noises like bombs, noises like the shot he'd heard in the middle of the night. The man was screaming and then, very swiftly, was not screaming. The straps came loose from the ceiling and his arms collapsed on his head. He pulled the blindfold away from his eyes, still shocked at how the fabric felt like the grace of some angel's wing, and saw what the earthquake had done, his friend Allie nothing but a pair of legs peering out from the concrete. *Take cover*, his brain warned, and as he turned to look for a place to hide he slipped on the sweat and saliva that'd pooled underneath him. He could no longer move, and he clasped his hands around a bloody rod of rebar that was in his way. It wouldn't budge. At first he simply thought *too heavy* and tried to move out from under it. But there was no more trying and no more moving. He touched the blood on his shirt. It belonged to him and it felt wrong to see it outside of him, so much of it. Even dying felt good throughout his body. But the word itself—*dying, to die*—tasted worse than the blood filling his throat. This was the last thing he'd done, the last place he'd seen, the last person he'd begged and thanked and told, in his own sad way, he loved. He began to breathe heavier, waiting for it. He'd waited so long, and despite what he'd always thought, he wanted to wait longer. Much longer. He would've promised anything, right then, to wait forever. But what to promise, and to whom, he couldn't say. And why—that he'd never been able to explain, not once.

Right away, the earth had loosened under the obelisk. Diane had seen it in time to move. Liam hadn't. She'd now seen the spilt brains of two men she loved, or thought she loved, and that was too much to ask in one lifetime. It was nothing like the other earthquake, which could've been a semi truck passing down a small street. This felt like someone had picked up her world and shaken it, no chance to start screaming. Even when his skull burst open—when Liam went from a man to a crushed, broken-up thing they'd have to sweep away with the rest of the city's ruin—there was no time for her to think, to mourn. She wrapped her hands around the roots of the nearest hedge and held on, hoping Colin, back at the motel, was doing the same.

When she got to her feet and clambered out of the garden it was as she thought. Part of the mansion had collapsed, its walls split down the middle. Cars in the parking lot had rolled into one another. A few people were crushed to death between them and more were on their way, dragging their clenched fists along the metal as though that might help. Farther out, it was worse. From the park she could see the entire panorama—downtown's hotels and office towers, some of which were missing or leaning to one side, and rightward all the way to the ocean, the beach they'd just cleaned of garbage and filth. Columns of smoke appeared all over the skyline. The roar and rush of traffic was gone, and in its absence not only the city's millions of car alarms and calls for help but all the birds that'd taken flight now returning to their trees, chittering among themselves. She wanted to feel something but she couldn't decide what. *I'm in shock*, she told herself, evaluating this trauma, how she herself could've died. But wasn't that what she wanted, all those times she looked to the sky for an asteroid or prayed for God to strike her down? When she dreamt of funnel clouds, when she drove through traffic wanting someone in the oncoming lane to be drunk? This was her opportunity, and she'd squandered it. This could've been her way out.

Her chin began to tremble, her lip threatening to curl and give her away. To what or to whom she couldn't say; who was watching her now? But what she thought was a heartful of sobs came out in laughter. It shook through her, violent as the earth, and seized every last part of her. She was alive, and glad for it. Glad to have made it. Glad to be looking at all this rather than crushed underneath it. Glad she could, after the emergency was over, go back home and tell everyone how it happened—her mother, Shannon, Tim, and whoever else was listening because it was something she would have to tell people, how she had lived. Soon she would climb back down into the city and make her way among the broken streets and the hissing hydrants, passing—because there was nothing to be done—the casualties and the victims and those whose time had come. She was sorry for them but not for herself, not sorry to be alive. She would find Colin, safe in the motel, and this they'd remember. This they'd share.

My family is strong, Alan had written. My wife is strong. She wouldn't refuse herself another life, another chance at love. They will all flourish without me, and that leaves me unguarded, unwatched, untethered. How long have I owned this gun, and I'm still writing? All these notes, all these facts, all these made-up pieces of life? Who's to say I won't invent one more reason to live just a little longer? One more need for myself? One more love, or fear?

But he hadn't, Alan. He shot himself in the head and it was she who was untethered and free. Even in this ruined, broken city—for what was perhaps the first time, she thought—she was happy to be alive.

So this is what it means to be grateful, she was thinking, when she noticed something wrong out there in the noise and the panic. There was something new, and she looked, everywhere, for an explanation. Even around her, the groans of the wounded and the dying were quieting, one by one. It was as if someone had switched on a small fan, its white noise swallowing them up. Then something in the ocean's light caught her eye, the sun's reflection bending in a way it shouldn't. It could've been something unexplained, a sea monster lifting itself spine-first out of the water and so many miles tall it would soon be everything she saw. People were screaming again. Those who could were clambering past her for higher ground. The water went on rising, higher and higher, as the noise grew to a roar louder than the earthquake itself. Its shadow came first, touching the beach and the first rows of houses as if to say, *This may hurt a little.* "Oh thank God," she said, when she understood.

Acknowledgments

To those at Graywolf Press: my immense gratitude for giving this novel such an enthusiastic and caring home; and with special thanks to Steve Woodward for his extensive, detailed edits, as well as his difficult questions during the final drafts.

Thanks to Dawn Frederick, who first read this book as a friend and then, later, as my agent, and who made me feel as if it might have a future after all. Thanks to Laura Zats for her careful edits and suggestions, and for forwarding all those encouraging e-mails.

Thanks to Marlon James for his careful eye on the opening pages, as well as encouraging me to pursue whatever ending I wanted.

Thanks to Nona, Martin, Diana, John, Jeffrey, Elias, Timothy, Heather, Sam, Maysa, and other early readers who helped shape this book's direction.

Thanks to Michael, who told the truth when the sixth draft was boring.

More than anyone, thank you to my parents and my family, without whom I obviously would not have written this book.

I'm so grateful for all of these people in my life, and others. I'm grateful for everyone's influence, and for the way everything came together, and for that day in the desert.

PATRICK NATHAN's short fiction and essays have appeared in *Gulf Coast*, *Boulevard*, *Real Life*, the *Los Angeles Review of Books*, and elsewhere. This is his first novel. He lives in Minneapolis.

The text of *Some Hell* is set in Adobe Caslon Pro.
Book design by Rachel Holscher.
Composition by Bookmobile Design & Digital
Publisher Services, Minneapolis, Minnesota.
Manufactured by Friesens Corporation on acid-free,
100 percent postconsumer wastepaper.